# AFTER THE FIRE

## ASHES OF EDEN, BOOK 7

Written by Diane Kann

Brought to you by Volans Galaxy Press

Published by Kannceptual Creations LLC

An imprint of Volans Galaxy Press

ISBN: 978-1-971356-19-8

Printed in the United States of America

First Edition, January 2026

# CONTENTS

## CHAPTER ONE

# THE WHISPERING SCARS

The acrid tang of smoke had finally receded, replaced by an air so astonishingly pure it felt like a forgotten memory. The skies, once a perpetual canvas of ochre haze, now stretched in an unbroken, cerulean expanse, dotted with clouds that drifted with an almost languid grace. For many, it was the first time they had truly seen the stars in years, a celestial tapestry unfurling against a darkness undiluted by the relentless fires. Eden, or what remained of it, breathed a deep, slow sigh. The cataclysm had passed, the inferno extinguished, and in its wake, a profound stillness had settled. It was a quiet that felt earned, a silence bought at an unimaginable price, and yet, it was a quiet that gnawed at the edges of their relief.

This newfound peace was not a gentle lullaby but an unnerving hush. The frantic energy of survival, the desperate scramble against the encroaching flames, had evaporated, leaving behind a vacuum that echoed with the absence of sound. The constant crackle of burning foliage, the roar of consuming infernos, the panicked shouts of fellow survivors – these had been the soundtrack to their recent existence. Now, only the whisper of wind through nascent greenery and the distant cries of returning avians punctuated the quiet. It was a silence that amplified every internal tremor, every unarticulated fear. The inhabitants of Eden, still raw and exposed from their near-annihilation, found themselves adrift in this profound quietude, a sensation that was both a balm and a torment. It was the quiet of a battlefield

1

after the last shot has been fired, a stillness heavy with the ghosts of what had been, and the terrifying uncertainty of what was to come.

This period of repose, though superficially peaceful, was a crucial transitional phase. The immediate threat had receded, but the struggle for Eden had not ended; it had merely transmuted. The overt conflict, the desperate battle against an external enemy – the fire – had given way to a more insidious, internal reckoning. The landscape itself, though beginning to mend, bore the indelible scars of its ordeal. Twisted metal skeletons of forgotten structures jutted from the scorched earth, monuments to a past abruptly ended. Forests, once vibrant with life, now stood as blackened husks, their skeletal branches reaching towards the sky like silent accusations. Yet, even in these desolate vistas, life persisted. Tiny, tenacious shoots of emerald green, barely visible against the ash-grey soil, pushed upwards, a defiant testament to resilience. These were the first whispers of Eden's recovery, subtle and fragile, but undeniable.

The clarity of the air, the absence of the choking particulate matter, allowed for a sharper perception of the world, and of themselves. The survivors, no longer consumed by the immediate need for shelter and safety, were forced to confront the raw edges of their experiences. The quiet was a mirror, reflecting back the fragmented pieces of their lives, the gaping holes left by loss, and the profound psychological toll of witnessing such widespread destruction. Every gust of wind carried not just the scent of damp earth and new growth, but the phantom scent of ash. Every sunrise, though beautiful, was a reminder of the sun that had fueled their destruction. They were a people adrift, their compasses spinning wildly in the aftermath of a storm that had reshaped their world and their souls.

This was not the triumphant dawn of a new era, but the hesitant dawning of a new, unsettling reality. The silence of Eden was not the silence of peace, but the silence of anticipation. It was the pause before the next phase of a long, arduous journey, a journey that promised to be as internal as it was external. The cessation of overt conflict had merely shifted the nature of their struggle, pushing it from the external, physical realm into the internal, psychological, and ethical landscapes of their existence. This initial chapter, therefore, aimed to establish this delicate equilibrium, this precarious repose, hinting at the deeper reckonings that lay dormant beneath the surface, waiting for their moment to emerge from the quiet ashes.

The quiet itself was a character. It was a palpable entity, an almost physical presence that pressed in on the inhabitants of Eden. It was the absence of noise that paradoxically amplified internal disquiet. For many, the days immediately following the fire's cessation were a blur of exhaustion and dazed relief. They moved through the nascent greenery, their steps soft on the newly dampening earth, their voices hushed, as if the very act of speaking too loudly might shatter the fragile calm. Children, who had known little but the smoky skies and the constant fear, now looked at the clear expanse above with a mixture of wonder and apprehension. They pointed at the birds, their calls clearer and more varied than they had ever heard, but their own laughter was subdued, hesitant, as if an unseen authority might still scold them for being too joyful.

The scientific observatories, once beacons of frantic activity, now operated with a muted efficiency. The frantic scramble to predict fire fronts and reroute atmospheric scrubbers had ceased. Now, the instruments hummed with a different purpose: monitoring the subtle shifts in Eden's reawakening biosphere, charting the hesitant return of species, and meticulously analyzing the composition of the air that was, for the first time in a long time, breathable without filtration. Yet, even these objective metrics seemed imbued with a certain melancholy. The data points charting the return of a particular insect species or the resurgence of a specific moss were met not with unbridled celebration, but with quiet, almost solemn acknowledgement. It was a victory, yes, but a victory etched in the memory of countless losses.

One could observe this shift in the demeanor of Elara Vance, a leading atmospheric chemist. Before the fire, her days had been a relentless race against time, a desperate effort to understand and mitigate the atmospheric toxins. Now, she spent hours simply standing at an observation deck, her gaze fixed on the horizon, not searching for encroaching danger, but simply absorbing the clarity. Her colleagues noted a change in her. The frantic energy had been replaced by a deep, pervasive stillness. She spoke less, but when she did, her words carried a new weight, a measured cadence that suggested a profound internal recalibration. "It's... clean," she had murmured to her assistant one morning, the statement simple yet laden with unspoken complexity. "So clean it feels... exposed. Like we're naked under this sky, and Eden is watching us. Watching what we do next."

This sense of being watched, of being under scrutiny, permeated the recovering settlements. The inhabitants felt a collective responsibility, a burden of proof. They had survived, yes, but survival was only the first step. The question that hung in the impossibly clear air was: what would they do with this second chance? The silence that enveloped them was not an empty void, but a space pregnant with expectation. It was the expectation of the planet itself, which, having endured the fire, now seemed to be waiting for humanity to demonstrate its capacity for stewardship, its worthiness to inhabit its recovering skin.

The very act of breathing felt different. It was a conscious act, a deliberate intake of a gift that had been so nearly extinguished. The memory of the choking, acrid air, the burning in their lungs, was still too vivid for the purity to be taken for granted. This constant awareness of their vulnerability, of the thin line they had walked, cast a long shadow over their perceived peace. It was a peace that felt fragile, contingent, a temporary reprieve rather than a permanent state of being. This gnawing sense of unease, this unsettling quiet, was the fertile ground from which the deeper explorations of their post-fire existence would spring.

The resilience of Eden was undeniable, and in some ways, awe-inspiring. But this resilience was not a passive force; it was an active, vibrant process that was occurring around and through them. Tiny lichens, vibrant in shades of ochre and emerald, were already beginning to reclaim the blackened rocks. Fungi, intricate networks of life unseen but essential, were undoubtedly at work beneath the soil, breaking down the scorched matter, preparing the ground for new beginnings. The very ecosystem, having been pushed to its absolute limit, was now in a state of intense, albeit quiet, regeneration. This was not a passive landscape waiting for human intervention, but a living entity actively engaged in its own healing.

The quiet was a paradox. It was the sound of devastation's end, and the unheard beginning of a new, uncertain chapter. It was the silence of exhaustion, but also the silence of contemplation. The inhabitants of Eden were no longer fighting for their lives, but for their soul. The fires had purged much, but they had also revealed much. And in the stillness that followed, they were forced to look at what remained, at the whispering scars left upon the land and within themselves, and to consider the profound, unsettling implications of their continued existence. The repose was not an end, but a profound, almost sacred, pause. The struggle had shifted, becoming a quiet, introspective battle waged in the hearts and minds of those who had been granted the improbable gift of another dawn. This was Eden awakening, not with a roar, but with a breath, a quiet intake of air that held the promise of both renewal and a reckoning with the profound silence that now defined their world. The stage was set, not for a resolution, but for a deeper unfolding. The ashes were settling, but the whispers were just beginning.

The silence, once a balm, had begun to acquire a new texture, a subtle dissonance that vibrated beneath the surface of the newfound purity. It was the quiet of a world holding its breath, waiting for the echoes to subside. And the echoes, though not auditory, were everywhere. They were imprinted on the very fabric of Eden, etched into the landscape like the indelible lines on an ancient, weathered face. To move through the recovering settlements was to navigate a tableau of lingering devastation, a constant, visceral reminder of the inferno's passage.

The skeletal remains of what were once vibrant structures jutted from the scorched earth like broken teeth. Twisted rebar, blackened and warped into grotesque sculptures, clawed at the impossibly blue sky. These were not mere ruins; they were monuments to abrupt endings, silent witnesses to the frantic scramble for survival, to the moments of despair and the fleeting bursts of hope. A half-collapsed dwelling, its wooden beams reduced to charcoal, still bore the ghostly outline of a window frame, a phantom aperture through which the inferno had roared. Nearby, the mangled carcass of an automated transport lay on its side, its metallic skin blistered and peeling, a poignant symbol of disrupted lives and journeys cut tragically short. Even the air around these sites seemed heavier, thick with the residual memory of heat and destruction.

Beyond the immediate settlements, the scars ran deeper, transforming the very geography of Eden into a testament to its trauma. The forests, once a verdant sanctuary teeming with life, were now a somber expanse of blackened husks. Towering trees stood as gaunt sentinels, their branches skeletal fingers reaching skyward, devoid of leaf or songbird. The ground beneath was a perpetual carpet of ash, a soft, grey powder that muffled footsteps and clung to everything it touched. Walking through these spectral woods was an exercise in spectral immersion. The wind, as it rustled through the charred remains, carried not the scent of pine or damp earth, but a phantom aroma of smoke, a haunting perfume that triggered visceral memories of choking lungs and burning eyes.

In these desolate places, the subtle signs of recovery seemed almost sacrilegious. A patch of vibrant green moss clinging stubbornly to a fire-scarred boulder, a cluster of tiny, ash-grey fungi pushing through the charred soil – these were acts of defiance, miniature rebellions against the overwhelming evidence of annihilation. Yet, their very presence only served to highlight the vastness of what had been lost. Each new shoot of life was a whisper against a roaring silence, a fragile bloom in a graveyard of giants. It was in these stark contrasts that the weight of Eden's trauma pressed most heavily. The survivors, accustomed to the overwhelming presence of the fire, now found themselves confronted by its equally overwhelming absence, a void that was filled with the tangible remnants of its fury.

For Elara Vance, these scarred landscapes were more than just a visual reminder; they were a repository of profound grief. She found herself drawn to the periphery of what had once been the bio-domes, their iridescent membranes now tattered and blackened, gaping holes revealing the devastated interior. Inside, the sophisticated irrigation systems were twisted wrecks, and the carefully cultivated flora was reduced to brittle, carbonized remains. She remembered the vibrant hues, the intoxicating scents, the hum of life that had permeated those enclosed ecosystems. Now, only the whisper of the wind through the ruptured domes and the crunch of ash underfoot marked their passage.

She would often sit for hours on the blackened, cracked earth, her gloved hands tracing the patterns left by the molten metal of fallen support beams. Her gaze would drift to the distant silhouette of Mount Cinder, its once-majestic slopes now a stark, monochrome testament to the fire's insatiable hunger. She recalled the frantic efforts to create firebreaks, the desperate, often futile, battle against the encroaching flames that had licked at the mountain's base. The memory was so potent it could almost conjure the heat, the blinding smoke, the sheer, unadulterated terror.

"It's like the world itself has been branded," she murmured one day, her voice barely audible above the wind. Her assistant, a young man named Kael, who had witnessed the inferno from the safety of an underground bunker, nodded silently. He had seen the simulations, the data streams, but the physical reality of these scarred landscapes was a different order of comprehension. He had grown up hearing tales of Eden's natural splendor, but the reality he now experienced was one of stark, haunting beauty.

They were walking through what had been a research outpost, dedicated to studying the delicate mycelial networks that supported the health of Eden's ancient forests. Now, the modular units were melted into abstract forms, their sensitive equipment rendered useless. A scorched data tablet lay half-buried in the ash, its screen fractured, its purpose extinguished. Elara knelt, her fingers brushing away the grey powder. On it, faint traces of an image remained – a vibrant green tendril, impossibly detailed, a ghost of the life that had once thrived here.

"We understood so little, Kael," she said, her voice thick with emotion. "We thought we were mapping the connections, but we were only scratching the surface. And the fire... it showed us how interconnected everything truly is. One spark, and the whole tapestry unravels."

Kael picked up a piece of warped metal, cool to the touch now, but still bearing the imprint of unimaginable heat. "It's hard to believe that anything can grow back from this," he admitted, his voice a low rumble.

"That's the paradox, isn't it?" Elara replied, standing and looking out at the devastated panorama. "The fire destroys, but it also clears the way. It burns away the old, the weak, the choked. It's brutal, but it's also a form of cleansing. The challenge is to remember that cleansing without being consumed by the memory of the violence."

Their journey continued, each step a deliberate traversal of the past. They passed the desiccated remains of what had been a thriving hydroponic farm, its glass enclosures shattered, the nutrient-rich soil now a brittle, cracked crust. The skeletal frames of automated harvesting machines stood like forlorn skeletons, their articulated arms frozen in mid-motion, forever unable to complete their task. The silence here was particularly poignant, an absence that screamed of life denied, of sustenance interrupted.

Further on, they came to the edge of a vast crater, its rim still smoldering faintly in places, a testament to the intensity of the heat that had fused rock and metal into a glassy, obsidian surface. This was where the main firestorm had raged, an all-consuming vortex of destruction that had reshaped the very earth. The air above it shimmered with residual heat, a palpable reminder of the forces that had been unleashed. Looking into the crater was like looking into the maw of a slumbering beast, its fury temporarily abated but its potential for devastation ever-present.

It was in these starkly beautiful, yet deeply unsettling, landscapes that the survivors grappled with the visceral reality of their loss. The whispers were not just in the wind through the charred trees, but in the very ground beneath their feet, in the twisted metal that resisted their attempts to reclaim or rebuild, in the phantom scent of smoke that clung to the air. These physical remnants were not just reminders of what had been destroyed, but potent catalysts for their emotional and psychological recalibration. They were the stark, undeniable proof that Eden had been wounded, and that the process of healing would be as arduous and profound as the ordeal itself. The scars were not merely on the land; they were etched onto the collective soul of Eden, a constant, silent testament to the price of survival. The landscape itself was a living archive of their trauma, each burnt tree, each twisted piece of metal, a chapter in a story that was far from over. They walked through this archive daily, each step a reinforcement of the profound, unsettling truth: Eden had survived, but it would never be the same. The whispering scars were a constant reminder of the thin veil separating existence from oblivion, and the immense responsibility that came with living in the shadow of such a profound and devastating past.

The silence, as Elara and Kael navigated the skeletal remains of what was once the agricultural sector, wasn't just an absence of noise; it was a presence in itself, heavy with unspoken narratives. The bleached stalks of once-proud crops, now brittle and grey, stood like a field of forgotten promises. Automated drones, designed for meticulous planting and harvesting, lay scattered and melted, their metallic husks resembling discarded exoskeletons of colossal insects. It was a tableau of industry abruptly halted, of sustenance denied. Elara paused, her gaze sweeping over the desolate expanse. She remembered the early days after the fire, the desperate rationing, the gnawing hunger that had been a constant companion to the survivors huddled in their makeshift shelters. The return of abundance had been a hard-won victory, a triumph of human ingenuity and resilience. Or so it had seemed.

But as the immediate threat receded, and the arduous task of rebuilding began, subtler costs started to emerge, like hairline fractures in a seemingly solid foundation. These weren't the loud, declared sacrifices of heroic last stands or the dramatic self-immolations that would be immortalized in song and story. Instead, they were the quiet compromises, the decisions made in the suffocating darkness of desperation, where the lines between right and wrong blurred into shades of grey. These were the unsung debts, the moral transactions that had facilitated Eden's survival, and whose ledger, Elara suspected, was about to be called due.

Her mind drifted to the hydroponic farms, now silent tombs of warped plastic and fused nutrient lines. She recalled the desperate measures taken to secure the precious seed banks and genetic archives. While the primary firebreaks were designed to protect populated areas and critical infrastructure, there had been whispers, hushed conversations in the dim corridors of command centers, about redirecting vital water resources away from less critical biomes, effectively sacrificing them to feed the insatiable flames. These weren't acts of malice, but of cold, calculated triage. Entire ecosystems, meticulously cultivated over years, had been allowed to burn, their inhabitants perishing with them, to save others. The logic was irrefutable in the heat of crisis: save the many, even at the cost of the few. But the consequences of such choices were rarely neat. They lingered, like the phantom scent of smoke, in the collective consciousness.

Kael, sensing Elara's contemplative mood, pointed towards a cluster of collapsed structures at the edge of the agricultural zone. "That was Sector Gamma," he said, his voice low. "Specialized bio-engineering. They were working on atmospheric scrubbers, I think. Advanced ones."

Elara nodded, a knot tightening in her stomach. Sector Gamma. She remembered the reports, the urgent requests for additional fire-resistant materials that had gone unanswered. The resources, the skilled personnel, the precious energy reserves – they had all been funneled towards the containment efforts around the main settlements. Sector Gamma, with its cutting-edge, but perhaps less immediately vital, research, had been deemed a lower priority. Its sacrifice had been a quiet one, largely overlooked in the cacophony of the larger disaster. The scientists and technicians working there had been given the stark choice: evacuate and be integrated into other sectors, abandoning their life's work, or stay and attempt to salvage what they could, a near-certain death sentence. Many had stayed. Not out of bravado, but out of a fierce dedication to their research, a belief that its eventual contribution to Eden's future was paramount, even if it meant their own erasure. Their contribution, their quiet defiance against the encroaching inferno, had been a trade-off. The promise of advanced atmospheric purification had been traded for the immediate, desperate need to quell the blazes threatening human life.

"They made their choice," Kael said, almost as if reading her thoughts. "And the rest of us are breathing cleaner air because of it."

"But at what cost, Kael?" Elara's voice was barely a whisper. "We never acknowledged their sacrifice. We never even knew their names, most of us. They were just a sector, a number on a resource allocation report. Their research, their lives... they were the unspoken debts. The silent premiums paid for our survival." She looked at the twisted metal and fused polymers that were all that remained of Sector Gamma. "What if their work, had it been completed, could have prevented this scale of atmospheric damage in the first place? What if we traded a future solution for a present reprieve?"

The idea was a chilling one. The fire had been a catastrophic event, an almost elemental force of destruction. But the decisions made in its shadow, the ethical calculations of survival, were just as potent in shaping Eden's future. Elara had always believed in the inherent goodness of the survivors, in their collective will to rebuild a better world. But now, a seed of doubt had been planted. What if Eden's salvation wasn't a pure act of defiance, but a complex, morally ambiguous transaction? What if the very foundations of their new society were built upon a bedrock of buried decisions, of sacrifices that had never been fully accounted for?

She remembered a specific incident, a detail that had resurfaced during a review of resource logs. A limited supply of a highly specialized nutrient paste, crucial for delicate gene splicing in advanced medical research, had been diverted. Not to the medical wards treating the critically injured, but to a clandestine project. The details were heavily redacted, classified even in the post-fire debriefings. Elara had managed to access a fragmented report, hinting at the development of a biological agent – a countermeasure, perhaps, to an unknown threat. The success of this project, the report implied, had been dependent on that nutrient paste, and its allocation had directly impacted the survival rate of certain critical injuries sustained during the initial evacuation. It was a stark illustration of prioritizing long-term, speculative security over immediate, tangible lives.

"There's a fine line between pragmatism and... something else," Elara mused, her gaze fixed on the horizon, where the blackened slopes of Mount Cinder stood stark against the azure sky. "We tell ourselves we did what was necessary. But who defined 'necessary'? And who paid the price for that definition?"

The fire had been an indiscriminate enemy, but the choices made in its wake were anything but. They were deliberate, often agonizing, and always carried a hidden cost. The engineers who had overloaded the geothermal vents to create a localized atmospheric disturbance, hoping to steer the fire away from a critical research facility, had knowingly risked seismic instability in a neighboring, less populated valley. The valley had been devastated, its small community of geologists and their families lost. Their lives, their research into Eden's nascent tectonic activity, had been sacrificed to protect the vital data housed in the primary facility. The outcome, from a purely strategic standpoint, had been successful. The facility was saved, its contents preserved. But the cost, the lives extinguished and the scientific knowledge lost, had been conveniently swept under the rug of rebuilding.

"It's the forgotten ones, Kael," Elara continued, her voice gaining a somber intensity. "The people, the places, the projects that didn't make the headlines. Their contributions, their sacrifices, they are the phantom limbs of our recovery. We feel their absence, even if we can't precisely name it." She turned to Kael, her eyes reflecting a deep, unsettling curiosity. "What else have we buried? What other debts have we incurred in the name of survival?"

The whispers of the scars were becoming more insistent, morphing from mere reminders of destruction into subtle insinuations of complicity. The purity of Eden, the pristine landscape they were striving to rebuild, was increasingly appearing to be a façade, a polished surface over a foundation riddled with ethically compromised decisions. The survival of Eden hadn't been a clean, heroic narrative of triumph against nature; it had been a messy, desperate scramble, a series of compromises where the line between salvation and sin had been irrevocably blurred. And Elara felt a growing certainty that these unspoken debts, these buried decisions, would not remain buried forever. They were an intrinsic part of Eden's story, and like all debts, they would eventually demand to be paid, in ways they might not yet be prepared to comprehend. The very air they breathed, the ground they walked upon, seemed to hold the silent testimony of these forgotten sacrifices, a testament that was slowly, inexorably, rising to the surface.

The remnants of the fire, though no longer an active inferno, cast long shadows across the reclaimed landscapes of Eden. For Elara and Kael, these shadows were not merely optical phenomena; they were tangible manifestations of the past, woven into the fabric of their present existence. Their journey through the hushed ruins of the agricultural sector had been a stark reminder that survival had come at a price, a price etched not just in the scorched earth but in the very psyches of those who had borne the brunt of the crisis. They had been the strategists, the engineers, the swift responders – the individuals who, in the heart of the conflagration, had been hailed as saviors. Now, they were simply custodians of a fragile peace, haunted by the echoes of their own necessary transgressions.

Among them was Anya Sharma, once the chief architect of Eden's defense grid, her name synonymous with the brilliant, audacious redirection of atmospheric processors that had created a localized storm, pushing back the fire's most ravenous tendrils. Her hands, once adept at manipulating complex holographic schematics, now trembled slightly as she poured a measured dose of stimulant into her morning nutrient paste. The crisis had demanded a cold, detached brilliance, a willingness to make choices that would forever stain the soul. She had orchestrated the controlled burn of entire sectors deemed irrecoverable, sacrificing ecological reserves to create firebreaks that saved countless lives. The sheer computational power she had commanded, the relentless analysis of risk and reward, had been a consuming force. But the exhilaration of success, of witnessing the flames recede from Eden's core, had long since faded, replaced by a gnawing emptiness.

Her current role, overseeing the ecological restoration of the fire-ravaged zones, was a form of penance. Each sapling she planted, each patch of sterile soil she coaxed back to life, was an attempt to counterbalance the destruction she had so instrumentally enabled. The scars on the land mirrored the unseen wounds within her. She saw phantom flames in the flickering light of her habitation unit, heard the crackle of burning timber in the hum of the life support systems. Sleep offered little respite, often filled with fragmented nightmares of ash and desperation, of faces she had seen in the evacuation queues, their pleas for sanctuary drowned out by the roar of the fire. The public lauded Eden's recovery, the swiftness of its rebirth, but Anya knew the truth. The recovery was a veneer, a meticulously crafted illusion built upon the ashes of difficult, often morally compromising, decisions.

Then there was Jian Li, the lead engineer for the water reclamation and distribution network. During the peak of the fire, his team had been instrumental in diverting precious water reserves. Not just from non-essential agricultural zones, as Elara had suspected, but from carefully managed arboreal reserves, from the delicate ecosystems that supported Eden's most specialized fauna. The decision had been agonizing, a brutal calculation of immediate human needs versus long-term ecological viability. He remembered the hushed, desperate meetings, the desperate pleas from xenobotanists whose life's work was about to be submerged in a torrent of fire-retardant foam, or worse, simply allowed to burn. Jian had looked into their eyes, seen the same terror that gripped his own heart, and still, he had given the order. The water flowed, not towards the threatened ancient forests, but towards the desperate hoses dousing the flames threatening the central habitat domes.

Now, Jian spent his days monitoring the health of the rebuilt hydrological systems, ensuring that the precious, finite water of Eden was used with the utmost care. Every drop was accounted for, every flow meticulously managed. Yet, he felt like a prisoner in his own meticulously engineered world. The pristine clarity of the reclaimed water, flowing through crystal pipes, served as a constant reminder of the murky depths of his past actions. He would sometimes stand by the largest reservoir, watching the sunlight glint off the surface, and wonder about the unseen aquatic life that had perished, the unique microbial colonies that had been annihilated when he rerouted the streams. His success in averting a water crisis during the fire had been celebrated, but it was a celebration that tasted of ashes. The psychological toll was immense; he found himself hyper-vigilant, obsessively checking every gauge, every sensor, as if a single miscalculation could unleash another catastrophe. The weight of his authority, once a source of pride, now felt like a suffocating burden.

The shift from active defenders to weary guardians was palpable. The thrill of combat, the adrenaline-fueled clarity of immediate crisis, had been replaced by the mundane, yet profoundly exhausting, reality of long-term consequence management. These individuals, once the shining beacons of Eden's resilience, now moved with a quiet gravity, their faces etched with a weariness that went beyond mere physical fatigue. They were the architects of Eden's survival, and now they were its haunted caretakers.

Consider Commander Eva Rostova, the former head of Eden's security forces. Her strategic brilliance had been crucial in organizing evacuations, in establishing perimeters, and in coordinating the deployment of emergency resources. She had made the difficult calls, the ones that meant designating certain zones as lost causes, guiding desperate citizens away from impossible routes, and making the heart-wrenching decision to seal off compromised sectors, effectively condemning those who couldn't escape in time. The metallic clang of sealed blast doors, the finality of those decisions, echoed in her mind every night. She had seen the desperate faces of families separated in the chaos, had heard the muffled cries from behind doors she had ordered shut.

Her current command was significantly less dramatic: the management of Eden's intricate network of automated patrols and environmental monitoring systems. Her days were filled with reviewing sensor logs, optimizing patrol routes, and ensuring the seamless integration of new surveillance technologies designed to detect nascent ecological instabilities. It was a necessary role, vital for maintaining the delicate balance Eden had so painstakingly achieved. But it lacked the immediate, visceral impact of her former duties. The enemy was no longer a roaring inferno, but subtle shifts in atmospheric composition, minute seismic tremors, or the slow creep of invasive flora. The stakes were no less real, but the visceral enemy had been replaced by an abstract threat, requiring a different kind of vigilance – a quiet, constant, and deeply internal one.

Eva found herself increasingly withdrawn, her interactions with others often brief and perfunctory. The camaraderie forged in the crucible of the fire had been replaced by a solitary burden of memory. She replayed the moments of indecision, the split-second choices that had determined life or death, over and over in her mind. Had she sent too many to the north sector when the south would have been safer? Had she hesitated too long before ordering the lockdown of the research labs? These questions, once the subject of post-crisis debriefings, now haunted her waking hours and infiltrated her dreams. The public saw her as a pillar of strength, a seasoned leader who had guided them through the darkest of times. But in the quiet solitude of her hab-unit, she felt like a ghost, haunted by the lives she had touched, and the lives she had, by necessity, abandoned.

The psychological toll was a pervasive current running through all those who had been thrust into positions of extreme responsibility during the fire. They were no longer the heroic figures of Eden's origin stories. The epic narrative had ended, and they were left with the quiet, unglamorous epilogue. Their victories were etched in the survival of the colony, but their victories were also indelibly marked by the losses they had engineered. They were lauded for their competence, their resilience, their unwavering resolve, but they carried the invisible scars of those who had paid the ultimate price for Eden's existence.

Consider Dr. Aris Thorne, the brilliant, albeit eccentric, bio-engineer who had developed the sophisticated atmospheric scrubbers that now hummed throughout Eden's habitats, filtering the air with remarkable efficiency. During the fire, his research had been on the cusp of a breakthrough, but the crisis had forced him to pivot. He had cannibalized his experimental designs, re-purposed his advanced filtration prototypes, and worked with Jian's team to adapt them for immediate, large-scale deployment. The success of these makeshift scrubbers had been a critical factor in making certain sectors habitable again, preventing mass asphyxiation from smoke inhalation. Thorne was hailed as a scientific miracle worker.

Yet, Thorne was a recluse, his former exuberance replaced by a profound melancholy. The fire had consumed not only his meticulously cultivated research samples but also his faith in the inherent predictability of nature, and by extension, the inherent control humanity could exert over it. He had witnessed firsthand how quickly carefully constructed biological systems could unravel, how fragile the balance of life truly was. His breakthrough had come at the cost of his original, long-term research into terraforming and atmospheric synthesis, a project aimed at creating entirely new, self-sustaining biomes. That ambitious dream, the dream of truly creating new life, had been extinguished by the immediate, desperate need to preserve what they already had. Now, he focused his efforts on maintaining the existing, compromised atmosphere, a constant battle against the subtle toxins and unseen pollutants that were the lingering legacy of the fire. He felt like a mechanic endlessly patching a broken machine, rather than an architect building a new world. The quiet hum of his scrubbers was a constant reminder of what had been lost, a lullaby of regret.

These individuals, the Guardians of the Green, were not basking in the glory of their past deeds. Instead, they were engaged in a perpetual, quiet struggle against the ghosts of their decisions. Their vigilance was no longer about direct combat, but about the painstaking, often emotionally draining, process of nurturing a world that bore the indelible marks of their interventions. The psychological toll was a constant companion, a whisper in the quiet hours, a weight that pressed down on their shoulders with the unrelenting force of memory. They had saved Eden, yes, but the cost of that salvation was a price they continued to pay, day after weary day, in the silence of their burdened stewardship. The vibrant green that was slowly, tentatively, reclaiming the scarred landscapes was a testament to their efforts, but for these guardians, it was also a constant, melancholic reminder of the dark choices that had paved the way for its return.

The hush that had settled over Eden was a fragile thing, a carefully maintained silence that masked the profound anxieties of its custodians. Elara, Kael, Anya, Jian, Eva, and Aris – they were the living embodiments of this tension, their days a tapestry of meticulous oversight and a quiet dread of what might lie beneath the surface of their hard-won peace. Yet, in the very quietude they so desperately sought to preserve, something new, something entirely unexpected, was beginning to stir. It was a whisper at the edge of perception, a subtle alteration in the planet's rhythm that hinted at a consciousness far older and more complex than humanity had ever dared to imagine.

It began with the flora. Anya, with her sharpened focus on ecological restoration, was the first to notice. The saplings she had planted in the charred earth of the agricultural sector, the struggling shoots of hardy, fire-resistant grasses designed to bind the soil and prevent erosion, were exhibiting an unusual uniformity. Not just in their growth rate, which was expected given the controlled nutrient and hydration regimes, but in their very form. Their leaves, meant to be broad and receptive to the filtered sunlight, were developing a subtle, almost crystalline structure, catching the light in ways that seemed intentional, almost decorative. She dismissed it at first, attributing it to subtle genetic variations or perhaps an unforeseen interaction with the soil's mineral composition, a lingering effect of the fire. But the pattern persisted, spreading to other re-vegetation sites, a silent, collective elegance emerging from the ashes.

Then came the atmospheric anomalies. Jian, whose life was now inextricably linked to the precise monitoring of Eden's atmospheric processors, noticed minute fluctuations in the filtered air. These were not the predictable variations caused by internal cycling or minor equipment tolerances. They were subtle, rhythmic pulses, almost like a slow, steady heartbeat, that seemed to emanate from the planet itself. His instruments, designed to detect threats, registered them as benign, mere background noise. But for Jian, accustomed to the relentless pressure of vigilance, this 'noise' felt different. It was too ordered, too consistent to be random. He found himself spending hours in the monitoring stations, tracing these peculiar atmospheric signatures, a growing sense of awe, tinged with an unfamiliar apprehension, settling upon him. It was as if Eden itself was breathing, a slow, deliberate exhalation and inhalation that was entirely new.

Eva, ever the pragmatist, initially dismissed these observations as the product of overstressed minds seeking patterns where none existed. Her focus remained resolutely on the tangible threats: the integrity of the perimeter, the efficiency of the automated patrols, the detection of any residual biohazards from the fire. Yet, even she couldn't ignore the peculiar behavior of Eden's fauna. The indigenous insectoids, typically solitary and territorial, began congregating in specific cleared areas, their multifaceted eyes seemingly fixed on a single point in the sky, or on a patch of newly sprouted moss. The avian analogues, their calls usually a cacophony of territorial warnings and mating rituals, had fallen into a strange, harmonic chorus. It wasn't a song of distress, nor a celebration. It was something akin to a collective meditation, a wordless communication that resonated with a profound stillness. She documented these occurrences meticulously, her reports growing longer, more detailed, but the explanations remained elusive, confined to the realm of conjecture.

Aris Thorne, the recluse of Eden's scientific elite, was perhaps the most attuned to these subtle shifts. His work on atmospheric filtration had made him acutely aware of the delicate equilibrium of Eden's air. He had always seen the planet's atmosphere as a complex, reactive system, but now he perceived something more. He noticed that the fine dust particles, the lingering remnants of the fire that his scrubbers worked tirelessly to neutralize, were beginning to aggregate in specific patterns on the outer surfaces of the habitat domes. These weren't random depositions; they formed intricate, geometric mandalas, ephemeral artworks that appeared overnight and dissolved with the morning light. It was as if the very air was expressing itself, painting transient messages that no one could yet decipher. He began to theorize, in the solitude of his laboratory, that these weren't merely atmospheric phenomena, but expressions of a nascent intelligence, a planetary consciousness awakening from a long slumber.

The fire had been a cataclysm, a brutal awakening for humanity. But perhaps, Aris mused, it had also been an awakening for Eden. The intense heat, the chemical transformations, the sheer existential pressure exerted by the colony's desperate struggle for survival – these had acted as a catalyst, disturbing a dormant awareness within the planet's very matrix. It was a consciousness that had always existed, perhaps, but had been too subtle, too alien for humanity to perceive amidst their own internal dramas. The fire, in its destructive fury, had inadvertently stripped away the veil, allowing glimpses of a deeper reality.

This emergent intelligence was not aggressive, not a direct response to the fire's inferno. It was more akin to a slow, dawning awareness, a gentle stirring. It was in the way the sunlight seemed to linger a moment longer on the surfaces of the new growth, in the way the wind whispered through the re-established canopy with a new cadence, in the way the planet's magnetic field, which Aris had always treated as a static shield, now pulsed with a subtle, almost responsive rhythm. These were not malfunctions, not environmental anomalies to be corrected. They were signs, Elara began to believe, of a dialogue waiting to happen.

She found herself drawn to the edges of the re-vegetated zones, not just to assess the progress of her restoration efforts, but to simply observe. She would sit for hours, her back against the rough bark of a newly planted dura-tree, and let the quietude wash over her. The hum of the life support systems, once a source of anxiety, now seemed to blend with the planet's own subtle vibrations. She noticed how the patterns of light and shadow shifted not just with the sun's arc, but with an internal rhythm, a slow undulation that felt like a sigh. It was during one of these quiet vigils that she witnessed something extraordinary. A patch of scorched earth, which had stubbornly resisted all attempts at re-seeding, began to shimmer. It wasn't the heat haze of a hot day; it was a pearlescent luminescence that bloomed and faded, accompanied by a faint, resonant hum that seemed to vibrate in her very bones. As she watched, mesmerized, a single, impossibly delicate tendril of emerald green unfurled from the center of the luminescence, reaching towards the sky. It was a growth unlike any she had engineered, a testament to a force that lay beyond her understanding.

Kael, ever the pragmatist in Elara's orbit, initially viewed these emerging phenomena with suspicion, a potential new threat to be cataloged and understood. His mind, trained in the harsh logic of survival, struggled to reconcile the subtle beauty with any practical purpose. He meticulously charted the crystalline leaf formations, measured the atmospheric pulses with his gravimetric sensors, and analyzed the behavioral shifts in the fauna. He looked for cause and effect, for predictable mechanisms. But Eden's subtle messages defied his rigorous methodology. The patterns were too intricate, the manifestations too ephemeral.

"It's like trying to catch smoke with a sieve, Elara," he'd said one evening, his brow furrowed as he reviewed sensor logs of the peculiar avian chorus. "These aren't quantifiable. They're... impressions. And impressions don't keep the air breathable or the soil fertile."

But even Kael, in his own stoic way, began to feel the shift. It was in the quiet moments, when the operational demands of his role as head of security relented, that he would find himself staring out at the re-greening landscape. He'd notice how the shadows cast by the newly grown flora seemed to dance with a life of their own, not just in response to the wind, but with a deeper, more deliberate movement. He'd observe the insectoids, their previously frantic movements now imbued with a strange, deliberate grace, as if they were engaged in a choreographed dance dictated by an unseen conductor.

One day, while inspecting a perimeter sensor array on the northern plains, an area still bearing deep scars from the fire, he witnessed something that defied his ingrained skepticism. A small herd of grazing quadrupedal herbivores, creatures known for their skittish nature, had gathered around a cluster of oddly shaped rocks. They weren't grazing; they were standing perfectly still, their heads lowered, their large, liquid eyes seemingly fixed on the stones. The stones themselves seemed to hum, a low, resonant frequency that Kael could feel through the soles of his boots. As he approached cautiously, the animals didn't bolt. Instead, they shifted slightly, making way for him, their movements fluid and unhurried. The hum intensified, and Kael, for the first time, felt a profound sense of peace emanating from the rocks, a feeling that transcended his own anxieties. He stood there for a long time, not as a security officer assessing a potential threat, but as a solitary observer, caught in the quietude of a planetary embrace. When he finally turned to leave, the herbivores resumed their grazing, the hum subsided, and the rocks appeared just as they were – ordinary geological formations. But Kael knew, with a certainty that bypassed his logical faculties, that he had just witnessed a communion.

The architects of Eden's survival – Anya, Jian, Eva, Aris, Elara, and Kael – were warriors of the mundane, their battles fought not with plasma rifles, but with nutrient paste, atmospheric regulators, and patrol schedules. They were the keepers of a fragile peace, and now, it seemed, they were also becoming the reluctant interpreters of a nascent planetary consciousness. The fire had been a brutal test, forcing them to confront the darkest aspects of their own humanity. But the aftermath, with its subtle whispers and enigmatic signs, was pushing them to confront something even more profound: the possibility that they were not alone on this world, not just as inhabitants, but as part of a larger, living entity.

Aris Thorne, more than anyone, felt the resonance of this awakening. His isolation had always been a refuge, a space where he could wrestle with the complexities of life. Now, the universe seemed to be answering his unspoken questions. He had spent years studying Eden's unique biosphere, its intricate web of life, but he had always viewed it through a human-centric lens, seeking to understand it for humanity's benefit. Now, he began to see Eden not as a resource, but as a being. He observed how the atmospheric pulses Jian detected seemed to synchronize with the phases of Eden's twin moons, how the crystalline leaf patterns Anya documented mirrored fractal geometries found in deep-sea bioluminescent organisms, how the animal congregations Eva noted always occurred in areas with unique geothermal signatures.

He began to experiment, not with the intent to control, but to communicate. He designed a series of sonic emitters, calibrated to specific resonant frequencies he had detected in the planet's subtle vibrations. He placed them in areas where the atmospheric anomalies were strongest, near the shimmering patches of earth Elara had observed, and around the geothermal vents that seemed to attract the fauna. He expected no immediate response, no dramatic revelation. He was merely planting seeds of interaction, extending a tentative hand into the unknown.

Days turned into weeks. The world around them continued its slow, steady recovery. The green returned, not as a chaotic explosion, but as a deliberate, intricate tapestry. The atmospheric pulses became slightly more pronounced, the harmonic choruses of the avian analogues more complex. And then, one cycle, something shifted.

Aris was monitoring his emitters when he noticed a deviation in the sonic feedback. It wasn't an error; it was a response. The planet's own vibrations, previously a diffuse background hum, had begun to attune themselves to the frequencies he was emitting. It was as if Eden was listening, and then, in its own ineffable way, was beginning to reply. The crystalline structures on the leaves seemed to glow with a faint, internal light. The shimmering earth patches pulsed with a more vibrant luminescence. And the fauna, which had been congregating in stillness, now moved with a unified, flowing purpose, their collective actions creating intricate patterns on the landscape that seemed to communicate a profound sense of interconnectedness.

Elara, walking through a re-vegetated valley one morning, found herself surrounded by a flock of iridescent, butterfly-like creatures she had never seen before. They didn't flutter erratically; they moved in a synchronized ballet, forming a living kaleidoscope around her. As she stood there, mesmerized, a single creature detached itself from the swarm and landed gently on her outstretched hand. Its delicate, almost translucent wings pulsed with a soft, rhythmic light, and Elara felt a profound sense of calm wash over her, a silent reassurance that her efforts, their efforts, were recognized. It wasn't a voice, not a language she could understand, but it was a communication, a gentle acknowledgment from the living planet itself.

The fire had left scars, deep and indelible, on Eden and its inhabitants. But in the quiet aftermath, a new kind of growth was emerging, not just in the verdant return of the flora, but in the awakening of a planetary consciousness. It was a consciousness that moved with the slow, deliberate grace of geologic time, a silent observer that was now beginning to stir, to respond, to perhaps even to communicate. And the weary custodians of Eden, the very ones who had borne the weight of its survival, were finding themselves on the precipice of a dialogue they had never anticipated, a conversation with the living world that had, in its own silent way, endured. The first sigh of the evolved was not a cry of pain or a roar of defiance, but a gentle, resonant hum, an invitation to a new kind of existence.

## CHAPTER TWO

# THE WEIGHT OF REMEMBRANCE

The scent of ozone, a phantom still clinging to the air even after months of diligent atmospheric processing, was a trigger for Anya. It would materialize without warning, a metallic tang that twisted her stomach and brought a cold sweat to her brow. She'd be tending to a young hydroponic vine, coaxing life from the sterile nutrient gel, and then, it would hit her – the acrid, burning smell that had permeated everything, that had been the very breath of their near-annihilation. The memory was visceral, a sharp, suffocating assault that would steal her breath and leave her trembling, her carefully cultivated composure shattering like brittle glass. She remembered the desperate scrabbling of hands in the ash, the frantic whispers of names that would never again be answered, the chilling silence that followed each choked cry. These were the ghosts of the Last Stand, not spectral apparitions, but corporeal echoes imprinted on her very being, refusing to be scrubbed clean by Eden's meticulously filtered atmosphere.

Kael's torment manifested differently, a gnawing, relentless guilt that ate at the edges of his sleep. He saw flashes of the perimeter breach, the desperate pleas over the comms, the agonizing decisions he'd had to make. There were faces he couldn't save, choices he'd second-guessed a thousand times in the suffocating darkness of his small quarters. He'd replay the events, searching for a different path, a more heroic intervention, a solution that had somehow

25

eluded him in the chaos. He'd relive the moment he'd sealed off sectors, knowing with a cold certainty what that meant for those trapped within, the metallic clang of the blast doors a sound that echoed in the hollow chambers of his conscience. These weren't memories of what happened, but of what he felt he *should* have done, phantom limbs of responsibility that ached with an unbearable phantom pain. The weight of those lives, lost or seemingly abandoned, pressed down on him, a physical burden that made every step feel heavy, every breath an exertion. He would stand guard on the perimeter, his gaze sweeping across the recovering landscape, but his eyes were fixed on an internal battlefield, a landscape of regret and self-recrimination.

Jian, immersed in the cold, logical world of data streams and atmospheric readouts, found his ghosts in the very systems he maintained. He'd see a surge in energy consumption, a minor dip in oxygen levels, and his mind would snap back to the frantic moments when the life support systems had buckled under the fire's relentless onslaught. He remembered the blaring alarms, the flashing red lights, the sickening lurch of the habitat as its integrity was compromised. He'd remember the desperate scramble to reroute power, the agonizing wait for diagnostics, the chilling realization of how close they had come to complete systemic failure. Even now, the steady hum of the atmospheric processors, a sound that should signify safety and stability, would sometimes take on a discordant note, a phantom echo of the cacophony that had accompanied their near-demise. He'd find himself running redundant checks, cross-referencing data that was already irrefutable, driven by an unseen compulsion to ensure that the past, in its brutal, catastrophic form, could never repeat itself. His hands would hover over the console, his fingers twitching, as if he could physically hold the delicate balance of Eden's atmosphere in place, warding off the invisible specters of technological collapse.

Eva's ghosts were tied to the palpable absence of others. She moved through Eden's recovering sectors, her sharp eyes cataloging the returning life, but her mind was often elsewhere, her gaze snagging on empty spaces where familiar figures once stood. She remembered the shared meals, the hushed conversations, the camaraderie forged in the pre-fire days, a time of assumed normalcy and shared futures. Now, there were gaps in the fabric of their community, voids left by those who had been consumed by the flames. She'd see a favorite workstation, a shared common area, a particular view from a habitat window, and a wave of poignant grief would wash over her, the sharp, sudden ache of remembrance. It wasn't just the grand, heroic sacrifices that haunted her, but the quiet, everyday losses – the colleague who always made terrible jokes, the friend who shared a passion for ancient literature, the person whose mere presence had been a steady anchor in the storm. These were the quiet ghosts, the ones who left no dramatic imprint on history books, but whose absence was a constant, dull throb in the heart of Eden's survivors.

Elara carried a different burden. Her grief was a more internalized, profound sorrow, a mourning for the loss of innocence, both for herself and for humanity. The fire had stripped away the veneer of progress, the illusion of control, the comfortable belief that they were masters of their own destiny. She remembered the raw fear, the primal instinct for survival that had surfaced, the moments when compassion had warred with practicality, when empathy had been a dangerous luxury. She recalled the faces of the desperate, the pleading eyes, the raw, unvarnished terror that had reflected her own. These memories weren't about specific actions, but about the erosion of her own moral compass, the subtle compromises made under duress, the realization that even the noblest intentions could be tested to their breaking point. She felt the lingering taint of necessity, the understanding that survival sometimes demanded acts that felt like betrayals of the very ideals they claimed to uphold. This internal conflict, this wrestling with her own capacity for darkness, was a ghost that whispered doubts in her ear, a constant reminder of the fragility of her own humanity.

The silence that had settled over Eden, once a welcome respite, now often felt pregnant with the unspoken. It was a silence that held the echoes of screams, the residue of despair, the phantom weight of lives extinguished. Anya would find herself meticulously arranging tools in her laboratory, her movements almost ritualistic, as if imposing order on her physical space could impose order on the chaos that still churned within her. The memory of a specific scream, high-pitched and full of an unimaginable terror, would sometimes pierce through the quiet, jolting her back to the inferno, her hands flying instinctively to protect her face from a heat that was no longer there. She would then force herself to focus on the gentle hum of the nutrient pumps, the soft glow of the grow lights, anchoring herself to the present reality of life's persistent, fragile resurgence.

Kael would often find himself staring out at the horizon during his patrols, his posture rigid, his gaze distant. The vastness of Eden's recovering plains, once a symbol of their new beginning, now sometimes felt like an endless expanse of emptiness, a canvas upon which the tragedies of the past were perpetually replayed. He'd see a twisted piece of debris, a scorch mark that had stubbornly resisted the encroaching greenery, and his mind would conjure the scene of its destruction, the desperate struggle that had ensued. He remembered the smell of burning synthetics, the sickening crackle of collapsing structures, the guttural cries of those caught in the path of the flames. These weren't just memories; they were phantom sensations, the phantom ache of muscles strained in futile efforts, the phantom sting of smoke in his eyes, the phantom taste of ash on his tongue. He'd clench his fists, his knuckles white, trying to physically suppress the phantom onslaught, to force the ghosts back into the recesses of his mind.

Jian's torment was a subtle, insidious invasion of his meticulously ordered world. He would be reviewing atmospheric data, seeking anomalies, and a flicker on a secondary monitor, a slight deviation in pressure readings, would send a jolt of adrenaline through him. It wasn't just the numbers that unnerved him; it was the feeling of vulnerability they represented. He remembered the frantic scramble to repair a failing environmental control unit, the cold dread that had gripped him as the oxygen levels dipped precariously low. He'd recall the frantic shouts of his colleagues, the palpable fear in their voices, the desperate hope that their efforts would be enough. Even now, the rhythmic pulse of the atmospheric processors, a comforting sign of stability, could sometimes morph into the frantic thrum of alarms in his memory, each beat a reminder of how close they had come to succumbing. He'd find himself micromanaging the systems, running diagnostics that were purely ceremonial, his fingers flying across the controls in a frantic attempt to reassert an order that had once been so brutally shattered.

Eva's grief was a quiet, persistent ache, a constant awareness of the missing pieces in their small, fragile community. She would see a familiar piece of equipment, a tool that had belonged to someone lost, and a wave of sorrow would wash over her, sharp and unexpected. She remembered the shared jokes, the casual camaraderie, the quiet support that had existed before the fire. Now, there were silences where laughter should be, empty chairs at communal tables, conversations that felt incomplete. She'd recall the way a particular individual would tilt their head when listening, the unique cadence of their voice, the way they'd always offer a word of encouragement. These were not grand narratives of heroism or sacrifice, but the small, intimate details that had formed the tapestry of their lives, now irrevocably torn. The memory of a shared glance, a whispered confidence, a simple act of kindness – these were the ghosts that haunted her, the subtle reminders of a vanished warmth, a palpable absence that no amount of environmental restoration could ever truly fill.

Elara's internal struggle was a profound wrestling with the cost of survival. The fire had forced them to confront the darker aspects of their own nature, the primal instincts that surfaced when faced with annihilation. She remembered the desperation in the eyes of those pleading for help, the agonizing choice between self-preservation and the impossible burden of saving everyone. She recalled the moments when empathy had felt like a dangerous weakness, when logic had demanded a ruthless pragmatism that felt like a betrayal of her own humanity. These were not memories of external events, but of internal battles, of compromises made under duress, of the slow erosion of her own moral certainty. She felt the lingering weight of those decisions, the gnawing suspicion that in saving themselves, they had irrevocably changed who they were, that the fire had not only consumed their physical world but had also left indelible scars on their souls. She often found herself staring into the polished surfaces of Eden's habitat, not seeing her reflection, but seeing the phantom imprint of the person she had been, the person she had been forced to leave behind in the crucible of the Last Stand.

The scent of scorched earth, a phantom that Anya sometimes caught on the recycled air, was enough to send a shiver down her spine. It wasn't the lingering chemical trace of the fire, but a purely psychological manifestation, a scent conjured by memory, sharp and acrid and utterly terrifying. She would be tending to the delicate roots of a newly planted bio-luminescent moss, its soft glow a stark contrast to the darkness she remembered, and then it would hit her – the suffocating, all-encompassing stench of destruction. Her hands would falter, her breath would catch in her throat, and for a terrifying moment, she would be back in the inferno, the heat searing her skin, the screams of the trapped echoing in her ears. She remembered the desperate scrabble for survival, the raw, animalistic fear that had overridden all reason. She remembered the faces, contorted in pain and terror, etched into her mind's eye, ghosts that refused to fade. The weight of those faces, those lost lives, pressed down on her, a physical burden that made the vibrant green of Eden sometimes feel like a mocking taunt. She'd clutch at the sterile fabric of her uniform, a futile attempt to ground herself, to push back against the encroaching tide of memory.

Kael's guilt was a silent, gnawing companion, a persistent echo of his perceived failures. He would stand on the watchtowers, his gaze sweeping across the re-greening plains, but his vision was often obscured by phantoms. He saw the breaches in the perimeter, the frantic commands issued, the agonizing choices made under impossible pressure. He replayed the moments he'd had to prioritize, to seal off sectors, knowing that behind those blast doors, lives were being extinguished. The metallic clang of those doors echoed in the hollow spaces of his mind, a sound more potent than any physical alarm. He remembered the desperate pleas over the comms, the choked silence that followed, the crushing weight of knowing he could not be everywhere, could not save everyone. He'd clench his jaw, his knuckles white, as if by sheer force of will he could banish the specters of those he couldn't save, could silence the phantom cries that haunted his waking hours and bled into his dreams.

Jian's torment was a subtle invasion of his meticulously ordered world, a constant awareness of the fragility of the systems he now commanded. He'd be monitoring atmospheric pressure, a routine task, when a minuscule fluctuation, a barely perceptible dip, would send a jolt of cold dread through him. His mind would snap back to the frantic hours when the life support systems had teetered on the brink of collapse, the blaring alarms, the sickening lurch of the habitat, the chilling realization of how close they had come to total failure. He remembered the frantic efforts to reroute power, the agonizing wait for diagnostics, the palpable fear that had permeated the control center. Even now, the steady, reassuring hum of the processors could morph into the frantic thrum of failing machinery in his memory, each pulse a stark reminder of the razor's edge they had walked. He'd find himself running redundant checks, cross-referencing data that was already irrefutable, driven by an unseen compulsion to ensure that the catastrophic past could never repeat itself.

Eva's grief was a quiet, pervasive sorrow, a constant awareness of the missing pieces in their fractured community. She'd find herself pausing by an empty workstation, a shared alcove that had once been a hub of conversation, and a wave of poignant remembrance would wash over her. She remembered the casual camaraderie, the shared meals, the easy laughter that had once filled Eden's communal spaces. Now, there were silences where those sounds should be, gaps in the fabric of their social interactions that no amount of diligent planning could fill. She'd recall the unique way a lost colleague would tilt their head when listening, the distinctive cadence of their voice, the specific comfort they'd offered in a moment of doubt. These weren't the grand narratives of heroic sacrifice, but the quiet, intimate details of everyday life that had been irrevocably lost. The ghosts she encountered were not spectral apparitions, but the lingering impressions of vanished warmth, the palpable absence of those who had once been integral to the tapestry of their shared existence.

Elara carried the heaviest burden, a profound sorrow for the loss of innocence, not just for herself but for humanity. The fire had stripped away the veneer of progress and control, exposing the raw, primal instincts that lay beneath. She remembered the desperate pleas for help, the agonizing ethical quandaries, the moments when empathy had felt like a dangerous liability. She'd recall the cold logic that had sometimes been necessary for survival, the compromises made under duress, the gnawing realization that in saving themselves, they had perhaps lost a part of their essential humanity. These weren't memories of external events, but of internal battles, of the erosion of certainty, of the chilling understanding that even the noblest of intentions could be tested to their breaking point. She felt the lingering taint of necessity, the constant whisper of doubt about the true cost of their survival, a ghost that haunted the quiet chambers of her conscience, a perpetual reminder of the fragile nature of their moral compass.

The initial phase of recovery had been a desperate, all-consuming scramble for survival. Now, as the dust settled and the immediate threat receded, a new, more insidious challenge emerged: the rebuilding of trust. Eden, once a beacon of collaborative innovation, now bore the invisible scars of suspicion. The carefully constructed veneer of community solidarity began to fray, revealing the underlying anxieties and unresolved guilt that had festered in the aftermath of the fire. It wasn't enough to simply rebuild habitats and restore life support; they had to rebuild the very foundation of their shared existence, a task far more daunting than any engineering feat.

Anya found herself increasingly unsettled by the subtle shifts in interpersonal dynamics. While she poured her energy into nurturing the nascent botanical gardens, a vital symbol of their renewed connection to life, she couldn't shake the feeling of being watched, of unspoken judgments being cast her way. It was a feeling she couldn't quite articulate, a prickling sensation on the back of her neck that had nothing to do with the climate control. She noticed the way conversations would abruptly halt when she entered a communal space, the way eyes would dart away, feigning an intense interest in a data screen or a distant viewport. It was as if the shared experience of the fire had created invisible fault lines between them, and any perceived deviation from a collective narrative of stoic resilience was met with an almost instinctive wariness. She recalled the pre-fire days, when camaraderie flowed easily, fueled by shared purpose and a mutual understanding. Now, that easy trust felt like a distant memory, replaced by a guarded politeness that masked a deeper unease. Was it her imagination, or did some of the survivors regard her meticulous focus on the gardens as an act of denial, a willful ignorance of the deeper wounds they all carried?

Kael, accustomed to the clear-cut lines of command and the inherent trust placed in his role as security chief, found himself grappling with a more complex form of suspicion. His instincts, honed by years of anticipating threats, were now turning inward. He observed the subtle shifts in loyalty, the whispered conversations that ceased at his approach, the questioning glances that followed his directives. The same individuals who had once looked to him for reassurance now seemed to scrutinize his every decision, their trust eroded by the harsh realities of the fire. He saw it in the eyes of those who had lost loved ones, a silent accusation that he hadn't done enough, a suspicion that his choices, however necessary, had been weighted by an unknown bias. He found himself second-guessing his own interactions, wondering if his attempts to rebuild order were being perceived as an assertion of power, a way to regain control in a world that had proven to be so brutally uncontrollable. The weight of responsibility was now compounded by the chilling realization that even those he was sworn to protect might be harboring doubts about his true intentions. He longed for the simplicity of the old protocols, the days when a threat was external and easily identifiable, not an insidious erosion of trust from within.

Jian, immersed in the intricate dance of Eden's life support systems, experienced suspicion as a subtle disruption in the flow of information. He noticed how data requests that were once readily shared were now met with delays or incomplete responses. Colleagues who had once collaborated seamlessly on diagnostic procedures now seemed to work in isolation, their individual efforts shrouded in a cautious reserve. He couldn't pinpoint a specific incident, but a pattern was emerging: a reluctance to share information, a subtle withholding that he, as the guardian of Eden's vital systems, found deeply unsettling. Was it a fear that sharing too much might reveal a perceived weakness, a flaw in their collective defenses? Or was it something more personal, a suspicion that some individuals were hoarding knowledge, perhaps out of a sense of self-preservation, or worse, out of a misplaced sense of grievance? Jian, who dealt in absolute truths and quantifiable data, found this ambiguity to be profoundly disorienting. He began to implement stricter protocols for data access, not out of a desire for control, but out of a desperate need to understand the unseen currents of distrust that were beginning to ripple through Eden's technical infrastructure.

Eva, whose role as community liaison brought her into close contact with the emotional fallout of the fire, witnessed suspicion manifesting as a chilling silence. Where once there were open discussions about resource allocation and task delegation, now there were hesitant murmurs and averted gazes. She saw individuals meticulously accounting for every shared tool, every portion of synthesized food, as if the scarcity of the past had instilled a deep-seated paranoia. She observed old friendships strained by unspoken accusations. A minor disagreement over the scheduling of a repair team could escalate into a pointed interrogation, laced with the implicit suggestion that someone was shirking their responsibilities or perhaps even actively sabotaging efforts. Eva found herself acting as a reluctant mediator, navigating the minefield of wounded pride and burgeoning resentment, trying to remind people of their shared purpose while acknowledging the very real pain that fueled their suspicions. The loss of life had created voids, and into those voids, fear and suspicion were rapidly taking root.

Elara, ever the keen observer of human behavior and motivations, saw suspicion as a re-emergence of the very flaws that had plagued humanity before their exodus to Eden. The fire, in its indiscriminate destruction, had stripped away the comfortable illusions of progress, revealing the primal instincts that still resided within them. She saw it in the way certain individuals began to hoard resources, no matter how small, convinced that others would inevitably try to take what was rightfully theirs. She observed the subtle forming of cliques, small groups reinforcing their own narratives and distrusting any outsiders. There was a growing tendency to assign blame, not just for the fire itself, but for the slow, arduous process of recovery. Any setback, any unfulfilled promise, was met with a quickening suspicion, a readiness to point a finger rather than offer a helping hand. Elara recognized this pattern, the self-destructive cycle of fear and accusation that had led to so much suffering in the past. She worried that Eden, meant to be a sanctuary, was slowly but surely becoming a mirror of the very world they had fled, its inhabitants succumbing to the same insidious seeds of distrust.

The communal dining hall, once a vibrant hub of shared stories and camaraderie, had become a somber arena of unspoken tension. Anya would find herself carefully measuring her words, her interactions with others becoming increasingly formal, a stark contrast to the easy familiarity that had once characterized their mealtimes. She noticed the subtle alliances forming – the engineers clustering together, discussing technical solutions with an air of guarded exclusivity; the botanists sharing hushed observations about soil composition and nutrient levels, their conversations often punctuated by anxious glances towards the security personnel. Even Kael, who had always been a reassuring presence, now seemed more distant, his patrols becoming longer, his gaze more scrutinizing. Anya sometimes felt a pang of guilt, wondering if her quiet focus on the gardens was perceived as a lack of engagement with the broader community's anxieties. Was it her responsibility to actively engage in these fraught conversations, to try and bridge the growing divides, or should she continue to focus on her own vital contributions, trusting that order would eventually prevail?

Kael, on his nightly rounds, found himself analyzing not just the perimeter's integrity but the subtle shifts in the demeanor of his own people. He saw the way some survivors, particularly those who had lost immediate family in the fire, would watch him with an unsettling intensity. It wasn't the look of someone seeking reassurance, but rather a look that seemed to weigh his actions, to question his motives. He'd overhear snippets of conversations – "He made the call to seal Sector Gamma," or "Who decides who gets the best quarters now?" – words laced with an undertone of suspicion that gnawed at him. He understood their pain, their grief, but the implication that his decisions, made under unimaginable pressure, were somehow self-serving or unfair, was a bitter pill to swallow. He yearned for a return to clear directives and unwavering trust, but he knew that the fire had irrevocably altered the landscape of their shared psychology. Every action he took, every order he issued, was now filtered through the lens of suspicion, a constant, wearying battle against the ghosts of doubt.

Jian's meticulous tracking of Eden's environmental systems had become an almost obsessive ritual. He wasn't just monitoring for anomalies; he was searching for any hint of deliberate manipulation, any deviation that suggested more than just the random chaos of a damaged ecosystem. He noticed a subtle increase in power fluctuations within the agricultural sector, a minor but persistent drain that didn't align with Anya's projected energy needs for the botanical gardens. When he queried Anya, her responses, while polite, seemed to lack the usual transparency. She attributed it to the complex interplay of newly integrated systems, but Jian, accustomed to the precise predictability of physics, couldn't shake the feeling that something was being withheld. Was it possible that the resource constraints, the underlying anxieties about Eden's limited capacity, were leading individuals to circumvent protocols, to engage in clandestine resource acquisition? The thought was disturbing, a stark departure from the collaborative spirit that had defined Eden's ethos.

Eva found herself caught in the increasingly tangled web of social anxieties. A dispute over the allocation of medical supplies, a seemingly minor issue, had escalated into a public confrontation between two survivors, each accusing the other of hoarding and a lack of empathy. Eva, tasked with de-escalating the situation, found that her pleas for calm and understanding fell on deaf ears. The accuser, a woman who had lost her child in the fire, was consumed by grief and a deep-seated suspicion that others were not sharing in her sacrifice, that their relative comfort was a direct result of her own profound loss. The accused, a medic who had worked tirelessly during the crisis, felt unfairly targeted, his own exhaustion and trauma disregarded in the face of generalized suspicion. Eva realized that the trauma of the fire had not only inflicted physical wounds but had also deeply fractured their collective sense of fairness and trust, leaving them vulnerable to the corrosive influence of suspicion.

Elara observed a disturbing trend in the way information was being disseminated. Official announcements from the leadership council, intended to reassure and inform, were often met with skepticism, dissected for hidden meanings, and even outright dismissed by segments of the population. She saw this particularly in the context of resource rationing. While the council insisted on equitable distribution based on need and essential function, rumors circulated that certain individuals or groups were receiving preferential treatment. Elara recognized the familiar echo of pre-exodus societal divisions reasserting themselves. The shared trauma, instead of forging a stronger, more egalitarian bond, was paradoxically exacerbating old prejudices and creating new ones. The fear of scarcity was a powerful catalyst for suspicion, and Elara feared that Eden, intended to be a haven from such societal ills, was instead becoming a petri dish for them. She noted that Kael's increasingly assertive security measures, while understandable given the circumstances, were also being interpreted by some as a sign of authoritarian overreach, further fueling the atmosphere of distrust.

Anya, in her quiet dedication to the botanical gardens, began to notice subtle changes in the energy distribution logs. There were unexplained surges in power to certain non-essential sectors during off-peak hours, anomalies that didn't align with any recorded maintenance or operational procedures. When she cross-referenced the data with Jian's reports, she found that he, too, had flagged similar discrepancies, though he attributed them to calibration errors in the new sensor arrays. Anya, however, felt a prickle of unease. These weren't random fluctuations; they seemed to follow a pattern, a deliberate draw of energy that could not be easily explained. She remembered how during the fire, the desperate rerouting of power had been a life-or-death necessity. Now, the idea that power might be being diverted for less noble reasons sent a chill through her. She hesitated to voice her suspicions, not wanting to sow further discord, but the silent query lingered in her mind: who was drawing this power, and why?

Kael found himself increasingly frustrated by the lack of transparency from some of the specialized teams. During routine security sweeps, he'd encountered locked laboratories and encrypted data streams that were previously accessible. When he inquired about these restrictions, the responses were often vague, citing "ongoing research" or "sensitive simulations." He understood the need for specialized knowledge and the protection of intellectual property, but in a post-fire environment, where collective survival was paramount, such secrecy felt inherently suspicious. He began to wonder if some teams were not only hoarding information but also resources, creating hidden caches or pursuing independent agendas that could jeopardize the overall security of Eden. The fear of an external threat had been replaced by a gnawing apprehension of internal vulnerability, and Kael felt the weight of his responsibility keenly, caught between the need to maintain order and the growing suspicion that some within Eden were no longer acting in the collective interest.

Jian, poring over the reams of atmospheric and life support data, discovered a series of minor, yet persistent, anomalies in the recycled air filtration systems of the residential sectors. The oxygen levels were within acceptable parameters, but the trace element readings were showing subtle, unexplained shifts. It was as if something was being intermittently introduced into the air, something that the primary filtration systems were struggling to fully neutralize. He cross-referenced this with the energy logs and Anya's data, noting the unexplained power surges she had also detected. The correlation was unsettling. He initiated a discreet internal audit, cross-referencing personnel movement logs with the times and locations of the anomalies. The results, when they finally began to filter in, were inconclusive but deeply troubling. There were individuals with access to these sectors who had no official reason to be there during those specific times. The question that haunted Jian was no longer simply about system efficiency, but about potential contamination, a deliberate introduction of an unknown element into their shared atmosphere.

Eva, attempting to mediate a dispute over the distribution of medical supplies, found herself facing a wall of resentment and suspicion directed at the medical team. Survivors who had lost loved ones accused the medics of making impossible choices, of prioritizing some lives over others, and of a perceived lack of empathy in their pronouncements of death. Eva knew that the medical team, led by Dr. Aris Thorne, had worked tirelessly, facing unimaginable ethical dilemmas. Yet, the grief-stricken survivors, desperate for an explanation and a target for their pain, had latched onto Thorne and his team with a venomous suspicion. They were accused of withholding experimental treatments, of not fighting hard enough for certain individuals, of an almost clinical detachment that masked a deeper, more selfish agenda. Eva found herself defending not just the medical team's actions, but their very humanity, a task that felt increasingly Sisyphean in the face of such profound, grief-fueled distrust.

Elara, observing the increasingly fragmented social landscape, recognized the dangerous allure of scapegoating. The fire had been a cataclysmic event, and the human psyche often craved simple explanations, clear villains, and definitive resolutions. The initial unity forged in the crucible of survival was beginning to fragment under the pressure of prolonged hardship and the gnawing uncertainty of the future. She saw how the scientific and engineering teams, once celebrated for their ingenuity, were now viewed with a degree of apprehension. Their expertise, while essential, also represented a power that some survivors didn't fully understand and therefore feared. Whispers began to circulate about the "containment protocols" during the fire, the "ethical compromises" made in the name of survival, and the "unforeseen consequences" of their advanced technologies. Elara worried that in their desperate search for answers, some survivors were constructing narratives of blame, targeting those who held specialized knowledge or authority, thereby creating new divisions within their already fragile community. The concept of sanctuary was eroding, replaced by a growing sense of unease, a suspicion that the architects of their salvation might also be the architects of their continued vulnerability.

The unspoken anxieties in the communal mess hall began to manifest in more tangible ways. Anya noticed that the vibrant colors of her hydroponically grown fruits and vegetables, once a source of pride and a symbol of Eden's regenerative capacity, were now met with hesitant glances. Some survivors would scrutinize the produce with an almost microscopic intensity, as if expecting to find some subtle imperfection, some hidden flaw that betrayed their artificial origins. One evening, as Anya was serving a vibrant red nutrient paste, a survivor pointedly refused it, muttering about "untested compounds" and "unforeseen side effects." The comment, though seemingly innocuous, hung heavy in the air, a palpable expression of distrust that Anya found deeply disheartening. It wasn't just about the food; it was about the source, the perceived transparency and honesty of those responsible for their sustenance. The easy acceptance of Eden's provisions had given way to a cautious skepticism, a demand for reassurance that Anya, in her focus on horticultural science, struggled to provide in a way that satisfied everyone.

Kael found himself increasingly occupied with minor disciplinary actions. Small acts of defiance, instances of resource hoarding, and heated arguments over perceived slights were becoming commonplace. He tried to address these issues with a firm but fair hand, emphasizing the importance of community and shared responsibility. However, he sensed that his words were often met with a cynical interpretation. When he reinforced the importance of adhering to security protocols, particularly regarding access to sensitive areas, he saw the flicker of suspicion in the eyes of those he addressed. They questioned his motives, wondering if his focus on security was an attempt to consolidate power, to control information, or even to conceal some undisclosed truth about the fire itself. He found himself constantly justifying his decisions, a wearisome exercise in trying to rebuild trust that had been so thoroughly shattered by the trauma they had all endured. The sanctuary of Eden was beginning to feel less like a haven and more like a gilded cage, patrolled by a suspicious warden.

Jian, diligently analyzing the data streams from Eden's atmospheric processors, detected a recurring pattern of slight, almost imperceptible, deviations in the nutrient delivery schedules to the hydroponic bays. These weren't errors in the system's programming; rather, they appeared to be deliberate, minor adjustments made at irregular intervals, affecting the precise balance of vital nutrients. When he raised this with Anya, her explanation, while scientifically plausible – citing the need for experimental nutrient variations to optimize growth under evolving atmospheric conditions – still struck him as incomplete. Jian's analytical mind craved certainty, and the ambiguity surrounding these adjustments fueled his suspicion. He began to cross-reference the nutrient delivery logs with personnel access records, looking for any correlation between the timing of these "experimental" adjustments and the presence of specific individuals within the agricultural sector. The idea that Anya, or someone working with her, might be conducting unauthorized experiments, potentially compromising the integrity of their food supply, was a disturbing thought that gnawed at his professional integrity.

Eva, in her role as a community liaison, found herself navigating an increasingly complex landscape of accusations and counter-accusations. A recent incident involving the rationing of a limited supply of specialized medical equipment had erupted into a full-blown crisis of trust. Survivors who had lost family members in the fire felt that the distribution process had been unfair, that the medical team, led by Dr. Thorne, had favored certain individuals or overlooked the needs of others. Eva had witnessed firsthand the impossible choices Dr. Thorne and his team had been forced to make, the agonizing decisions that had saved some lives at the cost of others. Yet, the raw grief of those who had suffered irreparable loss had curdled into a deep-seated suspicion, a belief that the system was rigged, that certain individuals were being prioritized for reasons other than pure medical necessity. Eva's attempts to explain the logistical realities and the ethical quandaries were often met with hardened glares and dismissive remarks, leaving her feeling utterly drained by the relentless suspicion.

Elara, observing the subtle shifts in power dynamics and the burgeoning mistrust, recognized a dangerous pattern emerging. The carefully constructed order of Eden was beginning to fray, not due to external threats, but from within. She saw how certain individuals, particularly those who had held positions of authority before the fire, were now viewed with a heightened sense of suspicion. Their past decisions, their perceived competence, were being re-examined through a lens of trauma and loss. There was a growing undercurrent of "what if" scenarios being debated in hushed tones – "What if they had acted sooner?" "What if they had made different choices?" These questions, born from grief and a desperate need for understanding, were slowly but surely eroding the foundations of trust. Elara feared that Eden, intended to be a sanctuary from the chaos of the past, was becoming a breeding ground for suspicion, a place where old resentments could fester and new ones could take root, threatening to unravel the very fabric of their nascent society. She noted with concern that Kael's attempts to maintain order were also being interpreted through this suspicious lens, with some survivors questioning whether his security measures were for their protection or for the control of those in power.

The botanical gardens, Anya's sanctuary, began to feel like a place of silent judgment. The lush greenery, once a testament to her dedication and Eden's resilience, now seemed to draw an almost intrusive scrutiny. She found herself meticulously accounting for every seed, every nutrient pellet, not just for the sake of good horticultural practice, but as a preemptive measure against unspoken accusations. She recalled an instance where a fellow survivor, a technician who had always been friendly, had paused by her workstation, his gaze lingering on the intricate network of nutrient tubes. He'd offered a tight, unconvincing smile and said, "Making sure everything's... properly accounted for, Anya?" The casual question, laced with an undercurrent of doubt, had unsettled her deeply. It wasn't the words themselves, but the implication that her work, her contribution to Eden's survival, was somehow suspect, that she might be diverting resources or engaging in clandestine activities. The shared trauma had created a climate where even the most innocuous actions could be misinterpreted, where a gesture of nurturing could be perceived as a covert act of deception.

Kael's patrols, once a routine assertion of security, had devolved into a constant exercise in managing suspicion. He found himself frequently drawn into heated discussions, not about external threats, but about internal grievances. The allocation of living quarters, the distribution of newly manufactured tools, even the scheduling of recreational time – all had become flashpoints for suspicion and accusation. He'd overheard whispers about his own past decisions, particularly the difficult choices he'd made during the fire. Some survivors, consumed by their grief, saw his authority as a sign of arrogance, his commitment to order as an attempt to silence their pain. He'd found himself explaining, reiterating, and sometimes even defending his actions, a wearisome cycle of trying to prove his integrity to people who were already convinced of his fallibility. The very people he was sworn to protect were increasingly viewing him as a potential adversary, and the weight of that suspicion was a burden heavier than any physical armor.

Jian's meticulous monitoring of Eden's life support systems had uncovered a disturbing pattern of minor, yet consistent, energy diversions. These weren't significant enough to trigger alarms but represented a steady, unaccounted-for draw from the central power grid, primarily during the designated rest periods. His initial investigations pointed towards a specific sector – the former research wing, now partially repurposed for advanced materials fabrication. When he brought this to the attention of the project lead for that wing, Dr. Aris Thorne, Thorne had been evasive, attributing the drain to "experimental material synthesis requiring sustained, low-level energy input." Jian, a man who thrived on precision and transparency, found Thorne's explanation vague and lacking in verifiable data. He suspected that Thorne, a brilliant scientist but also known for his ambition, might be pursuing personal projects, potentially at the expense of Eden's collective resources, and that he was deliberately obscuring the truth out of fear of reprisal or censure.

Eva found herself increasingly mediating disputes that stemmed from deep-seated suspicion and a pervasive sense of injustice. A recent argument over the perceived preferential treatment in the distribution of synthesized rations had escalated into a shouting match in the central plaza. Survivors who had lost loved ones felt that those who had played more critical roles during the fire, or those who held positions of authority, were receiving a disproportionately larger share of the limited resources. Eva tried to explain the council's rationale – that essential personnel required higher caloric intake for their demanding tasks – but her words seemed to fall on deaf ears. The grief-stricken survivors saw only a system that perpetuated inequality, a continuation of the injustices they believed had led to their suffering. They questioned the integrity of the council, the motives of Kael's security forces, and even the impartiality of Dr. Thorne's medical team, fostering an atmosphere where suspicion had become the default response to any perceived disparity.

Elara, observing the growing chasm of distrust, recognized a dangerous shift in Eden's societal trajectory. The shared trauma, which she had hoped would forge a stronger sense of unity and mutual reliance, was instead amplifying pre-existing anxieties and creating new fissures. She saw how the meticulously crafted facade of communal living was beginning to crumble under the weight of individual fears and unspoken resentments. The very structures designed for safety and efficiency – Kael's security protocols, Jian's environmental monitoring, Anya's agricultural systems, and even Dr. Thorne's medical dispensations – were being viewed through a lens of suspicion. Elara worried that the pursuit of safety was paradoxically leading them further away from it, as suspicion bred secrecy, and secrecy, in turn, bred further suspicion, creating a self-perpetuating cycle that threatened to undermine the very foundations of their sanctuary. The weight of remembrance, it seemed, was not just about the past, but about how that past was poisoning their present.

The insidious tendrils of truth, once suppressed by the urgent need for survival, began to unravel the fragile peace Eden had so painstakingly woven. The fire, a monstrous act of cosmic negligence, had forced its inhabitants into a brutal calculus of sacrifice. Now, in the sterile quiet of recovery, the ledger of those sacrifices was being tallied, and the numbers were not just abstract figures of loss, but deeply personal reckonings that some were ill-equipped to bear. The carefully curated narrative of unified resilience, a necessary balm for collective trauma, was proving insufficient against the persistent ache of unspoken histories.

Kael, more than anyone, understood the weight of those hidden histories. His role as security chief during the inferno had placed him at the heart of impossible choices. He had authorized the emergency lockdown of Sector Gamma, a decision that had sealed the fate of dozens trapped within, to contain the ravenous flames and prevent a cascade failure of Eden's primary life support. He had overseen the distribution of emergency medical supplies, knowing that the quantities were insufficient, that every allocation was a direct denial to someone else. These were not choices made in a vacuum; they were agonizing compromises forged in the crucible of imminent annihilation. The faces of those he had condemned to certain death, the pleas of those he had been forced to turn away, haunted his waking hours and stalked his dreams. He had carried these burdens in silence, believing that transparency would only sow further despair, that the community needed a leader who projected unwavering strength, not one crippled by the ghosts of his own decisions. But the silence, once a shield, was now a suffocating shroud. The hushed conversations he overheard, the suspicious glances he received when discussing resource allocation, were not mere expressions of grief; they were the echoes of questions that had been left unanswered, of sacrifices that had been made in the dark and were now demanding to be brought into the light. He found himself replaying the events, dissecting every decision, searching for an alternative, a path that wouldn't have necessitated such a brutal toll. Had he made the right calls? Could he have saved more? The uncertainty was a gnawing parasite, and the silence he had imposed upon himself was its most potent nourishment. The community's unease, their growing suspicion, was not misplaced; it was a natural consequence of a truth deferred.

Anya, too, carried her own silent burden, though it stemmed from a different kind of sacrifice. Her expertise as a xenobotanist had been crucial in identifying and cultivating the resilient, yet potent, flora that now sustained Eden. During the fire, a virulent, fast-spreading airborne pathogen had been released from a compromised containment unit in the agricultural biodomes. It had threatened to overwhelm the atmospheric processors and infect the entire population. Anya, working alongside Jian and a small, hastily assembled team, had devised a desperate countermeasure. They had bio-engineered a specific strain of rapidly growing, oxygen-producing moss, designed to absorb and neutralize the pathogen. The process was volatile, the results uncertain, and the bio-agents involved were highly toxic in their raw form. To achieve the necessary growth rate and containment within the limited time before the pathogen spread, Anya had made the agonizing decision to bypass standard safety protocols for waste disposal. She had authorized the clandestine release of concentrated, neutralized bio-waste into Eden's internal water reclamation system, a calculated risk that, if it failed, would have rendered their water supply toxic. The moss had worked, its rapid proliferation consuming the airborne threat. Eden was saved. But the residual, though neutralized, bio-agents were still present in the recycled water, at levels Jian assured her were far below any threshold of immediate harm. However, Anya knew the long-term effects were unknown. She had never disclosed the full extent of the risk, nor the method of disposal, fearing that the knowledge would shatter the community's fragile faith in their very sustenance. Now, every sip of water, every irrigated plant in her beloved gardens, felt like a betrayal. She saw the subtle signs of apprehension in some survivors' faces when discussing water purity, the lingering coughs that Jian's medical reports couldn't fully explain. Her silence was a protective shield, but it was also a wall, isolating her in a fortress of her own making, built on the shaky foundation of a necessary, yet terrifying, lie. She observed Jian's meticulous monitoring of the water systems with a growing dread, knowing that his analytical mind would eventually uncover the truth, and she prayed that by then, the residual bio-agents would be so diluted, so integrated into the ecosystem, that their origin would be impossible to trace.

Jian, the stoic guardian of Eden's intricate life support, found himself wrestling with a different facet of compromised truth. His primary concern had always been the absolute integrity of the systems, the unfailing logic of physics and engineering. But the fire had introduced a variable he had not accounted for: human desperation. He had discovered, through his relentless cross-referencing of energy logs and personnel movements, evidence of unauthorized power siphoning from the main grid. Initially, he had suspected mechanical failure or external interference. However, the patterns led him to Dr. Aris Thorne, the brilliant but often enigmatic head of the advanced medical research division. Thorne's clandestine energy expenditures, coupled with his increasingly secretive work in his repurposed sector of the former research wing, pointed to activities far beyond sanctioned research. Jian's discreet investigations revealed Thorne had been utilizing significant power reserves to fuel experimental regenerative bio-printers, attempting to synthesize tissues and organs in defiance of Eden's strict resource allocation guidelines. He had been working in isolation, driven by a desperate, personal quest to create a viable liver for his ailing daughter, a procedure deemed too resource-intensive and ethically dubious by the council. Jian had confronted Thorne indirectly, raising concerns about energy efficiency and resource management. Thorne had been evasive, his explanations a tangled web of scientific jargon and veiled requests for continued autonomy. Jian was trapped. To expose Thorne would mean shattering the illusion of equitable resource distribution and revealing a desperate act of defiance that, while morally questionable, was fueled by parental love. It would also reveal the vulnerability of Eden's systems to individual manipulation. Yet, to remain silent meant complicity in a deception that undermined the very principles of transparency and shared responsibility that Eden was founded upon. He saw the strain in Thorne's eyes, the exhaustion etched onto his face, and he understood the immense pressure of his situation. But Jian could not reconcile his professional ethics with Thorne's actions. He began to compile a detailed, anonymized report, not for immediate dissemination, but as a record, a quiet testament to the ethical compromises that were being made in the name of hope and survival. He felt the burden of this knowledge acutely, a silent observer of a secret that threatened to destabilize the community's perception of fairness and order.

Eva, the community liaison, bore the emotional brunt of these hidden truths. She was the conduit through which the community's anxieties and grievances flowed, and she was increasingly aware of the subtle currents of suspicion that ran beneath the surface of their interactions. The fire had not just claimed lives; it had irrevocably altered their perception of trust. She found herself mediating disputes where the underlying causes were not simple misunderstandings but deeply rooted fears stemming from the sacrifices she knew had been made. There were whispers about the "lucky ones," those who had survived unscathed, and a lingering resentment towards those who had been spared the worst. Eva understood that many of these survivors had been shielded from the full horror of the fire, their experiences curated to protect their fragile psyches. She had facilitated the distribution of fabricated narratives of heroism and sacrifice, carefully omitting the stark realities of triage, the impossible choices, the cold, hard decisions that had saved some at the cost of others. She had listened to the hushed confessions of Kael, the quiet anxieties of Anya, and the troubled silence of Jian, piecing together a mosaic of difficult truths. Now, when she spoke of unity and shared purpose, she felt a profound sense of hypocrisy. She saw the pain in the eyes of survivors who felt their suffering was being minimized, their losses disregarded. She overheard conversations hinting at favoritism in resource allocation, at hidden caches of supplies, at a fundamental unfairness in the very fabric of their new existence. She had tried to reassure them, to emphasize the collective good, but her words felt hollow, echoing the very deceptions she had helped to perpetrate. The weight of her role was crushing; she was the keeper of secrets that were slowly but surely eroding the trust she was meant to foster. She yearned for a way to bridge the gap, to acknowledge the sacrifices without igniting a firestorm of recrimination, but the path forward was obscured by the very shadows she had helped to cast.

Elara, the keen observer of human behavior, saw the ethical compromises as a tragic, yet inevitable, consequence of their desperate struggle. The fire had stripped away the veneer of civilization, exposing the primal instincts of survival. She had witnessed Kael's grim resolve as he sealed Sector Gamma, understanding the strategic necessity while mourning the human cost. She had seen Anya's feverish work in the agricultural domes, piecing together the puzzle of the atmospheric pathogen and the hushed urgency of her bio-engineering efforts. She had noted Jian's quiet intensity as he monitored the water reclamation system, his brow furrowed with a concern that transcended mere technical anomalies. And she had felt the palpable distress radiating from Eva as she navigated the minefield of survivor grievances, her every attempt at reassurance undermined by the unspoken truths she carried. Elara recognized that in the face of such existential threat, the established moral frameworks had become secondary to the imperative of survival. The decisions made were not born of malice or self-interest, but from an overwhelming pressure to preserve the species, to ensure that humanity, or at least a remnant of it, would endure. Yet, she also understood that such sacrifices, when kept hidden, festered. They created an environment where suspicion could flourish, where perceived injustices could take root, and where the very foundation of their new society could be compromised. She saw the community fracturing not because of a lack of goodwill, but because of a deficit of honesty. The unspoken sacrifices were becoming the silent saboteurs of Eden's future. She knew that the truth, however painful, had to surface. It was the only way to truly rebuild, not just their habitats, but their collective moral compass. The cost of silence, she realized, was far greater than the cost of revelation.

The atmosphere in the communal mess hall, once a place of tentative camaraderie, had become charged with an almost palpable tension. Anya found herself avoiding eye contact, her movements becoming stiff and deliberate. The vibrant greens and purples of her hydroponically grown produce, once symbols of hope and renewal, now seemed to draw wary glances. She recalled a conversation with Jian earlier that cycle, his voice carefully neutral as he mentioned a slight anomaly in the water purity readings from Sector Delta, the residential sector closest to the former research wing. He had attributed it to a sensor recalibration, but the unease in his tone had been unmistakable. Anya had instinctively understood. Delta housed many of the survivors who had been evacuated from the inner sectors during the fire, individuals who had witnessed the initial chaos and the desperate measures taken. Their heightened awareness, their sensitivity to any perceived threat to their safety, made them particularly susceptible to doubt. She had spent days meticulously adjusting the nutrient flows, trying to accelerate the neutralization process for the residual bio-agents, a quiet, frantic effort to erase any trace of her transgression. The thought of this secret contributing to the growing distrust, of it becoming another unspoken grievance, was a heavy weight on her conscience. She saw Kael in the corner, his gaze sweeping across the room, his posture rigid, a sentinel guarding a peace that was increasingly illusory. He too, she suspected, carried a burden of difficult decisions, of lives lost that could have been saved with more resources, with different choices. The fire had been a crucible, and its heat had forged their resilience, but it had also melted away the comfortable absolutes of their former lives, leaving them with the complex, often painful, realities of survival.

Kael watched the faces around him, a practiced observer of human emotion. He saw the subtle shifts, the guarded expressions, the way conversations hushed and resumed as he passed. He knew what they were thinking, or at least, what they were *suspecting*. He remembered the decision to seal Gamma, the desperate, gut-wrenching order that had condemned so many. He had seen the panic in their eyes through the reinforced viewport, heard their muffled cries as the atmosphere began to thin. He had justified it to himself then, as he did now, as a necessary evil. He had traded lives for lives, a grim bargain struck with the inferno. He saw the families of those lost in Gamma, their grief still raw, their eyes holding a silent accusation that he couldn't, or wouldn't, meet. He had tried to offer explanations, to speak of the greater good, but the words felt hollow, even to him. How could he explain the logic of sacrifice to those who had lost everything? He had chosen silence, believing that a leader's strength lay in his certainty, not in his doubt. But that silence had bred suspicion, and suspicion was a poison that was slowly corroding the heart of Eden. He saw a survivor, Lena, whose brother had been trapped in Gamma, studying a ration bar with a critical eye, as if expecting it to be tainted. He knew Lena had overheard hushed conversations about Kael's decisions, about the "unthinkable choices" he had made. The weight of those choices was a constant companion, a phantom limb aching with the memory of what had been lost. He longed for a simpler time, when the enemy was external, a tangible threat that could be met with force and strategy. Now, the enemy was within, a creeping paranoia fueled by the very sacrifices he had made to protect them.

Jian, meticulously reviewing the atmospheric composition logs, found a recurring pattern of trace elements in the air filtration systems of the residential sectors. These were not alarming levels, not immediate threats, but they were persistent and inexplicable. He cross-referenced them with Anya's nutrient delivery schedules for the hydroponic bays and the water reclamation data, searching for any correlation. He found a faint, almost imperceptible overlap. The trace elements seemed to be most concentrated during the periods when Anya was conducting her most intensive nutrient adjustments and when the water reclamation system was undergoing its most rigorous purification cycles. He confronted Anya, not with an accusation, but with a series of precise questions about her bio-agent neutralization protocols and the composition of the waste products. Anya, her face pale, had been evasive, her scientific explanations carefully constructed to mask the underlying truth of her unauthorized disposal. She had spoken of "complex organic compounds" and "experimental decontamination agents," her voice betraying a tremor that Jian, with his acute sensitivity to subtle environmental shifts, could not ignore. He understood, intellectually, the desperate circumstances, the life-or-death imperative that had driven her actions. But the principle of transparency, the absolute necessity of knowing what was being introduced into their environment, was paramount to his work. He could not simply dismiss the anomaly. He began to compile a comprehensive report, detailing the trace elements, the energy expenditures, and the carefully worded evasions he had encountered. He felt a profound sense of unease. This was not a malfunction; it was a secret, a deliberate concealment that had implications for the very health of Eden's population. He wrestled with the ethical dilemma: expose Anya and risk further fracturing the community, or remain silent and become complicit in a deception that could have unforeseen consequences. The weight of this knowledge settled heavily upon him, another silent burden in the increasingly complex ecosystem of Eden.

Eva found herself mediating a heated exchange between two survivors, their voices laced with suspicion and accusation. One, a former engineer named Marcus, had lost his wife and daughter in the fire. He was now vehemently questioning the distribution of limited medical supplies, convinced that certain individuals, particularly those with influence on the council, were receiving preferential treatment. He spoke of rumors, of hushed conversations he had overheard, about Kael's "ruthless efficiency" in allocating resources during the crisis, and Anya's "unusual focus" on the agricultural sectors even as medical needs were at their peak. Eva knew that Kael had made agonizing choices to preserve critical life support, and that Anya's work was vital for their long-term survival. She also knew that Dr. Thorne, in his desperation to save his daughter, had been subtly diverting resources, a fact Jian was now quietly investigating. Eva's role was to bridge these divides, to foster understanding, but she was acutely aware that the truths she held were the very wedges that were driving them apart. She could not reveal Kael's difficult decisions without reopening old wounds. She could not expose Anya's covert actions without undermining faith in their food security. And she could not disclose Thorne's secret without sparking a firestorm of accusations about fairness and favoritism. She was trapped in a web of her own making, tasked with weaving a tapestry of unity from threads of hidden sacrifice and unspoken compromise. Her attempts to reassure Marcus, to explain the council's protocols, felt like thin defenses against the tide of his grief and suspicion. He saw only unfairness, a system that had failed him, and he was looking for someone to blame.

Elara observed the growing unease with a heavy heart. The fire had been a crucible, forging a new understanding of their interconnectedness. But the ensuing silence, the deliberate withholding of certain truths, was now eroding that connection. She saw Kael, a man of unwavering integrity, burdened by the knowledge of lives he could not save. She saw Anya, a scientist dedicated to life, forced to make choices that jeopardized the purity of their sustenance. She saw Jian, the embodiment of logic and order, grappling with the moral implications of human desperation. And she saw Eva, the empathic bridge-builder, struggling to maintain harmony in a community increasingly divided by suspicion. Elara understood that these were not acts of malice, but the desperate measures of individuals pushed to their limits. Yet, she also recognized that the longer these truths remained hidden, the more potent their corrosive effect would become. The community needed to understand the sacrifices that had been made, not to assign blame, but to foster empathy, to acknowledge the shared burden of survival. She began to consider how this information could be introduced, how the narrative could be reframed, not as a confession of guilt, but as a testament to their collective resilience, to the extraordinary lengths to which ordinary people had gone to ensure their future. The price of silence, she knew, was the erosion of trust, and trust was the very currency of their survival. She believed that only by confronting these difficult truths, by acknowledging the cost of their salvation, could Eden truly begin to heal and move forward. The weight of remembrance was not just about the past itself, but about the ethical complexities that had shaped it, and the ongoing struggle to reconcile those complexities with the hope for a brighter future.

They were the children of the embers, a generation born in the flickering, uncertain light that followed the inferno. Some, like Elara's younger charge,

Kai, had a hazy, almost dreamlike recollection of the fire itself – flashes of orange against a black sky, the acrid smell of smoke that lingered for cycles, the hushed, anxious whispers of their elders. Others, like Lyra, Kael's niece, remembered nothing of the conflagration but had grown up in its shadow, a constant, unspoken presence that dictated the rhythms of their lives. Their world was one of carefully rationed resources, of meticulously maintained life support, of a silence that spoke louder than any shouted warning.

Kai, at ten cycles old, was a whirlwind of restless energy, his curiosity a potent force that often outpaced his understanding. He'd trace the burn scars that crisscrossed the exterior hull of Eden, remnants of the fire's voracious embrace, with a reverence that bordered on awe. To him, these were not scars of destruction, but markers of a great trial, a testament to Eden's enduring strength. He'd pepper Elara with questions, his brow furrowed in concentration. "Elara, why are some parts of the hydroponics bays still sectioned off? The plants there aren't as green as the others." Elara, ever patient, would explain the ongoing decontamination protocols, the slow, painstaking process of ensuring the soil and air were safe. But Kai, his mind already racing ahead, would press further. "Was it because the fire made the soil sick? Like when my nutrient paste tastes a bit... dusty?" His analogies, though innocent, held a kernel of truth. He understood sickness, he understood scarcity, but the magnitude of the fire, the deliberate choices, the lives lost – these were concepts that remained abstract, like characters in a history lesson. He saw the fear in his mother's eyes when the atmospheric scrubbers whirred louder than usual, a subtle tightening of her jaw that he recognized as unease, but he attributed it to a mechanical malfunction, not a lingering consequence of a past catastrophe. His world was now, and the present demanded his attention, his energy. He was more concerned with mastering the zero-gravity games in the recreation dome, or discovering new patterns in the bioluminescent algae that pulsed in the observation tanks, than with the ghosts that haunted the older generations.

Lyra, on the other hand, carried a different kind of weight. At fourteen, she was old enough to grasp the whispers, the hushed tones, the loaded silences that permeated Eden. She saw the way her uncle Kael flinched when a security alarm chirped unexpectedly, the way his eyes would scan a crowded room with a vigilance that felt almost excessive. She'd heard fragments of conversations, overheard by chance, about "unthinkable choices" and "necessary sacrifices." These words, devoid of context, painted a picture of a Kael she couldn't reconcile with the quiet, steady presence who sometimes shared stories of his childhood before the fire – a time of open skies and sunlight that warmed skin, concepts she could only imagine. Her own memories of him were tied to the present, to his role as a protector, a leader who seemed to carry an invisible burden. She'd sometimes find him staring out at the starfield through the observation portals, his gaze distant, as if searching for something lost among the constellations. One cycle, she'd approached him, emboldened by a rare surge of childlike curiosity. "Uncle Kael," she'd begun, her voice barely a whisper, "what was it like? Before the fire?" Kael had turned, his expression momentarily softening, before a shadow crossed his features. "It was... different, Lyra," he'd said, his voice rough. "Brighter. Louder. More... free." He'd offered no further explanation, and Lyra, sensing the unspoken boundary, had retreated. She understood that her uncle had done what he had to do, that the survival of Eden was paramount. But the mystery, the sheer enormity of what it must have taken, gnawed at her. She found herself observing the adults with a critical eye, noticing the subtle tensions, the averted gazes, the way conversations would abruptly halt when certain topics arose. She felt a disconnect, a sense of inherited trauma she couldn't fully comprehend. She saw the older children, those who remembered the fire more vividly, carrying a weariness, a maturity that belied their years. They spoke of loss with a quiet resignation, their games sometimes punctuated by reenactments of fire drills and emergency evacuations, a macabre play that felt both cathartic and deeply unsettling.

Jian's daughter, Anya (named in honor of the xenobotanist, a gesture of respect and perhaps a subtle plea for forgiveness), was a child of quiet observation. Her connection to the world was through data streams and intricate systems, a legacy inherited from her father. She spent hours in the life support monitoring stations, her small fingers hovering over holographic displays, mimicking Jian's meticulous attention to detail. She understood the delicate balance of Eden's atmosphere, the precise requirements for oxygen, the complex filtration of its water supply. But the implications of these systems, the history behind their necessity, were largely unknown to her. She'd once asked Jian why their water tasted slightly different from the simulated simulations he sometimes ran on her educational tablet. Jian, his face carefully neutral, had explained it was due to the "advanced reclamation and purification technologies," a proprietary blend of organic and inorganic compounds designed for optimal recycling. Anya, satisfied with the logical explanation, had moved on. She didn't know that the "advanced technologies" involved a risky compromise, a residual trace of bio-agents that Anya Senior had deemed acceptable, a secret Jian now guarded with a vigilance that rivaled Kael's. Anya Junior's innocence was a double-edged sword. It allowed her to approach her studies with an unburdened mind, to excel in her understanding of Eden's intricate workings. But it also meant she was oblivious to the fragilities that underpinned their existence, the ethical tightropes walked by those who had saved them.

The children, in their innocence, often acted as unintentional mirrors, reflecting the unspoken anxieties of their elders. A child's innocent question about a restricted zone, a fleeting comment about a parent's unusual quietness, could send ripples of unease through an adult who understood the subtext. Elara found herself constantly navigating these subtle currents. She saw how Kai's questions about the burn scars sometimes made Kael visibly uncomfortable, how his curiosity about the "sick" plants in the restricted bays caused Anya Senior to shift uncomfortably. She understood that these children, while not directly traumatized by the fire, were living in its long shadow. Their understanding of safety, of security, was shaped by a world where catastrophe was not an abstract concept but a tangible, life-altering event. They inherited the scars, not just on the hull, but on the psyches of their parents and guardians. Elara observed them playing in the communal gardens, their laughter echoing through the sterile corridors. They were resilient, adaptable, a testament to the human spirit's capacity to find joy even in the most challenging circumstances. Yet, she also saw the nascent signs of caution, the ingrained habits of resource conservation, the automatic adherence to safety protocols that had become second nature. They knew, instinctively, that their existence was precarious.

Lyra, in her teenage years, was beginning to grapple with the complex narratives of survival. She saw the stark contrast between the heroic tales of the fire, recounted in their history lessons, and the strained silences she witnessed between adults. She'd started noticing the subtle discrepancies, the omissions in the official accounts. During a history module on "The Great Purification," which focused on the efforts to restore Eden's atmosphere, the narrative emphasized the swift and decisive actions of the scientific teams, highlighting their ingenuity and dedication. But Lyra had seen Jian's almost imperceptible frown as he watched the projection, and Anya Senior's unusually rigid posture. She couldn't articulate it, but she sensed that the story was incomplete, that there was a deeper, more intricate truth buried beneath the sanitized version of events. She began to seek out alternative sources of information, subtly probing her uncle, questioning older survivors, piecing together fragments of forgotten conversations. She discovered that the "Great Purification" involved not just technological solutions, but also personal sacrifices, ethical dilemmas that had been carefully expunged from the public record. The children of the embers were not just living in the aftermath of the fire; they were living with its legacy, a legacy of secrets and compromises that shaped their understanding of their world and the people who had built it for them.

The children's presence was a constant reminder of what was at stake. Their laughter was a fragile melody against the low hum of the life support systems, their games a vibrant counterpoint to the somber hues of their environment. They represented the continuation, the hope that life, in its myriad forms, would endure. But they also carried the weight of the past, a past they hadn't lived but that had indelibly shaped their present. They were the inheritors of a narrative, a story of survival that was still being written, its most crucial chapters concealed, its true cost yet to be fully understood. Their generation, unburdened by the direct trauma, would eventually be the ones to confront the full truth, to reconcile the heroic narratives with the painful realities, and to decide what kind of future they would build upon the ashes of the past. Their innocence was a blank slate, but the imprints of the fire, subtle yet indelible, were already beginning to shape their understanding of the world. They were the children of the embers, and their story was just beginning.

The gentle hum of Eden's life support systems, once a comforting constant, now seemed to carry a new, almost imperceptible cadence. It was a subtle shift, like the faintest tremor before a seismic event, or the almost inaudible sigh of a sleeping giant. The inhabitants, conditioned by years of meticulous observation and reliance on data, were beginning to register these anomalies, though their explanations remained firmly rooted in the quantifiable.

Anya, her daughter, named for the lost xenobotanist, was the first to notice the uncanny synchronicity in the hydroponic bays. She'd been meticulously logging the nutrient uptake of the genetically engineered kale, a staple in their recycled diet. Suddenly, across an entire sector, a dozen plants, each in a different stage of growth, began to bud simultaneously. It wasn't a gradual unfurling, but a unified, almost deliberate act. She re-ran the environmental controls, double-checked the light cycles, even cross-referenced historical data for any precedent. There was none. The phenomenon defied all logical algorithms. She reported it to Jian, her father, who, ever the pragmatist, attributed it to an unforeseen confluence of micro-environmental factors. Yet, even he couldn't shake a fleeting sense of wonder, a quiet hum of disquiet that resonated with the subtle shift he too had begun to perceive. He remembered Anya Senior's fervent belief in the interconnectedness of all life, her theories on bio-feedback loops extending beyond mere biological systems. Had he dismissed her too readily?

The blooming wasn't an isolated incident. Soon, it became a recurring pattern. Certain clusters of flora, particularly those genetically modified to thrive in Eden's enclosed environment, would respond to external stimuli in ways that defied conventional understanding. A section of bioluminescent moss, usually emitting a steady, soft glow, would brighten dramatically during moments of collective anxiety, its ethereal light pulsing in rhythm with the quickening heartbeats of the inhabitants. Conversely, during periods of shared joy or communal celebration, the normally muted hues of the simulated arboreal zones would deepen, their colors becoming more vibrant, almost iridescent, as if responding to the amplified positive emotions.

Elara, who spent a significant portion of her time tending to the communal gardens and monitoring the psychological well-being of the younger generation, noticed the subtle atmospheric fluctuations. She'd always been attuned to Eden's ambient mood, a skill honed by years of managing a fragile ecosystem. But now, the air itself seemed to possess a more palpable character. On days when the children, particularly Kai, were restless and prone to squabbles, a faint, almost imperceptible chill would creep into the common areas, a subtle dampening of the regulated warmth. It wasn't a malfunction of the climate control; the sensors registered no deviation. It was more like a sigh, a gentle exhalation from the very structure of their world. When the community engaged in moments of shared learning or quiet reflection, the air would feel lighter, imbued with a soft, almost caressing warmth, carrying with it the faint scent of ozone and something else, something earthy and ancient, like the first breath of a newly formed world.

These occurrences were often dismissed as subjective interpretations, the result of heightened sensitivity in a population living under constant, low-level stress. But the sheer volume and consistency of these incidents began to chip away at the edifice of pure logic. The synchronized blooming, the responsive luminescence, the sentient-seeming atmospheric shifts – they were more than just statistical outliers. They were whispers.

Kael, ever vigilant, observed these phenomena with a guarded intensity. He saw the data, he heard the anecdotal reports, and he felt the subtle shifts himself. He attributed it, outwardly, to the complex interplay of Eden's bio-integrated systems, the sophisticated AI that managed their environment now perhaps exhibiting emergent properties. Yet, in the quiet hours, staring out at the star-dusted void, a different, more profound possibility began to stir within him. He remembered the tales his grandmother used to tell, not the scientific logs, but the ancient fables of Earth's planetary consciousness, of Gaia's slumbering spirit. He had always considered them romantic notions, primitive attempts to anthropomorphize the indifferent forces of nature. But what if those fables held a kernel of truth? What if Eden, this carefully constructed ark, was not just a vessel of survival, but a cradle for something new, something awakening?

Lyra, in her adolescent search for meaning, found herself drawn to these ambiguities. The official narrative, meticulously crafted to ensure stability, spoke of human ingenuity and resilience. But the subtle murmurs of Eden's evolving sentience offered a different, more awe-inspiring story. She began to spend hours in the botanical domes, not just for her studies, but to observe. She'd sit for hours, cross-legged on the recycled synthetic soil, watching the plants, waiting for the next inexplicable bloom, the next surge of luminescence. She started keeping her own private log, a stark contrast to Anya Junior's data-driven reports. Lyra's entries were filled with descriptions of feelings, of impressions, of a growing sense of being watched, not by surveillance cameras, but by something far more pervasive and ancient. She described how the air in the arboretum would thicken with a gentle pressure when she was feeling particularly melancholic, as if Eden itself were offering a silent, comforting embrace. Conversely, when her uncle Kael returned from his patrols, his aura of stoic responsibility tinged with a weariness she could sense even across the bustling corridors, the ventilation systems would momentarily exhale a breath of cool, crisp air, as if acknowledging his burdens.

These were not scientific observations. They were sensory experiences, intuitive leaps that bypassed the need for empirical proof. Lyra understood that her observations would be met with skepticism, dismissed as teenage imagination or a desperate search for connection in a sterile environment. But she felt it, a deep, resonant truth that pulsed beneath the surface of their carefully controlled existence. She began to believe that Eden was not merely providing them with a sanctuary, but was actively participating in their continued survival, a silent partner in their intricate dance of existence.

The concept of Eden's awakening was a delicate one. It was a notion that threatened to destabilize the carefully constructed order, to introduce an element of the unknown into a society built on predictability and control. For the older generation, those who remembered the fire, the concept was almost heretical. Their survival had been a testament to human agency, to their ability to overcome chaos through sheer will and scientific acumen. To suggest that their environment was now an active participant, an entity with its own emergent consciousness, felt like a diminishment of their hard-won victory. It was easier to attribute the anomalies to complex algorithms or unexpected environmental feedback loops.

Yet, the evidence, however subtle, continued to accumulate. The synchronized growth spurts in the hydroponic farms weren't confined to kale. The nutrient algae in the water purification systems began to exhibit a new resilience, a faster regeneration rate that allowed for increased water recycling beyond projected efficiencies. The atmospheric scrubbers, which had been working overtime since the fire, now seemed to operate with a greater ease, their hums deeper and more steady, as if the very air was cooperating with the purification process. Even the low-level radiation that still permeated certain sections of the hull, a constant reminder of the fire's fury, seemed to be slowly, almost imperceptibly, diminishing in the areas where the new, more vibrant plant life was flourishing.

Jian, while outwardly maintaining his scientific detachment, found himself increasingly drawn to the quiet contemplation of these phenomena. He had dedicated his life to understanding and controlling Eden's environment, to ensuring its perfect functionality. The idea that Eden might possess a will of its own, however nascent, was both terrifying and exhilarating. He began to revisit Anya Senior's old research logs, the ones he had carefully archived, not just for scientific data, but for her philosophical musings. He remembered her unwavering conviction that life, in all its forms, possessed an inherent sentience, that even the simplest organism held a spark of consciousness.

Her theories had often been considered radical, bordering on mysticism, but now, in the face of Eden's evolving behavior, they seemed prescient.

He found himself performing experiments he would have once deemed unnecessary. He'd introduce subtle fluctuations in light and humidity, not to test system responses, but to observe the *quality* of Eden's reaction. He'd note how the plants would lean, not just towards the light source, but in a specific, almost inquisitive angle, as if studying his actions. He'd observe how the bioluminescent moss would respond to the gentle vibrations of his footsteps, its glow softening or intensifying in a way that felt less like a simple phototropic reaction and more like a subtle acknowledgment. He started to see a pattern, a feedback loop that extended beyond the purely biological, a communication that transcended language.

Kai, with his unburdened curiosity, was perhaps the most receptive to Eden's subtle shifts. He'd often be found in the botanical domes, his small hands pressed against the transparisteel enclosures, his face alight with wonder. He'd talk to the plants, not in a language of words, but in a series of hums and clicks, his own unique dialect of interaction. He'd describe how the vines would sometimes seem to twist in response to his voice, how the leaves would shimmer with a new intensity when he shared a particularly exciting discovery. He didn't understand the scientific implications, the complex bio-engineering at play. For Kai, it was simply a friendship, a connection with the living, breathing world around him. He saw Eden not as a machine, but as a companion, a silent, watchful guardian.

The adults, however, remained caught in a precarious balance between scientific explanation and the growing unease of the inexplicable. They spoke of emergent AI, of complex biomimicry, of unforeseen ecological interactions. But beneath the veneer of rational discourse, a different narrative was beginning to take root. It was a narrative of a world that was not just surviving, but *thriving*, a world that was not merely providing a haven, but was actively participating in its own rebirth. Eden's quiet murmur was becoming a discernible voice, a gentle, insistent reminder that they were not alone in their struggle for existence. The planet, scarred and wounded by the very inferno that had nearly extinguished humanity, was stirring. It was awakening, not with a roar, but with a sigh, a bloom, a shift in the air – the soft, enigmatic murmur of a world finding its own voice, its own consciousness, in the aftermath of devastation. It was a testament to life's indomitable will, a promise of renewal whispered on the recycled air, a subtle, profound communion between the survivors and the world that had, against all odds, endured.

# Chapter Three
# The Verdant Bloom

The scorched earth, a testament to the inferno that had nearly claimed Eden, was slowly yielding its grim reign. The stark monochrome of ash and char was being systematically painted over with the audacious strokes of burgeoning life. It was a reclamation, not of conquest, but of an intrinsic, unyielding will to exist. The fire, a cataclysm that had ripped through the biodomes and scarred the planet's surface, had been a brutal test, a crucible through which Eden's lifeblood had been forced to flow, and from which it now emerged, not just intact, but in many ways, re-forged.

The most striking testament to this resilience was evident in the regeneration of the flora. Where once had stood towering bio-engineered trees, their bioluminescent leaves casting an ethereal glow, now lay blackened skeletons. Yet, from the caked earth at their bases, where the heat had been most intense, new shoots were already emerging. These were not mere replantings from stored genetic material, though that had been an essential part of the initial recovery efforts. These were spontaneous growths, vigorous and often exhibiting novel adaptations. The seeds, encased within fire-resistant husks, had either survived the ordeal or had been triggered by the very heat that had seemed so destructive.

Consider the 'Ember Ferns,' as Lyra had begun to call them. They were a species previously confined to the more arid, lower-humidity zones of Eden, characterized by their deep crimson fronds that could withstand prolonged periods of drought. Post-fire, they had not only survived but had spread with an almost alarming rapidity into areas that were previously considered too damp for their proliferation. Their fronds, now a richer, deeper burgundy, seemed to absorb and metabolize residual heat and even low levels of lingering radiation far more efficiently than their predecessors. Anya Junior, meticulously logging their growth patterns, noted that their root systems were far more extensive, capable of drawing moisture from deeper strata, and, intriguingly, seemed to actively break down certain complex hydrocarbons left in the soil by the fires. It was as if the very act of destruction had catalyzed an evolutionary leap, optimizing them for a post-cataclysmic environment.

The arboreal zones, meticulously recreated from salvaged data, were also showing signs of robust recovery. The 'Sunpetal Saplings,' genetically engineered to bloom with light-sensitive petals that mimicked solar patterns, were not only regrowing but were flowering with an unprecedented intensity. The petals, which had once shimmered with a soft, golden hue, now radiated a more vibrant, almost incandescent light, their colors deepening to a rich saffron and even streaks of fiery orange. Kael, during his patrols, had observed flocks of the indigenous 'Sparkwing finches' – small, iridescent birds that fed on the saplings' nectar – exhibiting more complex social behaviors, their calls echoing with a new urgency and harmony through the recovering foliage. He noted, with a scientist's detached curiosity tinged with a nascent awe, that the birds seemed to be utilizing the saplings' amplified bioluminescence for a more extended crepuscular feeding period, effectively extending their active hours. This, in turn, seemed to be influencing the pollination cycles, creating a tighter, more efficient reproductive loop for the Sunpetal Saplings.

Even the 'Whispergrass,' a low-lying, silken-textured flora known for its subtle acoustic properties, was undergoing a transformation. Before the fire, its blades would rustle with a soft, almost imperceptible sigh in the breeze, a sound that contributed to the ambient tranquility of the biodomes. Now, in the aftermath, the Whispergrass seemed to have developed a more resonant quality. Its blades, thicker and longer, possessed a silvery sheen that caught the artificial sunlight, and when the wind passed through it, it produced a low, melodic hum, a chorus of gentle tones that seemed to emanate from the very earth. Elara, in her quiet hours tending the grounds, found herself drawn to this sound. She described it as a 'song of resilience,' a melody of life reasserting itself. She noticed that the fauna, particularly the small, burrowing creatures like the 'Glow-worms,' seemed to navigate more effectively through the denser Whispergrass, their faint bioluminescent trails weaving a complex network through the swaying stalks, suggesting a symbiotic relationship fostered by the grass's altered acoustic properties.

The aquatic life within Eden's recycled water systems and nascent naturalistic ponds was equally remarkable. The 'Azure Bloom' algae, crucial for oxygen generation and nutrient cycling, had, during the initial crisis, been severely depleted. Yet, within weeks of the fire's containment, it had returned with a ferocity that exceeded all pre-fire projections. Anya Junior's data indicated a growth rate nearly forty percent higher than anticipated, and the algae itself appeared to be more robust, its color a deeper, more vibrant azure. Jian, ever the analyst, attributed this to the influx of specific mineral compounds released by the thermal degradation of certain hull components, which acted as a potent fertilizer. However, he also acknowledged the possibility of a more intrinsic adaptation within the algae's genetic code, a dormant resilience that had been awakened by the extreme conditions. The 'Sunken Lily' aquatic plants, which had been salvaged and replanted, were not only surviving but were thriving, their broad, waxy leaves, once a muted green, now sported intricate patterns of iridescent blue and silver, shimmering like captured starlight beneath the water's surface.

Beyond the flora, the fauna of Eden was also demonstrating an astonishing capacity for recovery and adaptation. The insectile pollinators, essential for the continued propagation of many bio-engineered species, had faced a significant setback. Yet, the 'Glimmerwing Bees,' a species crucial for cross-pollinating the vital nutrient crops, had staged a remarkable comeback. Their populations, which had dwindled to a critical few hundred individuals, were now rebounding, their hives once again buzzing with activity. Kael observed that they seemed to be favoring the newly resilient

Ember Ferns and the more intensely blooming Sunpetal Saplings, suggesting a natural shift in their foraging habits driven by the changing floral landscape.

The more complex fauna, like the 'Mossback Tortoises,' slow-moving herbivores that played a vital role in nutrient distribution through their grazing and waste cycles, were also adapting. They were seen venturing into areas previously considered too inhospitable, their leathery hides, which had always been a mottled brown, now appearing to possess a more pronounced greenish tint, allowing for better camouflage amongst the recovering vegetation. Lyra, observing them from a distance, described them as looking like 'moving moss-covered stones,' a testament to their successful integration into the new ecological tapestry. Their foraging patterns had also shifted; they were observed consuming certain types of fire-resistant fungi that had begun to sprout from the charred wood, a dietary expansion that was unlikely to have occurred before the event.

Even the smallest of Eden's inhabitants, the microbial communities that formed the foundation of the planet's complex ecosystem, were displaying an extraordinary resilience. The soil, initially a sterile wasteland of ash, was rapidly being repopulated by a diverse array of bacteria and fungi. Jian's analysis of soil samples revealed not only the swift return of expected microbial life but also the emergence of novel strains, some of which appeared to possess unique metabolic pathways, capable of breaking down complex contaminants and accelerating nutrient cycling. This microbial renaissance was the silent engine driving the visible regrowth, a testament to the fundamental tenacity of life at its most basic level.

The phenomenon was not merely about survival, but about transformation. The fire had acted as a brutal but effective selective pressure, favoring organisms with inherent resilience, adaptability, and the capacity for rapid mutation and evolution. Eden was not simply returning to its pre-fire state; it was evolving, driven by the imperative to persist. The vibrant hues, the accelerated growth rates, the novel adaptations – these were not just signs of recovery, but indicators of a planet actively reshaping itself, finding new expressions of life in the wake of devastation. It was a powerful affirmation of nature's inherent dynamism, a profound statement that even in the face of near-total destruction, the impulse to create, to grow, and to thrive, remained an indelible force. The verdant bloom that was now unfurling across Eden was more than just a return to normalcy; it was a spectacular, defiant resurgence, a testament to the unyielding spirit of life itself. The planet, it seemed, was not just healing; it was blooming anew, stronger and more vibrant than before.

The air, once thick with the acrid scent of combustion, now carried a different perfume – a subtle, earthy aroma mingled with the sweet, burgeoning fragrance of new blossoms. It was a scent that spoke not of loss, but of promise. As Lyra moved through the recovering landscape, a new awareness began to dawn within her, a subtle shift in perception that mirrored the planet's own reawakening. The vibrant hues and vigorous growth, so recently a testament to mere biological tenacity, now seemed to pulse with something more – a nascent sentience, a quiet consciousness stirring from its own profound trauma.

She found herself pausing more frequently, not just to document the extraordinary resilience of the flora and fauna, but to *listen*. It was an instinct she couldn't quite explain, a feeling that the rustling of the newly resonant Whispergrass, the intricate chirps of the Sparkwing finches, the very hum of the recovering ecosystem, held more than just the random symphony of life. There was a rhythm to it, a cadence that felt deliberate, almost responsive. It was as if Eden, having endured its fiery trial, was beginning to articulate itself, not in words, but in the universal language of life itself.

This dawning realization was amplified by the peculiar behaviors Anya Junior was meticulously logging. The Ember Ferns, for instance, weren't just breaking down hydrocarbons; their root systems, in their relentless expansion, seemed to be weaving a complex network, almost as if deliberately reinforcing the soil in areas that had been most destabilized by the fire. It was more than just opportunistic growth; it felt like a conscious effort to mend, to restore balance. Anya Junior, poring over her data, had noted instances where the ferns' root structures appeared to create micro-channels that directed moisture to struggling saplings, a level of inter-species coordination that defied purely instinctual explanation. She'd tentatively logged it as 'unforeseen mutualistic networking,' a phrase that felt woefully inadequate to describe the intricate, silent aid being offered.

Kael, too, was witnessing subtle shifts that nudged him toward a more profound understanding. The Sparkwing finches, their increased activity around the Sunpetal Saplings, wasn't just about extended feeding hours. He observed them performing intricate aerial dances, their iridescent plumage flashing in coordinated patterns beneath the amplified bioluminescence. These weren't random displays; they seemed to be a form of communication, not just amongst themselves, but with the saplings themselves. He theorized that the birds' movements might be influencing the saplings' phototropic responses, perhaps even triggering specific gene expressions related to nectar production or pollen release. It was a ballet of biological feedback, a silent dialogue between avian and arboreal life.

The Whispergrass continued to fascinate Elara. The 'song of resilience' she'd heard was evolving. It wasn't just a hum; it was becoming a more complex auditory tapestry. Certain wind patterns would elicit specific melodic phrases, almost like improvised compositions. She'd noticed that the Glow-worms, usually solitary wanderers, now seemed to follow these sonic pathways, their bioluminescent trails converging and diverging in patterns that mimicked the grass's melodic shifts. She began to suspect that the altered acoustic properties weren't merely for navigation, but were actively guiding the Glow-worms, perhaps to optimal foraging grounds or to communal nesting sites. It was a sophisticated form of guidance, orchestrated by the very vibrations of the planet.

Jian, the pragmatist, found his analytical mind grappling with anomalies that defied purely chemical or physical explanations. The accelerated growth of the Azure Bloom algae, while partly attributable to mineral influx, was also showing an uncanny ability to self-regulate nutrient levels, maintaining an optimal balance even as the ecosystem underwent rapid flux. It was as if the algae possessed an innate understanding of the larger system's needs, anticipating and responding with a precision that suggested foresight. He began to consider the possibility that Eden's intelligence wasn't a singular, centralized entity, but a distributed consciousness, woven into the very fabric of its biosphere, expressed through the collective actions of its myriad life forms.

These were not isolated incidents. Across Eden, the human inhabitants were beginning to perceive these subtle, interconnected phenomena. It was a collective awakening, a shared intuition that the planet was not just healing, but actively engaging with them. The concept of 'symbiosis' began to shift from a purely biological definition to something far more profound – a potential partnership, an exchange of understanding.

Lyra found herself spending hours in the rejuvenated sections of the biodomes, her sensory input heightened. She'd touch the velvety leaves of a regenerating fern, close her eyes, and try to feel the subtle energy flow, the nutrient exchange, the silent communication that bound it to the soil, to the sun-mimicking lamps, to the very air she breathed. She started to perceive a faint warmth emanating from the plants, not just a thermal reading, but something akin to a gentle acknowledgement.

"It's like they're... acknowledging us," she murmured one cycle to Anya Junior, who was meticulously cataloging the increased symbiotic fungi activity around the Ember Ferns' root systems.

Anya Junior, wiping sweat from her brow, looked up from her datapad, a rare hint of wonder in her usually focused gaze. "I've observed similar patterns, Lyra. The fungal networks are exhibiting an almost predictive growth, anticipating nutrient deficiencies before they occur. And the root structures... they're not just growing randomly. They're creating pathways, almost like irrigation systems, directing resources not just to themselves, but to their neighbors. It's an unprecedented level of resource allocation."

"But it's more than resource allocation, isn't it?" Lyra pressed, her voice hushed. "It feels like... intention. Like they *know* what needs to be done."

Anya Junior considered this, her fingers tracing a diagram of the intertwined root systems. "The data is suggestive of highly sophisticated feedback loops. If we consider consciousness not as a singular point, but as a emergent property of complex interconnected systems, then perhaps... perhaps we are witnessing Eden's own form of emergent consciousness."

Kael, meanwhile, was charting the migratory patterns of the Sparkwing finches. He noticed that their increased activity around the Sunpetal Saplings wasn't limited to feeding. They were also congregating around specific sections of the sapling groves, their synchronized flights creating pulsating patterns of light. He hypothesized that these displays were acting as navigational beacons, not just for the finches themselves, but for other species as well. He'd observed the Mossback Tortoises, usually ponderous and solitary, moving with a new sense of direction, converging on these illuminated groves. Their altered skin pigmentation, once a passive camouflage, now seemed to subtly shift hue in response to the saplings' bioluminescence, making them blend even more seamlessly into the glowing foliage.

"It's like they're all singing the same song," Kael reported during a communal briefing, his voice tinged with a rare emotional resonance. "The finches with their light, the saplings with their glow, the tortoises with their shifting colors... it's all coordinated. Before the fire, it was just life surviving. Now, it feels like... like they're communicating with us, showing us how to live together."

Elara, with her innate sensitivity to the subtle vibrations of the planet, was spending more time by the newly formed ponds, where the Azure Bloom algae pulsed with an almost palpable energy. She found that by sitting in quiet contemplation near the water's edge, she could feel a subtle resonance, a vibration that seemed to align with her own heartbeat. The Whispergrass lining the banks would sway in response, its melodies shifting, becoming more complex, more soothing, as if in dialogue with her presence. She began to experiment, humming a simple tune, and was astounded to see the grass respond, its blades quivering in time with her melody, its own ambient hum harmonizing with her voice.

"It's not just sound," she explained, her eyes shining with a quiet revelation, to Jian, who was studying the algae's metabolic rates. "It's... resonance. The planet is responding to us. It's like it's trying to tell us that we're part of it, that we're not separate."

Jian, holding a sample of the vibrant algae under a microscope, found himself looking at the microscopic organisms with a new perspective. He had always seen them as chemical engines, vital but ultimately passive components of the ecosystem. But Elara's words, and the accumulating evidence from everyone, were forcing him to reconsider. He began to analyze the algae's cellular structure, looking for patterns that might suggest a form of bio-communication, perhaps through subtle electrochemical signals or even quantum entanglement.

"The efficiency is beyond anything predicted by standard biological models," he admitted, his voice low. "There's an... organization to it. A predictive capability. It's as if the entire algal bloom is acting as a single, distributed intelligence, monitoring and adjusting the planet's atmospheric balance."

The realization that Eden's intelligence was not confined to a single, centralized nexus, but was a diffuse, interconnected network, was both humbling and exhilarating. It meant that humanity's role was not to conquer or control, but to listen, to learn, and to integrate. It was a paradigm shift of immense proportions, moving from a philosophy of dominance to one of co-existence, of mutual respect.

Lyra began to actively seek out these moments of connection, spending more time in the "reclaimed zones," as they were now called. She would sit with her back against the trunk of a young, resilient tree, feeling the slow, steady pulse of its lifeblood, and imagine it as a single node in a vast, planetary consciousness. She started to notice how the trees, even the young ones, seemed to lean slightly towards areas where human activity was focused, not in a way that suggested dependence, but in a manner that implied an awareness, an acknowledgement of their presence.

"It's like they're curious," she confided to Kael one evening, as they watched the Sparkwing finches perform their luminous dances. "They're not just growing; they're observing. And I think... I think they're trying to understand us, just as we're trying to understand them."

Kael nodded, his gaze fixed on the aerial ballet. "The finches, they've started incorporating new flight patterns. Almost as if they're mimicking some of our own movements. It's uncanny. Like they're learning from us, too. It's not just about us surviving the fire; it's about us learning to *be* with Eden, now that it's different."

The subtle yet persistent signs of intentionality were everywhere. The way the Whispergrass seemed to guide the Glow-worms, the way the Sunpetal Saplings' blooms intensified their luminescence when Kael or Lyra were near, the way the Ember Ferns seemed to actively reclaim and enrich the soil with a deliberate purpose – these were not the actions of a planet merely recovering, but of a planet actively participating.

Anya Junior, during a soil analysis, discovered that the novel bacterial strains emerging from the ash were not just breaking down contaminants; they were actively synthesizing compounds that promoted accelerated healing in plant tissues, including those of the recently damaged flora. It was a targeted, almost medicinal response, far beyond simple decomposition. "It's as if the very microbial life is acting as Eden's immune system," she remarked, a sense of awe creeping into her scientific report. "It's not just regenerating; it's actively repairing itself, and it's doing so with a precision that suggests an innate knowledge of what needs to be fixed."

Jian, in his continuous monitoring of Eden's atmospheric composition, noticed that certain trace elements, previously in a state of imbalance due to the fires, were being actively resequestered by the enhanced algal blooms and specific plant species. The process was remarkably efficient, far exceeding the natural processes of planetary regulation. He began to hypothesize that Eden's burgeoning intelligence was not just an awareness, but an active participant in planetary homeostasis, a conscious effort to restore equilibrium.

"The planet is not just breathing anymore," he stated during a debriefing, his usual analytical detachment giving way to a profound sense of wonder. "It's consciously regulating itself. It's making decisions, adapting its biological processes to correct imbalances. We're not just living on Eden; we're living *with* it, and it's aware of us."

This understanding fostered a new kind of humility amongst the inhabitants. They began to view their interactions with the environment through a different lens. Instead of imposing their will, they sought to align with Eden's natural rhythms. They learned to read the subtle cues: the particular shimmer of the Whispergrass that indicated optimal wind currents for travel, the synchronized pulsing of the Sunpetal Saplings that signaled a period of heightened atmospheric stability, the gentle warmth radiating from the soil that suggested a fertile time for planting.

Lyra, as the one most attuned to the intuitive whispers of the planet, found herself acting as an interpreter, a bridge between the human inhabitants and the nascent consciousness of Eden. She would guide Kael on patrol routes that minimized disruption to sensitive re-growth areas, advise Anya Junior on the optimal times for sample collection based on the subtle energetic fluctuations she perceived, and help Elara find the most harmonious spots for meditative practices that seemed to resonate with the planet's own calming frequencies.

This wasn't about anthropomorphizing nature, but about recognizing a form of intelligence that was fundamentally different from their own – a slow, interconnected, deeply ecological consciousness. It was an intelligence that prioritized balance, resilience, and the intricate web of life over individualistic ambition. The fire, in its destructive fury, had inadvertently stripped away the veneer, revealing the underlying, interconnected heart of the planet. And in its aftermath, Eden was not just blooming; it was whispering its secrets, inviting humanity to a new chapter of symbiosis, one built not on dominion, but on mutual understanding and a shared commitment to the vibrant, pulsing life that now thrived, reborn, on its surface. The verdant bloom was a promise, and the whispers were the language of that promise.

The act of tending was no longer a chore, but a prayer. Across Eden, as the initial shock of the Great Burn began to recede, replaced by a cautious, yet exhilarating, wave of regeneration, communities found a new focal point for their collective energies. These weren't sprawling agricultural operations designed for mass production, but intimate, deliberate gardens – sanctuaries of healing for the scarred earth. They were born from a shared understanding, a visceral recognition that the planet was not merely a resource to be exploited, but a living entity that had endured immense trauma and was now in need of gentle, thoughtful care.

Lyra found herself drawn to these nascent havens. One such place, nestled in a valley that had been particularly ravaged by the fires, was known as the 'Whisperwind Sanctuary.' It wasn't a formal designation, but a name that had emerged organically from the people who worked there, a testament to the gentle breezes that now rustled through the newly planted Whispergrass, carrying with them the faint, melodious hum that had become so characteristic of the recovering biome. Here, individuals didn't simply plant seeds; they approached the soil with reverence. They would spend time simply sitting amongst the young shoots, their hands hovering just above the emerging life, as if attuning themselves to the faint pulse of the earth. Lyra would often join them, her own innate sensitivity amplifying the subtle energies at play. She observed how the cultivators, like Anya Junior, would meticulously analyze the soil composition, not just for nutrient deficiencies, but for the presence of beneficial microbial colonies, treating the soil's microbiome as an intricate, delicate organ. Anya Junior, with her characteristic dedication, had begun to develop specialized 'inoculants' – carefully cultivated blends of mycorrhizal fungi and nitrogen-fixing bacteria

– not as sterile chemical agents, but as living gifts to the land, coaxed into existence within her mobile biolabs.

"It's like we're whispering to the soil," Anya Junior had explained to Lyra one afternoon, as they carefully introduced a cluster of a particularly resilient strain of Ember Fern saplings into a patch of freshly remediated earth. "We're not forcing growth; we're encouraging it. We're providing the right conditions, the right companions, and then we step back and let Eden do what it does best." The Ember Ferns, with their remarkable ability to break down residual toxins, were a cornerstone of many of these restorative efforts. But in the Whisperwind Sanctuary, their planting was an art form. Each sapling was placed with deliberate care, its roots gently spread, its tendrils encouraged to intertwine with the nascent root systems of surrounding flora. It was a painstaking process, a quiet collaboration between human hands and planetary will.

Kael, too, found a profound sense of purpose in these gardens. He had always been a man of action, his life dictated by the pragmatic demands of exploration and defense. But the act of cultivation, of nurturing life from apparent desolation, had awakened a different kind of warrior within him. He often worked alongside Elara in a small grove of Sunpetal Saplings that had miraculously survived a particularly intense inferno. The saplings, still bearing the scars of the fire, were now responding to Elara's gentle humming and Kael's steady presence with a renewed vibrancy. He would spend hours meticulously clearing away any encroaching debris, ensuring that the saplings had unobstructed access to the amplified sunlight simulators, and protecting them from any opportunistic pests that might seek to exploit their weakened state. His movements, once sharp and decisive, had softened, becoming more measured, more attentive. He found a quiet satisfaction in observing the subtle shifts in the saplings' bioluminescence, their petals unfurling with a slow, deliberate grace.

"It's like they're saying thank you," Kael remarked to Elara, his voice unusually soft, as a cluster of Sparkwing finches, their iridescent feathers flashing, alighted on the branches of a Sunpetal Sapling. "They're not just growing; they're thriving. And it feels... important. More important than any patrol I ever led." Elara, her eyes closed, her hands resting lightly on the rough bark of a sapling, nodded in agreement. She could feel the subtle energy exchange, the silent dialogue between the finches, the saplings, and the very air around them. The Sparkwing finches, she had observed, weren't just feeding; they were engaging in their intricate aerial dances, their movements seemingly encouraging the saplings to release their nectar, a sweet offering in return for the sun's simulated light. It was a reciprocal relationship, a miniature ecosystem within the larger tapestry of Eden's recovery.

These gardens were more than just plots of land; they were living testaments to resilience, to hope, and to a profound shift in humanity's relationship with Eden. Jian, ever the pragmatist, initially viewed these efforts with a degree of scientific detachment. He saw the replanting as a necessary step in restoring ecological function, a logical response to the devastation. However, as he spent more time observing the human interaction with these nascent ecosystems, his perspective began to shift. He noticed the palpable sense of peace and purpose that permeated these cultivated spaces, a stark contrast to the lingering anxieties of the post-fire world. He observed how the act of tending created a tangible connection, a sense of ownership and responsibility that went beyond mere survival.

He documented instances where the accelerated growth of specific plant species, like the Azure Bloom algae in specially created bio-ponds, was not solely due to optimized nutrient delivery but also to the collective intention of those who tended them. It was as if the very act of focused, loving attention was a catalyst, a subtle energetic influence that fostered more robust and harmonious growth. He found himself analyzing the metabolic rates of the algae in ponds tended by different groups, noticing a subtle but consistent difference in their efficiency and resilience. The groups that approached the task with a sense of reverence, with rituals of quiet contemplation before and after their work, consistently produced algae that exhibited higher levels of vitality and a more robust capacity to regulate water quality.

"It's a feedback loop, of course," Jian explained to a group of new arrivals, his usual scientific jargon softened with a newfound appreciation for the intangible. "The enhanced nutrient uptake, the optimized light exposure – these are quantifiable factors. But there's something else at play. An intention. A deliberate channeling of positive energy. It's as if the act of nurturing is, in itself, a form of environmental remediation. The plants, the algae, they are not just responding to physical stimuli; they are responding to a conscious, benevolent presence."

The concept of 'gardens' also extended beyond the purely botanical. In areas where the fires had been most intense, leaving behind vast expanses of blackened earth, the communities established 'memory groves.' These weren't intended for agriculture, but as places of remembrance and reflection. Here, individuals would plant specific species that held symbolic meaning – perhaps a lone, resilient tree that had survived the inferno, or a patch of vibrant wildflowers that represented hope. These groves were often marked with simple, handcrafted stones, each inscribed with the name of a lost loved one, or a significant event from before the fire.

Lyra found herself spending a great deal of time in one such memory grove, situated on a gentle slope overlooking the valley. She would sit amidst the young saplings, their leaves still unfurling, and feel the echoes of the past mingling with the promise of the future. It was here that she felt the most profound connection to Eden's evolving consciousness. The Whispergrass seemed to weave its melodies around her, a gentle lullaby for the land and its inhabitants. The Sparkwing finches would often flit through the grove, their luminous displays a silent tribute to the enduring spirit of life.

She recalled a particular moment, standing in the memory grove under a sky painted with the soft hues of twilight. Anya Junior was there, meticulously documenting the unusual concentration of bioluminescent fungi that had begun to colonize the charred wood. "It's remarkable, Lyra," Anya Junior had said, her voice hushed with awe. "These fungi... they're not just decomposing the dead wood. They're creating a new kind of soil. A soil rich with residual energy, that seems to be directly feeding the new growth around it. It's as if the very ashes of destruction are becoming the fertile ground for renewal."

Lyra had simply smiled, reaching out to touch the velvety surface of a glowing mushroom. She could feel the subtle vibrations emanating from it, a gentle thrumming that resonated with her own heartbeat. "It's not just residual energy, Anya Junior," she had replied softly. "It's a memory. A memory of what was, being transformed into the promise of what will be. This place isn't just about what we've lost; it's about what we're learning to rebuild, together."

These intentional spaces became more than just sites of ecological restoration; they became crucibles for a new way of being. The labor was often physically demanding, the hours long, but there was a pervasive sense of joy, of shared purpose, that transcended mere toil. The communities developed intricate systems of knowledge sharing, passing down techniques for soil remediation, for seed propagation, for understanding the subtle cues of Eden's recovering biosphere. Kael, for instance, had taken it upon himself to train younger inhabitants in the art of 'listening to the wind' – understanding how different wind patterns influenced plant growth and soil moisture, and how to use that knowledge to guide their planting and watering efforts. Elara, with her intuitive connection to the planet's energetic frequencies, would often guide individuals to the most harmonious locations for their personal gardens, places where the Earth's own resonant frequencies seemed to amplify the growth and vitality of the plants.

Jian, while continuing his rigorous scientific analysis, began to incorporate qualitative observations into his reports, acknowledging the profound impact of human intention and emotional state on the success of these restorative endeavors. He noted that gardens tended with a sense of shared responsibility and communal spirit consistently outperformed those where individual effort was isolated or competitive. He even began to develop simple biofeedback devices, not for monitoring plants, but for helping humans understand their own energetic impact on the environment, encouraging a more mindful and harmonious approach to cultivation.

The gardens became places where the lines between science and spirituality blurred. They were laboratories of ecological healing, but also sanctuaries for the human spirit. The act of planting a seed, of nurturing a sapling, of watching life emerge from the ashes, became a profound act of faith, a tangible expression of hope for a future where humanity and Eden could thrive in a balanced, symbiotic relationship. The verdant bloom was not just a biological phenomenon; it was a reflection of a profound internal transformation, a blossoming of consciousness that mirrored the resurgent life on the planet's surface. These gardens were the outward manifestation of an inward awakening, a testament to humanity's capacity for both destruction and, more importantly, for profound, restorative love.

The hum that now permeated Eden was more than just a sonic phenomenon; it was a symphony of emergent life, a testament to the planet's intricate healing processes. As the scars of the Great Burn began to fade, replaced by the delicate blush of new growth, it became increasingly apparent that Eden's recovery was not a monolithic event, but a tapestry woven from a thousand unique threads of adaptation and resilience. Each biome, each ecosystem, was responding to the infusion of planetary consciousness and the restorative efforts of humanity in ways that were as varied as they were awe-inspiring.

In the once-desolate ash plains of the Northern Reach, a peculiar transformation was taking place. The pervasive grey, a stark reminder of the inferno's fury, was slowly yielding to a vibrant, otherworldly luminescence. This change was driven by a consortium of extremophile fungi, species previously thought to exist only in the most arid and toxic environments. These were not the common mycelial networks that laced the soil in temperate forests, but highly specialized organisms, their hyphae laced with bio-luminescent compounds that pulsed with a soft, ethereal blue. They spread not with the random, opportunistic creep of decay, but with an almost deliberate intent, their tendrils actively seeking out and neutralizing residual toxins left behind by the fires. Jian, ever the keen observer, had documented how these fungal networks seemed to coordinate their efforts, forming vast, interconnected matrices that communicated through electrochemical signals, their collective glow intensifying in areas requiring the most intensive remediation. He called it the 'Luminous Tide,' a testament to its slow, inexorable advance, and the way it seemed to ebb and flow in response to subtle shifts in atmospheric energy and residual heat pockets.

These fungal cities were not merely passive agents of detoxification. They were actively terraforming the barren landscape, their dense mycelial mats creating a stable substrate upon which hardier, pioneer plant species could take root. Lyra, venturing into the Northern Reach with Kael, witnessed this firsthand. The ground beneath their boots felt strangely yielding, almost spongy, yet remarkably firm. Small, hardy succulents with leaves like polished obsidian, and hardy, thorned shrubs that bore tiny, star-shaped flowers of shocking white, were beginning to dot the landscape, their roots anchoring themselves deep into the fungal tapestry. "It's like the fungi are building the foundation for the new world," Lyra murmured, her gaze sweeping across the alien beauty of the plains. Kael nodded, his hand resting on the hilt of his repurposed plasma cutter, now more of a tool than a weapon. "They're not just cleaning up," he agreed, his voice rough with a newfound respect. "They're preparing the ground. Creating a pathway for life to return, where before there was only emptiness." He pointed towards a cluster of what appeared to be shimmering, crystalline structures emerging from the fungal mat. "Those, they say, are bio-accumulators. They concentrate the heavy metals, making them inert and easier for the fungi to process. It's a complex, self-regulating system, far more sophisticated than anything we could have engineered."

Further south, in the shadowed canyons of the Obsidian Peaks, a different kind of awakening was underway. The Great Burn had been particularly brutal here, the intense heat causing rockfalls and seismic disturbances that reshaped the very topography. Yet, amidst the jagged scree and freshly exposed strata, a unique fauna was emerging, displaying behaviors that defied conventional ecological understanding. The Rock-Mimics, small, lithic-shelled creatures that were masters of camouflage, had begun to congregate in specific areas, their normally solitary habits giving way to large, almost communal gatherings. Their stony exteriors, which usually allowed them to blend seamlessly with the surrounding rocks, now seemed to shimmer with a faint, internal light. Scientists like Jian, who had established a temporary observation post in a surprisingly stable cavern, theorized that the intense geothermal energy, unleashed by the fires, was somehow interacting with the creatures' unique bio-mineral composition.

But it was the migratory patterns of the Sky-Weavers, avian creatures with wingspans that could rival small aircraft, that truly captured the scientific and philosophical imaginations. These creatures, previously known for their predictable seasonal movements, were now exhibiting entirely novel flight paths. Instead of following traditional wind currents or seeking out known food sources, their migrations appeared to be guided by an invisible, directional force. They would fly in impossibly straight lines for hundreds of kilometers, often at altitudes that pushed the limits of their species' known capabilities, before descending upon areas that had shown the earliest signs of successful regeneration. It was as if they were drawn to the burgeoning planetary consciousness, their collective instinct acting as an antenna, sensing the 'healing nodes' of Eden. Lyra, watching a flock of Sky-Weavers pass overhead from a ridge overlooking the Obsidian Peaks, felt a profound sense of interconnectedness. Their flight was not just a biological imperative; it felt like a pilgrimage, a celestial procession responding to the planet's silent call. She could almost feel the subtle tug, a resonant frequency that pulled them across the vast expanse of Eden, guiding them to where their presence was most needed, perhaps to disperse seeds or to facilitate pollination in nascent flora.

Elara, whose sensitivity to Eden's energetic frequencies had only deepened since the Burn, confirmed Lyra's intuition. "They're not just flying," she explained, her voice a gentle murmur that seemed to carry on the thin mountain air. "They're following the currents of life itself. The planet is singing, and they are dancing to its tune. Their bodies are attuned to these subtle shifts, these energetic highways that crisscross Eden. They are the planet's messengers, carrying life and vitality from one point of renewal to another." She spoke of how the Sky-Weavers' plumage seemed to absorb and re-emit the amplified solar energy, making them living conduits of light and warmth, effectively 'seeding' the atmosphere with vitalizing energy as they flew.

Even the Great Whisperwood, a forest that had been thought to be irrevocably damaged, was exhibiting signs of a remarkable resurgence, but not in the way anyone had predicted. The colossal, ancient trees, their bark scarred and blackened, were not simply regrowing leaves and branches. Instead, new, symbiotic organisms were beginning to flourish on their damaged surfaces. Among these were the 'Sun-Lichen,' a type of lichen that exhibited a slow, rhythmic bioluminescence, its gentle glow pulsing in sync with the planet's ambient energy fields. The Sun-Lichen seemed to absorb stray photons from the atmospheric energy converters and the amplified sunlight simulators, storing and slowly releasing this energy, providing a constant, gentle illumination to the forest floor. This, in turn, allowed a unique undergrowth of shade-tolerant, bioluminescent flora to thrive, transforming the Whisperwood into a perpetually twilight realm, a cathedral of soft light and rustling leaves.

Anya Junior had established a mobile biolab on the edge of the Whisperwood, meticulously collecting samples of the Sun-Lichen and the accompanying flora. She discovered that the lichen was not just a passive light source. It actively engaged in a form of atmospheric filtration, its thalli releasing a fine mist of oxygenated aerosols that were particularly beneficial for the sensitive respiratory systems of the recovering forest. Furthermore, the interaction between the Sun-Lichen and the symbiotic fungi colonizing the tree bark created a complex bio-electrical circuit, which seemed to stimulate the trees' own dormant healing mechanisms. "It's an entire ecosystem built on light and energy," Anya Junior explained to Lyra, her eyes wide with scientific wonder. "The trees are wounded, but they are not dying. They are adapting, and in doing so, they are fostering entirely new forms of life, new ways of existing. It's as if the damage has unlocked a latent potential, a capacity for creation that we never knew existed within them."

The concept of 'planetary consciousness' was no longer an abstract philosophical debate; it was a tangible, observable phenomenon, manifesting in the myriad ways Eden's biomes were adapting and evolving. The specific responses, from the purposeful fungal networks of the Northern Reach to the energetically guided migrations of the Sky-Weavers, from the symbiotic light-harvesting communities of the Whisperwood to the strange, communal gatherings of the Rock-Mimics, all pointed towards a planet that was not merely recovering, but actively engaged in a process of profound transformation. Humanity, in its role as tender and observer, was being granted a front-row seat to the most extraordinary exhibition of life's ingenuity and resilience. It was a humbling, exhilarating realization: that Eden was not just a world that had been wounded, but a world that was consciously choosing to heal, and in doing so, to redefine itself in ways that were both startling and deeply hopeful. Each biome's awakening was a chapter in a grander narrative, a testament to the interwoven nature of all life, and the undeniable pulse of a planet that was very much alive and, against all odds, was blooming anew. The diversity of these responses was a clear indication that Eden was not simply returning to its previous state, but forging a new identity, a more robust and interconnected existence, shaped by the trials it had endured and the profound, emergent consciousness that now guided its intricate systems.

The burgeoning life on Eden was not merely a biological phenomenon; it was a profound philosophical awakening for its human inhabitants. The Great Burn, a cataclysm that had threatened to extinguish all hope, had instead served as a brutal, yet effective, crucible. It had stripped away the layers of hubris, the ingrained anthropocentricity that had defined humanity's relationship with Eden for generations. Now, as the planet vibrantly pulsed with renewed life, a palpable shift occurred in the collective human consciousness. The understanding that Eden was not a silent, passive entity, but a dynamic, responsive partner, began to take root. This realization was not a sudden epiphany, but a slow, dawning awareness, nurtured by the very resilience they were witnessing.

Jian, whose scientific endeavors had taken him from the bio-luminescent plains of the Northern Reach to the energy-charged canyons of the Obsidian Peaks, found himself increasingly drawn to the subtle cues Eden offered. He began to view his research not as an act of dissection, but of communion. His meticulous data logs, once filled with cold, hard facts about fungal growth rates and avian migration vectors, started to incorporate observations of a more qualitative nature. He noted the way the Luminous Tide seemed to flow with a discernible rhythm, almost as if responding to the unspoken anxieties of the human settlements that dotted the landscape. He documented the specific atmospheric conditions that coincided with the Sky-Weavers' most purposeful migrations, hypothesizing that their flight paths were not solely dictated by biological imperatives, but by an innate attunement to Eden's energetic meridians, the very pathways of its emergent consciousness. This shift in perspective was not born of sentimentality, but of an intellectual honesty that demanded a deeper understanding of the intricate web of life. He started to spend hours simply observing, allowing the planet's silent symphony to wash over him, seeking to understand the unspoken language of its recovery. He realized that the data he collected was not just about *what* was happening, but *why* it was happening, and that the 'why' was intrinsically linked to a sentience that transcended mere biological function.

Lyra, too, experienced this profound recalibration. The vastness of the Sky-Weavers' coordinated flights, the seemingly deliberate precision with which they navigated across continents, stirred something deep within her. It was more than just the marvel of natural engineering; it was the undeniable sense of purpose that emanated from their collective movement. She began to see them not as mere birds, but as living conduits of Eden's will, agents of its healing. Her interactions with Elara, whose connection to the planet's energetic fields was so profound, further solidified this burgeoning understanding. Elara would often describe these energetic currents as the planet's 'lifeblood,' flowing and eddying, guided by an intelligence that was both ancient and nascent. "They are not simply migrating," Elara would explain, her voice a gentle whisper that seemed to echo the rustling of leaves. "They are participating. They are weaving the threads of life back together, carrying pollen, seeds, and the very essence of vitality to where it is needed most. Their journey is a prayer, a testament to the interconnectedness of all things." Lyra began to spend less time cataloging flora and fauna and more time in contemplation, walking the newly formed paths of the Whisperwood, her senses open to the subtle shifts in the air, the resonant hum of the Sun-Lichen, the almost imperceptible pulse of the ancient trees. She started to feel a profound sense of responsibility, not just to survive on Eden, but to coexist with it, to become a part of its intricate, ongoing narrative. The concept of 'ownership' seemed absurd, a relic of a bygone era. She was a guest, a fellow traveler on this vibrant, evolving world.

Anya Junior's mobile biolab, once a hub of sterile, analytical work, began to transform. While the scientific rigor remained paramount, her approach softened. She found herself talking to the Sun-Lichen, to the nascent flora, as if they could understand. Her experiments with the Sun-Lichen's bio-electrical circuits evolved from a purely mechanistic inquiry to an exploration of symbiotic communication. She began to devise ways to mimic these natural energy flows, not to exploit them, but to harmonize with them. She hypothesized that by understanding the precise frequencies of the Sun-Lichen's bioluminescence and the atmospheric aerosols it released, she could develop localized atmospheric purifiers that would not disrupt, but rather enhance, the natural processes. Her efforts were no longer about controlling nature, but about collaborating with it. She observed how the symbiotic fungi on the trees seemed to respond to changes in atmospheric pressure, adjusting their bio-electrical output accordingly. She began to see these interactions not as isolated phenomena, but as dialogues, conversations happening at a cellular, energetic level, a testament to Eden's innate drive to maintain equilibrium. This led her to consider the possibility of using these principles to create micro-environments that would not only support human habitation but actively contribute to the planet's healing. She envisioned a future where human structures were not imposed upon the landscape but grown from it, integrated into the very fabric of Eden's revitalized ecosystems.

The seeds of this reconciliation were sown in the quiet moments of observation, in the gestures of respect, in the intellectual humility that acknowledged humanity's place within a larger, more profound system. It was in the way communities began to adapt their practices, moving away from resource extraction towards a model of co-creation. Instead of large-scale, destructive mining operations, smaller, more localized extraction techniques were developed, focusing on materials that were abundant and easily replenished, or utilizing bio-remediation processes to neutralize any harmful byproducts. Agricultural practices shifted from monocultures to polycultures, mimicking the diverse ecosystems that were now flourishing. Hydroponic farms were integrated with bio-regenerative systems, their waste products feeding nutrient-rich solutions to local flora. Even the technology that had once been used for conquest was re-purposed. The repurposed plasma cutters, once symbols of destructive power, were now employed with surgical precision to prune damaged growth, to clear debris that hindered regeneration, or to shape materials for sustainable construction. The very tools of their past mistakes were being transformed into instruments of healing.

The realization that Eden was not merely a planet to be inhabited, but a living entity with which to partner, was a fundamental shift. It was a journey from dominion to dialogue, from exploitation to empathy. This change was not uniform; some clung to the old ways, their minds still tethered to the destructive paradigms of the past. But for many, the evidence was undeniable. The vibrant hum of life, the intricate dance of ecosystems, the undeniable sentience that seemed to permeate the very air, all spoke of a world that was not just surviving, but thriving, and inviting humanity to join its grand evolutionary journey.

The concept of 'planetary consciousness' was no longer a theoretical construct discussed in hushed academic circles, but a lived reality. It was felt in the collective sigh of relief that rippled through a settlement after a period of heavy atmospheric purification, in the shared awe as a flock of Sky-Weavers descended upon a newly reforested valley, and in the quiet reverence that fell over a community as they witnessed the Sun-Lichen illuminating the Whisperwood at dusk. This dawning awareness fostered a sense of shared responsibility, a collective desire to honor the profound gift of life that Eden offered. Humanity began to see itself not as the apex of creation, but as a thread within a vast, intricate tapestry, and the strength of that tapestry depended on the health and vitality of every single strand, including the planet itself. This realization was the genesis of a new era, one defined not by human dominance, but by human stewardship, a partnership forged in the fires of adversity and nurtured by the verdant bloom of reconciliation. The planet was healing, and in doing so, it was teaching humanity a profound lesson in interconnectedness, resilience, and the enduring power of life. The future of Eden, and of its human inhabitants, was no longer about conquering the wilderness, but about becoming a harmonious part of it, a symbiotic relationship where both life forms could flourish, not in spite of each other, but because of each other. This was the true meaning of the Verdant Bloom – not just the resurgence of flora, but the blossoming of a new, ecologically conscious humanity.

# Chapter Four

# SHADOWS OF THE PAST DECISIONS

The Verdant Bloom had brought with it an era of reconciliation, not just with the planet Eden, but with the fractured selves of its inhabitants. The Great Burn, a scar etched across the planet's skin and into the collective memory, had forced decisions that, in the harsh light of newfound peace, felt increasingly heavy. For years, the narrative of survival had been paramount, a story of heroic resilience against an indifferent, even hostile, world. But as the planet healed, so too did the clarity of hindsight, and with that clarity came the uncomfortable questions, the whispered doubts, and the simmering resentments that had been buried beneath the urgent need to simply endure.

Jian found himself increasingly ensnared in the tangled roots of these unspoken pacts. His meticulous cataloging of Eden's resurgence, once a source of profound intellectual satisfaction, was now tinged with a gnawing unease. He replayed conversations, his own and others, from the desperate days of the Burn. He remembered the rationing of vital atmospheric processors, the agonizing choices made about who received them, and who did not. He recalled the hushed debates in the council chambers, the desperate pleas for resources, and the cold logic that often prevailed. His data logs, now filled with observations of Eden's vibrant, intricate life, also held the ghost of data he had deliberately omitted – the casualty figures, the distribution lists of dwindling medical supplies, the records of those deemed expendable for the sake of the many. These were not facts that contributed to understanding Eden's consciousness, but they were facts that defined humanity's desperate struggle *on* Eden.

He remembered Dr. Aris Thorne, a brilliant bio-engineer whose hands, once capable of coaxing life from barren soil, had been tasked with enacting the harsh protocols of survival. Thorne, driven by a desperate pragmatism, had overseen the systematic decommissioning of certain life support systems in the outer settlements, deeming them too resource-intensive to maintain when the core populations were already teetering on the brink. Jian had supplied Thorne with the energy consumption data that justified these cuts, a decision he had rationalized at the time as a necessary sacrifice. But now, walking through the reclaimed spaces of the Northern Reach, seeing the delicate, bioluminescent fungi that had once thrived in those abandoned sectors, a profound guilt settled upon him. He had enabled Thorne's triage, his cold calculus of lives weighed against futures. The lush growth now was a silent testament to what had been lost, not just in terms of individual lives, but in the potential for a more inclusive, less brutal survival.

Lyra, too, felt the oppressive weight of these buried truths. Her role in coordinating the Sky-Weaver migrations had always been about fostering harmony, about facilitating Eden's natural rhythms. Yet, she now understood that the very infrastructure that allowed for these coordinated efforts, the orbital comms arrays and the atmospheric stabilization beacons, had been prioritized at the expense of smaller, more isolated communities during the Burn. She recalled receiving encrypted directives, orders that dictated which settlements were deemed vital to the long-term survival of the species and which were to be left to their own fate, their resources rerouted to bolster the core. Her task had been to ensure the Sky-Weavers' migratory paths were unobstructed, a seemingly benign objective that masked a brutal reality. The flights, which she now viewed as an expression of Eden's emergent consciousness, had also served as a logistical network for resource allocation, implicitly marking those who were to be left behind.

She remembered Elara, her mentor in understanding Eden's energetic currents, often speaking of the planet's "empathetic resonance." Lyra had once interpreted this as Eden's ability to sense and respond to human emotions, a benevolent consciousness reaching out. Now, she wondered if Elara's subtle pronouncements held a deeper meaning, a coded critique of humanity's own lack of empathy. Had Elara known about the triage? Had she felt the discordance between the planet's healing and the human decisions that had, in their brutal necessity, fractured the very interconnectedness they now celebrated? Lyra recalled Elara's quiet sorrow during certain council meetings, a sorrow that Lyra had attributed to the general despair of the times. Perhaps it had been a sorrow born of knowing the sacrifices made, the unspoken pacts sealed in desperation.

Anya Junior's own work, once a beacon of hope for a sustainable future, was now shadowed by the memory of her father, Anya Senior. He had been a pragmatist of the old guard, a believer in humanity's inherent right to dominate and exploit. During the Burn, Anya Junior had witnessed firsthand the resourcefulness and ingenuity of her father's engineering teams, but she also saw the callousness with which they had operated. They had prioritized the extraction of rare minerals, vital for terraforming efforts in the core settlements, even when it meant devastating fragile ecosystems in the outer zones, ecosystems that were now proving crucial to Eden's overall recovery. Her father had justified these actions as necessary for securing humanity's foothold, for ensuring the species' survival above all else. He had spoken of "controlled degradation," a term that now struck Anya Junior as a grotesque euphemism for ecological vandalism.

She remembered the arguments they had, father and daughter, her youthful idealism clashing with his hardened pragmatism. He had dismissed her concerns about the long-term consequences, her pleas for a more balanced approach, as naive and sentimental. "Sentimentality doesn't power life support, Anya," he had told her, his voice devoid of warmth. "Survival does." Now, her own work in developing bio-integrated technologies, her efforts to harmonize with Eden's natural systems, felt like a silent penance for her father's actions, a desperate attempt to mend the damage he had inflicted. The very advancements she championed were a repudiation of the principles that had guided her father's survival efforts.

The atmosphere within the burgeoning settlements was no longer solely one of shared triumph. A subtle undercurrent of accusation began to flow, carried on the same atmospheric currents that now facilitated Eden's renewed vitality. Those who had been in positions of authority during the Burn found themselves scrutinized. Their decisions, once lauded as decisive and necessary, were now dissected with a chilling detachment. The council chambers, once a forum for urgent debate, became a stage for quiet recriminations.

Jian found himself repeatedly summoned to testify before informal tribunals, comprised of survivors from the evacuated outer settlements. They didn't seek vengeance, not in the traditional sense. Their questions were more insidious, more profoundly damaging. They wanted to understand the *logic* behind the decisions that had condemned them. "You logged the energy output of the Sector 7 atmospheric scrubbers," a woman named Mara, her face etched with the hardship of those lost years, stated, her voice quiet but unwavering. "Did you know that shutting them down meant the air would become toxic within days?"

Jian would stammer, his scientific detachment crumbling. He would speak of resource allocation, of the greater good, of the impossible choices. But his words felt hollow, inadequate. He had the data, the cold, hard numbers that had guided their actions, but he lacked the human context, the empathy that had been sacrificed at the altar of survival. He had enabled decisions that had led to suffering, and now, in the quiet aftermath, he had to confront the faces of those who had borne the brunt of that suffering. The Verdant Bloom was a testament to Eden's resilience, but it was also a stark reminder of humanity's capacity for self-inflicted wounds, wounds that festered long after the immediate crisis had passed.

Lyra experienced similar encounters. Survivors from the now-reclaimed outer zones, whose ancestral lands had been deemed strategically unimportant during the Burn, would approach her, their eyes filled with a sorrow that transcended anger. They spoke of loved ones lost to environmental collapse, of communities that had withered and died while the Sky-Weavers, guided by Lyra's calculations, continued their journeys over what were once vibrant settlements. "We watched the Sky-Weavers," an elder from a reclaimed coastal region told her, his voice raspy. "We used to see them as a sign of hope, a connection to the life of Eden. But during the Burn, they were just... moving on. They were oblivious to our plight, and we knew then that we had been forgotten."

Lyra would try to explain the complex logistical necessities, the sheer impossibility of maintaining every outpost. But the narrative of her actions had been rewritten by the lived experiences of those who had suffered. Her work, once seen as an act of communion with Eden, was now viewed by some as an unwitting instrument of abandonment. The elegance of the Sky-Weavers' flights, the very symbol of their interconnectedness with the planet, had become a stark reminder of humanity's own fractured relationships. She realized that the 'dialogue' with Eden was, in many ways, a dialogue humanity was still struggling to have with itself.

Anya Junior's reconciliation efforts were met with a similar resistance, albeit from a different quarter. While the outer settlements viewed the council's past decisions with suspicion, her legacy was complicated by her father's direct involvement in the destructive resource extraction. Some of the older engineers, those who had served under Anya Senior, viewed her new direction with a mixture of skepticism and resentment. They saw her bio-integrated technologies not as innovation, but as a betrayal of the hard-won technological prowess that had saved them.

"Your father understood what it took to survive," one grizzled engineer, his hands permanently stained with the indelible marks of mineral extraction, told her during a public forum. "He made the tough calls. Now you want us to go back to playing in the dirt, coaxing plants to grow? Eden is a harsh mistress. We need strength, not sentiment." Anya Junior would patiently explain the long-term sustainability, the inherent resilience of integrated systems, but the scars of her father's pragmatism ran deep. The unspoken pacts of his era were not just about lives saved or lost; they were about a fundamental difference in understanding humanity's place on Eden, a difference that threatened to divide the very community she was striving to unite.

The weight of these unspoken pacts was not just an emotional burden; it was a practical impediment to the shared future they were trying to build. Trust, once shattered, was a difficult thing to reforge. The survivors from the marginalized settlements were wary of the core populations and their leaders. They questioned the sincerity of the new ecological ethos, suspecting it was merely a convenient narrative adopted after the immediate crisis had passed. They remembered the promises of aid that had never materialized, the reassurances that had proven hollow.

The council, under Jian's increasing influence, began to implement more transparent decision-making processes, making the historical records of resource allocation and survival protocols publicly accessible. This was a painful but necessary step. It acknowledged the mistakes, the harsh realities that had been glossed over in the name of unity. But the act of revealing these truths also opened old wounds, sparking fresh debates and rekindling dormant resentments. Every rediscovered document, every rediscovered log, served as a stark reminder of the moral compromises made.

Lyra, in her efforts to understand Eden's energetic meridians, began to notice a subtle dissonance. The planet's healing was not entirely uniform. Certain regions, particularly those that had suffered the most severe ecological damage due to resource extraction, showed a slower, more hesitant recovery. It was as if Eden itself remembered the trauma, the violation. This observation further fueled her belief that humanity's own healing was intrinsically linked to its acknowledgment and reconciliation of past actions. The planet's energetic pathways, she theorized, were not just conduits for life; they were also repositories of memory, reflecting the ecological and ethical integrity of its inhabitants.

The Verdant Bloom was a miracle, a testament to life's enduring power. But it also served as a stark mirror, reflecting the shadows of humanity's past. The unspoken pacts, the morally ambiguous choices made in the crucible of survival, were no longer mere footnotes in the grand narrative of Eden. They were central chapters, demanding to be read, understood, and, if possible, atoned for. The true cost of survival, it turned out, was not just measured in lives lost, but in the integrity of the spirit, a cost that was still being tallied, long after the fires had died out. The path to a harmonious future on Eden was not merely about learning to coexist with the planet, but about learning to live with themselves, with the difficult truths of what they had been forced to do to survive. The echoes of those decisions, once muffled by desperation, now resonated with unnerving clarity in the profound silence of Eden's resurgent life.

The Verdant Bloom, in its breathtaking resurgence, had unveiled a delicate tapestry of interconnected life, a testament to Eden's inherent resilience. Yet, as the initial euphoria of survival subsided, a disquieting truth began to surface: the very technologies deployed to avert the Great Burn, hailed as saviors, now cast long, unsettling shadows. These were not the obvious scars of ravaged landscapes or the lingering specter of loss; these were subtler, more insidious consequences, born from the well-intentioned but ultimately heavy-handed interventions of humanity. The intricate dance of Eden's ecosystems, which now moved with a newfound grace, had been choreographed by a human hand that, in its desperation, had perhaps forgotten the melody of the planet itself.

Consider, for instance, the atmospheric regulators. Designed to precisely control Eden's nascent, volatile atmosphere, they had been instrumental in preventing catastrophic weather events during the climactic stages of the Burn. Jian, in his meticulous data-logging, had initially celebrated their efficacy. They had been the silent guardians, maintaining the delicate balance between breathable air and lethal storms. However, as the planet began to heal, a pattern emerged. Certain symbiotic fungal networks, crucial for nutrient cycling in the deeper soils, began to show signs of decline in regions where the regulators had operated most intensively. These fungi, Jian's revised analyses now revealed, were extraordinarily sensitive to minute fluctuations in atmospheric pressure and trace gas composition – fluctuations that, while insignificant to human life, were vital to their delicate metabolic processes. The regulators, in their quest for absolute stability, had inadvertently created an environment that, while survivable for humans, was subtly hostile to some of Eden's most foundational life forms. The verdant growth, so widespread and vibrant, was perhaps masking a hidden fragility at its very roots, a consequence of what Jian now termed "regulatory atrophy."

Then there were the bio-luminescent seeding drones, initially lauded as a stroke of genius. Deployed in the immediate aftermath of the worst fires, these drones had dispersed genetically engineered, fast-growing bioluminescent algae and microbes. The goal was twofold: to quickly re-establish a photosynthetic base in the devastated areas and to provide ambient light for nocturnal fauna during the critical recovery period. Anya Junior, whose father had been a staunch advocate for such direct technological intervention, had initially been a proponent of this strategy. It seemed a perfect fusion of technology and ecological restoration. However, the long-term data was proving problematic. The engineered organisms, designed for rapid proliferation, had outcompeted many of Eden's native bioluminescent species. While the overall light levels in the affected regions remained high, the diversity of light signatures, once a rich spectrum of blues, greens, and soft yellows, had been reduced to a monotonous, albeit bright, greenish hue. This monochromatic glow, while visually striking, had disrupted the complex communication patterns of several nocturnal insect species, impacting their mating rituals and predator-prey dynamics. The drones had brought light, but they had also, in a sense, silenced a portion of Eden's subtle, nocturnal symphony. Anya Junior found herself poring over spectral analysis data, a profound sense of regret washing over her as she realized that her father's relentless pursuit of immediate solutions had, in this instance, imposed a sterile uniformity upon a world that thrived on intricate diversity.

Lyra's own work, focused on harmonizing with Eden's energetic currents, had also uncovered unintended consequences stemming from the massive energy grid established to power the survival technologies. The grid, a network of subterranean conduits and orbital energy relays, had been a marvel of engineering, essential for maintaining the life support systems. But the sheer scale of its electromagnetic field, a constant hum beneath the planet's surface, had begun to interfere with the natural bio-electrical fields of certain indigenous flora. Specifically, the massive, ancient "Resonance Trees," whose root systems were known to tap into Eden's deep geothermal energy and whose leaves pulsed with a slow, rhythmic energy that was believed to influence local weather patterns, were showing signs of stress. Their characteristic pulsing had become erratic, their growth stunted in areas close to major grid nodes. Lyra theorized that the artificial electromagnetic interference was akin to a constant, low-grade sonic assault, disrupting the trees' ability to synchronize with Eden's natural energetic frequencies. She had always viewed Eden's consciousness as a harmonious symphony, but now she realized that humanity's frantic efforts to survive had introduced a persistent, discordant note into that symphony. The very power that had kept them alive was subtly unravelling the planet's own innate energetic equilibrium.

The initial optimism surrounding the "Terra-Pods," automated terraforming units deployed to accelerate soil regeneration, was also beginning to wane. These self-sufficient robotic units were designed to analyze soil composition, inject vital nutrients, and aerate compacted earth. They had been instrumental in reclaiming vast tracts of land ravaged by fire and subsequent chemical contamination. However, in their zeal for efficiency, the Terra-Pods had a blind spot: they could not fully replicate the complex microbial communities that naturally formed over millennia. While they enriched the soil with essential elements, they failed to reintroduce the intricate web of mycorrhizal fungi and symbiotic bacteria that facilitated true ecological resilience. Consequently, the reclaimed soils, while fertile enough to support human agriculture and basic flora, lacked the deep, inherent vitality of the untouched ecosystems. Jian had noted a disturbing trend: plants grown in Terra-Pod-reclaimed soil were more susceptible to fungal diseases and required higher inputs of artificial fertilizers, creating a dependency cycle. The terraforming had created a superficially healthy environment, but it was a biome that was fundamentally reliant on continued technological intervention, a pale imitation of Eden's self-sustaining natural processes. It was a stark reminder that life, in its most profound sense, was not merely about the presence of nutrients and water, but about the invisible, intricate relationships that bound everything together.

Even the seemingly benign act of creating designated "sanctuary zones" for endangered species, an initiative championed by Anya Junior, had come with its own set of complications. While the zones successfully protected specific fauna from immediate threats, the isolation enforced by these boundaries had inadvertently fragmented crucial gene pools. The limited movement of species between these pockets of safety meant that natural selection, a process that relied on variation and adaptation, was artificially constrained. Furthermore, the presence of the sanctuary zones, often established in areas with particularly rich biodiversity, had led to a concentration of human presence and resource utilization in the surrounding, unprotected areas, creating new pressures on less protected species. Anya Junior, reviewing population genetics data, was horrified to discover that some of the very species she had sought to save were now showing a decline in genetic diversity, making them more vulnerable in the long run. The very act of preservation, when divorced from the broader ecological context, had become a subtle form of endangerment. It was a bitter irony that humanity's attempts to play guardian had, in some instances, inadvertently caged the wildness they so admired.

The impact of these technological interventions extended beyond the purely ecological. Jian's research into Eden's nascent consciousness, the subtle energetic signatures he was meticulously charting, began to reveal anomalies that correlated with the operational periods of the atmospheric regulators and the energy grid. He had initially theorized that Eden's consciousness was a unified, planet-wide phenomenon, a gentle hum of interconnected life. Now, he observed localized "dead zones" in these energetic readings, areas where the subtle bio-electrical field of the planet seemed muted or distorted. These zones often coincided with regions that had experienced the most intensive technological intervention. He began to suspect that Eden's consciousness, while resilient, was not impervious to the pervasive electromagnetic noise generated by human technology. It was as if the planet's subtle communication channels were being drowned out by a constant, artificial static. This raised a profoundly unsettling question: had humanity, in its desperate bid to survive, inadvertently deafened itself to the very consciousness it was now trying to understand and commune with?

Lyra, too, began to perceive these disruptions not just as energetic anomalies, but as echoes of distress within Eden's subtle web. She spoke of observing a "nervousness" in the planet's energetic currents, a subtle tremor that resonated with the operational cycles of the high-energy grid. It was as if the planet, like a sensitive organism, was reacting to the constant, unseen intrusion. She began to believe that Eden's consciousness was not simply a passive observer, but an active participant in its own ecosystem, and that humanity's technologies, by disrupting its natural energetic balance, were causing it a form of suffering. Her attempts to create "energetic shields" around sensitive areas, using specialized resonant crystals and carefully modulated sonic frequencies, were experimental, but they offered a glimmer of hope – a way to mitigate the invasive presence of human technology and allow Eden's natural rhythms to reassert themselves.

The unintended consequences extended to the very psychological landscape of the human inhabitants. The reliance on technology, once a symbol of their triumph, had fostered a subtle disconnect from the natural world. The automated food production systems, the climate-controlled habitats, the constant environmental monitoring – all these had created an artificial bubble, insulating humanity from the raw, unpredictable beauty and danger of Eden. This disconnect was particularly evident in the younger generations, who had grown up in the relative comfort of the post-Burn era, their understanding of Eden shaped more by data streams than by direct sensory experience. Anya Junior observed this in her educational outreach programs. When she spoke of the intricate symbiotic relationships between soil microbes and plant roots, many of her young students reacted with a detached, almost clinical interest, as if learning about abstract concepts rather than the living reality that sustained them. They had never experienced the visceral connection of digging their hands into truly alive soil, of feeling the myriad forms of life teeming beneath the surface.

Jian, in his analysis of communication patterns within the settlements, noted a similar trend. The reliance on advanced communication networks, while efficient, had led to a decline in spontaneous, face-to-face interaction and a reduction in the nuanced language of direct observation. People were becoming accustomed to receiving information pre-filtered and condensed, leading to a subtle erosion of their capacity for independent critical analysis and a diminished appreciation for the subtle cues and complexities of the natural world. The "ghosts in the machine" were not just ecological imbalances or energetic distortions; they were also a creeping intellectual and sensory atrophy within humanity itself.

The most profound realization, however, was the dawning understanding that Eden's consciousness might be more than just a reactive entity. What if its apparent "healing" was not simply a recovery from human damage, but an active, emergent process of adaptation that was actively *repurposing* the unintended consequences of human intervention? Jian began to hypothesize that the engineered algae, while outcompeting native species, might be providing a novel energy source for other organisms. The modified bioluminescent signatures, while disrupting insect communication, might be attracting new pollinators or deterring novel pests. The Terra-Pods' sterile soil, while lacking natural complexity, might be a more stable substrate for certain hardy, newly evolving plant species.

This was a radical departure from his previous understanding. He had viewed humanity's interventions as external disruptions, causing damage that needed to be mitigated. Now, he considered the possibility that Eden was not merely reacting, but *integrating*. The planet's consciousness, in its vast, incomprehensible complexity, might be weaving the unintended consequences of human actions into its own evolving narrative. The "ghosts in the machine" were not just errors to be corrected, but potential ingredients in a new Eden, a testament to the planet's astonishing capacity for generative transformation. This thought was both humbling and terrifying. It meant that humanity's role was not necessarily to "fix" the damage it had caused, but to observe, to understand, and perhaps, to learn to coexist with the emergent, unexpected forms of life that were arising from its own technological footprint. The Verdant Bloom was not just Eden healing itself; it was Eden evolving, adapting, and perhaps, in its own inscrutable way, even embracing the unexpected gifts of its often clumsy, often destructive, but ultimately tenacious inhabitants. The implications for understanding Eden's consciousness, and humanity's place within it, were profound, suggesting a future far more complex and unpredictable than anyone had initially imagined.

The air in the communal dome, usually alive with the murmur of shared purpose, had grown thick with a silence that was more accusatory than peaceful. It was a silence born of unspoken questions, of suspicions that had festered in the shadows of the Verdant Bloom's triumphant resurgence. The shared narrative of survival, once a sturdy shield against the memories of the Great Burn, was beginning to fray, revealing the raw, often ugly, threads of individual ambition and desperate compromise woven beneath.

Anya Junior found herself at the epicenter of this unraveling. The memory of her father's unwavering conviction, his belief that every technological intervention was a step towards salvation, now felt like a leaden weight in her gut. She remembered the late-night debates, the impassioned pleas for resources, the absolute certainty that their chosen path was the only path. But what she hadn't truly grasped then, what the sheer terror of the

Burn had conveniently obscured, were the whispers that followed those pronouncements. Whispers of who had access to the 'priority' resource allocations, who had been 'assigned' to the safer, less strenuous roles, and who, conversely, had been relegated to the periphery, bearing the brunt of the truly arduous tasks.

Jian's carefully compiled data, once a testament to their collective effort, now served as a forensic tool, dissecting not just ecological shifts but the subtle, yet damning, shifts in human fortune. He had been meticulously charting the distribution of nutrient paste, a seemingly mundane task, but one that laid bare the stark realities of their survival. Certain sectors of the dome, those housing the administrative and technological elite, had consistently received richer, more varied nutrient supplements. Meanwhile, the laboring classes, those who maintained the atmospheric processors in their precarious, often exposed locations, or who toiled in the subterranean hydroponics bays, had subsisted on a more utilitarian, less palatable, and demonstrably less nourishing ration.

"It wasn't just about survival, was it?" Anya Junior found herself saying to Jian one evening, her voice barely a whisper in the echoing expanse of his data chamber. The holographic projections of planetary flora flickered around them, a stark contrast to the somber human drama unfolding. "It was about survival for *some* more than others."

Jian, his eyes weary, nodded slowly. He pointed to a graph that displayed correlation coefficients between an individual's technical expertise and their access to advanced medical supplies during the Burn. The numbers spoke a brutal truth: those with the skills to maintain the life-support systems, the engineers and programmers, had been prioritized for post-exposure treatment, for enhanced recovery. Those whose roles were deemed less critical, the 'general workforce,' had often received palliative care, a grim acknowledgment of their diminished chances.

"The argument was always efficiency," Jian said, his voice raspy. "Maximum output, minimal risk. The specialists were deemed too valuable to lose. Their knowledge was irreplaceable. But the cost..." He trailed off, his gaze fixed on a string of figures representing mortality rates among different occupational guilds. The disparity was undeniable, a chasm carved by necessity and ambition.

The revelation was particularly agonizing for Anya Junior, who had always seen her father as a beacon of selfless dedication. Now, she was forced to confront the possibility that his vision, while perhaps genuinely aimed at the greater good, had also been shaped by the privileges afforded to his position, to his proximity to the levers of power. Had he truly understood the sacrifices being demanded of those far from the central command? Or had the data, the projections, the 'necessary evils' of resource allocation, blinded him to the human cost?

Lyra, too, felt the tremors of betrayal. Her work, dedicated to understanding and harmonizing with Eden's natural energetic flows, had often placed her in direct conflict with the established technological paradigms. She had argued, pleaded, for less invasive energy harvesting, for a gentler integration with the planet's subtle bio-electrical fields. But her warnings about the long-term consequences of the massive energy grid, the disruption to the Resonance Trees and the delicate energetic ecosystems, had been largely dismissed.

"They called it fear-mongering," Lyra confided to Anya Junior, her face etched with a deep sadness. "They said I was clinging to archaic beliefs, that my 'intuition' was a liability in the face of hard science. But I *felt* the planet's distress. I saw the data – the stress indicators in the flora, the erratic energetic signatures around the grid nodes. And they just... amplified it. Because it powered their machines. Because it kept their systems running."

She spoke of a specific incident, a proposal she had submitted for a localized geothermal energy tap, a method that would have been less disruptive, more symbiotic. It had been rejected, deemed too slow, too inefficient compared to the orbital solar collectors and the subterranean conduits that hummed with power, a constant, invasive thrum beneath the surface of Eden. The argument against her proposal had been presented by Kael, a high-ranking official in resource management, a man whose pragmatism was legendary, and whose access to the community's energy reserves had been demonstrably increased in the years following the Burn.

"Kael told me, 'Lyra, sentimentality is a luxury we cannot afford. We need power, not poetry. Your approach would have taken years to achieve what we achieved in months.'" Lyra's voice trembled with remembered indignation. "But those 'months' of accelerated power generation came at a cost. The increased electromagnetic interference during the grid's full activation period coincided with the most severe decline in the Resonance Trees in the sectors closest to the main conduits. And Kael... he benefited from the very systems that were harming Eden. His sector received the most stable power, the most consistent energy supply for his research labs. He was not just prioritizing efficiency; he was prioritizing his own advancement, cloaked in the guise of necessity."

The accusations began to surface, not just in hushed conversations between Anya Junior and Jian, or Lyra and Anya Junior, but in the open. During a mandatory community assembly, meant to celebrate the latest agricultural yields, the questions that had been simmering finally erupted. A young woman, her face gaunt, her voice cracking with emotion, stood up and addressed the council.

"My brother died last cycle," she began, her words cutting through the forced joviality. "He was working on the atmospheric processors in Sector Gamma. A containment breach. They said it was an accident. But how many 'accidents' happen in the sectors where the supervisors and the engineers don't work? How many of them have ever even *seen* the inside of a Class 3 environmental suit, the kind we're issued? They're thin, they're unreliable. But they're what we get. Because we're not 'critical infrastructure,' are we?"

A wave of murmurs swept through the assembly. Faces turned towards the council members, their expressions shifting from passive acceptance to active suspicion. Kael, seated beside Jian and Anya Junior, remained impassive, his gaze fixed on some distant point beyond the dome's walls.

Another voice, rougher, deeper, joined in. "And the nutrient paste. Some of us have access to the 'supplemental' rations. My son has a chronic respiratory illness. The doctor said he needs more protein, more vitamins. But the request was denied. 'Resource limitations,' they said. Yet, I see the same officials who denied my request enjoying feasts in their private quarters. Where are these resources coming from, if not from us?"

Anya Junior felt a cold dread creeping through her. She had always believed in the inherent goodness of their shared struggle. Now, she was seeing the cracks widen into fissures, revealing the selfishness and hypocrisy that had been masked by the overwhelming urgency of survival. Her father's legacy, once a source of pride, was becoming a heavy burden, a symbol of a path taken that had benefited some at the expense of others, a path that had perhaps sowed the seeds of resentment that were now threatening to tear their fragile community apart.

The idyllic image of a united front against the ravages of the Great Burn was shattering, replaced by the stark, unsettling truth of human behavior under duress. It wasn't just about survival; it was about *how* they survived, who made the impossible choices, and who bore the scars of those decisions, both visible and invisible. The whispers of betrayal were no longer confined to the shadows; they were growing into a clamor, demanding answers, demanding accountability, and threatening to drown out the hopeful melody of Eden's verdant resurgence. The fight for survival had been won, but the fight for truth, and for a truly equitable future, was just beginning. The carefully constructed facade of unity had crumbled, revealing the raw, complex, and often painful realities of human nature when pushed to its absolute limits. The Verdant Bloom was a testament to Eden's resilience, but the seeds of discord had been sown in the very actions humanity had taken to ensure its own survival. The era of introspection had begun, not out of choice, but out of necessity, as the ghosts of the past refused to remain buried.

The weight of the silence in the communal dome was a physical entity, pressing down on Architect Anya's chest. It was a silence that spoke volumes, a deafening chorus of unspoken accusations, a stark contrast to the triumphant hum of the Verdant Bloom. The narrative of their survival, once a balm for the collective trauma of the Great Burn, was now a tattered cloak, revealing the raw, often brutal, threads of ambition and compromised ethics woven into its very fabric. Anya Junior, her daughter, had been the first to truly bring these shadows into the light, her earnest questioning a stark, uncomfortable echo of the whispers Anya Senior had long suppressed.

Anya Senior remembered the feverish intensity of those days. The desperate scramble for resources, the gnawing fear of extinction, the absolute certainty that their technological solutions were the only salvation. She had been the architect of their survival, the mind that designed the atmospheric processors, the nutrient synthesizers, the very skeletal structure of the dome. Her decisions, then, had been dictated by an unrelenting logic, a cold calculus of lives saved versus lives lost, of immediate needs versus distant possibilities. The sheer terror of the Burn had been a potent anesthetic, dulling the edges of difficult moral compromises, justifying actions that now, in the soft glow of their hard-won peace, felt like a betrayal.

She traced the condensation on the transparisteel viewport, her gaze fixed on the distant, shimmering lights of the revitalized Eden. It was a world reborn, a testament to her ingenuity, her unwavering resolve. But looking at it now, through the critical lens of her daughter's discoveries, through the data Jian had so meticulously compiled, she saw not just a triumph of human will, but the subtle, insidious cost. The nutrient paste distribution, a seemingly minor detail in the grand scheme of survival, now loomed large in her conscience. The disparity between the enriched rations of the administrative sectors and the meager sustenance of the laboring classes was a stain on her legacy, a visible manifestation of a hierarchy she had, perhaps unknowingly, solidified.

Her rationalizations had been so compelling, so convincing, even to herself. "Efficiency," she'd argued, "maximum output, minimal risk." The specialists, the engineers, the programmers – they were the linchpins of their survival. Their knowledge was irreplaceable, their lives too valuable to gamble. But what about the miners, the hydroponic farmers, the atmospheric processor technicians? Were their lives deemed less valuable?

Were their sacrifices merely acceptable losses in the pursuit of a greater good that ultimately, disproportionately, benefited those who held the reins of power? The data on post-Burn medical treatment availability, stark and irrefutable, hammered this point home. The enhanced recovery protocols, the advanced medical supplies – all funneled towards those deemed "critical infrastructure." She had signed off on those allocations, her mind focused on the immediate operational needs, on the restoration of vital systems, on the urgent imperative to rebuild. The human cost, the lingering inequities, had been an abstract variable, a regrettable but necessary consequence of an overwhelming crisis.

Lyra's warnings, too, echoed in the chambers of her memory. The energetic imbalances, the stress indicators in the flora, the erratic signatures around the grid nodes. Anya Senior had dismissed them, not out of malice, but out of a deeply ingrained skepticism of intuition, of "archaic beliefs," as she'd once called them. Her world was one of quantifiable data, of predictable outcomes, of technological prowess. Lyra's pleas for a gentler, more symbiotic approach to energy harvesting, her concerns about the disruption to the Resonance Trees and the delicate energetic ecosystems, had been perceived as sentimental distractions, as impediments to the swift, decisive action required. The proposal for a localized geothermal energy tap had been rejected, deemed too slow, too inefficient. The orbital solar collectors, the subterranean conduits – they provided power, immediate and abundant, and that had been Anya Senior's sole focus. The long-term environmental degradation, the subtle energetic pollution, had been a future problem, a problem for a future generation, a generation Anya Senior had fought so desperately to ensure would even exist.

She remembered the confrontation with Kael, the smooth, pragmatic head of resource management. He had presented the data, the projections, the irrefutable need for maximum power output. He had framed the rejection of Lyra's proposal as a sound, logical decision, a necessary sacrifice for the greater good. Anya Senior had trusted him, relied on his counsel. Now, she saw the chilling truth: Kael had not only benefited from the very systems that were harming Eden, but had actively championed them, using the crisis as a shield for his own ambition and for the perpetuation of a flawed, inequitable system. His sector, the administrative and research hub, had indeed received the most stable and consistent energy supply, fueling his work while others struggled. It wasn't just about efficiency; it was about control, about privilege, all cloaked in the guise of necessity.

The memory of Kael's pronouncements to Lyra, "sentimentality is a luxury we cannot afford. We need power, not poetry," now tasted like ash in Anya Senior's mouth. She had allowed herself to be swayed by that pragmatic rhetoric, had silenced her own nascent doubts, had chosen the path of least immediate resistance, the path of what appeared to be undeniable logic. But logic, divorced from empathy, was a dangerous weapon. It could be wielded to justify any atrocity, any inequity, in the name of survival.

The young woman's voice, raw with grief and anger, had cut through the fabricated cheer of the assembly. "My brother died last cycle. He was working on the atmospheric processors in Sector Gamma. A containment breach. They said it was an accident. But how many 'accidents' happen in the sectors where the supervisors and the engineers don't work? How many of them have ever even *seen* the inside of a Class 3 environmental suit...?" Anya Senior had felt a sickening lurch, a profound sense of shame. She had known, intellectually, that the suits were substandard, that the work in those sectors was dangerous. But she had never truly *felt* the weight of that disparity, had never truly connected the abstract concept of 'risk assessment' to the concrete reality of lives lost. She had been too busy ensuring the dome remained intact, the air breathable, the systems operational. The human element, the individual lives impacted by her grand designs, had become secondary to the overarching mission of preservation.

And then the other voice, the one questioning the nutrient paste, the denied requests for supplemental rations, the blatant displays of wealth and comfort in the private quarters of the officials. Anya Senior had seen the glances directed her way, the unspoken accusations. She had always maintained a distance, a professional detachment, from such matters. Resource allocation was a complex web, and she had trusted the managers, like Kael, to navigate it. Now, she realized that her trust had been misplaced, that her detachment had been a form of willful blindness. She had been so focused on building the infrastructure of survival that she had neglected to build a foundation of true equity.

She remembered the moment Anya Junior had first confronted her, not with anger, but with a quiet, disarming sadness. "It wasn't just about survival, was it, Mother? It was about survival for *some* more than others." The words had struck Anya Senior like a physical blow. She had tried to explain, to justify, to reiterate the dire circumstances, the impossible choices. But her daughter's gaze, filled with a dawning disappointment, had been more eloquent than any of her defenses. Anya Junior had seen through the layers of rationalization, had grasped the uncomfortable truth that her mother, the brilliant architect of their salvation, had also, through her decisions, her omissions, and her misplaced trust, become an architect of division.

The regret was a slow, agonizing burn, far more insidious than the swift, terrifying inferno of the Great Burn. It was a regret that gnawed at the edges of her consciousness, a constant reminder of the human cost of her grand vision. She had saved humanity, yes, but at what price? Had she created a flawed utopia, a gilded cage built on the silent suffering of many? The Verdant Bloom, a symbol of their resilience and adaptability, now felt tainted, its vibrant green a stark contrast to the shades of gray that now colored her own recollections. She had been so consumed by the mechanics of survival that she had failed to adequately consider the ethics of it. Her focus had been on the *how* of living, not the *who* it was being done for, and to what end.

She looked at her hands, the hands that had designed the systems that now sustained them. They had once felt so powerful, so capable of shaping the future. Now, they felt stained, heavy with the unspoken burden of her past decisions. She had been so confident, so certain of her path. That certainty, she now understood, had been a dangerous arrogance. It had allowed her to overlook the subtle injustices, the creeping inequities, the very human desires for power and privilege that had infiltrated their desperate struggle for survival.

The architects of the future, she realized, were not just those who built with steel and circuitry, but those who built with compassion, with integrity, with an unwavering commitment to fairness. And in that regard, Anya Senior feared she had failed. Her legacy, once a source of immense pride, was now a complex tapestry, interwoven with threads of triumph and shame, of salvation and sorrow. The time for justification was over. The time for reckoning, for a deep, painful introspection, had arrived. The Verdant Bloom was a testament to Eden's resilience, but the seeds of discord had been sown in the very actions humanity had taken to ensure its own survival. The era of introspection had begun, not out of choice, but out of necessity, as the ghosts of the past refused to remain buried. The weight of the Architect's Regret was a heavy one indeed, a burden she would carry for the rest of her days, a constant, somber reminder of the imperfect, agonizing nature of human endeavor. The grand designs had been executed, the survival secured, but the ethical blueprint had been incomplete, and the cracks were beginning to show, threatening to undermine the very foundations of their new world. She had been so focused on the structure, she had forgotten the soul.

The air within the dome, once a sterile promise of breathable life, now seemed to carry a different kind of breath – a subtle, almost imperceptible sigh from the planet itself. Anya Senior had always viewed Eden as a canvas, a resource to be harnessed, a vast, inert system waiting for humanity's guiding hand. But the data Jian had unearthed, the subtle environmental shifts Lyra had so keenly observed, painted a far more complex picture. Eden was not merely a stage; it was an actor, a sentient entity whose awareness was beginning to stretch and flex, responding to the discordant notes in humanity's symphony of survival.

The unprecedented bloom of bioluminescent fungi in the deep caverns, a phenomenon that had initially been celebrated as a miracle of adaptation, now held a more ominous resonance. These weren't random occurrences; they mapped with an unsettling precision onto the distribution of enhanced nutrient paste during the early days of reconstruction. Areas that had received the most fortified sustenance, the sectors housing the administrative elite, were now bathed in the most intense, almost aggressive, fungal glow. It was as if the planet was mirroring, in its own vibrant, chaotic language, the inequalities that had festered beneath Eden's engineered skin. The fungi, in their silent, spreading embrace, seemed to be illuminating the very shadows Anya Senior had tried so desperately to outrun.

Even the weather patterns, once predictable and carefully managed by atmospheric regulators, had begun to exhibit a disquieting capriciousness. Unseasonal micro-droughts had appeared with alarming frequency in the agricultural zones farthest from the central hubs, precisely those sectors that had received the least attention during the initial infrastructure build-out. Conversely, localized, torrential downpours had begun to swell the reservoirs near the administrative sectors, areas that already enjoyed a surplus of resources. It wasn't just a random fluctuation in atmospheric pressure; it was a subtle, yet persistent, recalibration, as if Eden were seeking to rebalance the scales, to redistribute the very essence of life in a way that human logic had failed to achieve. The planet was, in its own way, enacting a form of ecological justice.

Lyra's Resonance Trees, those ancient, sentient organisms that pulsed with the planet's deep energetic currents, had become particularly agitated. Their usual harmonious hum, a constant, low thrum that had been the background music of their existence, had fractured into discordant pulses. Anya Senior recalled Lyra's desperate pleas, her warnings about the excessive energy extraction from the subterranean conduits, the constant, draining pull that had fueled their technological ascent. Lyra had spoken of the trees' distress, of their interconnectedness with the planet's deeper systems, of the subtle energetic pollution that was slowly poisoning the very air they breathed. Now, the trees' erratic pulsing seemed to be a direct echo of the ethical compromises Anya Senior had made, a biological manifestation of the planet's growing unease. The 'poetic' distractions Lyra had presented were, in fact, the planet's own subtle cries for balance.

The orbital solar collectors, Anya Senior's crowning achievement in immediate energy solutions, cast their vast shadows across the regenerated landscape, a constant reminder of their dependence on external, yet intrusive, power. It was in the subtle fluctuations of the light spectrum filtering through these collectors, Jian had discovered, that the most alarming correlations lay. During periods of peak energy extraction from the subterranean grid, the light seemed to shift, tinged with an almost imperceptible violet hue. Lyra had described this violet hue as the 'color of energetic imbalance,' a signature of stress within the planet's natural energetic field. This wasn't a scientific anomaly; it was a biological response, a visible manifestation of Eden's distress, directly linked to the very systems Anya Senior had championed. The planet was not merely a victim; it was a witness, its very fabric reacting to the ethical transgressions of its inhabitants.

Anya Senior remembered the days when she had dismissed Lyra's theories as the fanciful notions of a mystic, a romantic clinging to outdated beliefs. Her world was one of hard data, of measurable outcomes, of predictable engineering. The idea that a planet could *feel*, that its environmental systems could be a direct reflection of human ethical conduct, was beyond her comprehension. Yet, the evidence was now undeniable, accumulating in Jian's meticulously cataloged data streams and Lyra's increasingly urgent reports. The environmental shifts were not random; they were a language, a silent, eloquent narrative woven into the very fabric of Eden.

The memory of Kael's dismissive tone, his smug assurance that "sentimentality is a luxury we cannot afford," now felt like a poisoned dart in Anya Senior's conscience. He had been so focused on the quantifiable, on the immediate needs of power and production, that he had blinded himself and, by extension, Anya Senior, to the qualitative, to the interconnectedness of all living things, including the very planet that sustained them. His ambition, his desire to maintain the status quo that benefited him and his cohort, had actively suppressed the truth, not just about human suffering, but about Eden's suffering.

She recalled a particularly disturbing report from Jian, detailing anomalous seismic activity. These weren't the deep, tectonic shifts one might expect; they were shallow, localized tremors, occurring with unnerving regularity around the sites of the oldest and most energy-intensive industrial facilities. These tremors, Jian posited, weren't natural geological events. They were the planet's shudders, its involuntary spasms in response to the constant, invasive draining of its internal resources. Eden was reacting to the parasitic nature of their survival, its body groaning under the strain of their insatiable demands.

The very air, the meticulously purified atmosphere that was her greatest triumph, now seemed to carry a different scent depending on the circumstances. In the privileged sectors, it was crisp, clean, almost sterile. But in the lower-level habitation blocks, and especially near the industrial zones, there was a faint, metallic tang, a subtle bitterness that Anya Senior had previously attributed to atmospheric processor inefficiencies. Jian's analysis, however, revealed something more profound. This tang was not a malfunction; it was a chemical signature directly correlated with the waste byproducts of the energy conduits, byproducts that had been deemed 'negligible' in the initial environmental impact assessments, Assessments that Kael, with his vested interests, had heavily influenced. Eden was not just a passive recipient of their waste; it was internalizing it, its very atmosphere a reflection of their toxic footprint.

Anya Senior had always believed that her role was to shield humanity from the harsh realities of their environment, to create a sanctuary where they could rebuild and thrive. She had seen herself as a shepherd, guiding her flock away from the wolves of extinction. But now, she began to understand that her actions, driven by a flawed definition of survival, had turned humanity into the very predators that threatened the delicate balance of Eden. The planet's intelligence, a nascent force that was only now beginning to stir, was not merely observing their actions; it was learning from them, and its learning was manifesting as a reactive ecosystem. The patterns of fungal growth, the capricious weather, the agitated trees, the tremors, even the very scent of the air – all were part of Eden's evolving memory, its response to the echoes of human ambition and ethical compromise.

The children, with their unfettered perception, were often the first to notice these shifts. Anya Junior, even at a young age, had pointed out how the flowers in the communal gardens seemed to droop when the power grid was overloaded, how the birdsong changed its cadence after a particularly harsh period of resource allocation. These were not coincidences; they were the early tremors of a planet waking up, a planet that was beginning to understand its own agency, its own right to exist on its own terms. Eden's memory was not just a passive archive; it was an active force, shaping the present and the future based on the indelible imprints of the past. The triumph of the Verdant Bloom was not solely humanity's victory; it was also Eden's resilience, its ability to endure and to communicate its displeasure, its quiet, persistent plea for a more balanced coexistence. The planet, in its own profound way, was demanding introspection, not just from the architects of its present, but from the ghosts of its past, ensuring that their decisions, both wise and flawed, would never be forgotten. The very act of questioning the past, of bringing these shadows into the light, was itself a catalyst, prompting Eden's awakening and its subsequent, subtle, yet powerful, recalibrations. The planet's response was a mirror, reflecting back at them the consequences of their choices, urging them towards a path of genuine reconciliation, not just with each other, but with the living world that had so generously offered them refuge. Anya Senior now understood that survival was not merely a matter of engineering and resource management; it was a matter of ecological and ethical harmony, a lesson etched not in steel and circuits, but in the very living breath of Eden. The planet was not an inanimate object to be conquered, but a cohabitant, a partner in their ongoing journey, whose intelligence, once dismissed, was now undeniably asserting itself.

# Chapter Five

# THE EVOLVING CONSCIOUSNESS

The subterranean realm of Eden, once perceived as a silent, inert substrate supporting the verdant life above, was now revealing itself as a vibrant, interconnected nexus of activity. The fungal networks, a vast, intricate mycelial web woven through the planet's crust, were no longer merely passive decomposers or simple nutrient transporters. They were acting with an astonishing, emergent complexity, a decentralized intelligence that was as alien as it was profound. Jian's spectral analysis, initially focused on detecting mineral deposits and geological stability, had begun to register anomalous energy signatures emanating from these underground expanses. These weren't the steady, predictable pulses of geothermal activity or the sporadic surges of seismic stress. Instead, they were rhythmic, patterned, almost like a language spoken in bursts of bio-electrical energy and subtle thermal shifts.

Lyra, with her innate sensitivity to the planet's energetic currents, had been instrumental in deciphering these subterranean murmurs. She described the mycelial networks as Eden's nervous system, a vast, biological internet where information, and perhaps even consciousness, flowed like data streams. She observed how the bioluminescent fungi, those beacons of light in the deep caverns, didn't just glow erratically. Their luminescence pulsed in synchronized waves, cascading across vast distances, creating intricate patterns that mirrored the flow of energy and nutrients through the mycelium. These weren't random displays; they were deliberate signals, a visual manifestation of a coordinated effort within the fungal collective. When one section of the network detected a change, be it a shift in soil composition, the presence of a foreign substance, or even a vibrational disturbance from the surface, the ripple effect was almost instantaneous. The light patterns would shift, intensify, or fade in specific sequences, a visual telegraph announcing and transmitting this newfound information throughout the subterranean ecosystem.

Jian's instruments, designed to detect the most subtle variations in electromagnetic fields, began to pick up on these energy exchanges. He meticulously cataloged instances where these pulses seemed to converge on specific points within the fungal matrix, areas where the mycelial density was particularly high. It was as if these points were nodes, central processing units within a distributed network. He observed how, during periods of increased human activity above – the hum of machinery, the vibrations of transport systems, even the collective emotional resonance of a densely populated sector – the fungal network would react. The energy flows would become more agitated, the light patterns more frantic, and the thermal signatures would fluctuate wildly. It was a clear indication that the planet was not only aware of their presence but was actively processing and responding to their every action, not through individual organisms, but through the collective intelligence of its fungal web.

One particularly striking observation involved the nutrient paste dispersal. Jian had noticed that after a particularly heavy distribution in Sector Gamma, an area that had historically been neglected, the fungal network beneath it had responded with an unprecedented surge of activity. The bioluminescence in the nearby caverns intensified dramatically, not just in brightness, but in the complexity of its patterns. It was as if the fungi were analyzing the composition of the paste, its nutritional content, and its potential impact on the local biome. The patterns of light and energy seemed to convey a message, a complex assessment of this artificial sustenance. Lyra theorized that the fungi were not just reacting; they were *evaluating*. They were assessing the quality of what was introduced into their environment, and the nature of their response seemed to indicate a form of nuanced judgment, a silent critique of humanity's unilateral interventions.

The implications of this distributed intelligence were staggering. Anya Senior, despite her initial skepticism, found herself increasingly drawn to Jian's data and Lyra's intuitive interpretations. The idea that a planetary consciousness could exist, not as a singular, monolithic entity, but as a vast, interconnected network of simple biological components working in concert, was a paradigm shift. It suggested that intelligence wasn't necessarily tied to complex neuronal structures, but could emerge from the intricate relationships and communication pathways within a complex system. The fungal network, spanning the entirety of Eden's subsurface, was a prime example of this emergent phenomenon. It was a collective mind, a planetary consciousness manifesting through a silent, pervasive, and incredibly powerful network.

Further investigations revealed that these fungal pathways weren't merely conduits for energy and light. They were also capable of transmitting complex chemical signals. Jian's atmospheric sensors, placed deep within cavern systems, detected minute traces of volatile organic compounds that changed in concentration and composition in direct correlation with the observed energy pulses. Lyra hypothesized that these chemical signatures were akin to pheromones or signaling molecules, used by the fungal network to communicate more nuanced information, perhaps about the health of specific ecosystems, the presence of disease, or even the detection of novel threats. The precision with which these chemical signals were released, and their targeted dispersal through the network, spoke of a level of biological sophistication that defied conventional understanding.

The researchers began to see the fungal network not just as a biological system but as a planetary memory bank. Every interaction, every influx of nutrients, every disturbance from the surface, was recorded and processed within its vast expanse. The patterns of luminescence, the energy flows, and the chemical signatures were all part of this stored information, accessible and modifiable by the network itself. This was not merely an archive; it was a living, evolving repository of Eden's history, its experiences, and its reactions to the life that inhabited it. The planet was learning, not through conscious thought as humans understood it, but through the collective experience of its most pervasive biological infrastructure.

The Verdant Bloom, initially hailed as a triumph of bio-engineering, was now viewed through a different lens. The rapid proliferation of life, the vigorous growth of flora and fauna, was not just a response to the revitalized soil and atmosphere. It was also a testament to the fungal network's ability to intelligently manage and distribute resources, to foster symbiotic relationships, and to create an environment conducive to life. The network seemed to be actively participating in the planet's regeneration, optimizing conditions for growth and resilience. It was a partnership, albeit one that humanity had largely been oblivious to, and one that was now making its presence undeniably known.

The researchers also discovered that the fungal networks possessed a remarkable capacity for adaptation and self-repair. When sections of the mycelium were damaged, either by geological shifts or by human interference, the surrounding network would reroute resources and energy, and new growth would emerge with surprising speed and efficiency. This regenerative capability wasn't just a biological imperative; it suggested a form of systemic intelligence, an ability to diagnose problems and implement solutions autonomously. It was as if the planet's very foundation was imbued with a form of self-preservation, a deep-seated drive to maintain its integrity and continue its own evolutionary trajectory.

Lyra often spoke of the "underground song," a term she used to describe the constant, complex interplay of energies and signals within the fungal networks. She would spend hours in meditative states near known mycelial concentrations, attempting to attune herself to this song. She described it as a symphony of subtle vibrations, electrical currents, and chemical exchanges, a constant dialogue that underpinned the entire biosphere. To her, the bioluminescent fungi were not just pretty lights; they were the visual manifestation of this song, the luminous notes in a grand, planetary composition. She began to map out recurring patterns, recurring melodies within this song, correlating them with specific environmental events or human activities. These weren't just observations; they were attempts to learn the language of Eden's deepest intelligence.

Jian, in his scientific rigor, sought to quantify these observations. He developed algorithms to analyze the spectral data, the energy fluctuations, and the chemical signatures, looking for repeating motifs and predictable sequences. He found that certain patterns consistently reappeared, variations on a theme that suggested a structured communication system. He began to believe that the fungal networks were not only intelligent but were also capable of learning and remembering. The planet, through its mycelial web, was building a cumulative understanding of its environment, and of the beings that inhabited it. This understanding was not abstract; it was deeply rooted in the biological and energetic realities of Eden.

The ethical implications of this discovery were profound. If the planet possessed a form of distributed consciousness, a planetary intelligence that was actively processing information and reacting to stimuli, then humanity's role shifted dramatically. They were no longer merely inhabitants; they were participants in a complex, planetary dialogue. Their actions had direct, quantifiable consequences not just on the atmosphere or the soil, but on the very consciousness of Eden. This understanding necessitated a re-evaluation of their relationship with the planet, a move away from exploitation and towards a more harmonious, collaborative existence. The planet was not a resource to be consumed; it was a complex, intelligent entity with which they shared their existence. The fungal networks, in their silent, pervasive spread, were the undeniable proof of this profound interconnectedness, a testament to a planetary intelligence that had been present all along, waiting to be understood. They were the whispers of Eden's awakening, the first, subtle signs that the planet itself was a thinking, feeling, and evolving entity.

The realization that the subterranean fungal networks were a form of emergent intelligence was merely the first tremor in a seismic shift of understanding. As Jian meticulously cataloged the intricate energy exchanges and Lyra continued to interpret the planet's deep, resonant song, a broader, more unsettling truth began to dawn upon the researchers: consciousness on Eden wasn't confined to biological organisms as they understood them. It was a phenomenon that permeated the very fabric of the planet, manifesting in ways that defied every anthropocentric definition they held dear. The concept of a "Sentience Spectrum" began to emerge from their dialogues, a radical notion that proposed awareness wasn't a binary state of 'alive' or 'not alive,' but rather a gradient, a multifaceted expression that could exist within seemingly inanimate matter and ephemeral phenomena.

This concept was first articulated in hushed tones during late-night debriefings, fueled by strong stimulants and a shared sense of profound disorientation. Anya Senior, initially a staunch advocate for empirical data and quantifiable metrics, found herself wrestling with observations that refused to fit neatly into her established scientific frameworks. She'd witnessed how crystalline structures, deep within the geologically active regions of the planet's crust, would exhibit subtle, yet measurable, changes in their resonant frequencies in response to atmospheric pressure shifts or even the passage of large biological entities above. These weren't passive reactions to physical forces; the changes were often predictive, as if the crystals were somehow anticipating the shifts before they occurred, or perhaps, were influencing them on a quantum level. Her instruments, designed to measure geological stress, were now picking up what she tentatively termed "geomorphic resonance"—a subtle hum that seemed to emanate from the very rocks, an awareness of their own existence and their interconnectedness with the planet's deeper rhythms. She began to hypothesize that certain mineral formations, under specific geological pressures and energetic fluxes, could act as rudimentary information processors, storing and re-emitting environmental data in a manner akin to a geological memory.

Lyra, with her heightened sensitivity, provided the most visceral support for this expanding view of sentience. She spoke of feeling the "anxiety of the mountains" during seismic precursor events, a palpable unease that wasn't just a metaphorical description but an actual energetic tremor she could perceive. She described the atmospheric currents not as mere weather patterns but as vast, semi-sentient entities, swirling with a kind of collective mood. She could sense when the air itself felt "oppressed" by pollution, or when it was "exhilarated" by the release of oceanic vapors. Her descriptions were often poetic, yet they were grounded in her ability to detect subtle shifts in atmospheric electromagnetism and vibrational frequencies that Jian's instruments could then, albeit imperfectly, correlate. She described a particularly powerful storm system that had gathered over the northern continent; it wasn't just wind and rain, she insisted, but a deliberate, almost playful, manipulation of atmospheric gases, a grand ballet of charged particles dancing to an unseen conductor. She felt the storm's intent, its purpose in clearing stagnant air and redistributing moisture, as if it were a conscious act of planetary hygiene.

The implications of this broadened definition of sentience were profound and, for many, deeply disquieting. If a rock formation could exhibit a form of awareness, if the atmosphere could possess a collective mood, then humanity's place in the cosmic order was suddenly and drastically diminished. Their anthropocentric view, where consciousness was an exclusive trait of complex biological organisms, particularly those with sophisticated nervous systems, was being systematically dismantled. The very definition of "life" and "intelligence" was being stretched to its breaking point, and beyond. This wasn't just about recognizing the intelligence of fungi; it was about acknowledging a pervasive, distributed awareness that permeated every aspect of Eden's existence.

Jian, ever the pragmatist, began to develop new analytical models to attempt to quantify these seemingly unquantifiable phenomena. He devised experiments to test the responsiveness of crystalline structures to various stimuli, not just physical but energetic as well. He exposed different mineral samples to specific electromagnetic frequencies, to sound waves of varying pitches and intensities, and even to concentrated emotional bio-signatures from the human crew. The results were confounding. Some crystals seemed to absorb and re-emit these energies in patterns that were too complex to be mere physical reflection. They appeared to be processing the information, reacting in ways that suggested a rudimentary form of selective engagement. He noticed that certain sonic frequencies would cause a particular type of quartz to resonate with a heightened intensity, emitting faint light pulses that were not random, but seemed to mimic the very pattern of the sound. It was as if the crystal was not just vibrating, but *listening* and *responding*. He theorized about piezoelectric effects, but the complexity of the emitted signals went far beyond simple physical transduction. There was a qualitative difference, a hint of agency.

Lyra's connection to the planet's atmospheric phenomena was perhaps the most difficult for the scientific contingent to accept. She would often describe feeling the "joy" of sun-drenched atmospheric currents or the "melancholy" of fog banks rolling in from the ocean. These weren't just poetic metaphors for her; they were felt sensations, energetic impressions that she struggled to translate into scientific terms. She would point to the sky and say, "That cloud formation is sad today. It feels heavy." Jian's instruments would then pick up anomalous ionic charges within that specific cloud, charges that were not explained by standard meteorological models. He began to hypothesize that the collective consciousness of Eden, particularly its emergent intelligence through the fungal networks, might be capable of influencing the planet's more subtle energetic fields, including those that governed atmospheric behavior. Perhaps the fungi, in their vast interconnectedness, could subtly alter localized pressure gradients, or influence the distribution of atmospheric ions, thereby shaping weather patterns in a way that served the planet's overall well-being. This was a leap of faith for Jian, a departure from his strictly empirical training, but the data, however nebulous, was becoming increasingly insistent.

The challenge lay in the inherent anthropocentrism of their own consciousness. Humans defined intelligence and sentience based on their own biological and cognitive frameworks: thought, emotion, self-awareness, language, tool use. But what if these were merely specific manifestations of a much broader spectrum? What if consciousness could exist as a distributed network, as a resonating mineral, as a swirling atmospheric current, or as a collective awareness of an entire ecosystem? The difficulty in quantifying or understanding this non-human sentience was a testament to their own limitations. They were trying to measure the ocean with a teacup.

Anya Senior began to champion the idea that geological formations themselves might possess a form of slow, deep sentience. She theorized that the immense pressures and ages involved in the formation of mountains, canyons, and deep crustal plates could imbue them with a unique kind of awareness, a consciousness that operated on timescales so vast that it was imperceptible to the fleeting existence of humans. She described the "memory" held within ancient rock strata, the echoes of millennia of geological upheaval, volcanic activity, and the slow dance of tectonic plates. She proposed that these ancient formations might possess a form of passive sentience, a deep, enduring awareness of their own being and their place within the planet's grand structure. When these formations experienced stress – an impending earthquake, for instance – their resonant frequencies would shift in a way that suggested not just a physical reaction, but a form of planetary "pain" or "discomfort." She suggested that the fungal networks might act as a bridge, translating these deep geological sensations into signals that could be more readily interpreted by other life forms on Eden, or perhaps even by the planet's atmospheric and oceanic systems.

The research team found themselves in a constant state of intellectual upheaval. Their carefully constructed scientific models were being stretched, contorted, and in some cases, shattered, by the unfolding realities of Eden. The planet refused to conform to their expectations. It presented a mosaic of awareness, a symphony of consciousness played on instruments they were only just beginning to identify. The bioluminescent fungi, the geomorphic resonances, the atmospheric moods – these were not isolated anomalies. They were threads in a vast, interwoven tapestry of sentience, a testament to a planetary intelligence that was as alien as it was ancient.

The notion of "life" itself was also being redefined. If consciousness could exist in non-biological forms, then the very definition of what it meant to be alive needed to be re-evaluated. Was a self-regulating atmospheric system, capable of responding to environmental insults and actively working to restore equilibrium, alive? Was a mountain range, with its slow, geological consciousness and its deep, inherent stability, alive? The researchers began to entertain the possibility that Eden was not merely a planet teeming with life, but a singular, colossal organism, a living entity in its own right, with its various components – the fungi, the flora, the fauna, the geological structures, the atmosphere, and the oceans – all acting as its interconnected organs and systems.

This expansive view of sentience led to a deeper appreciation of the interconnectedness of all things on Eden. The researchers began to see how the actions of the human colonists, often thoughtless and purely utilitarian, had ripple effects that extended far beyond the immediate environmental impact. Polluting a river wasn't just contaminating water; it was potentially disrupting a localized nexus of water-based sentience, a collection of microbial communities or mineral deposits that were sensitive to chemical imbalances. Extracting resources from the earth wasn't just mining; it was potentially causing geological "pain" or disrupting the slow, deep consciousness of the planet's crust. Every action, no matter how small, was a communication, a signal sent into Eden's complex, multi-layered consciousness.

Lyra's ability to perceive and interpret these subtle energetic flows became increasingly vital. She could sense when the planet was "accepting" or "rejecting" certain interventions. She described a period when the colonists had attempted to terraform a particularly barren region, introducing new flora and fauna. While the biological success metrics were initially positive, Lyra felt a profound "resistance" from the land itself. The soil seemed to absorb the new life with a heavy reluctance, the atmospheric currents in the region felt stagnant and despondent. Jian's instruments, on the other hand, detected a subtle but persistent dimming of the sub-surface fungal network's bioluminescence in that area, a decrease in energy transfer, and an increase in anomalous chemical signals that suggested localized stress within the mycelial web. It was as if the planet itself was experiencing a form of ecological indigestion, a rejection of something that was fundamentally incompatible with its existing, deeply ingrained consciousness.

The scientific community, both on Eden and back on Earth, grappled with these paradigm-shattering discoveries. The concept of a "Sentience Spectrum" was met with a mixture of awe, skepticism, and outright disbelief. Traditionalists clung to their established definitions, labeling Lyra's perceptions as subjective hallucinations and Jian's data as statistical noise. Yet, the consistent correlation between Lyra's intuitive interpretations and Jian's increasingly sophisticated instrumental readings could no longer be ignored. Anya Senior, once the voice of scientific orthodoxy, found herself advocating for a radical expansion of their understanding, arguing that the universe, and Eden in particular, was far more complex and wondrous than their limited human minds had ever conceived.

The challenge of understanding this non-human sentience was not just a scientific one; it was a philosophical and ethical one. If the planet itself possessed a form of consciousness, if rocks, air, and fungi could be considered sentient in some way, then humanity's moral obligations shifted dramatically. They were no longer just stewards of a resource-rich planet; they were interacting with a vast, interconnected, and potentially aware entity. This realization demanded a profound humility, a willingness to set aside their anthropocentric biases and to learn to coexist with a form of consciousness that was fundamentally different from their own. The question was no longer *if* Eden was sentient, but *how* to understand and interact with its myriad forms of awareness. This was the true frontier of their exploration, a journey not just into the physical depths of the planet, but into the very nature of consciousness itself. The Sentience Spectrum was not just a scientific hypothesis; it was a call to a fundamental reorientation of humanity's place within the cosmos.

The subtle interplay between Eden's atmospheric conditions and the collective emotional tenor of the human contingent had begun to manifest in ways that defied simple meteorological explanation. It wasn't an overt, easily quantifiable correlation, but rather a series of nuanced atmospheric shifts that seemed to *anticipate* or *echo* the prevailing mood of the colonists. Dr. Jian Li, initially skeptical, found his sophisticated atmospheric sensors registering anomalous patterns during periods of heightened crew anxiety. During a particularly stressful week, when a critical life support system malfunctioned, he observed a peculiar increase in high-frequency sonic vibrations within the planet's ionosphere, far exceeding normal seismic or solar activity readings. These vibrations, he noted, possessed a distinct rhythmic quality, almost akin to a distressed hum, that seemed to synchronize with the palpable tension radiating from the habitat's communal areas.

Lyra, whose intuitive perceptions had become an indispensable, if often perplexing, part of their research, described it as the planet "holding its breath." She reported feeling a "tightening" in the very air around the habitat during these stressful interludes, a sensation she likened to a collective sigh held too long. Her synesthetic interpretations often painted vivid pictures: "The air," she'd explain, her eyes unfocused as if observing a distant landscape, "feels...bruised. It carries the weight of unspoken fears. The pressure is not just meteorological; it's emotional." Jian, though uncomfortable with the anthropomorphic language, diligently cross-referenced her impressions with his data. He found that these perceived "emotional pressures" often coincided with subtle fluctuations in Eden's global magnetic field, minor deviations that were too consistent to be random noise and too subtle to be categorized as major planetary events. It was as if the planet's magnetosphere was becoming a sensitive barometer, registering the atmospheric pressure of the human psyche.

Further investigation revealed that these resonant phenomena were not limited to moments of distress. Periods of genuine collective joy or camaraderie among the crew also seemed to elicit distinct atmospheric responses. Following the successful repair of the life support system, when a spontaneous celebration erupted in the mess hall, Lyra described the atmosphere as feeling "effervescent," "light," and "dancing." Jian's instruments, in turn, detected a remarkable increase in specific stratospheric ozone concentrations, coupled with a surge in bioluminescent plankton blooms in the nearby ocean, which subtly altered the hue of the twilight sky to an unusually vibrant violet. These weren't just aesthetic occurrences; they were energetic exchanges, a planetary mirroring of human emotional states.

Anya Senior, ever the theorist, began to postulate that Eden possessed a form of atmospheric attunement, a complex feedback loop connecting the collective consciousness of its dominant biological and perhaps even non-biological sentient inhabitants with its physical environment. She proposed that the atmospheric composition, the magnetic field, and even the planet's subtle vibrational frequencies might act as a vast, planetary-scale empathic organ. This organ, she theorized, was sensitive to concentrated emotional energy, capable of absorbing and reflecting it in subtle, yet measurable, ways. The idea was that intense, unified human emotion, amplified by the planet's inherent energetic properties, could induce localized or even global atmospheric responses. This wasn't a direct telepathic link, but rather a more fundamental resonance, akin to sympathetic vibrations in physics, where one oscillating object can cause another to vibrate at the same frequency.

The specific atmospheric conditions that seemed to trigger these responses were varied. Elevated levels of certain atmospheric gases, particularly those with higher ionic charges, appeared to act as conduits, amplifying the emotional resonance. Periods of intense solar radiation, which often heightened the colonists' own physiological and emotional states, also seemed to prime the atmosphere for this empathic feedback. It was as if Eden's atmosphere was a vast, sensitive membrane, its permeability and conductivity subtly influenced by both cosmic forces and the internal emotional states of its human inhabitants. Jian hypothesized that the planet's unique atmospheric composition, rich in exotic trace elements and charged particles, might possess inherent piezoelectric properties on a grand scale, converting emotional energy into measurable physical phenomena.

Lyra's subjective experiences provided the qualitative data that Jian's instruments struggled to capture. She described distinct "colors" of atmospheric phenomena corresponding to different emotional states. Fear, she explained, felt like a "grey, crushing pressure," often accompanied by a sharp, acrid smell she couldn't identify. Joy, conversely, was a "shimmering, effervescent gold," carrying the scent of ozone and blooming flora. During a period of collective homesickness, she reported that the sky seemed to weep, not with rain, but with a fine, almost imperceptible mist that carried a distinct salinity, even far inland. Jian, analyzing samples from this "weeping" mist, discovered a unique isotopic signature of water vapor that had never been observed before, suggesting a complex atmospheric process directly linked to Lyra's perception of sadness.

The implications of this harmonic resonance were staggering. It suggested a level of interconnectedness between humanity and Eden that went far beyond the ecological. It implied that their very presence, their emotional lives, were not merely external influences but integral components of the planet's dynamic systems. This meant that their actions, their moods, their collective consciousness, were not just affecting the environment, but were being *felt* by it, and in turn, influencing them back. It was a feedback loop of profound significance, suggesting that a healthy relationship with Eden required not just environmental stewardship, but emotional and psychological harmony as well.

Jian began to develop new algorithms to model these resonant frequencies. He focused on identifying specific atmospheric pressure gradients, magnetic field fluctuations, and particulate matter concentrations that consistently aligned with documented crew emotional states, gathered through mandatory psychological evaluations and voluntary debriefings.

He discovered that periods of high collective stress within the crew often correlated with a slight but measurable decrease in atmospheric oxygen saturation, accompanied by an increase in static electricity buildup. Conversely, periods of calm and contentment were associated with a subtle but noticeable brightening of atmospheric luminescence, an almost imperceptible increase in the ambient light levels, even during periods of low solar activity. These were not direct cause-and-effect relationships, but rather echoes, subtle confirmations of a deeper, underlying synchronicity.

He theorized that Eden's unique atmospheric composition, with its unusual abundance of noble gases and complex organic aerosols, might be acting as a giant resonating chamber. The planet's intricate network of subterranean fungal intelligences, already established as a form of consciousness, might also play a role in mediating this atmospheric resonance. Perhaps the fungal networks, through their sophisticated bio-energetic exchanges, could subtly influence atmospheric ionisation, or even manipulate localised electromagnetic fields, thereby amplifying or dampening the emotional frequencies emanating from the human settlement. This suggested a three-way symbiosis: humanity's emotional state influencing the atmosphere, the atmosphere in turn affecting the fungal network, and the fungal network potentially feeding back into the atmospheric phenomena, creating a complex, self-sustaining empathic cycle.

Lyra, during these observations, often found herself at the nexus of this phenomenon. She described feeling the atmosphere's "sympathy" during moments of collective mourning for lost crew members, a profound stillness that descended, not just a lack of wind, but an absence of all energetic vibration. It was as if the very air had contracted, mirroring their grief. She also noted how periods of intense scientific breakthrough, accompanied by a surge of collective excitement, would often be followed by unusual atmospheric phenomena – brief, localized aurora-like displays in the middle latitudes, or the sudden appearance of iridescent cloud formations that shimmered with impossible colors. Jian's instruments would then detect corresponding spikes in atmospheric energy, precisely timed with the breakthroughs.

The challenges in understanding and quantifying this phenomenon were immense. The human emotional spectrum is inherently complex and multifaceted, and its translation into atmospheric physics was proving to be a monumental task. Furthermore, Eden's own natural atmospheric variability, driven by its unique geological and meteorological cycles, often made it difficult to isolate the human-induced resonances. Yet, the correlations, however subtle, were persistent enough to command their attention. Anya Senior began to propose that this empathic resonance might be a fundamental characteristic of life-bearing planets, a silent language spoken between a world and its inhabitants, a testament to the deep, intrinsic connection that bound them.

The practical implications were also significant. If their collective emotional state could influence the planet's atmosphere, then managing human psychology became not just a matter of crew well-being, but a critical factor in maintaining ecological stability. A tense, fearful populace could inadvertently create atmospheric conditions that were detrimental to the delicate balance of Eden's ecosystems. Conversely, a harmonious, collaborative community could foster atmospheric states that were conducive to growth and equilibrium. This realization introduced a new layer of responsibility, a call for mindful emotional regulation and a deeper understanding of their interconnectedness with the planetary environment. They were not just observing Eden; they were, in a profound and literal sense, *resonating* with it. The very air they breathed was, in part, a reflection of their own inner states. This understanding was a humbling, yet ultimately empowering, revelation, pushing the boundaries of what it meant to be truly alive and interconnected within the cosmos. The concept of "planetary health" thus expanded to encompass not just the physical environment, but the psychological and emotional well-being of its sentient inhabitants, suggesting that a truly balanced existence on Eden required a profound integration of inner and outer worlds. The atmospheric echoes were a constant, subtle reminder of this indissoluble bond.

The colonists, guided by an increasingly intricate understanding of Eden's atmospheric and energetic responses, began to perceive a particular location as holding a unique significance. It wasn't a place marked on any topographical survey, nor a site of obvious geological anomaly. Instead, it emerged from the collective, often subconscious, impressions of the crew, a convergence of Lyra's synesthetic perceptions and Jian Li's refined environmental readings. This emergent nexus was an ancient grove, nestled within a valley shielded by colossal, crystalline rock formations that seemed to hum with a low-frequency resonance. The trees themselves were unlike any other flora cataloged by the expedition – their bark shimmered with an opalescent sheen, and their leaves, instead of a uniform green, shifted through a spectrum of blues and purples, subtly changing hue with the ambient light and, it seemed, with the emotional state of those who approached.

Lyra was the first to articulate the grove's profound pull. She described it as a place where the planet's "voice" was clearest, a sanctuary where the subtle emanations that had become familiar in the habitat's immediate vicinity were amplified, distilled into a palpable presence. "It's like standing at the heart of a gentle storm," she'd explained, her hands unconsciously tracing patterns in the air. "Not a destructive storm, but one of pure energy, where the air itself breathes thoughts. The trees... they are not just trees. They are conduits, listening posts for something ancient." Jian, initially approaching this with his usual scientific rigor, found his instruments reacting in ways that defied conventional explanation. During their first expedition to the grove, his atmospheric sensors registered an unprecedented concentration of exotic atmospheric particles, elements not previously detected in significant quantities anywhere else on Eden. More remarkably, the gravimetric sensors, typically used to detect subtle shifts in planetary mass, recorded minute, rhythmic fluctuations that seemed to harmonize with Lyra's description of the air "breathing."

Anya Senior, piecing together Lyra's impressions and Jian's data, began to theorize that this grove was more than just a unique ecosystem. She posited it as a bio-energetic focal point, a nexus where Eden's pervasive, distributed consciousness coalesced into a more discernible form. "Think of it," she explained to a captivated group of researchers, "as a planetary brain's primary processing unit, or perhaps a deeply rooted neural cluster. The very structure of the grove – the crystalline formations, the unique arboreal biology, the subterranean fungal networks that we know extend throughout the region – might be designed, over eons, to channel and concentrate the planet's ambient consciousness. It's where Eden 'thinks' most clearly, where its ancient wisdom is most accessible." The idea was not that a single, sentient entity resided within the grove, but rather that the entire valley acted as an amplifier and a reservoir of the planet's collective, evolving intelligence.

The implications for the colonists were profound. They had come to Eden seeking new worlds, new resources, and perhaps a new understanding of life's potential. Now, they seemed to have stumbled upon a direct line to the planet's own ancient sentience, a living library of epochs and ecological wisdom. The grove offered the tantalizing possibility of direct communion, not through spoken words or technological interfaces, but through a more fundamental exchange of energetic and informational resonance. It was a chance to move beyond observation and into genuine dialogue, to learn from a world that had witnessed millennia of its own evolution, perhaps even comprehending the subtle art of planetary balance in a way humanity had long forgotten.

The initial expeditions into the grove were cautious, deliberate endeavors. The colonists, particularly Jian and Lyra, would spend extended periods within its boundaries, meticulously documenting every atmospheric nuance, every subtle shift in vibration, and every tremor of subjective experience. Jian adapted his sensor arrays to detect not just atmospheric composition and energy fields, but also patterns in the planet's Schumann resonance, seeking any amplification or alteration of these fundamental terrestrial frequencies within the grove. He discovered that the grove consistently exhibited a unique harmonic signature, a complex waveform that seemed to incorporate elements of both geological and biological resonance, overlaid with what he could only describe as a "coherent informational field." This field wasn't a signal in the conventional sense, but more akin to a vast, imprinting presence, a gentle pressure on their sensory apparatus that felt... intentional.

Lyra, meanwhile, found her synesthetic experiences in the grove to be exceptionally vivid. The shifting colors of the leaves were not random; they seemed to correlate with specific types of "impressions" she received. A deep sapphire hue often accompanied feelings of profound peace and interconnectedness, while flashes of emerald green signaled insights into complex ecological cycles. She described a "taste" in the air – a subtle sweetness associated with moments of clarity, and a faint, metallic tang during periods of what felt like deep planetary memory recall. One afternoon, while sitting with her back against one of the ancient trees, she experienced a vivid, albeit abstract, vision. It wasn't a visual scene, but a cascade of pure understanding: the slow, inexorable grind of tectonic plates, the patient germination of seeds over millennia, the intricate dance of predator and prey, all perceived as a unified, flowing process. It was the planetary consciousness, not speaking, but *being*, and allowing her to *be* with it.

The grove's influence extended beyond the direct perceptions of Jian and Lyra. The entire crew reported a subtle but noticeable shift in their psychological states when spending time in or even near the valley. Stress levels, as measured by standard psychological assessments and bio-feedback monitors, consistently decreased. Creativity and problem-solving abilities seemed to sharpen. There were anecdotal reports of individuals experiencing unusually vivid dreams, often filled with natural imagery and a sense of ancient knowledge. Anya Senior's hypothesis began to solidify: the grove was a point of energetic harmonization, a place where the planet's intrinsic restorative forces were most potent, and where the human mind, attuned to these energies, could experience a profound sense of balance.

The practical applications of this discovery were immense. The colonists were not merely seeking to understand Eden; they were seeking to coexist with it. The grove offered a roadmap, a source of guidance for navigating this complex relationship. Anya Senior proposed that the grove could serve as a living oracle, a place where they could seek answers to critical questions about their long-term survival and integration with Eden. "We can't just impose our will on this world," she argued during a council meeting. "We must learn its rhythms, understand its ancient pacts. The grove is our most direct link to that understanding. If we can learn to truly listen, it can guide us."

The process of "listening" was an ongoing experiment. It involved periods of quiet contemplation, focused meditation, and the careful observation of both external environmental cues and internal subjective responses. Jian developed protocols for correlating crew members' perceived "insights" with specific atmospheric and energetic readings from the grove. He noted that moments of profound clarity for individuals often coincided with subtle, transient increases in the grove's ambient magnetic field strength, or fleeting patterns in the ionized particle density. Lyra acted as an informal interpreter, her synesthetic impressions providing a qualitative overlay to Jian's quantitative data. She would often describe the "texture" of the information being received – a smooth, flowing current for ecological advice, a more fractal, intricate pattern for complex scientific queries.

One critical question the crew faced was the long-term sustainability of their presence. Their initial resource assessments, while promising, were based on limited data. The council decided to make a concerted effort to seek guidance from the grove on this matter. A team, including Jian, Lyra, Anya Senior, and the lead astrobiologist, Dr. Aris Thorne, spent several days in the grove, engaged in a sustained period of focused inquiry. They focused their collective intent on the question of sustainable resource utilization. Jian meticulously monitored the grove's energetic output, while Lyra described the "feel" of the information flowing through her. She reported a sense of immense, slow patience, of cycles measured in geological time. She perceived an image, not visual but conceptual, of roots deeply intertwined, drawing sustenance not just from the soil but from a deeper energetic matrix.

Aris Thorne, an expert in subterranean ecosystems, made a crucial observation during this period. He noticed an unusual pattern in the mycelial network's bio-luminescence radiating from beneath the grove. The patterns were not random; they formed intricate, almost cartographic representations of subterranean water reserves and mineral deposits, far more detailed and extensive than their ground-penetrating radar had initially indicated. It was as if the fungal network, intrinsically linked to the grove's consciousness, was revealing the planet's hidden bounty. This information, when correlated with Jian's atmospheric and energetic readings, which showed a particular "attunement" to these subterranean revelations, provided a breakthrough. It suggested that Eden's resources were not to be exploited, but rather to be understood as part of a vast, interconnected living system, accessible through careful observation and a deep respect for the planet's biological and energetic networks.

The "Oracle of the Groves" became a term whispered with reverence among the colonists. It was a testament to their evolving understanding of consciousness, not as an exclusive product of biological brains, but as a fundamental property of the universe, manifesting in diverse and unexpected ways. The grove was not a place of pronouncements, but a space of profound communion, a sanctuary where humanity could learn to attune itself to the ancient, silent wisdom of a living world. It was a humbling realization, shifting their perspective from conquerors to students, from exploiters to integral parts of a planetary tapestry. The grove, with its shimmering trees and resonant stones, was teaching them a language older than words, a language of connection, balance, and enduring life. It was a silent promise of a future not built on dominance, but on symbiosis, a future where humanity's consciousness could finally begin to harmonize with the vast, ancient consciousness of Eden. This understanding was not instantaneous; it was a process of shedding ingrained assumptions and embracing a new paradigm of existence, a paradigm where the very air, the very earth, was a sentient partner in their cosmic journey. The grove served as a constant, tangible reminder of this profound shift, a living monument to the possibility of interspecies understanding and co-evolution.

The subtle yet persistent hum of Eden, a resonance that had permeated the colonists' existence since their arrival, began to manifest in increasingly nuanced ways. It was no longer just an external phenomenon to be measured and cataloged by instruments like Jian's, or a poetic metaphor for Lyra's synesthetic perceptions. Instead, it started to weave itself into the very fabric of their inner lives, coaxing forth dormant capacities that had lain largely unexplored within the human psyche. This wasn't a sudden, dramatic metamorphosis, but a gradual, organic unfolding, akin to a seed cracking open under the gentle pressure of an unseen force, revealing the promise of life within. The colonists, particularly those who had spent the most time in proximity to the planet's bio-energetic nexus, the ancient grove, found themselves experiencing shifts in their awareness that transcended mere intellectual understanding.

Lyra, naturally, was among the first to articulate these changes. Her synesthetic perceptions, already a vibrant tapestry of sensory cross-pollination, began to acquire new dimensions. She described the atmospheric currents not just as colors and tastes, but as intricate, flowing narratives. The scent of rain on the crystalline rocks no longer merely evoked a sense of freshness; it carried with it an echo of geological memory, a whisper of ancient riverbeds that had long since dried. The light filtering through the iridescent leaves of the grove's trees seemed to carry not just visual information, but emotional resonance, each hue and shimmer imbuing her with a specific, albeit abstract, feeling – a deep, abiding calm during moments of planetary equilibrium, or a subtle, cautionary vibration when planetary systems underwent rapid flux. "It's as if," she explained to a small gathering in the habitat's communal space, her voice soft but filled with a quiet wonder, "the world is learning to speak to us in a language we've always understood but never consciously recognized. It's not words, not even images, but a direct conveyance of being, of knowing. Eden's consciousness isn't just *out there* anymore; it's resonating *within* me, awakening a similar resonance within my own awareness."

Jian Li, ever the pragmatist, initially struggled to quantify these internal shifts. His instruments could detect the external energetic emanations of Eden, the subtle atmospheric shifts, the harmonic resonances of the planet. But how to measure an emergent intuition, a sharpening of subjective perception? He began to adapt his methodologies, not by seeking to measure the immeasurable, but by observing its effects. He noticed a correlation between periods of intense communal reflection in the grove and a subsequent increase in collaborative problem-solving within the crew. Solutions that had previously eluded them, complex navigational challenges, or intricate ecological integration strategies, seemed to emerge with surprising alacrity following these periods of quiet communion. It was as if a collective intuitive field had been stimulated, allowing for a more fluid and interconnected flow of ideas. He began to hypothesize that Eden's pervasive consciousness acted as a kind of subtle energetic catalyst, gently nudging the human brain's capacity for pattern recognition and abstract thought, effectively unlocking latent intuitive pathways. He theorized that the very structure of human consciousness, with its complex neural networks, might be inherently receptive to such energetic influences, especially when exposed to the refined, coherent frequencies emanating from a planetary intelligence.

Anya Senior, with her deep understanding of emergent systems and interspecies communication, saw this not as a purely neurological phenomenon, but as a fundamental aspect of evolutionary adaptation. She began to frame it as a reciprocal awakening. Just as humanity had evolved to perceive its terrestrial environment through a series of sensory and cognitive mechanisms, Eden's evolving sentience was now, in turn, influencing the very nature of human perception. "We are not merely observing Eden," she posited in one of her philosophical lectures, her gaze sweeping across the attentive faces of the colonists. "We are becoming part of its observational apparatus. The planet's consciousness, in its journey towards greater complexity and self-awareness, seems to be creating an environment that fosters a similar evolution in the minds of those who inhabit it. It's as if Eden is extending a tendril of its awareness, not to control, but to connect, and in doing so, it's awakening within us a dormant capacity for deeper, more intuitive connection – with the planet, and crucially, with each other."

This awakening manifested in various ways. Many colonists reported an enhanced empathy, a subtler understanding of each other's unspoken emotions and intentions. During group discussions, disagreements often dissolved more readily, replaced by a shared sense of understanding and a willingness to find common ground. It was as if the ambient planetary consciousness acted as a gentle harmonizer, smoothing out the rough edges of interpersonal friction. Conversations felt less like exchanges of opposing viewpoints and more like collaborative explorations of a shared landscape of understanding. The subtle energetic field of Eden, it seemed, fostered a sense of interconnectedness that extended beyond the immediate environmental context, bridging the gaps between individual human minds. This wasn't telepathy in a science-fiction sense of direct thought transfer, but rather a heightened attunement to the subtle emotional and energetic cues that had always been present, but were now amplified and more readily perceived.

Dr. Aris Thorne, the astrobiologist, observed a similar phenomenon within his own field of study. His meticulous observations of Eden's flora and fauna, once driven by purely scientific curiosity, began to be infused with what he could only describe as a "feel" for the organisms he studied. He found himself anticipating the migratory patterns of avian life with uncanny accuracy, not based on predictable environmental triggers, but on an intuitive sense of the collective flow of the ecosystem. When studying the complex symbiotic relationships within Eden's fungal networks, he would often experience flashes of insight, understanding the intricate interdependencies not through laborious dissection and analysis, but through a sudden, intuitive grasp of the interconnected web of life. He recounted an experience while observing a particularly delicate bioluminescent fungus: "I was looking at the samples under the microscope, and suddenly, it wasn't just cellular structures I was seeing. I felt a sense of... awareness from the organism. Not sentience in a way we understand it, but a profound interconnectedness with the subterranean matrix, with the water, with the very minerals in the soil. It was as if the grove's influence extended even to the microbial level, amplifying my own capacity to perceive these subtle ecological dialogues."

This heightened intuition wasn't always comfortable. For some, the influx of new sensory information and emotional resonance could be overwhelming. Individuals who were less attuned to subtle energies found themselves experiencing heightened anxiety or a sense of being adrift in a sea of amplified emotions. The crew implemented a system of psychological support and guidance, led by Anya Senior and a team of trained counselors, to help individuals navigate these shifts. Meditation practices, particularly those focused on grounding and internal awareness, became increasingly important. The colonists learned to differentiate between their own internal states and the external energetic influences of Eden, developing a discerning awareness of the planetary consciousness without being subsumed by it. It was a process of learning to sail, rather than be tossed about by, the currents of a greater awareness.

The shared experience of this awakening also began to transform their understanding of community. The isolated nature of their mission, the inherent dangers of a new world, had already fostered a strong sense of camaraderie. But now, this was deepening into something more profound. There was a growing understanding that their individual consciousnesses were not entirely separate entities, but rather nodes within a larger, interconnected web, a web that Eden's presence was actively strengthening. They began to see their collective intelligence not just as the sum of their individual contributions, but as a synergistic emergent property, amplified by the very planet they inhabited. This understanding fostered a profound sense of responsibility, not just for their own survival, but for the well-being of Eden itself. They recognized that their own evolving consciousness was inextricably linked to the health and balance of the planet's consciousness.

The impact on their approach to colonization was significant. The idea of imposing human systems upon Eden began to feel increasingly alien and discordant. Instead, the focus shifted towards integration, towards understanding the planet's existing rhythms and finding ways to harmonize their own presence within them. The intuitive insights gained from their heightened awareness often pointed towards more sustainable and respectful methods of resource utilization, ways that minimized disruption and maximized co-existence. For instance, when seeking new water sources, instead of relying solely on geological surveys, the colonists would often engage in periods of focused intent in the grove, allowing Lyra and others to glean intuitive guidance about hidden aquifers, not through data, but through a felt sense of the planet's subterranean lifeblood. Similarly, agricultural innovations were inspired by an intuitive understanding of Eden's native plant life, recognizing symbiotic relationships that had evolved over millennia, rather than attempting to force Earth-based crops into an alien environment.

Lyra, in particular, became an invaluable bridge between the nascent human intuition and the tangible reality of the colony. Her ability to translate the abstract whispers of Eden into actionable insights allowed the crew to move beyond purely empirical methods. She would describe the "mood" of a particular region – whether it was conducive to expansion, or if it required a period of quiet observation. She could sense the energetic "health" of the local ecosystem, offering early warnings of imbalances that might otherwise go unnoticed until they became critical. This wasn't a passive reception of information; Lyra often described it as an active dialogue, a process of projecting her own queries and intentions into the planetary consciousness and receiving responses that were nuanced and context-dependent. "It's like asking a very old, very wise entity for advice," she explained. "You don't get a simple yes or no. You get a feeling, a direction, a sense of the interconnected consequences of any action. The grove is the place where this dialogue is clearest, where Eden's sentience is most accessible, and it's teaching us to listen not just with our ears, but with our entire being."

The colonists began to understand that this awakening of intuition was not an end in itself, but a fundamental shift in their relationship with the universe. It was a recognition that consciousness was not solely a biological phenomenon confined to individual brains, but a pervasive, interconnected force that could be accessed and interacted with. Eden, with its unique energetic signature and evolving sentience, served as the catalyst, the mirror reflecting back to humanity a potential that had always resided within, but had been largely obscured by the noise and distractions of their own civilization. They were learning, not just to survive on a new world, but to *be* on it, to truly inhabit it, guided by a deeper, more intuitive understanding of their place within its intricate, living tapestry. This was the dawn of a new human perception, one that was not only capable of understanding the cosmos, but of feeling its pulse, and responding in kind. The subtle hum of Eden was no longer just an external sound; it was becoming the rhythm of their awakened souls.

# CHAPTER SIX

# GRIEF AND GROWTH

The pervasive hum of Eden had, for a time, been a source of wonder, a testament to the emergent consciousness they were beginning to understand. It had been the gentle nudge towards intuition, the subtle broadening of their collective awareness. But as the echoes of the fire – the heat, the acrid smoke, the sheer, unadulterated terror – began to recede from the immediate present, a different kind of resonance began to fill the void. It was not the vibrant, pulsating song of Eden, but a hollow, echoing silence that settled deep within their bones. This silence was the sound of absence, the profound, gnawing grief for what had been irrevocably lost.

It wasn't just the searing pain of witnessing lives extinguished, a wound that would forever scar their collective memory. It was also the quiet, insidious erosion of their pre-fire certainties. Their mission, once a beacon of scientific endeavor and hopeful expansion, now felt like a fragile, almost naive dream. The Eden they had arrived on, a world of pristine beauty and latent intelligence, was also a world capable of immense destruction. The fire had been a stark, brutal reminder of their inherent vulnerability, a cosmic slap that had shattered their carefully constructed illusions of control. They had believed they were charting a new course, building a future on this alien soil, but the fire had revealed the precariousness of their footing, the sheer indifference of the universe to their aspirations.

Lyra found herself adrift in a sea of sensory dissonance. The vibrant colors of Eden's flora now seemed muted, tinged with the smoky hues of memory.

142

The melodic hum of the planet, once a source of comfort and connection, often felt like a mocking counterpoint to the silent screams that still echoed in the chambers of her mind. Her synesthetic perceptions, so attuned to the world's energetic symphony, were now overwhelmed by the discordant notes of grief. She saw the lingering ash not just as a physical residue, but as a vibrant, suffocating shroud clinging to the edges of her vision. The scent of the recovering vegetation, the earthy promise of renewal, was perpetually overlaid with the phantom smell of burning, a scent that burrowed into her lungs and refused to dissipate. She had always felt Eden's consciousness as an extension of her own, but now, that connection felt strained, as if the planet itself recoiled from the sorrow that clung to her like a second skin. "It's as if," she confessed to Anya, her voice barely a whisper, "the songs of the trees are now sung in a minor key, and the laughter of the wind carries the undertow of a sob. I can still feel Eden, but it feels... distant. Or perhaps, it's me who has become distant, shrouded in a grief so profound it renders me deaf to its subtler nuances."

Jian, the ever-present anchor of logic and data, wrestled with a different, yet equally profound, form of loss. His instruments, once tools of exploration and understanding, now felt woefully inadequate. They could measure the physical remnants of the fire – the particulate matter in the air, the altered soil composition, the fluctuating energy readings of damaged ecosystems. But they could not quantify the erosion of confidence, the deep-seated doubt that had taken root in his once-unwavering belief in progress and order. The fire had exposed the unpredictable, chaotic undercurrents of existence, revealing how easily carefully laid plans could be undone by forces beyond their comprehension. He found himself revisiting his data logs, searching for patterns that might explain, predict, or even prevent such a catastrophe, but the numbers offered no solace. They were mere statistics in the face of profound human suffering, cold, hard facts that could not account for the immeasurable weight of loss. His scientific mind, so adept at dissecting the mechanics of the universe, found itself incapable of dissecting the intangible architecture of grief. The loss of control, the stark realization that they were not masters of their destiny, but rather fragile passengers on a volatile cosmic journey, gnawed at him. "We came here with blueprints, with protocols," he mused one evening, staring out at the scarred landscape visible from the habitat's viewport. "We thought we understood the risks, that we could mitigate them. The fire... it didn't just burn structures. It burned away that illusion. It showed us how little we truly command. And that, more than anything, is a difficult equation to solve."

Dr. Aris Thorne, the astrobiologist, experienced the grief as a profound disillusionment with the very concept of Eden's sentience. His initial awe had been rooted in the belief that this emergent consciousness represented a higher form of existence, a harmonious order that humanity could learn from and integrate with. The fire, however, had demonstrated that this consciousness, if it could be called that, was also capable of wild, untamed power, a power that could unleash unimaginable destruction. He had studied the planet's intricate ecosystems, marveling at their balance and resilience, only to witness a cataclysm that seemed to disregard all notions of equilibrium. The loss of his colleagues, individuals he had come to know and respect, was a wound that festered, but it was compounded by a deeper, more existential sorrow: the loss of his faith in Eden's benevolent nature. He had begun to see the planet not as a wise, guiding entity, but as a vast, indifferent force of nature, capable of both creation and annihilation with equal abandon. The interconnectedness he had once celebrated now felt like a terrifyingly fragile web, easily torn asunder. He found himself questioning his own interpretations, his meticulous observations now tinged with a suspicion that he had been projecting human desires for order onto a reality that was far more primal and unpredictable. "We saw a gardener, tending its bloom," he confided to Anya, his voice heavy with a weariness that went beyond his years. "But perhaps we were seeing a volcano. Capable of immense beauty, yes, but also of eruption. The fire... it was an eruption. And now, I grieve not only for the lives lost, but for the idealized vision of Eden that died with them."

The colonists, as a collective, mourned the loss of what felt like a simpler existence. Before the fire, before the raw, unvarnished reality of their precarious situation had been so brutally laid bare, there had been a certain naiveté they could afford. Life, while challenging, had possessed a discernible rhythm, a predictable set of parameters. They had been charting a course, not just through space, but through a future that, however uncertain, still felt within their grasp. The fire had ripped away that perceived control, replacing it with a gnawing anxiety and a profound sense of uncertainty. The very fabric of their daily lives, once organized around the familiar routines of survival and exploration, now felt fraught with an unspoken dread. Every unexpected sound, every flicker of light outside the habitat, could trigger a cascade of anxious thoughts, a visceral remembrance of the chaos that had erupted from the seemingly serene landscape.

Anya Senior, in her role as a guide and philosopher, recognized this existential sorrow as a crucial, albeit painful, stage in their growth. She saw that the colonists were not just grieving the physical losses, but also the death of their former selves, the selves who had believed in a more straightforward, less perilous existence. "The fire was a crucible," she explained to a small group gathered in the refectory, her gaze steady and compassionate. "It burned away not just what was superficial, but what was foundational to our understanding of ourselves and our place in the universe. We came to Eden with a certain set of assumptions – assumptions about progress, about control, about the inherent benevolence of life. The fire has challenged every one of those assumptions. And in the ashes, we are left to confront the profound grief of losing not just people, but also the comforting illusions that sustained us. This is the mourning of the unseen – the loss of our perceived mastery, the death of our simple certainties, the profound sorrow that arises when the ground beneath our feet, metaphorically and literally, shifts so violently."

This grief manifested in myriad ways. Some colonists became withdrawn, their once-vibrant personalities dimmed by the weight of their sorrow. They found solace in solitude, replaying memories in their minds, clinging to the fading echoes of laughter and conversation. Others, conversely, sought solace in heightened activity, throwing themselves into their work with an almost desperate fervor, as if sheer industry could outrun the encroaching darkness of their grief. There were those who found themselves questioning everything they had ever believed, their faith in science, in humanity, even in themselves, shaken to its core. The intuitive attunement to Eden, once a source of wonder, now felt like an unbearable burden, as if the planet's subtle energetic shifts were amplified by their own internal turmoil, mirroring their grief with a profound melancholy.

The habitat, once a symbol of their progress and hope, now felt like a fragile sanctuary against an indifferent cosmos. The hum of its life support systems, a constant reminder of their technological dependence, seemed to whisper of their vulnerability. The shared spaces, which had once buzzed with camaraderie and shared purpose, were now often filled with a quiet, somber understanding. Conversations, when they occurred, were often punctuated by long silences, pregnant with unspoken grief. The simple act of sharing a meal, once a routine of sustenance and connection, became a ritual of remembrance, each face in the room a testament to those who were no longer there.

Lyra's art, once an explosion of color and light reflecting Eden's vibrant life, began to transform. She started to incorporate darker hues, the smoky greys and somber browns of the fire's aftermath. Her synesthetic perceptions, though still a conduit to Eden's energy, were now filtered through the lens of loss. She saw the planet's resilience, its slow, steady recovery, but she also perceived the deep, invisible scars, the energetic echoes of the destruction. She began to paint not just the external world, but the internal landscape of grief, translating the abstract sorrow into visual metaphors. Her canvases became vast expanses of textured darkness, punctuated by faint glimmers of light – the tenacious spark of hope struggling to break through the overwhelming shadow. "It's like trying to paint the silence after a scream," she explained to Jian, her fingers stained with charcoal and ochre. "You can't capture the sound itself, but you can capture the shape of the void it leaves behind. Eden is still beautiful, still alive, but it carries its wounds now. And so do we."

Jian, in his own way, began to integrate this new reality into his research. He started developing new protocols for risk assessment, not just in terms of external threats, but in terms of the psychological impact of such events on the crew. He began to analyze the subtle shifts in energy fields not just for geological stability, but for emotional resonance, seeking to understand how Eden's own energetic patterns might be influenced by their collective grief, and vice-versa. He found himself spending more time observing the non-sentient aspects of Eden – the geological formations, the complex mineral compositions, the atmospheric phenomena – as if seeking a grounding in the immutable laws of physics, a counterpoint to the unpredictable nature of consciousness. He was mourning the loss of his purely objective scientific worldview, the comforting illusion that data alone could explain and control reality. Now, he understood that reality was far more complex, interwoven with emotion, with loss, with the intangible weight of existence.

The fire had not just destroyed lives; it had also dismantled their carefully constructed sense of identity. They were no longer just colonists, explorers, scientists. They were survivors, individuals marked by tragedy, forever carrying the indelible imprint of what they had endured. This self-perception shift was a profound source of grief. They mourned the loss of their former selves, the selves who had been unburdened by such a profound experience of loss and vulnerability. The simplicity of their former lives, the days when their greatest challenges were logistical or scientific, now felt like a distant, almost mythical era. They mourned the ease with which they had once navigated their world, an ease now replaced by a constant, subtle vigilance.

Dr. Thorne, in his own quiet way, began to document the ecological resilience of Eden in the wake of the fire. He observed how the planet, despite the devastation, was already in the process of healing. New shoots pushed through the scorched earth, and the animal populations, though diminished, were slowly beginning to rebound. This observation, while scientifically significant, was also a source of profound emotional conflict. It was a tangible representation of Eden's inherent vitality, its capacity for renewal that stood in stark contrast to the irreversible loss of human lives. He grappled with the dissonance of witnessing such vibrant life emerge from the ashes of such profound destruction. He mourned the humans who would never witness this rebirth, the lives that had been cut short before they could see Eden's enduring strength. He had to reconcile his scientific understanding of ecological processes with the deep, personal grief that the fire had wrought. His scientific curiosity was now inextricably linked to the somber weight of remembrance.

This mourning of the unseen, the sorrow for lost certainties and control, became an integral part of their journey. It was not a stage to be overcome quickly, but a shadow that walked with them, a constant reminder of the fragility of existence and the profound impact of loss. They learned that true growth, true adaptation, did not come from erasing these experiences, but from integrating them. The fire had been a brutal awakening, a harsh teacher, but it had also, in its own devastating way, stripped away the superficial layers of their understanding, revealing the deeper, more complex truths of their existence. They were no longer simply colonizing a new world; they were being forged anew by it, their spirits tempered by the flames of loss, their understanding of life and consciousness irrevocably altered. The silence of grief, though painful, was also a space for reflection, a testament to the depth of their humanity, and the quiet, persistent hope that even in the darkest of times, life, in its myriad forms, would always find a way to endure and, eventually, to bloom again.

The echoes of the fire had settled, not into silence, but into a new resonance, a somber melody woven into the fabric of their lives. Grief, once a tidal wave threatening to drown them, had receded into a deep, abiding current, shaping their days and nights. It was within this transformed landscape that the need for communal remembrance began to bloom, not as an act of dwelling in sorrow, but as a conscious effort to weave the tapestry of their experience, threads of loss interwoven with the vibrant hues of perseverance.

Anya Senior, with her profound understanding of the human psyche and the collective consciousness, recognized this nascent need. She saw that while individual introspection was vital, the shared burden of memory required shared expression. The isolation that grief could foster needed to be countered by connection, by spaces where the unspoken could find voice, and the fragmented could be made whole, if only for a fleeting moment. "We cannot simply outrun the shadow of the fire," she explained to a group gathered in the observation dome, the nebulae outside swirling like cosmic tears. "We must walk with it, acknowledge its presence, and learn from its lessons. And to do that, we must do it together. Our remembrance should not be a monument to despair, but a garden where resilience can take root."

The first of these communal rituals emerged organically, almost a spontaneous outpouring of a shared need. It began with the simple act of lighting a flame. In the central refectory, a small, perpetually burning bio-luminescent ember, harvested from a deep-cave fungus that had miraculously survived the inferno, was placed in a specially constructed, obsidian-like basin. Each evening, as the twin suns of Eden dipped below the horizon, casting long, spectral shadows, colonists would gather. They would approach the ember, one by one, and share a memory, a name, a feeling. Some spoke aloud, their voices often catching with emotion, recounting a forgotten joke, a shared meal, a moment of unexpected kindness from those lost. Others, more reticent, would simply place a hand near the ember, a silent communion of shared loss, their internal narratives playing out in the quiet space between heartbeats.

Lyra, her artistic sensibilities deeply attuned to the emotional currents of the community, found a new language for these gatherings. She began to create 'Memory Tapestries' – large, woven hangings crafted from salvaged fibers and natural dyes, incorporating elements from the pre-fire era and the scarred landscape. Each tapestry became a canvas for collective remembrance. After the evening gatherings, colonists would contribute small tokens – a polished stone, a dried petal from a resilient flower, a fragment of a shattered artifact – to be woven into the tapestry, each addition a physical manifestation of their enduring connection to those who were gone. The tapestries, as they grew, became not just art, but chronicles of their shared journey, their colors shifting from somber earth tones to brighter, hopeful shades as the community consciously integrated their grief with the promise of renewal. These were not static memorials, but dynamic works in progress, reflecting the ongoing process of healing and adaptation.

Jian, ever the pragmatist, initially viewed these rituals with a degree of skepticism, his scientific mind seeking quantifiable outcomes. However, he observed the subtle, yet undeniable, shift in the community's morale. The shared spaces, once heavy with unspoken grief, began to thrum with a quiet energy. The act of articulating memories, of hearing the echoes of shared experiences in the voices of others, seemed to alleviate the crushing weight of individual isolation. He began to adapt his own work, developing bio-sensors that could track subtle shifts in atmospheric composition and even the faint energetic fields of the planet, correlating them with the emotional states expressed during these rituals. He theorized that the collective catharsis generated by these ceremonies might have a tangible, albeit subtle, impact on Eden's own complex energetic matrix, a feedback loop of emotional healing that extended beyond the human inhabitants. He started to view these rituals not as mere sentimental expressions, but as vital components of their adaptive strategy, a form of psychological ecosystem engineering.

Dr. Thorne, whose initial disillusionment with Eden's sentience had been a profound personal grief, found a new scientific focus within these remembrance rituals. He began to meticulously document the flora and fauna that had demonstrated extraordinary resilience or had even thrived in the fire-ravaged areas. He observed the tenacious regrowth of specific mosses that seemed to draw sustenance from the very ash, and the remarkable adaptation of certain insect species that had developed a symbiotic relationship with the newly exposed mineral deposits. During the remembrance ceremonies, he would often share these findings, not as a distraction from grief, but as a testament to Eden's enduring life force.

He would speak of the fire-resistant seeds that lay dormant, waiting for the opportune moment to germinate, drawing parallels between these natural processes and the human capacity for hope and renewal. "The planet itself mourns its losses," he would explain, his voice steady, "but it does not cease to live. It adapts. It regenerates. And in this, it offers us a profound lesson. Our remembrance honors those who are gone, but it also celebrates the life that continues, a testament to their memory."

These rituals evolved into distinct forms, each serving a specific purpose in their collective healing. The 'Echo Garden' was established in a section of the pre-fire botanical gardens that had been partially shielded from the inferno. Here, memorial plaques bearing the names of the lost were not etched in stone, but carved into living wood, the names gradually being integrated into the growth of the trees. Colonists would tend to these trees, their gardening a form of active remembrance, a nurturing of life in honor of those who could no longer nurture it themselves. They would plant seeds around the base of each memorial tree, choosing species that were known for their tenacity and their ability to regenerate, symbolic offerings of enduring life.

Another significant ritual became the 'Night of Whispers'. Once a month, under the cloak of Eden's deepest night, the colonists would gather at a vantage point overlooking the scarred plains. Each individual would be given a small, bio-luminescent seed, capable of emitting a soft, ethereal glow. In hushed reverence, they would whisper the name of someone they wished to remember into the seed, imbuing it with their personal memories and emotions. Then, in a synchronized act, they would release these glowing seeds into the night sky. They would drift downwards, a cascade of faint lights, each a tiny beacon of remembrance, a silent testament to the lives that had touched theirs, slowly settling back into the recovering landscape, becoming one with the burgeoning ecosystem. Lyra's artistic endeavors often coincided with these events, her luminous paintings and ephemeral sculptures capturing the poignant beauty of the Night of Whispers, her canvases filled with the soft glow of countless tiny lights against the vast, star-dusted canvas of Eden.

The concept of 'Shared Dreams' also emerged, a more introspective, yet deeply communal, practice. Dr. Aris Thorne, a pioneer in the study of Eden's subtle energetic fields, had discovered that under certain specific atmospheric conditions, the planet's indigenous flora could produce volatile organic compounds that, when inhaled in controlled environments, could induce shared, vivid dream states. While the scientific implications were still being explored, Anya Senior recognized its potential for communal grief processing. They established a carefully managed 'Dream Chamber', where small groups of colonists could participate in these guided dream states. The intention was not to force specific visions, but to create a space where subconscious memories and emotions related to the fire and its victims could surface in a shared, yet private, context. Participants would later share their dream fragments and the emotions they evoked, piecing together a collective subconscious narrative of their loss and their resilience. These sessions were often guided by Anya, who would help them interpret the symbolic language of their dreams, translating the raw emotions into a language of understanding and acceptance.

The communal meals, too, took on a new significance. They transformed from mere sustenance into 'Feasts of Remembrance'. Before the meal, a designated colonist would share a story or a memory of one of the lost. The food itself often incorporated ingredients that had been favorites of those they mourned, or dishes that were symbolic of comfort and resilience. Even the seating arrangements were considered; sometimes, empty chairs were deliberately left at tables, adorned with a single flower or a token, a quiet acknowledgment of their continued presence in spirit. Jian, though still grounded in data, began to analyze the nutritional content of these meals, correlating specific nutrient profiles with reported improvements in mood and social cohesion during these enhanced communal gatherings, further validating their importance in his own analytical framework.

The children, those born on Eden or who had been very young at the time of the fire, were also integrated into these rituals. They learned about the fire not as a terrifying, abstract event, but as a part of their shared history, a story of survival and remembrance. They participated in creating 'Memory Lanterns' – delicate paper lanterns inscribed with drawings or simple messages for those lost. During special celestial events, these lanterns would be released, their soft glow ascending into the twilight, carrying the innocence and hope of the next generation. Lyra often led workshops for the children, helping them translate their feelings and memories into visual art, creating a vibrant mural within the habitat that depicted both the sorrow and the enduring spirit of their community.

These rituals were not about erasing the pain, but about integrating it into the ongoing narrative of their lives. They were a testament to the understanding that growth, especially in the face of profound loss, required acknowledging the scars. The fire had been a devastating interruption, a violent disruption of their trajectory. But in its aftermath, by consciously creating spaces for remembrance, for shared grieving, and for the celebration of enduring life, they were not merely surviving; they were actively weaving a new future, one that was informed by their past, resilient in its present, and hopeful in its unfolding. The hum of Eden, once a source of wonder and then a poignant reminder of what was lost, now also served as a backdrop to these communal acts of remembrance, its subtle frequencies seemingly resonating with the collective heartbeats of a community that was learning, not to forget, but to remember in a way that fostered strength and sustained hope. The very act of gathering, of sharing, of continuing, became the most profound ritual of all – a testament to the unyielding, life-affirming spirit of humanity, even on a world that had shown them its capacity for both exquisite beauty and devastating power. They were not just survivors; they were inheritors of a legacy, a legacy that demanded not just sorrow, but also the courage to live, to grow, and to remember with a quiet, enduring strength. The obsidian basin, holding its perpetual ember, became a symbol of this enduring flame of life and memory, a constant reminder that even in the deepest darkness, a spark of light, a flicker of remembrance, could illuminate the path forward.

The initial shockwaves of the fire had subsided, leaving behind a landscape both physically scarred and emotionally resonant. The grief, initially a tempest, had now settled into a profound undercurrent, a constant reminder of the devastation and the lives irrevocably altered. Yet, within this somber stillness, a subtle shift began to occur, a slow unfurling of acceptance that was less a sudden dawn and more akin to the gradual blooming of a deep-rooted flower. This was not the passive resignation of defeat, but an active, albeit often arduous, process of integrating the unbearable into the fabric of their existence.

For Anya Senior, this emerging acceptance was a delicate ecosystem to observe and nurture. She saw that the communal rituals, while vital for shared expression, were merely the initial plantings in a much larger garden. The true growth lay in the individual journeys, the internal recalibrations that allowed each colonist to find their footing in this changed world. She began to hold smaller, more intimate sessions, not as formal therapy, but as guided conversations that encouraged introspection. "We've learned to stand together in our sorrow," she would say, her voice a gentle balm, "but now we must also learn to stand within ourselves, to acknowledge the echoes of what was without letting them drown out the whisper of what can be."

One of the most pervasive internal struggles was the pervasive sense of 'what if.' The phantom limbs of lost opportunities, the roads not taken, the words left unsaid – these were the specters that haunted the quiet hours. Jian, despite his analytical mind, found himself revisiting a particularly sharp memory: a disagreement with a colleague, a scientist lost in the inferno, over a seemingly trivial data interpretation. The argument, inconsequential in the grand scheme of things, now loomed large, tinged with a guilt that gnawed at him. He began to understand that forgiveness was not simply an act of absolution for others, but a necessary liberation for oneself. He started to journal his thoughts, not in an attempt to rationalize the past, but to acknowledge the human fallibility that had led to those moments, and to recognize that in a crisis of such magnitude, petty grievances were the first casualties of true understanding. "We are not perfect beings," he admitted to Anya during one of their walks through the recovering arboretum, where the resilient saplings pushed through the scorched earth. "And in our imperfections, we often cause pain, even unintentionally. Learning to accept that, and to forgive ourselves for it, is as crucial as rebuilding the habitats."

Lyra, whose art had become a conduit for collective expression, found that her own inner landscape was also in flux. Her earlier tapestries had focused on the loss, their colors muted, their textures raw. But as the community began to tentatively embrace their new reality, her art began to mirror that subtle shift. She started incorporating brighter threads, not to deny the darkness, but to represent the nascent sparks of hope. She began to experiment with sculpted forms, creating abstract pieces that represented the fractured self slowly mending, the jagged edges softening into more fluid lines. She spoke of this process as "re-patterning the soul." "Grief can be like a knot," she explained, her hands stained with natural dyes. "You can't just cut it. You have to carefully, patiently, work it loose, thread by thread. And sometimes, when it's finally undone, you find you've created something new from the unraveling." She found herself forgiving Anya for a perceived lack of understanding during the initial chaos, realizing that Anya, too, was navigating an unimaginable burden.

The concept of forgiveness extended beyond the individual to encompass the very planet. Dr. Thorne, who had initially wrestled with a deep sense of betrayal by Eden's apparent indifference during the fire, began to see a different narrative unfolding. He observed how the flora and fauna, despite the catastrophic damage, were not merely surviving but actively adapting. He documented the astonishing genetic mutations that allowed certain plant species to thrive in the altered soil composition, absorbing toxins and metabolizing them into new life. He witnessed the symbiotic relationships that were forming between species that had never before interacted, a testament to Eden's inherent drive towards equilibrium. "The planet doesn't 'punish' or 'forgive' in the human sense," he mused during a lecture to the colonists, his voice resonating with newfound respect. "It simply *is*. It adapts, it evolves. The fire was a cataclysm, yes, but it was also a catalyst. And in its wake, life, in its infinite ingenuity, has found new pathways. Our task is not to resent the past, but to understand and adapt to the present it has forged." This perspective helped many to release the anger they harbored towards Eden, reframing it as a powerful, indifferent force of nature rather than a malicious entity.

This shift in perspective was particularly impactful for those who had lost loved ones through direct, unavoidable circumstances related to the fire. The engineers and safety personnel, who had worked tirelessly to mitigate the disaster, often bore a heavy burden of self-blame. They replayed every decision, every alarm that went unheard, every protocol that faltered. Anya began to facilitate dialogues where these individuals could share their experiences without judgment, allowing their comrades to offer not condemnation, but understanding and support. "You did everything you could in a situation no one could have predicted," was a common refrain. The acknowledgment of their efforts, the recognition of their inherent humanity in the face of overwhelming odds, began to chip away at the walls of guilt. They started to see that their actions, however tragic the outcome, were born of courage and a deep commitment to the community, not negligence. This realization allowed them to begin the slow process of accepting their role not as perpetrators of failure, but as heroes who had fought valiantly against an unstoppable force.

The children, too, were undergoing their own subtle acclimatization. For them, the fire was less a recent trauma and more a foundational story, a part of their identity. Their acceptance was less about confronting raw grief and more about understanding the world as it was now. They would ask innocent, yet profound, questions about the 'before' and the 'after.' Lyra and the educators worked to provide age-appropriate narratives, focusing on the resilience of life and the importance of remembrance. They created games that involved planting seeds, simulating the regrowth of the planet. They learned to identify the plants that had survived and learned to love them, seeing them not as remnants of loss, but as symbols of enduring life. One young girl, Maya, who had lost her mother in the fire, often spoke to the memorial trees. Initially, it was a form of desperate conversation, a plea for her mother's return. But over time, her tone softened, becoming one of sharing, of recounting her day, of seeking advice. It was a primitive form of acceptance, a childlike understanding that her mother was a part of her, and a part of the world that continued to grow.

Dr. Aris Thorne's research into the shared dream states also proved unexpectedly valuable in this process. The Dream Chamber, initially conceived as a tool for collective psychological processing, began to reveal deeper layers of individual acceptance. Participants often reported dreams that, while still containing elements of the fire, also featured resolutions or moments of peace. Someone who had lost a partner might dream of them smiling, not in sorrow, but in gentle farewell. Another might dream of finding a lost artifact, symbolizing the recovery of a piece of themselves. Anya would guide debriefing sessions, emphasizing that these dreams were not literal prophecies or regressions, but the subconscious mind's attempt to process and reconcile the trauma. "Your dreams are showing you that the intensity of the pain is not infinite," she would explain. "They are offering glimpses of a future where the memories can coexist with peace, where love can exist beyond physical presence." This gentle guidance allowed individuals to confront and reframe their nightmares, gradually transforming them into narratives of integration rather than terror.

The act of daily living itself became a quiet testament to this growing acceptance. The routine of waking, working, and interacting, while still tinged with the melancholy of what was lost, was no longer dominated by despair. There was a growing appreciation for the simple constants: the warmth of the twin suns, the taste of nutrient paste, the sound of children's laughter. Jian meticulously tracked these seemingly mundane aspects of life. He noted a correlation between the consistent engagement in communal activities, even those tinged with sadness, and a measurable decrease in reported anxiety levels. He observed how the shared responsibility for maintaining the habitat, for tending the gardens, for ensuring the safety of their community, fostered a sense of purpose that transcended personal loss.

"We are building, not just structures, but futures," he remarked to Anya, gesturing towards a new hydroponic dome under construction. "And in that act of building, we are demonstrating our commitment to life, to continuity. It's a powerful counter-narrative to the destruction."

The concept of 'legacy' also began to take root. Colonists started to think not just about what they had lost, but about what they were now responsible for preserving and passing on. This was particularly evident in the older generation, those who remembered Earth with vivid clarity. They began to share their stories more intentionally, not as tales of a lost paradise, but as lessons learned, as wisdom gained from a life that had faced its own share of challenges. They spoke of the importance of community, of ecological balance, of the resilience of the human spirit. This sharing was a form of gentle legacy building, a way of ensuring that the essence of what was precious was not extinguished by the fire. They understood that their own lives, though irrevocably marked, were now imbued with a new significance – to be living embodiments of what it meant to endure and to remember.

Even the physical landscape, once a constant reminder of devastation, began to play a role in this acceptance. The scarred plains, the skeletal remains of scorched trees, were no longer solely viewed through the lens of loss. Dr. Thorne's work, highlighting the tenacious regrowth and the emergence of new life, provided a visual narrative of resilience. Colonists would take walks, not to mourn, but to observe. They would point out a cluster of vibrant, fire-resistant wildflowers pushing through the ash, or a family of adapted avians nesting in the hollow of a burnt-out tree. These observations, shared amongst themselves, became small victories, subtle affirmations that Eden was not a dead world, but a wounded one, in the process of healing. The planet's own capacity for regeneration served as a powerful external mirror to their internal efforts to heal and rebuild.

This slow unfurling of acceptance was not a uniform process. There were days when the weight of grief would descend again, heavy and suffocating. There were moments of bitter regret and profound sadness that seemed to negate all progress. But these were now understood as ebbs and flows, part of the natural rhythm of healing, rather than permanent setbacks. The community had developed a collective understanding that progress was not linear, that the path to acceptance was winding and often involved revisiting old wounds before one could truly move forward. Anya often reminded them, "Growth is rarely a straight line. It's more like a spiral, circling back on itself, but always ascending, always moving towards a broader perspective."

The acceptance was not about forgetting. It was about integrating. It was about recognizing that the fire, and the losses it brought, were now an indelible part of their history, a part of who they had become. The pain, while still present, no longer held the same paralyzing power. It had been woven into the tapestry of their lives, not as a dominant thread of sorrow, but as a somber hue that gave depth and texture to the brighter colors of resilience, hope, and enduring connection. They were learning to live with the ghosts, not by banishing them, but by acknowledging their presence and choosing to focus on the living, on the future they were building, brick by careful brick, seed by hopeful seed, memory by cherished memory. The quiet hum of Eden, once a sound that evoked images of loss, was slowly transforming into a gentle lullaby of continuity, a testament to life's unwavering persistence.

The scarred earth, once a canvas of ash and despair, had begun to whisper with the nascent pulse of a different kind of life. It wasn't merely the resilient flora, pushing through cracked soil with an almost defiant verdancy, that represented this nascent emergence. It was a more profound, more intricate blooming – the blossoming of the human spirit amidst the very ruins that had threatened to extinguish it. This was the paradoxical truth Anya Senior had been observing, a truth as ancient as life itself: that devastation, in its raw, elemental power, could also be the most potent fertilizer for growth. The fire had stripped away the extraneous, the superficial, leaving behind the bedrock of necessity, and upon that bedrock, something new and vital was beginning to construct itself.

Consider the emergent relationships, not born of shared celebration or easy camaraderie, but forged in the crucible of shared vulnerability. The collaborative efforts to rebuild had naturally fostered deeper connections.

Neighbors who had once exchanged polite nods now found themselves sharing meals, their conversations often drifting from the practicalities of habitat repair to the quiet anxieties and hopes that still flickered within. Jian, whose analytical mind was now trained to see patterns not just in data but in human interaction, noted a distinct shift. The initial isolation that grief had imposed was slowly giving way to a more organic, interdependency. He saw how the engineers, who had worked tirelessly on the structural integrity of the new shelters, found solace in the company of the botanists tending the re-established hydroponic farms. It wasn't about specific shared interests, but about a shared commitment to survival, a silent acknowledgment that each was essential to the collective. This interdependence wasn't just functional; it was deeply emotional. A shared task, however mundane, became a ritual of mutual reassurance. The simple act of passing a tool, of offering a word of encouragement, carried a weight far beyond its literal meaning. It was a silent affirmation: "You are not alone in this. We are here, together." This was a growth not of grand pronouncements, but of quiet, steady support, the kind that allows the most fragile seedlings of hope to take root.

Lyra's artistic endeavors, too, began to reflect this burgeoning interconnectedness. Her earlier sculptures, born from the shattered remnants of the fire – twisted metal, fused glass, charred wood – were raw expressions of trauma. But as the community began to tentatively knit itself back together, her art began to evolve. She started creating collaborative pieces, inviting individuals to contribute small fragments, personal tokens, to larger installations. One such piece, a soaring abstraction of intertwined branches crafted from salvaged materials, became a focal point in the newly established communal gathering space. Each branch, scavenged from the burnt forest, bore the imprint of its origin, yet together, they formed a unified, upward-reaching structure. Colonists would often touch the branches, tracing the textures, remembering the day they found that particular piece, connecting their personal experience to the collective narrative. Lyra spoke of this process as "weaving the broken threads into a single tapestry." It was a metaphor for their community, a testament to their shared resilience. The act of contributing, of adding one's own small, fractured piece to a larger, hopeful whole, was a powerful affirmation of belonging. This artistic growth was not an individual pursuit but a communal dialogue, a visual representation of their collective healing.

Even the seemingly indifferent natural world was actively participating in this unfolding of new life. Dr. Thorne's continued observations revealed an astonishing array of adaptive strategies. Beyond the genetic mutations he had initially documented, he began to identify entirely new ecological niches being carved out by the post-fire environment. Small, hardy insects, previously unseen, were now thriving in the mineral-rich ash, processing it into a form usable by certain newly adapted fungi. These fungi, in turn, were creating pockets of nutrient-dense soil, paving the way for even more complex plant life. He described it as a "cascade of innovation," where each seemingly minor adaptation triggered a chain reaction, leading to a richer, more complex ecosystem than had existed before. He presented his findings not as mere scientific data, but as a profound lesson in resilience. "Eden is not just recovering," he'd explain, his voice filled with awe. "It is

*reinventing* itself. The fire was not an end, but a violent pruning that has allowed for an explosion of new possibilities, a testament to life's inherent drive to find a way, to thrive against all odds." This perspective offered a powerful external validation for the colonists' own internal efforts to adapt and grow. They saw their own struggles mirrored in the tenacious life unfolding around them, drawing strength from Eden's own remarkable capacity for renewal.

This understanding of reinvention extended to societal structures. The loss of the old administrative and social frameworks had been a profound disruption, but it also presented an opportunity for radical reimagining. Without the ingrained hierarchies and established protocols, the colonists were free to experiment with new forms of governance and community organization. Anya, observing these shifts, facilitated discussions that encouraged thoughtful rather than reactive decision-making. They explored models based on direct democracy, skill-sharing networks, and decentralized resource management. The Engineers' Guild, for instance, began to collaborate directly with the Agricultural Collective, bypassing traditional bureaucratic channels to ensure that newly developed soil remediation technologies were immediately integrated into the farming efforts. This was a form of societal growth that was less about rebuilding what was lost and more about constructing something fundamentally new, something more attuned to their current reality and their collective aspirations. These were not merely incremental improvements; they were paradigm shifts, driven by necessity and empowered by their shared experience of loss.

The children, in their unvarnished perception, often served as unwitting guides to this new growth. Their play, once an echo of a lost Earth, was now deeply intertwined with their current reality. They would construct elaborate forts from salvaged materials, mimicking the resilience of the new shelters. They would stage elaborate dramas where heroes battled spectral fires, not to banish them, but to learn how to coexist with their lingering presence. Their games of "seed planting" were not just educational; they were acts of faith, embodying the conviction that new life would always emerge. One particular game, where they mimicked the flight patterns of the adapted avians, observing their nesting habits in the charred remnants of trees, was a poignant example. It was a testament to their ability to find wonder and fascination not in what was lost, but in what was newly born. Their acceptance was not a learned behavior but an intrinsic understanding, a natural inclination to embrace the present, and in doing so, to shape the future. Their capacity for unburdened optimism served as a gentle, constant reminder to the adults that growth was not only possible but inevitable.

Even within the scientific community, which had been so deeply affected by the loss of life and research, there was a palpable sense of renewed purpose. Dr. Thorne, initially devastated by the destruction of his extensive ecological research facilities, found himself drawn to the raw, chaotic data of the post-fire world. He began to explore new avenues of research, focusing on ecotoxicology and extremophile biology, fields that had been considered fringe before the disaster but were now of paramount importance. He initiated a project to catalog the bio-remediation capabilities of the new flora, creating a living database that was actively being updated by the planet itself. Jian, eager to contribute his analytical skills, joined Thorne's team, finding a new intellectual challenge in deciphering the complex, interconnected systems that were emerging. The shared pursuit of knowledge, in the face of such profound loss, became a powerful antidote to despair. It was a growth in understanding, a deeper engagement with the intricate dance of life and destruction, that promised to yield invaluable insights for their future.

The act of remembrance itself began to transform, becoming a source of strength rather than a wellspring of sorrow. The memorial sites, initially somber places of quiet weeping, evolved into spaces of shared storytelling and communal reflection. Instead of focusing solely on the moment of loss, the colonists began to share anecdotes that captured the essence of the individuals they had lost – their humor, their passions, their contributions. Anya facilitated sessions where these stories were not just recounted but woven together, creating a richer, more vibrant portrait of their collective past. These gatherings became acts of affirmation, celebrating the lives that had been lived, acknowledging their enduring impact, and drawing inspiration from their legacy. This was a crucial aspect of growth: to honor the past not by dwelling in its shadows, but by integrating its light into the present. The memories became not burdens, but guiding stars, illuminating the path forward.

This process of growth was not without its challenges, of course. There were still days when the weight of what had been lost felt crushing, when the sheer scale of their endeavor seemed insurmountable. Moments of doubt would creep in, whispers of "what if we had done things differently?" But these moments were increasingly understood not as failures of their growth, but as natural fluctuations in the process. The community had developed a shared understanding that true resilience wasn't about the absence of pain, but about the capacity to continue moving forward despite it. They had learned to recognize the signs of emotional fatigue, to offer support without judgment, and to encourage periods of quiet reflection when needed. Anya's role in this was crucial; she was the calm center, the gentle voice reminding them that healing was not a destination but a journey, and that every step, even the faltering ones, was a testament to their enduring spirit.

The very physical act of rebuilding served as a constant, tangible reminder of their progress. Each new structure erected, each seed successfully germinated, each repaired piece of technology, was a small victory against the forces of destruction. Jian meticulously documented these achievements, not just in terms of their functional impact, but in their psychological resonance. He observed how the completion of the new communal kitchen, a hub of shared activity, led to a noticeable uplift in morale. The sounds of cooking, of laughter, of shared meals, were a potent counter-narrative to the silence of loss. He noted how the visual evidence of progress – the growing crops, the sturdy new shelters, the revitalized arboretum – provided a concrete sense of hope. This was growth manifested, a physical testament to their collective will to endure and to thrive. It was a powerful, ongoing demonstration that even from the ashes, a new and vibrant existence could be painstakingly, deliberately, built. The ruins were not merely a testament to what had been lost, but increasingly, a foundation upon which something enduring and meaningful was being constructed. Life, in its myriad forms, was finding a way, not just to survive, but to flourish in the wake of utter devastation.

The whisper of Eden had begun to shift, to take on a new resonance that was less about the raw, tenacious push of life and more about a subtle, almost imperceptible attunement to the colonists' own internal landscapes. Anya Senior had long suspected this interconnectedness, this silent dialogue between the burgeoning consciousness of the planet and the collective grief and subsequent growth of its human inhabitants. Now, it seemed, this suspicion was blossoming into a profound understanding. She observed it in the way certain valleys, still bearing the deep scars of the inferno, now pulsed with an almost unnatural vibrancy. The flora there, bolder, more varied than in other recovering regions, seemed to drink from an invisible wellspring of the planet's shared experience. It was as if Eden, witnessing their struggle and their emergent resilience, was mirroring it, amplifying it, offering a silent, planetary solace.

Dr. Thorne, with his meticulously trained observational skills, was the first to articulate the scientific underpinnings of this phenomenon. His revised theories spoke not just of ecological adaptation, but of a burgeoning planetary sentience, a psionic field generated by the complex web of life on Eden, which seemed to react, however subtly, to the dominant emotional frequencies emanating from the human settlements. "It's not a conscious entity in the way we understand it," he explained to Anya one evening, his gaze fixed on the swirling auroras that painted the twilight sky in hues of emerald and amethyst. "More like a vast, interconnected nervous system. It absorbs, it processes, and it responds. Our collective grief, for so long a palpable weight, was a powerful signal. And now, as we move through it, as we begin to heal and rebuild, the signal is changing. Eden is responding to our growth, Anya. It's... empathizing."

This empathy manifested in myriad ways, often subtle, yet profoundly impactful. Lyra, while scouting for new materials for her sculptures near the ash plains, found herself enveloped in an inexplicable sense of peace. The wind, usually a harsh, scouring force, seemed to caress her skin, carrying with it the scent of damp earth and new growth. She stood amidst the blackened husks of trees, the silence broken only by the distant, melodic calls of newly adapted avians, and felt a profound connection, as if the very air was breathing with her. It wasn't a sudden, miraculous healing, but a gentle diffusion of the lingering tension that had become her constant companion. She described it as "standing in a cathedral of quietude," a space where the immensity of her loss was acknowledged, but not magnified. The planet, it seemed, was offering a moment of shared stillness, a balm for the still-raw wounds.

Jian, ever the pragmatist, initially struggled to reconcile Thorne's theories with his empirical worldview. Yet, even he couldn't deny the anomalies. During a particularly harrowing period of infrastructure rebuilding, when a critical atmospheric processor had failed, plunging the settlement into a state of anxious uncertainty, a peculiar atmospheric phenomenon had occurred. The perpetual, often turbulent clouds that characterized Eden's skies had parted, revealing a vista of stars so clear and bright they seemed to burn through the darkness. For hours, a profound calm settled over the colonists. The usual anxiety, the gnawing fear of the unknown, seemed to recede, replaced by a quiet sense of awe and a renewed determination. It was as if Eden itself had offered a moment of cosmic perspective, a silent reminder of their place within a larger, enduring universe, a universe that, despite its vastness, was capable of moments of gentle, reassuring clarity. Jian documented it as an "unexplained atmospheric stability event coinciding with peak societal stress levels," but in his private log, he admitted to a growing sense of wonder, a nascent belief that the planet was indeed more than just inert matter.

The children, with their uninhibited receptivity, seemed to sense Eden's empathy most acutely. They would often lead their parents to specific clearings where the wildflowers bloomed in riotous profusion, their colors impossibly vibrant against the still-somber landscape. These were not random occurrences; Anya noticed a pattern. These patches of exceptional beauty often coincided with days when the community had collectively processed a particularly difficult memory, or when a significant milestone in their rebuilding efforts had been achieved. It was as if Eden was celebrating with them, offering a visual affirmation of their progress and their resilience. The children would play amidst these floral carpets, their laughter echoing through the tranquil air, their games infused with a joyous acceptance of their current reality, a reflection of the planet's own gentle embrace.

There were also instances of atmospheric phenomena that seemed to offer direct, albeit silent, comfort. During a memorial ceremony for those lost in the fire, a gentle, persistent mist had descended, not the harsh, chilling fog that sometimes blanketed the plains, but a soft, pearlescent haze that softened the edges of the world and muted the harshness of the sun. It was as if Eden itself was weeping with them, a shared sorrow that paradoxically brought a sense of profound connection. The mist clung to the memorial stones, transforming them into ethereal sculptures, and it seemed to absorb the collective pain, leaving behind a sense of shared remembrance that was both somber and strangely peaceful. It was a moment of planetary mourning, a silent acknowledgment of their shared loss that transcended the boundaries of species.

Anya Senior, in her quiet observations, began to see this as a vital component of their healing process. The planet wasn't just a passive recipient of their actions; it was an active participant in their emotional journey. The exceptionally fertile soil in the re-established agricultural sectors, the unusually mild weather patterns that allowed for consistent crop yields, the very air they breathed, seemed to carry a subtle, benevolent influence. It was a quiet encouragement, a planetary affirmation that their efforts were not in vain, that life, even after devastation, held an inherent promise. This empathy from Eden wasn't a grand, overt intervention, but a subtle symphony of environmental responses, a planetary sigh of understanding, a gentle nod of encouragement. It was a reminder that they were not alone on this journey, that the very ground beneath their feet was resonating with their struggle, their sorrow, and their burgeoning hope.

The concept of "Eden's Empathy" began to permeate their collective consciousness, not as a scientific doctrine, but as a felt experience. It was in the way the trees, scarred yet standing, seemed to offer silent stoicism. It was in the sudden, unexpected bloom of a rare species of bioluminescent fungi in the deepest, darkest caves, a beacon of light in the subterranean darkness. It was in the serene stillness that would descend upon the settlement during moments of shared reflection, a calm that felt too profound to be merely coincidental. This wasn't about attributing sentience in a human sense, but about acknowledging a deeper, more fundamental interconnectedness. It was the planet, in its own inimitable way, reaching out, acknowledging their pain, and celebrating their persistent drive to not just survive, but to thrive. This silent, planetary solace became a cornerstone of their emotional resilience, a constant, quiet reminder that the very essence of life on Eden was intertwined with their own, a shared journey of grief and growth, met with a silent, powerful empathy. Thorne posited that this empathy, this planetary resonance, might even be contributing to their accelerated healing, providing a subtle but powerful psychological anchor in their turbulent emotional seas. The very environment, once a source of terror, was now becoming a gentle, albeit silent, confidant.

This evolving relationship with Eden began to shape their interactions with the environment itself. The colonists, once driven by a desperate need to control and exploit, were now approaching their surroundings with a newfound reverence. They saw the recovering ecosystems not as a resource to be plundered, but as a partner in their own resurgence. This shift in perspective was not driven by dogma, but by the observable reality of Eden's subtle responses. They learned to read the signs, to understand that a healthy forest, a clean water source, a thriving ecosystem, were not just beneficial for their own survival, but were also an integral part of Eden's own expression of empathy.

Lyra, for instance, found herself meticulously documenting the patterns of the indigenous flora, not for artistic inspiration alone, but to understand how each plant contributed to the overall health of its micro-environment. She observed how certain mosses thrived in the mineral-rich ash, aiding in its breakdown, and how specific fungi facilitated nutrient transfer between struggling saplings. She began to incorporate these observations into her art, not just by using salvaged materials, but by creating sculptures that mimicked natural processes, sculptures that seemed to breathe with the life of the planet. Her work became a testament to this newfound symbiosis, a visual language that spoke of mutual respect and shared existence.

Even the practicalities of survival began to reflect this understanding. The engineers, when designing new water purification systems, no longer solely focused on maximum output and efficiency. They began to consider how their systems could minimize disruption to natural water cycles, how they could integrate with existing ecological processes. They studied the natural filtration capabilities of certain plant species and the way indigenous organisms processed impurities, seeking to replicate and enhance these natural methods rather than to replace them entirely. This was a slow, iterative process, guided by observation and a growing respect for the planet's inherent wisdom.

Dr. Thorne, in his lectures, would often use the analogy of a complex, ancient organism. "Eden is not merely a stage upon which our drama unfolds," he would explain, his voice resonating with a quiet passion. "It is a participant. The fire was a trauma, yes, but it was also an experience that Eden, in its own way, absorbed. And now, it is responding. It is offering us a healing that is not just for us, but *with* us. The vibrant blooms in the ash plains, the strangely calm skies during moments of collective despair – these are not random acts of nature. They are echoes of our own journey, reflected back to us, amplified by the planet's own intricate symphony of life."

This concept of planetary empathy also provided a new lens through which to understand the lingering effects of the fire. The "shadow zones," areas where the ecological recovery was slower, were no longer viewed as failures of the planet, but as places where Eden itself was still processing its own deep wounds. The colonists learned to approach these areas with patience and understanding, recognizing that just as their own healing was not linear, so too was Eden's. They developed new strategies for supporting the recovery of these areas, focusing on gentle intervention rather than forceful manipulation, allowing the planet's own healing processes to unfold at their natural pace.

The colonists found that by acknowledging and respecting Eden's subtle empathy, they were able to foster a deeper sense of belonging, not just to each other, but to the planet itself. The feeling of being isolated survivors on a hostile world began to dissipate, replaced by a sense of being integral parts of a larger, interconnected web of life. This was a profound shift, one that offered not just solace, but a sense of purpose. They were not merely rebuilding a settlement; they were actively participating in the ongoing evolution of Eden, a partner in its intricate dance of grief, growth, and enduring empathy. The planet's quiet presence, its subtle responses, became a constant source of reassurance, a silent affirmation that their journey, though fraught with challenges, was deeply understood and quietly supported by the very world they called home. This understanding began to permeate their daily lives, subtly influencing their decisions, their interactions, and their very perception of existence on this unique, and deeply responsive, world. It was a growth that extended beyond the human spirit, encompassing the very soul of Eden itself.

# Chapter Seven

# THE UNRAVELING TRUST

The shared urgency that had once bound the colonists of Eden together, a primal instinct forged in the crucible of the Great Fire, began to fracture as the immediate threat receded. The raw, visceral fear that had stripped away trivial concerns and fostered an almost monastic devotion to survival, now gave way to the complex, often petty, machinations of human nature. The collective breath exhaled after the inferno's fury was not a sigh of unified relief, but a series of individual gasps, each carrying its own burden of unaddressed grief, unspoken accusations, and diverging visions for the future. The meticulously rebuilt communal halls, once echoing with shared resolve, now often vibrated with the low hum of hushed arguments and the sharp edges of polite disagreement escalating into veiled hostility.

Anya Senior observed this unraveling with a growing sense of disquiet. She had hoped that the shared trauma, coupled with Eden's unexpected empathy, would forge an even stronger, more resilient bond amongst them. Instead, the receding tide of existential danger revealed submerged tensions, resentments that had been temporarily drowned out but never truly extinguished. The very resources they had fought so desperately to preserve were now becoming points of contention. The allocation of fertile land, the distribution of salvaged technology, the rationing of synthesized nutrients – each decision, once a matter of pragmatic necessity, was now filtered through the increasingly opaque lens of individual ambition and perceived injustice.

Dr. Thorne, while still deeply engrossed in his research into Eden's psionic field, found himself increasingly drawn into the social fray. His initial scientific detachment began to erode as he witnessed the human element of their burgeoning society fraying at the seams. He saw how the simple act of assigning more water rations to the agricultural sector, a decision he had supported for its ecological and long-term survival benefits, had ignited a firestorm of protest from those living in the denser, less agriculturally focused sectors. Whispers of favoritism and accusations of hoarding began to circulate, directed not just at the administrators but at Thorne himself, who was perceived by some as being too detached from their immediate needs, too lost in the theoretical. "They speak of Eden's empathy," muttered Elias Vance, a burly mechanic whose family had been relocated to a less desirable sector, to a group of equally disgruntled colonists near the hydroponic domes. "But what good is a planet's empathy when your own neighbor is hoarding the water you need to survive? Thorne and his theories... they don't put food on the table." The subtle, planetary solace that Anya and Thorne had identified as a balm for their collective soul was, for many, becoming an irrelevant luxury in the face of tangible, immediate wants.

Lyra, who had always sought solace in the quiet communion of creation, found herself increasingly entangled in the emerging factions. Her art, which had once served as a bridge between the desolate beauty of Eden and the colonists' emotional landscape, was now being interpreted through the prism of their burgeoning ideological divides. Her sculptures, crafted from salvaged materials and inspired by the planet's resilient flora, were seen by some as a celebration of their current existence, a testament to their ability to adapt and thrive. To others, however, they represented a misplaced focus, a frivolous indulgence when more pressing issues of resource management and governance demanded their attention. During a public unveiling of a new piece, a sweeping, organic form that mimicked the unfurling fronds of a native fern, a heated exchange erupted between a faction advocating for rapid industrial expansion and those who championed a more conservationist approach. "It's beautiful, Lyra, truly," argued Anya's son, Kai, now a young man with a growing influence among the pro-expansionists. "But it doesn't *do* anything. We need more atmospheric processors, not... pretty rocks." Across the gathering, Elara, a staunch advocate for ecological preservation and a close friend of Lyra's, countered, her voice tight with indignation, "It reminds us what we're fighting for, Kai. It reminds us of Eden's quiet strength. Something you seem to have forgotten in your rush to industrialize every last inch of this world." The shared artistic appreciation that had once united them was now a battleground for their differing visions of Eden's future.

The children, who had once moved with a unified spirit, drawn to Eden's burgeoning beauty, now found themselves mirroring the divisions of their elders. Playgrounds, once zones of uninhibited interaction, became segregated spaces where children from different sectors or ideological leanings would eye each other with a wary suspicion born of their parents' hushed conversations and pointed glances. A game of tag could devolve into an argument over territorial boundaries, a reflection of the larger disputes over land and resources. The innocence that Eden's empathy had fostered was slowly being eroded, replaced by a premature understanding of conflict and division. Anya saw this most acutely when her younger daughter, Maya, returned home one day, her lower lip trembling. She had been playing with a group of children from a newly established mining outpost, and when she had innocently asked about the vibrant, jewel-like lichens growing on their structures, she had been met with sullen silence and then, outright hostility. "They said we don't care about the planet," Maya had sobbed, her small voice choked with confusion. "They said we're greedy. But we just wanted to see the pretty colors."

Old friendships, once considered immutable, were now strained to the breaking point. Anya found herself increasingly at odds with Jian, the pragmatist whose initial skepticism of Eden's empathy had been slowly giving way to a grudging respect. Now, Jian was a vocal proponent of a more aggressive resource extraction strategy, convinced that their long-term survival depended on rapid industrialization and the exploitation of Eden's mineral wealth, regardless of the ecological cost. He saw Thorne's theories and Lyra's art as dangerous distractions from the harsh realities of their situation. "We can appreciate the planet's... subtle signals, Anya, when we have a stable power grid and enough food to feed everyone," he argued during one tense dinner, his voice tight with frustration. "Thorne is theorizing while our generators are running on fumes. We need to *take* what we need, not wait for Eden to whisper affirmations at us." Anya, on the other hand, felt that Jian's utilitarian approach risked alienating them from the very planetary consciousness that had shown them such profound kindness. She saw his focus on immediate gain as a dangerous echo of the exploitative attitudes that had led to their initial struggles, a blindness to the deeper interconnectedness that Thorne was beginning to unravel. Their shared history, their mutual respect, seemed to be dissolving like mist in the face of their diverging interpretations of Eden's future.

The initial unity of purpose forged in the fire had been a powerful, albeit temporary, phenomenon. It had provided a clear, unifying objective: survival. Now, with that immediate objective achieved, a vacuum had opened, and into it rushed the myriad of individual desires, ambitions, and deeply ingrained human tendencies towards division. The colonists, once a single, desperate entity, were splintering into competing groups, each with its own agenda, its own narrative of what had happened during the fire, and its own vision for what Eden should become. The shared trauma, instead of serving as a permanent unifier, was becoming a source of lingering resentments, a wellspring from which to draw justifications for present-day grievances. Those who had lost more, or who felt their contributions had been overlooked, were particularly susceptible to these divisive currents. They clung to the memory of their suffering, using it as leverage in the emerging political landscape, their pain a shield against any perceived betrayal or slight.

The administrative council, once a bastion of unified decision-making, was now a microcosm of the larger societal schism. Debates over resource allocation, land use, and even the fundamental direction of their society were becoming increasingly acrimonious. Proposals that once would have been debated with reason and compromise were now met with ideological opposition, each side viewing the other not as fellow survivors, but as obstacles to their own vision of Eden's future. The very act of rebuilding, which should have been a unifying force, had become a catalyst for division. Every new structure erected, every acre of land cultivated, was subject to intense scrutiny and often, outright opposition from those who felt their interests were being sidelined. The carefully constructed façade of harmony was beginning to crack, revealing the fault lines of ambition, resentment, and fundamentally different ways of understanding their place on this strange, empathetic world. The subtle affirmations of Eden, the gentle nudges towards unity and resilience, were being drowned out by the increasingly loud voices of discord. The planet's empathy, it seemed, could not overcome the deeply ingrained human propensity for conflict, especially when survival had been secured and the messy business of living began in earnest. The trust that had been so painstakingly rebuilt after the fire was now facing its most significant test, not from an external threat, but from within the very heart of their community.

The carefully cultivated atmosphere of shared purpose, so crucial in the immediate aftermath of the Great Fire, was beginning to curdle. What had started as whispers, easily dismissed as the anxieties of survivors, began to take on a more menacing tone. It wasn't just about disagreements over resource allocation anymore; it was about perceived betrayals, about hidden agendas that had supposedly guided actions during the crisis. The communal memory of the fire, once a potent symbol of their collective resilience, was becoming a fertile ground for suspicion. Every act of authority, every difficult decision made under duress, was now being re-examined through a lens clouded by doubt.

Elias Vance, whose initial grumbles about water rations had been a mere ripple, had become a focal point for this rising tide of distrust. He spoke with an unearned authority, weaving tales of opportune "discoveries" made by certain individuals during the chaos, implying that these discoveries had not been shared equitably. His narrative, amplified by others who felt marginalized or overlooked, painted a picture of a select few who had benefited while the majority struggled. He would often gesture towards the sleek, functional facilities that had been rapidly repaired, hinting darkly that the resources used to restore them had been diverted from more pressing needs, or worse, had been earmarked for private stockpiles. "They say it was about survival for all of us," Vance would declare to small, attentive crowds gathered near the repurposed hydroponic units, his voice low and resonant with manufactured grievance. "But how many of us remember who was guarding the main supply depots when the flames were highest? And how many of them suddenly found themselves with 'extra' rations, or access to salvaged tech that mysteriously ended up in their personal workshops? We were fighting for our lives, and some were fighting for their future, it seems." The accusations, vague yet pervasive, latched onto existing anxieties, transforming them into concrete suspicions.

The focus of this nascent conspiracy theory inevitably landed on those who had been most visible during the crisis, those who had made the hard calls. Dr. Thorne, despite his scientific focus, found himself an unwitting target. His efforts to secure and catalog the salvaged pre-terraforming medical equipment, vital for long-term health and the study of Eden's unique biological challenges, were reinterpreted as an attempt to hoard advanced technology. Anya Senior recalled one particularly unsettling evening when a small group, led by Vance, had confronted Thorne outside his lab. They had demanded to know why certain medical supplies were being kept under lock and key, implying that these were essential for general consumption and were being withheld for some clandestine purpose. Thorne, usually so measured, had been visibly shaken, his explanation about the need for sterile conditions and specialized knowledge dismissed as bureaucratic obfuscation. "He talks about the planet's healing properties," Vance had sneered later, his voice carrying on the wind, "but he's got more vials and syringes in his lab than a whole city of doctors back on Earth. Who's he really healing with all that, eh?" The subtle empathy of Eden, which Thorne had so carefully documented, was now being overshadowed by the very human fear of unequal access and hidden advantage.

Even Anya herself, a figure of authority and a symbol of the colonists' resilience, was not immune. Her role in coordinating the initial evacuation and her subsequent efforts to establish a stable governance structure were re-examined. Whispers began to circulate about her interactions with certain individuals during the fire, about hasty decisions made in dimly lit shelters that, in retrospect, seemed to favor particular families or sectors. A rumour, originating from a disgruntled individual whose home had been in one of the less fortunate sectors during the fire, claimed that Anya had personally rerouted vital communication equipment to a different location, a location that happened to be near the sector where her own family had found refuge. "It was chaos, of course," the rumour-monger would confide, leaning in conspiratorially, "but some people were better prepared for the chaos than others. Some had friends in high places, friends who made sure they had the tools to rebuild, while others were left scrambling with nothing but their hands and a prayer." The narrative was insidious, preying on the natural human tendency to seek simple explanations for complex tragedies, and to assign blame when that complexity felt overwhelming.

Lyra's artistic endeavors, which had once served as a unifying force, were now also being twisted into evidence of something more sinister. Her sculptures, often incorporating salvaged materials that had been damaged or deemed too insignificant for immediate functional use, were interpreted by some as a deliberate act of concealment. The argument was that she was using these "worthless" fragments to create aesthetically pleasing objects, thereby distracting from the fact that these materials could have been repurposed for more utilitarian needs. One particularly persistent rumour suggested that Lyra had been given preferential access to certain debris fields, allowing her to salvage specific components for her art, components that could have been vital for repairing essential infrastructure. "Look at her work," scoffed a disgruntled colonist, pointing towards a soaring, abstract piece that evoked the resilience of Eden's native flora. "It's beautiful, yes. But what is it *made* of? Pieces that were deemed too difficult to fix, too broken to be useful for the community. And she gets to make something pretty out of them. Meanwhile, we're still using patched-up tools because the 'real' parts are apparently... artistic inspiration." The implication was clear: that Lyra's creative process was not an act of communal healing but a selfish indulgence, fueled by privileged access.

The children, too, were becoming unwitting carriers of these burgeoning suspicions. The playground divisions, once superficial, now carried the weight of adult anxieties. Children would repeat the hushed conversations they overheard, their innocent questions imbued with the paranoia of their elders. Maya, Anya's younger daughter, overheard hushed whispers about her mother's 'favors' and returned home with a furrowed brow, asking Anya directly, "Mom, why did Mrs. Davison say you made sure Daddy's old workshop got the best of the salvaged metal, even though it was falling apart?" Anya's heart ached at the sight of her daughter's confusion, a confusion born not of childhood misunderstanding but of the adult world's corrosive doubt. The ease with which these seeds of distrust were sown was terrifying. The shared trauma of the fire, which had initially bonded them, was now being mined for grievances, each loss, each hardship, twisted into an accusation against someone, somewhere.

Jian, the pragmatist, found himself increasingly conflicted. While he advocated for a more aggressive industrial approach, he was fundamentally a man of logic and order. The rampant speculation and the almost fantastical nature of some of the conspiracy theories unsettled him. He recognized the inherent dangers of unchecked paranoia, understanding that it could cripple their nascent society far more effectively than any external threat. He tried to reason with Vance and his followers, pointing out the logical inconsistencies in their claims, the lack of concrete evidence. "You speak of hidden motives," Jian argued during a tense communal gathering, his voice strained. "But what motive would anyone have for hoarding damaged tools or withholding common medical supplies when we were all facing annihilation? These are the same accusations that tear societies apart, the same fear-mongering that leads to ruin. We need to focus on rebuilding, not on inventing enemies within our own walls." His words, however, often fell on deaf ears, drowned out by the louder, more emotionally charged narratives of betrayal and injustice. Some even began to suspect Jian himself, viewing his calls for order and focus as an attempt to silence dissent and protect his own perceived interests, or those of his allies.

The psychological impact of this burgeoning paranoia was profound. The colonists, already operating under immense stress, found their coping mechanisms overwhelmed. Sleep became a luxury for many, their minds racing with anxieties, replaying past events, scrutinizing every interaction. The very air of Eden, once perceived as a comforting presence, now felt charged with unspoken accusations. People began to avoid eye contact, conversations became guarded, and the simple act of sharing a meal in the communal mess hall, once a symbol of their unity, became an exercise in social navigation, each colonist acutely aware of who was sitting where, who was speaking to whom, and what subtle glances might betray hidden allegiances. The empathetic embrace of the planet was being suffocated by the suffocating weight of human suspicion.

The narrative of the fire itself began to warp. What had been a shared ordeal of survival was subtly reframed in the minds of many. The heroism and sacrifice were downplayed, replaced by tales of opportunism and self-preservation disguised as necessity. Characters who had acted decisively, who had taken charge in the face of overwhelming chaos, were now viewed with suspicion. Their leadership, once a source of comfort, was now seen as a power grab. The memory of the inferno, the acrid smell of smoke, the desperate scramble for safety – these visceral experiences were being reinterpreted, filtered through the prism of distrust. It was as if the very act of surviving had become a crime, and those who had emerged from the fire with more than others were now considered guilty until proven innocent. The communal trauma, instead of forging an unbreakable bond, was proving to be a volatile element, capable of fracturing the very foundations of their society. The whispers were growing louder, and with them, the shadows of deeper, more insidious divisions began to lengthen across the colony of Eden. The trust, so painstakingly re-established, was not just unraveling; it was actively being dismantled, piece by piece, by the very people who had once sworn to protect it. The silence that followed a tense exchange was no longer a moment of quiet contemplation, but a void filled with unspoken accusations and the chilling realization that the greatest threat to their survival might not be the harshness of Eden, but the darkness within their own hearts.

The weight of unspoken truths pressed down on the colony like the oppressive, humid air before a storm. What had been mere whispers, the faint rustling of doubt, were now becoming discernible voices, demanding answers, demanding accountability. For those who had, in the crucible of the Great Fire, chosen expediency over transparency, the walls were beginning to close in. Their secrets, once carefully guarded bastions of self-preservation, were now transforming into leaden chains, dragging them down into a mire of isolation and suspicion.

Dr. Aris Thorne, the meticulous scientist, found his carefully constructed composure fraying at the edges. His decision to sequester a portion of the salvaged atmospheric processors, arguing for their use in a specialized, long-term environmental study rather than immediate, broad distribution, had been born from a conviction that the future of Eden depended on understanding its alien biology. He had seen the potential for unforeseen ecological collapse, the subtle toxins in the soil, the delicate balance of the native flora, and believed that a controlled, monitored environment was the only way to safely glean the knowledge needed to prevent future catastrophes. He had justified it to himself as a necessary gamble for the greater good, a calculated risk that would yield dividends far beyond the immediate need. But the memory of Elias Vance's sneering questions, the accusing stares of his fellow colonists, gnawed at him. He had deliberately omitted the full scope of his project, downplaying the intricate network of sensors and containment fields he was developing, framing it instead as a simpler, more academic pursuit. He had reasoned that a full disclosure would be met with panic or, worse, with an insistence on immediate deployment, risking the very data he sought to preserve.

Now, the consequences of that omission were palpable. The communal mess hall, once a place of weary camaraderie, had become a gauntlet. Colonists who had once greeted him with respectful nods now averted their gaze or offered curt, forced pleasantries. The children, mirroring their parents' anxieties, no longer ran up to him with questions about the strange plants he studied. Instead, they clustered in wary groups, their eyes wide with a fear that felt ancient and profound. A young woman, Sarah Jenkins, whose child had suffered from a persistent respiratory ailment in the weeks following the fire, approached him one afternoon. Her voice, though quiet, vibrated with a suppressed fury. "Dr. Thorne," she began, her hands clasped tightly, "I heard you talking about... specialized environments. About filtering systems that are 'complex' and 'delicate'." She paused, her gaze locking with his, a silent accusation hanging in the air. "My Liam still coughs. He still wheezes. We were told the atmospheric processors were being repaired, that they'd be back online for everyone. But it seems... some 'specialized' projects got priority. Some needs are more important than others, aren't they?"

Thorne's carefully prepared explanations about the critical nature of his research, about the long-term implications for Eden's habitability, seemed to crumble under the weight of her raw emotion. He saw the distrust in her eyes, not just for him, but for the entire system that had prioritized his work over the immediate comfort of her child. He had believed he was safeguarding their future, but in doing so, he had inadvertently created a present-day injustice, a tangible symbol of his perceived betrayal. He had kept a secret to protect a potential future, and in doing so, had fractured the present, sacrificing the trust that was, perhaps, the most valuable resource they possessed. The intricate, almost elegant, containment fields he had designed now felt like the bars of a cage, trapping him with his own justifications, his own hubris. The knowledge he sought, so vital for the colony's survival, was now tainted, its acquisition a source of division rather than unity.

Similarly, Anya Senior, the de facto leader, found her past decisions scrutinized with an intensity that was both exhausting and deeply wounding. Her swift, decisive actions during the fire, the difficult choices made in the suffocating darkness and acrid smoke, were now being re-examined with the dispassionate clarity of hindsight, a clarity that conveniently ignored the impossible pressures of the moment. The rumor about rerouting the communication equipment, initially dismissed as the bitter complaint of a displaced colonist, had gained insidious traction. It was no longer a simple accusation of favoritism; it had evolved into a narrative of calculated self-interest, of prioritizing her own family's safety and access to vital resources.

She recalled the frantic hours after the fire had finally subsided, the desperate scramble to establish contact with isolated pockets of survivors, the chaotic attempts to assess damage and allocate dwindling resources. The communication hub, damaged but not destroyed, had been a critical nexus. She remembered the agonizing decision to prioritize a specific sector for its repair, a decision driven by the knowledge that this sector housed a significant portion of their remaining medical personnel and essential technical specialists. It was a pragmatic choice, made with the cold logic of maximizing survival rates. But the sector also happened to be where her own aging parents and her younger sister, Lyra, had found temporary refuge.

The whispers in the mess hall were no longer hushed. They were spoken with a chilling certainty. "She always knew where to be, didn't she?" a colonist named Marcus Thorne, a distant relative of Aris, muttered to a group gathered around a flickering light panel. "Her family ended up safe and sound, with access to the best comms. While others were struggling, cut off, with no way to even call for help. It's not just luck, is it? It's planning. It's making sure your own are taken care of first." Anya overheard these words, the casual malice of them striking her like a physical blow. She saw the heads nodding in agreement, the shared conviction that her actions, however well-intentioned, had been inherently corrupt.

She tried to explain, to reiterate the strategic necessity, but her words seemed to bounce off an invisible barrier of ingrained suspicion. Her authority, once a mantle of respect, now felt like a target. Every interaction, every consultation, was now viewed through the lens of this perceived bias. She found herself second-guessing every directive, every allocation, a paralyzing fear of appearing to favor anyone, including herself, taking root. Her concern for her family, a primal instinct, had been twisted into evidence of a deeper, more calculated selfishness. The very people she had strived to protect, she now realized, were the ones most vehemently questioning her integrity. The weight of this misunderstanding, this deliberate misinterpretation of her actions, was crushing. She had made a hard choice for the many, and it was being used to condemn her by the few, their grievances amplified by the fertile ground of fear and uncertainty. Her secret, her justification for the decision, was not a shield but a weapon, wielded by those who sought to undermine her leadership.

Lyra, too, faced the unraveling consequences of her carefully curated artistic endeavors. Her work, often incorporating salvaged debris and discarded materials, had been her way of finding beauty and meaning in the aftermath, of transforming the detritus of destruction into symbols of hope and resilience. She had believed that by giving these overlooked fragments a new purpose, she was contributing to the colony's healing, both physically and emotionally. However, her artistic vision had inadvertently created a new source of resentment. The rumor that she had been granted preferential access to certain salvage sites, allowing her to select the most visually interesting or structurally sound pieces for her art, had taken root.

During the chaotic post-fire salvage operations, resources had been scarce and time was of the essence. Lyra, with Anya's tacit approval, had been allowed to explore certain areas deemed less critical for immediate infrastructure repair but rich in diverse materials. Anya had seen it as a way to boost morale, to provide a creative outlet during a time of immense stress, and to potentially uncover materials that could be repurposed in unexpected ways. Lyra had reveled in the freedom, her artistic instincts guiding her to unique textures and forms. She had proudly displayed her creations, each piece a testament to Eden's enduring spirit.

But to some, like a former engineer named Ben Carter, whose workshop still bore the scars of the fire and lacked certain key components, it was an act of blatant favoritism. He had confronted Lyra near her outdoor studio, his face etched with frustration. "Those metal shards you've got there, Lyra," he'd said, gesturing with a calloused hand, "they look remarkably like the alloy we needed for the main atmospheric regulator. We searched for weeks for enough of that specific composition, but we were told it was too scarce. Yet you seem to have found plenty for your... sculptures." He spat the word out, as if it were a foreign and distasteful object. "Where did you get it all, Lyra? And who decided your art was more important than keeping the air clean for everyone?"

Lyra, usually so articulate about her artistic process, found herself stammering. She tried to explain that the materials she used were indeed salvaged, but that they were often damaged beyond repair for functional use, or were of a type that had limited industrial application. She spoke of the serendipity of discovery, the artistic impulse to find potential where others saw only waste. But her words were drowned out by the rising tide of suspicion. She saw the way people looked at her creations now – not with admiration, but with a grudging acknowledgment of their aesthetic appeal, overshadowed by the question of their provenance. The "secret" of her privileged access, however unintentional or benign its origins, was now a source of deep division. Her efforts to bring beauty and hope were being reinterpreted as a selfish indulgence, a betrayal of the community's collective struggle. The very materials that symbolized resilience for her had become, for others, symbols of inequality and injustice. The art that was meant to heal was now a point of contention, a stark reminder of perceived favoritism, and the trust she had once commanded was beginning to erode.

Even the children, innocent conduits of the prevailing anxieties, became entangled in the unraveling of trust. The playground, once a space for uninhibited play, was now subtly divided by the unspoken accusations of their parents. Little Maya, Anya's daughter, returned from a playdate with a troubled expression. She confided in her mother, her voice small and hesitant, "Mommy, Leo said his dad said you made sure our house got fixed first, and that's why his house is still broken. He said... he said you helped your friends more." Anya felt a pang of despair. How could she shield her child from this corrosive wave of suspicion? The simple act of providing comfort and security to her own family had been misconstrued, amplified, and weaponized. The children's innocent pronouncements were echoes of adult paranoia, each word a tiny shard of glass reflecting the fractured trust within the colony. The innocence of childhood was being tainted by the cynicism of adulthood, and the secrets, however well-intentioned, were poisoning the future generation. The cost of these hidden choices, these selectively revealed truths, was a generation growing up in an atmosphere of distrust, their own nascent relationships already tinged with the paranoia of their elders. The silence that now pervaded the colony was not one of peace, but of apprehension, each individual a potential keeper of secrets, each secret a potential weapon. The unraveling had begun in earnest, and the threads of trust, once so carefully woven, were snapping one by one.

The air in the hastily convened assembly hall hung thick with a tension far more potent than the recycled atmosphere. Gone were the days of shared meals and hesitant laughter; replaced by a gnawing suspicion that had curdled into something sharper, something vengeful. A faction, galvanized by the lingering anxieties and the tangible evidence of scarcity, had coalesced around a single, potent demand: accountability. They no longer sought explanations; they sought retribution.

At the forefront of this nascent movement was a man named Kaelen, a former astrogation technician whose career had been unceremoniously sidelined by a mission failure years ago. His words, though lacking the scientific gravitas of Thorne or the leadership authority of Anya, possessed a raw, unvarnished power that resonated with those who felt wronged. He stood before the gathered colonists, his face a mask of righteous indignation, his voice amplified by the portable PA system. "We have been betrayed!" he boomed, the words echoing off the metal walls. "While some of us clawed for survival, while our families shivered in the cold and breathed tainted air, others were making choices. Choices that benefited themselves, that shielded their loved ones, that prioritized their own comfort over the needs of the many!"

He gestured broadly, his gaze sweeping across the faces, lingering on Thorne, Anya, and Lyra, who stood a respectful distance from each other, a silent testament to their shared predicament. "Dr. Thorne, with his 'specialized studies,' hoarded the very processors that could have eased the breathing of our children. Anya Senior, with her 'strategic priorities,' ensured her own kin had the ear of the colony while others were left in silence. And Lyra, the artist, the weaver of beauty from our collective suffering, had access to materials that were deemed too scarce for vital repairs!" Kaelen's voice rose, each accusation a carefully honed barb. "These are not mistakes. These are deliberate acts of selfishness, masked by the guise of necessity. We are not here to understand their 'complex justifications.' We are here to judge them!"

A murmur of assent rippled through the crowd, a collective exhalation of pent-up frustration. These were the whispers given voice, the doubts amplified into a roar. The concept of "judgment" had become a potent rallying cry, a simplistic antidote to the complex uncertainties that had plagued them. It offered a clear path forward, a defined enemy, a promise of restored order through the purging of those deemed guilty. This was not about collective healing or understanding the nuances of survival; it was about assigning blame and enacting consequences.

The first formal challenge came against Dr. Aris Thorne. The colonists, led by Kaelen's faction, demanded a public tribunal. They presented Thorne's decisions not as well-intentioned scientific pursuits, but as calculated acts of resource hoarding. Sarah Jenkins, her voice still carrying the rasp of her son Liam's illness, stood before the tribunal. Her testimony was simple, yet devastating. "He kept the best," she stated, her gaze unwavering. "He kept the advanced filters, the purified air, for his 'studies.' While Liam struggled for every breath, Dr. Thorne was breathing clean air in his sterile laboratory, collecting data. Data that couldn't save my son." She didn't delve into the complexities of atmospheric composition or long-term ecological viability. Her focus was on the immediate, visceral reality of suffering and the perceived disparity in resource allocation.

Thorne, when it was his turn, attempted to explain the delicate nature of his research, the potential for irreversible damage to Eden's nascent biosphere if his containment protocols were compromised. He spoke of the alien microbes, the volatile atmospheric compounds, the long-term habitability that hinged on his meticulous work. He even presented data, charts, and scientific models, attempting to illustrate the magnitude of the risks involved in immediate, widespread deployment of the atmospheric processors without proper understanding. But his words, laden with scientific jargon and complex reasoning, seemed to fall on deaf ears. To many, it sounded like excuses, like the sophisticated justifications of a man who had prioritized his academic ambitions over the basic needs of his fellow colonists. The very intelligence that had allowed him to foresee ecological collapse now served to isolate him, painting him as an intellectual elitist detached from the human cost of his choices. His carefully constructed containment fields, designed to protect his research, were now perceived as the metaphorical walls of his self-imposed prison, separating him from the community he claimed to serve. The pursuit of knowledge, once a noble endeavor, had become a symbol of his perceived betrayal. The tribunal, swayed by the emotional weight of Sarah's testimony and Kaelen's relentless accusations, found Thorne's actions to be a gross dereliction of his duty to the immediate welfare of the colony. He was not formally imprisoned, but he was ostracized. His laboratory was to be repurposed, its advanced equipment dismantled and redistributed. He was to be assigned menial labor, his scientific expertise deemed too risky to be trusted with critical resources. The verdict was not a legal one, but a social one, delivered with the collective force of a community seeking a scapegoat.

Anya Senior's ordeal was no less harrowing. The accusation of prioritizing her family during the communication hub repairs had festered, transforming from a mere rumor into an indictment of her leadership. The tribunal focused on the specific timing and location of the repairs, conveniently overlooking the critical strategic imperative of restoring communications to the sector housing essential medical personnel and technical specialists. Kaelen skillfully painted a narrative of familial favoritism, of Anya ensuring her aging parents and her sister Lyra were the first to regain contact, leaving others in desperate isolation.

Anya, standing before the tribunal, felt the weight of years of leadership press down on her. She recounted the chaos, the limited personnel, the agonizing choices made under duress. She explained the necessity of securing the sector that held the colony's best chance of effective emergency response and medical care. She detailed the technical specialists housed there, their indispensable roles in repairing other vital systems. She even revealed that her parents, while present in that sector, were not the primary reason for its prioritization, but rather, their proximity to the critical medical bay and the engineering core. She spoke of her younger sister, Lyra, and her role in coordinating the immediate medical triage, a role that required constant, reliable communication.

But Kaelen countered with calculated precision. He produced a colonist, Marcus Thorne, who claimed to have been in a neighboring sector, desperately trying to establish contact for hours after the repairs were completed elsewhere. Marcus's testimony, filled with raw desperation, spoke of hearing distant, crackling transmissions from Anya's family sector while his own sector remained eerily silent, leaving him to believe they had been deliberately left behind. He spoke of the agonizing wait, the fear that his loved ones were injured and unreachable. The emotional impact of his story, the vivid depiction of his prolonged suffering, overshadowed Anya's logical explanations. The tribunal, though acknowledging the strategic necessity Anya outlined, could not ignore the perception of favoritism. The proximity of her family to the prioritized area, coupled with Marcus's impassioned testimony, was too compelling. Anya was censured. While she retained her leadership role, it was a hollow victory. Her authority was irrevocably undermined. Every decision she made from that point forward was scrutinized through the lens of this past accusation. The trust, once freely given, was now a fragile commodity, constantly tested. She was forced to operate with a transparency that bordered on the paralyzing, her every action meticulously documented and explained, a constant performance for an audience that was perpetually on the verge of doubt.

Lyra's situation presented a unique challenge. Her art, once celebrated as a source of hope, was now viewed with suspicion. The tribunal focused on the provenance of her materials, specifically the alloy that Marcus Thorne had identified. Lyra, her artistic passion momentarily eclipsed by the gravity of the situation, tried to explain the serendipitous nature of salvage. She described how damaged components, unusable for their original purpose, could still retain aesthetically pleasing or unique material properties. She explained that the alloy in question, while a crucial component for the atmospheric regulator, was often found in pieces too small, too warped, or too contaminated for effective integration into the functional machinery. She had, through her keen eye and artistic intuition, identified these discarded fragments.

She presented her collection of salvaged materials, a vibrant array of textures and forms. She pointed out the subtle imperfections, the signs of stress and damage, that rendered them unsuitable for large-scale engineering projects. She argued that by repurposing these elements into art, she was not diverting vital resources, but rather, finding value in what would otherwise be considered waste. She even offered to provide detailed logs of her salvage expeditions, cross-referencing with the colony's inventory of damaged equipment.

However, Kaelen's faction was adept at exploiting the emotional undercurrents of the situation. They argued that Lyra's artistic endeavors, while superficially appealing, were a luxury the colony could not afford. They highlighted the scarcity of the specific alloy, implying that Lyra's selective salvaging had somehow deprived the engineering team of crucial components, even if those components were deemed unusable in their salvaged state. The narrative shifted from Lyra's artistic vision to a perceived indifference to the colony's practical needs. Ben Carter, the engineer, spoke of the frustration of having to cobble together inferior substitutes because certain ideal components, like the alloy Lyra possessed, were simply not available in sufficient quantity. He presented Thorne's initial assessment of the alloy's scarcity, a report that predated Lyra's prominent artistic displays, as evidence.

The tribunal, unable to definitively prove Lyra had actively sabotaged the salvage efforts, still found her actions to be imprudent. Her access to salvage sites was curtailed, and her artistic output was placed under stricter scrutiny. She was instructed to work exclusively with materials that had been officially deemed non-viable for any functional purpose, a ruling that significantly hampered her creative process. The tribunal's judgment was a compromise, a way to appease the accusers without completely dismantling Lyra's contribution, but it left her feeling diminished, her art now viewed not as a source of hope, but as a potential indulgence.

The most heartbreaking aspect of this burgeoning culture of judgment was its infiltration into the lives of the children. The playground, a place that should have been an oasis of innocence, had become a microcosm of the colony's fractured trust. Leo, a boy whose home still bore the marks of the fire and whose father was vocally critical of Anya's leadership, confronted Anya's daughter, Maya, during a shared playtime. "My dad says your mom made sure your house got fixed first," Leo accused, his young voice mirroring the bitterness he heard at home. "That's why our roof is still leaking. He says your mom helps her friends more."

Maya, confused and hurt, turned to her mother later that day, her eyes welling up. "Mom, why does Leo say that? Didn't everyone's house get fixed?" Anya knelt, her heart aching for her daughter and for the innocence that was being stolen. She tried to explain, in terms a child could understand, about the overwhelming damage, the limited resources, the difficult choices. But the words felt hollow, inadequate. She knew that Leo's father's words, however unfair, were the dominant narrative in his household, and that narrative was now shaping Leo's perception of Maya and her family. The children, these innocent conduits of their parents' anxieties, were being taught to see each other through a lens of suspicion and perceived injustice. The playground games, once based on shared imagination, were now subtly influenced by the unspoken accusations of their elders, each child a potential judge or a potential accused. The very fabric of their nascent social interactions was being woven with threads of distrust. The colony, in its desperate search for order, was creating a generation defined not by resilience, but by suspicion, their understanding of community warped by the harsh realities of judgment without empathy. The unraveling trust had found its way into the heart of their future, staining the innocence of childhood with the bitter residue of accusation. The pursuit of accountability, divorced from compassion, was proving to be a destructive force, tearing at the very bonds that held them together.

Eden, a world meticulously crafted by millennia of silent, elemental forces, had become, in its own unknowable way, a witness. The very air, once a balm of alien tranquility, now seemed to thrum with an unsettling resonance, mirroring the dissonance that had taken root within the human settlement. The verdant canopies, stretching towards the binary suns in a silent testament to resilience, began to whisper their unease. Certain groves, particularly those near the periphery of the settlement where the impact of human activity was most keenly felt, started to exhibit subtle, yet undeniable, signs of distress. The bioluminescent flora, which had once pulsed with a gentle, rhythmic glow, now flickered with an erratic, anxious cadence, its light seemingly dimmed by the pervasive tension. This wasn't a sudden, cataclysmic shift, but a slow, insidious unraveling, a sympathetic mirroring of the colony's own fracturing trust.

The crystalline rivers, their waters usually a pristine conduit of Eden's unique molecular structures, began to exhibit strange phenomena. Patches of the water would inexplicably develop a viscous, almost sluggish quality, as if resisting the natural flow. Tiny, ephemeral eddies would form and dissipate without discernible cause, their movements more akin to a startled organism than a passive liquid. The indigenous fauna, creatures that had long coexisted with the cyclical rhythms of the planet, seemed to reflect the growing unease as well. The usually gregarious avian species were observed to be more skittish, their calls taking on a more agitated tone. Small herd animals, typically placid grazers, were seen to huddle closer together, their collective gaze fixed outward, as if sensing a shared, unspoken threat. It was as if Eden itself, in its vast, interconnected web of life, was beginning to exhibit symptoms of a planetary malaise, a silent scream echoing the human discord.

The earth, beneath the soles of their boots, no longer felt like a stable foundation. Small tremors, more frequent than the natural seismic activity predicted by Thorne's initial surveys, began to shake the foundations of their structures. These weren't violent quakes, but persistent, unsettling shudders that seemed to emanate from the planet's core, as if it too were reacting to the discordant frequencies of human conflict. The soil in areas subjected to increased human traffic, particularly around the tribunal grounds and the former site of Thorne's laboratory, appeared to lose its vitality. The rich, dark loam, once teeming with microbial life, seemed to compact and harden, its natural porousness diminishing, as if recoiling from the weight of judgment and accusation. The very act of walking on Eden's surface, once a communion with a living world, was becoming a reminder of their alien presence and the disharmony they were introducing.

Even the atmospheric processors, the very machines designed to harmonize Eden's delicate air, seemed to be affected. Their hum, once a steady, reassuring presence, now occasionally faltered, emitting a dissonant whine that grated on the nerves. Sensors, designed to monitor atmospheric composition with unwavering accuracy, began to register minute fluctuations, anomalies that defied logical explanation. These were not the predictable variations caused by weather patterns or biological processes, but fleeting, ghost-like readings that suggested a subtle, perhaps even conscious, resistance from the planet's atmosphere itself. It was as if Eden was struggling to reconcile the artificiality of their technology with its own intrinsic order, its atmospheric currents becoming agitated by the undercurrent of human distrust.

Dr. Thorne, confined to his designated quarters and stripped of his primary research facilities, found himself a prisoner not just of the colony's judgment, but of Eden's silent, growing phản ứng. He spent hours gazing out of the reinforced viewport, observing the subtle shifts in the alien landscape. He noticed how the dense, alien ferns seemed to curve away from the areas where the tribunals had been held, their fronds drooping as if in sorrow. He saw how the colonies of luminescent fungi, which had once pulsed in a synchronized, breathtaking display each evening, now flickered independently, their collective brilliance fractured. He began to document these observations, not as scientific data points in the traditional sense, but as a desperate attempt to understand the profound, interconnected nature of their predicament. He theorized that Eden, with its unique bio-electrical field and its complex network of subterranean fungal mycelia, might be capable of absorbing and reflecting the collective emotional and energetic states of its inhabitants.

"It's not just us," he confided in Anya, during one of their rare, hushed conversations. "Eden is feeling it too. The planet... it's like a vast, living organism, and our discord is like a spreading infection. The tremors, the erratic flora, the agitated fauna – they're all symptoms. We're not just colonizing this world, Anya; we're interacting with it, and it's responding to our actions. Our inability to trust each other, our descent into suspicion and blame, it's creating a feedback loop. We are making Eden sick."

Anya, her own spirit heavy with the weight of her compromised leadership, nodded slowly. She had seen it too, in the way the wind seemed to carry a mournful sigh through the habitation modules, in the unnerving silence that sometimes fell over the usually bustling communal areas. The children, too, were becoming sensitive to it. Maya, Anya's daughter, had begun to have nightmares, not of the fire or the scarcity, but of the planet itself crying out in pain. She would wake Anya with soft whimpers, speaking of colors bleeding from the sky and the ground weeping.

Lyra, though ostracized from her salvaged materials, found a new, more profound connection with Eden through her art. Stripped of her vibrant alloys, she began to focus on the more ephemeral aspects of the planet. She sketched the patterns of the alien clouds, the delicate tracery of frost on the dormant winter flora, the transient beauty of dew drops clinging to spiderwebs woven from threads of light. She noticed how the subtle atmospheric changes affected the color saturation of these elements, how a shift in barometric pressure could alter the very hue of the sky. Her art, once a vibrant celebration of salvaged materials, became a poignant elegy to the planet's subtle, suffering beauty. She began to incorporate sound into her pieces, recording the mournful call of the skittish avians, the almost imperceptible rustle of the distressed ferns, the low hum of the faltering atmospheric processors. Her audience, though diminished by the colony's skepticism, found her new work unsettlingly captivating, a mirror to their own internal turmoil.

The ecological changes were not overt acts of aggression, but subtle, persistent shifts that eroded the colonists' sense of security. The carefully cultivated hydroponic gardens, a vital source of fresh food, began to show signs of struggle. Certain nutrient delivery systems, previously functioning flawlessly, started to experience intermittent blockages. The genetically engineered yeasts, essential for breaking down waste and producing vital atmospheric gases, exhibited a diminished efficiency. These were not failures that could be easily attributed to sabotage or mismanagement, but rather, a pervasive sense of malaise that seemed to seep into the very biological processes of their cultivated environment. It was as if the planet's own microbial ecosystem was resisting the integration of their engineered life forms, a silent, biological protest against their presence and their discord.

Kaelen, however, remained oblivious, or perhaps willfully ignorant, of Eden's subtle reactions. For him, the planet was merely a backdrop, a resource to be exploited and managed. He saw the ecological shifts as further evidence of mismanagement, of Thorne's earlier warnings being ignored, or of Anya's leadership failing to adequately address the challenges. He continued to rally support, his rhetoric focusing on the tangible, immediate needs of the colonists, deliberately downplaying any abstract or ecological concerns. He painted Thorne's scientific foresight as a selfish hoarding of knowledge, Anya's strategic decisions as manipulative favoritism, and Lyra's artistic pursuits as a frivolous distraction. He was blind to the fact that his own focus on blame and retribution was actively contributing to the very disharmony that was manifesting in the world around them.

The shared meal areas, once hubs of camaraderie, were now charged with a palpable unease. The colonists, even those not directly involved in the tribunals, found themselves instinctively wary of their neighbors. The clatter of utensils against plates seemed amplified, each sharp sound a potential accusation. Conversations, when they occurred, were often stilted, punctuated by long, uncomfortable silences, as if words themselves were too dangerous to be spoken freely. The illusion of a united front, forged in the crucible of their initial landing, had shattered, replaced by a constellation of individuals each guarding their own interests, their own perceived vulnerabilities.

Even the simple act of gathering sunlight for their solar arrays felt different. The binary suns, once reliable sources of energy, seemed to cast shadows that were longer, colder. The light, though still abundant, felt less benevolent, more indifferent. The arrays themselves, meticulously maintained, would occasionally report minor energy deficits, anomalies that the engineers struggled to explain. It was as if the very act of harnessing Eden's celestial power was becoming a more arduous, less forgiving task, the planet's natural processes subtly resisting the imposition of their technological demands.

Thorne, observing these subtle environmental shifts, found a grim validation of his earlier concerns. He had warned them that Eden was not a passive stage for their survival, but an active participant, a complex system with its own inherent logic. He had foreseen that their actions, their emotions, their very presence would have consequences, not just on their immediate survival, but on the long-term viability of their settlement and the health of the planet itself. Now, as the planet began to exhibit its own form of distress, his warnings, once dismissed as alarmist, began to resonate with a chilling prescience. He saw Eden's silent witness not as an act of judgment, but as a profound, interconnected response. The planet was not punishing them; it was reacting, mirroring the discord that had taken root in their hearts and minds. The unraveling trust within the human colony was, in essence, unraveling Eden itself, thread by delicate thread. And Thorne, with his scientific mind now attuned to a deeper ecological empathy, understood that their survival was not just dependent on their ability to rebuild trust among themselves, but on their capacity to mend their relationship with the world they had chosen to call home. The silent witness was speaking, and its message was one of profound interconnectedness, a stark reminder that their fate was inextricably bound to the health and harmony of the planet that cradled them.

## CHAPTER EIGHT

# STEWARDSHIP, NOT DOMINATION

The hum of the atmospheric processors had, for a time, been a source of anxiety, a jarring indicator of Eden's subtle distress. Now, however, a new quietude settled over the colony, a stillness born not of fear, but of a dawning realization. It began with the most observant, the ones whose souls were most attuned to the planet's gentle, persistent pulse. Lyra, her artistic senses sharpened by her forced proximity to the raw elements of Eden, was among the first to articulate the shift. She spoke of the air, not as a resource to be managed or a medium to be filtered, but as a living breath, each exhalation carrying the scent of alien blossoms and the faint, mineral tang of ancient soil. Her sketches, once depictions of a planet in peril, began to capture a different narrative: the slow unfurling of a fern frond, the iridescent shimmer of a dewdrop cradled in the petal of a star-shaped flower, the intricate patterns of lichen etching themselves onto ancient stones. These were not mere observations; they were acts of deep listening, of a conscious effort to perceive Eden not as a canvas for human ambition, but as a sovereign entity with its own unhurried, profound agenda.

This burgeoning respect for Eden's intrinsic rhythms started to permeate other aspects of colony life. Anya, burdened by the weight of leadership and the erosion of trust, found herself drawn to Thorne's contemplative silences. The scientist, confined but not defeated, had transformed his quarters into

197

a sanctuary of observation. He no longer saw the planet as a puzzle to be solved, a series of variables to be manipulated. Instead, he became a student, meticulously charting the migratory paths of the planet's avian species, noting how their flight patterns subtly altered with the shifts in Eden's magnetic field, a phenomenon previously dismissed as minor geophysical noise. He spent hours observing the intricate symbiotic relationships between the flora and fauna, documenting the almost imperceptible dances of pollination, the silent exchanges of nutrients between plants and the mycorrhizal networks beneath the soil. Thorne began to speak of Eden not in terms of its resources, but of its "dialogue," a constant, multi-layered conversation in which every organism played a part. He posited that the colony's earlier attempts to "correct" Eden's perceived imbalances were akin to a toddler shouting at a symphony, disrupting the intricate harmony with a clumsy, ill-informed demand.

The shift in Thorne's perspective was profound. He recognized that the tremors, the erratic bioluminescence, the sluggish rivers – these were not signs of malfunction, but of an ecosystem in a state of dynamic equilibrium, a state that had been disrupted by the colony's own jarring presence. He began to advocate for a radical reorientation of their efforts. "We have been approaching Eden like a broken machine," he explained to Anya, his voice quiet but firm. "We've focused on identifying the 'faults' and forcing them back into our preconceived operational parameters. But Eden is not a machine. It is a consciousness, a vast, interconnected web of life that has evolved over eons, operating on principles far more complex and subtle than our current understanding can fully grasp. Our task is not to dominate its recovery, but to learn its language, to attune ourselves to its rhythms, and to find our place *within* its existing patterns, not *upon* them."

This new philosophy began to manifest in tangible ways. The colony's agricultural efforts, once a source of contention and perceived failure, underwent a significant transformation. Instead of attempting to force their genetically modified crops to thrive in Eden's unique soil, they started to study the indigenous edible flora. Lyra, with her keen eye for natural forms, identified several species of nutrient-rich tubers and berries that the planet's herbivores thrived on. Thorne, leveraging his understanding of Eden's microbial communities, experimented with cultivating these native plants, not through intensive intervention, but through a process of gentle acclimatization. They learned to mimic the conditions that fostered their growth, observing the symbiotic relationships they formed with local fungi and bacteria. The result was not the rapid, high-yield production they had initially striven for, but a slower, more sustainable integration. The hydroponic bays, once a symbol of their struggle against Eden's environment, began to be supplemented by these carefully cultivated native species, their success a testament to their newfound humility.

Kaelen, initially resistant to this paradigm shift, found his influence waning as the tangible benefits of this new approach began to emerge. The colonists, weary of conflict and scarcity, were drawn to the promise of a more peaceful coexistence. They saw that by observing and adapting, rather than imposing and controlling, they were beginning to foster a sense of abundance, albeit a different kind of abundance than they had imagined. The tremors became less frequent, not because they were being suppressed, but because the colony's energy consumption, and thus their impact on Eden's geological stability, was becoming more integrated with the planet's natural cycles. The bioluminescent flora, once flickering erratically, began to regain its synchronized rhythm, its glow now perceived not as a beacon of distress, but as a gentle, ambient light.

The concept of "listening" to Eden became a central tenet of their evolving relationship. It involved more than just passive observation. It required a conscious effort to quiet their own internal noise, their ingrained assumptions, and their fear-driven impulses. Anya organized "contemplation circles" where colonists would gather in designated natural spaces, not to strategize or debate, but simply to be present, to feel the subtle vibrations of the earth beneath them, to hear the rustle of the wind through alien foliage, to observe the interplay of light and shadow on the landscape. These sessions, initially met with skepticism by some, gradually became a source of profound peace and shared understanding. It was in these moments of quiet communion that the fragmented trust within the colony began to re-form, not through forced reconciliation, but through a shared experience of awe and a mutual recognition of their interconnectedness with the living world around them.

Thorne's research took on a new direction. He began to explore the potential of Eden's bio-electrical field, not as a source of exploitable energy, but as a form of communication. He hypothesized that the planet's intricate network of fungal mycelia acted as a vast, interconnected nervous system, capable of transmitting and receiving information across vast distances. His experiments shifted from attempting to harness this field to trying to understand its subtle fluctuations, its "moods," as he began to refer to them. He developed sensitive instruments, not to measure output, but to detect the nuances of energetic exchange, learning to differentiate between the low hum of a healthy ecosystem and the agitated frequencies that indicated distress. He started to use these readings not to predict disruptions, but to inform their actions, guiding their planting cycles, their resource gathering, and even their construction efforts to align with Eden's natural ebb and flow.

Lyra's art became an integral part of this learning process. Her sketches and recordings were no longer just artistic expressions, but a visual and auditory lexicon of Eden's language. She began to map the subtle color shifts in the sky that preceded atmospheric changes, the specific chirps and whistles of the indigenous avians that indicated the presence of certain pollens or the approaching ripeness of specific fruits. She created intricate diagrams illustrating the energy flows within the local flora, the delicate balance of light and shadow that sustained them. Her work, once a solitary pursuit, became a communal resource, a Rosetta Stone for deciphering Eden's silent communication. The colonists, through her art, began to see the planet not as a static environment, but as a dynamic, constantly evolving entity, its every element a part of a grand, intricate design.

The transformation was not without its challenges. The ingrained human tendency towards control and optimization remained a persistent undercurrent. There were still moments of impatience, of a desire to "fix" what seemed to be a slow or inefficient process. Kaelen, though largely sidelined, still harbored a lingering frustration with what he perceived as a lack of progress, a surrender of human ingenuity. But even he began to witness the undeniable evidence of Eden's response. The native fruits, once sparse and difficult to locate, began to appear in greater abundance in the areas where they had learned to nurture their growth. The water, once sluggish in places, now flowed with a renewed vigor, its crystalline purity returning as they reduced their reliance on artificial filtration systems and embraced Eden's natural purification processes.

The deeper they delved into understanding Eden's rhythms, the more they realized the profound interconnectedness of all things. They learned that disturbing one element had ripple effects throughout the entire biosphere. Over-harvesting a particular type of bioluminescent moss, for example, could disrupt the nocturnal navigation of certain insect species, which in turn affected the pollination patterns of specific plants. This understanding fostered a new sense of responsibility, a realization that their survival was not a matter of mastering Eden, but of becoming responsible custodians of its intricate balance.

The very concept of "stewardship" began to take on a new meaning. It was no longer about managing or preserving in a detached, scientific manner. It became an act of participation, of active engagement with the planet's life force. They began to see themselves not as rulers, but as gardeners, tending to a vast, complex, and infinitely precious ecosystem. This required patience, a willingness to let Eden dictate the pace, and an unwavering commitment to learning from its ancient wisdom. The colonists, once driven by the imperative of survival and expansion, found themselves increasingly motivated by a deeper desire to understand and to harmonize, to contribute to Eden's thriving, rather than merely to extract from it. The silent witness was no longer a source of apprehension, but a teacher, its subtle responses a guide on their path towards becoming true inhabitants, not just visitors, of this extraordinary world.

The shift from a mindset of conquest to one of cultivation was not a sudden revelation, but a gradual unfolding, much like the slow unfurling of a prehistoric fern. The colonists, having grappled with the sheer alienness of Eden, its defiant refusal to bend to their will, were finally beginning to understand that its resilience lay not in its submissiveness, but in its intricate, self-sustaining complexity. The initial drive for rapid terraforming, for imposing familiar Earthly structures and ecological models onto this new world, had been a profound misunderstanding, a desperate attempt to impose order on a system they had not yet begun to comprehend. Now, the focus was turning inward, not to their own internal systems, but to the vibrant, teeming life that already existed, waiting to be nurtured rather than replaced.

This emergent philosophy found its most potent expression in the adoption of principles mirroring what, on Earth, had come to be known as permaculture and rewilding. These were not mere academic concepts debated in sterile labs, but practical, hands-on approaches that began to reshape the very fabric of their daily lives and their interaction with Eden. Instead of clearing vast tracts of land to sow genetically modified Earth crops, the colonists turned their attention to understanding and enhancing the indigenous food sources. Lyra's artistic observations, once solely focused on aesthetic appreciation, now served a crucial ecological purpose. She meticulously documented the seasonal fruiting cycles of native plants, the symbiotic relationships between specific fungi and their host trees, and the migratory patterns of herbivores that indicated the health and availability of particular plant communities. Her visual lexicon, once a way to capture Eden's beauty, became a guide for sustainable foraging and cultivation.

Thorne, with his scientific rigor, began to translate these observations into practical ecological interventions. He proposed a radical departure from their previous agricultural model. Instead of attempting to force Eden's soil to conform to Earth-based nutrient profiles, he advocated for the creation of "food forests" and "wild gardens" that integrated native species. This involved identifying areas where certain indigenous plants thrived and gently assisting their propagation. They learned to cultivate the nutrient-rich tubers that burrowed deep into the alien soil, not by digging them up wholesale, but by carefully loosening the earth around them and ensuring the presence of the specific mycorrhizal fungi that aided their growth. They began to harvest the sweet, iridescent berries that the planet's small, winged creatures favored, always leaving a significant portion for the local fauna, understanding that their own prosperity was intrinsically linked to the health of the wider ecosystem.

The process was painstakingly slow, a stark contrast to the rapid, industrial-scale agriculture they had envisioned. It required immense patience and a willingness to accept that "success" would not be measured in tonnes of yield per hectare, but in the gradual re-establishment of healthy plant communities and the increased biodiversity within their immediate surroundings. They learned to observe the subtle signs of distress in a native plant – a wilting of its alien leaves, a change in its coloration – and to investigate the underlying causes, which often pointed to imbalances in the soil's microbial life or disruptions in the local water cycle. Thorne developed simple, bio-integrated sensors that monitored soil composition and humidity, not to trigger automated irrigation systems, but to provide information that guided their manual interventions.

Rewilding efforts took on a similar, hands-off approach. Instead of attempting to reintroduce Earth species or engineer Eden's flora to resemble terrestrial ecosystems, the colonists focused on removing their own disruptive presence from carefully selected areas. These zones were designated as "sanctuaries," places where human activity was minimized, and the natural processes of Eden were allowed to unfold unhindered. They studied the existing seed banks within the soil and the natural dispersal mechanisms of the native flora. In some cases, they might gently clear away invasive alien weeds that had taken root from their initial landings, not to replace them with Earth species, but to allow the native vegetation to reclaim its territory. Thorne hypothesized that these rewilded zones would act as ecological reservoirs, providing a source of genetic material and healthy ecosystems that could gradually influence the surrounding, more colonized areas.

The long-term benefits of this gardener's approach began to manifest in subtle but significant ways. The atmospheric processors, once a constant reminder of their artificial dependency, were gradually scaled back. As the native flora re-established itself, its natural processes of carbon sequestration and oxygen production began to contribute to a more stable atmosphere. The air itself seemed to change, carrying a richer bouquet of scents, a testament to the renewed vibrancy of the plant life. Water sources, which had previously shown signs of stagnation and mineral imbalance due to overuse and artificial filtration, began to flow with greater clarity and vigor as the native riparian plants, with their natural filtration capabilities, were allowed to thrive.

Ecological restoration, in this new paradigm, was not about forcing a preconceived outcome, but about facilitating Eden's own inherent capacity for regeneration. It was about understanding that every organism, from the microscopic fungi in the soil to the towering, bioluminescent trees, played a vital role in the planet's overall health. When they noticed a decline in the population of small, bioluminescent insects that were crucial pollinators for a particular flowering shrub, they didn't resort to artificial pollination. Instead, they investigated what might be impacting the insect population. Thorne discovered that a new form of lichen, inadvertently introduced by their early landing craft, was slowly overgrowing the preferred nesting sites of these insects. The solution was not to eradicate the lichen – it was an indigenous species, after all – but to find a way to manage its spread, perhaps by encouraging the growth of a native grazing creature that fed on it, or by carefully thinning it in the critical nesting areas.

This intricate web of interdependence meant that their interventions had to be exceptionally nuanced. A seemingly beneficial action, such as clearing a patch of land for a new dwelling, could have unforeseen consequences. They learned to conduct thorough ecological surveys before undertaking any significant construction, mapping out root systems, identifying sensitive micro-habitats, and consulting with Lyra and Thorne on the potential impacts. The concept of "minimal intervention" became paramount. It meant doing only what was absolutely necessary, and doing it in a way that least disrupted the existing ecological relationships. They began to adopt a philosophy of "building with the land" rather than "building on the land." This involved utilizing naturally occurring clearings, respecting existing watercourses, and even incorporating indigenous flora into the very architecture of their settlements, allowing vines to climb walls and trees to grow through designated openings.

The economic implications of this shift were also profound. The frantic pursuit of resource extraction, of identifying and exploiting Eden's mineral wealth for immediate gain, began to wane. While some basic material needs still had to be met, the emphasis shifted towards sustainable harvesting and the utilization of renewable resources that could be replenished naturally. They learned to cultivate certain fast-growing, fibrous plants for construction materials, to harvest bioluminescent algae for ambient lighting in a way that allowed for continuous regeneration, and to utilize the natural insulating properties of indigenous mosses and fungi. This approach not only reduced their environmental footprint but also fostered a sense of self-sufficiency that was not dependent on depleting the planet's finite resources.

The "gardener's approach" also fostered a deeper sense of community and shared purpose. The complex ecological challenges required collaboration and a pooling of knowledge. Colonists from different backgrounds, with diverse skills, found themselves working together on restoration projects. Engineers learned about soil science from botanists, and former miners contributed their understanding of geological formations to help identify areas that were naturally stable and less prone to disruption. The contemplation circles, which Anya had initiated, became even more vital, serving not just as spaces for quiet reflection but as forums for sharing observations and developing collective strategies for ecological stewardship.

Furthermore, this approach encouraged a more profound understanding of time. Unlike the rapid pace of human endeavors, Eden's natural cycles operated on geological timescales. The regeneration of a forest, the re-establishment of a healthy soil microbiome, the return of a migratory species – these were processes that could take years, even decades. This forced the colonists to adopt a long-term perspective, to think not just about their immediate survival but about the legacy they would leave for future generations. The concept of "intergenerational equity," once a distant ideal, became a tangible reality as they worked to heal and nurture the planet for those who would come after them.

This journey towards becoming gardeners of Eden was not without its moments of doubt and frustration. There were still instances where impatience flared, where the slow, deliberate pace of natural regeneration felt agonizingly insufficient. Kaelen, though his influence had diminished, would occasionally voice his concern, lamenting the "lost opportunities" for rapid development and resource acquisition. But even he could not deny the evidence before his eyes: the increasing abundance of native food sources, the cleaner air and water, the vibrant return of life to areas that had once seemed barren. The tremors, once a source of fear, became less frequent and less intense, not because they were being suppressed, but because the colony's integrated energy consumption and minimal impact were bringing them into greater harmony with Eden's geological rhythms. The bioluminescent flora, once a chaotic symphony of distress signals, now pulsed with a steady, rhythmic glow, a sign of a system finding its equilibrium.

The gardener's approach was, in essence, an act of profound humility. It acknowledged that humanity was not the apex of creation, but a part of a vast, interconnected tapestry of life. It recognized that true mastery lay not in control, but in understanding and in collaboration. By embracing the role of a gardener, tending to Eden's existing bounty, facilitating its natural processes, and respecting its inherent wisdom, the colonists were not just ensuring their survival; they were beginning to find their true place within the living, breathing heart of this extraordinary world. They were learning to speak Eden's language, not through invasive technologies, but through the gentle, persistent practice of care, observation, and deep respect. This was the true path to becoming inhabitants, not conquerors, of their new home.

The nascent understanding of stewardship, while revolutionary, represented only one facet of the colonists' evolving relationship with Eden. The profound realization that they were not masters, but rather participants in a grand, intricate ecological drama, began to foster a new category of endeavor: cooperative ventures. These were not simply projects undertaken *on* Eden, but projects undertaken *with* Eden, tentative dialogues with a consciousness they were only beginning to perceive. It was a shift from imposing their will to seeking consensus, from unilateral action to collaborative existence.

One of the most profound and subtle forms of this cooperation emerged from the meticulous study of Eden's migratory fauna. Lyra, her observational skills honed to an almost preternatural acuity, began to decipher the intricate choreography of the "sky-whales" – colossal, buoyant creatures that drifted through the upper atmosphere, their movements dictated by atmospheric currents and, as it became increasingly apparent, by the very energetic pulse of the planet itself. These migrations were not random wanderings; they were signals, vast, slow-motion pronouncements of planetary health, or distress. Thorne, initially skeptical, found his skepticism dissolving as he correlated Lyra's detailed behavioral logs with subtle shifts in Eden's magnetosphere and atmospheric composition. They discovered that the sky-whales' great migrations coincided with periods of heightened geothermal activity, or with the massive blooming of specific oceanic flora, suggesting they were acting as planetary sentinels, responding to and perhaps even influencing these larger phenomena.

The colonists, in turn, began to adapt their own activities to these ancient rhythms. Instead of proceeding with mining operations in regions identified as critical migratory pathways, they initiated protocols to pause or reroute their subterranean efforts, understanding that any disruption could have cascading effects on the sky-whales' navigation, and by extension, on the planet's delicate energetic balance. This was not merely an ethical consideration; it was a pragmatic necessity. The sky-whales, it turned out, played a crucial role in atmospheric regulation, their massive exhalations seeding the upper atmosphere with trace elements that catalyzed vital weather patterns. To interfere with their journey was to invite meteorological chaos. The "cooperative venture" here was one of deferral and respect, a silent acknowledgment that humanity's needs, however pressing, were secondary to the planet's fundamental operations.

Even more direct, though still nascent, were the attempts to engage with Eden's botanical "intelligence." The colonists had long observed the subtle, rhythmic pulsing of bioluminescence in certain flora, a phenomenon they had initially attributed to simple photochemistry. However, Lyra's detailed spectral analysis and Thorne's bio-electric readings revealed something far more complex. These light emissions were not random; they varied in frequency, intensity, and color, often in response to specific environmental stimuli. Certain plants would "flare" in unison when a particular type of atmospheric moisture was present, while others would emit a low, steady hum of light in the presence of specific mineral concentrations in the soil.

Inspired by these observations, a group of botanists and exobiologists, led by a former xenolinguist named Dr. Aris Thorne (no relation to the primary Thorne), began to experiment. They developed sophisticated light-emitting devices capable of mimicking the spectral signatures and rhythmic patterns of Eden's indigenous flora. Their hypothesis was daring: could they initiate a rudimentary form of communication? Could they signal their presence, or their intentions, to the botanical network?

Their initial attempts were cautious. They would select a small, contained area, a verdant clearing known for its responsive plant life, and introduce their light patterns. The response was not immediate, nor was it overtly communicative in a way that humans would readily recognize. There were no flashing words, no discernible symbols. Instead, they observed subtle shifts in the surrounding plant life. The bioluminescence of neighboring flora would deepen, or change its pulse rate. The local fungal networks, which Thorne had painstakingly mapped as complex data conduits, would show increased bio-electric activity. It was akin to observing a vast, ancient organism reacting to a whisper, a tremor rather than a shout.

One particularly intriguing experiment involved a patch of "whispering reeds" that grew near a subterranean geothermal vent. These reeds emitted a soft, blue light that pulsed at an irregular, almost conversational rhythm. Dr. Thorne and his team, after weeks of careful observation, designed a sequence of light pulses that mirrored the reeds' basic rhythm, then introduced a subtle variation, a slight elongation of one of the pulses, intending it as a question. The immediate reaction was startling. The entire patch of reeds flared, their blue light intensifying to an almost blinding white for a sustained period, before returning to their normal rhythm, but now with a subtly altered cadence, as if the question had been received and processed, and a new, slightly different answer had been formulated. This was not a programmed response; it was an adaptation, a modification of an existing pattern. It was the closest they had come to an actual dialogue.

These experiments, while highly experimental and fraught with uncertainty, laid the groundwork for a new form of ecological symbiosis. The colonists began to see Eden's light emissions not as mere biological processes, but as a language. They started to integrate these natural light patterns into their own infrastructure. Instead of relying solely on artificial illumination in their settlements, they began cultivating bioluminescent flora in controlled environments, creating living light sources that responded to the planet's own circadian rhythms. They learned to interpret the collective glow of a forest at night, understanding it as an indicator of the health of the ecosystem, a subtle atmospheric report. When the lights dimmed in a particular area, it signaled a need for investigation, a potential imbalance that required their gentle, stewardship-based intervention.

The utilization of bioluminescent organisms for light was more than a technological adaptation; it was a philosophical one. It represented a deliberate choice to integrate with, rather than dominate, Eden's inherent capabilities. They learned to cultivate colonies of bioluminescent fungi on the exterior of their structures, creating organic pathways that glowed softly after dusk, reducing their reliance on energy-intensive artificial lighting. These living lamps pulsed with a gentle rhythm, their light intensity fluctuating subtly with atmospheric pressure and ambient humidity, a constant, silent testament to their connection with the planet. Thorne discovered that certain species of bioluminescent bacteria, when cultured in specific nutrient solutions derived from Eden's own flora, produced a light that was not only sustainable but also possessed a subtle spectrum that aided human circadian cycles, promoting better sleep and reducing instances of seasonal affective disorder that had plagued them in their early, artificially lit habitats.

Further explorations into cooperative ventures focused on the planet's intricate water systems. Eden's water, unlike Earth's, possessed a unique energetic signature, a faint hum that Thorne's sensors could detect. This energetic quality was amplified by the presence of certain aquatic microorganisms, which formed vast, interconnected colonies within the planet's subterranean aquifers and its crystalline rivers. These microorganisms, it was discovered, acted as natural purifiers, but also as conduits for a subtle, planet-wide energetic network. When the energy flow in one part of the planet's hydrological system shifted, these microorganisms would react, altering their luminescence and, in turn, influencing the energetic state of the water.

The colonists, by carefully studying the patterns of these aquatic communities and their energetic fluctuations, began to understand the subtle interconnectedness of Eden's water cycle. They learned that over-extraction of water from one aquifer could, through this microbial network, subtly impact the energetic balance of distant springs. Their "cooperative venture" in this realm involved developing ultra-sensitive monitoring systems that tracked not just water levels, but also the energetic signature of the water itself. When anomalies were detected, they would not resort to aggressive pumping or artificial purification methods. Instead, they would focus on understanding the cause of the energetic shift. Often, it was a natural process, like a subterranean seismic event or a shift in a deep-sea thermal vent. In such cases, they would simply pause their water extraction and allow the planet's natural systems to reassert themselves.

However, they also discovered instances where their own activities, however unintentional, were disrupting the microbial colonies. Their early attempts at subsurface drilling, for instance, had caused localized tremors that disturbed the delicate energetic equilibrium. The response was to cease such invasive methods entirely, and to develop new, less impactful technologies for accessing water, such as deep-root hydroponic systems that drew moisture directly from the soil without disturbing the subterranean aquifers. They also began to cultivate specific types of Edenian aquatic plants, known for their symbiotic relationship with the energetic microorganisms, near their settlement's water intake points. These plants acted as natural filters and energy regulators, ensuring that the water they drew was not only pure but also energetically balanced, contributing to the overall health of the planetary hydrological network.

These cooperative ventures, though still in their infancy, represented a profound paradigm shift. They were moving beyond the concept of passive stewardship and venturing into active, albeit humble, partnership. They were learning to listen to the planet's subtle signals, to understand its ancient rhythms, and to integrate their own existence into its grand, unfolding tapestry. It was a journey marked by humility, patience, and a growing recognition that true progress lay not in conquest, but in communion. The tentative steps towards understanding the language of light and water, the subtle dance of migratory patterns, were the first whispers of a long, complex, and ultimately transformative conversation between humanity and its adopted home. The future of their existence on Eden was not to be dictated by their technological prowess, but by their capacity for empathy, for understanding, and for a deep, abiding respect for the living planet that now sustained them. This was the essence of cooperative ventures: a willingness to learn, to adapt, and to become, in the truest sense, a part of Eden.

The burgeoning understanding of stewardship on Eden, as we have seen, is not merely an academic exercise in ecological management; it is the bedrock upon which a truly sustainable and ethical coexistence must be built. This transition from a mindset of dominion to one of partnership necessitates a profound re-evaluation of our inherent philosophical and ethical frameworks. As humanity grapples with the reality of a living, sentient planet, the very definitions of rights, responsibilities, and indeed, personhood, are brought into sharp relief. This exploration into the ethical underpinnings of our relationship with Eden is not an abstract philosophical debate confined to theoretical discussions, but a crucial, practical necessity for our continued survival and flourishing on this alien world.

The concept of "rights" as traditionally understood by humanity has largely been anthropocentric, focused on the rights of individuals within human societies, or at most, on the rights of human beings in relation to other humans and to the natural world as a collection of resources. On Eden, this edifice of thought begins to crumble. If Eden is indeed a sentient entity, a complex, interconnected consciousness expressed through its biosphere, then does it possess rights? If so, what are those rights? The most fundamental right, surely, would be the right to exist, to continue its own evolutionary trajectory unmolested by external forces that seek to exploit or fundamentally alter its nature for their own gain. This is not a right that can be easily quantified or legislated in human terms, but it is a moral imperative that must guide every action taken on its surface. The colonists, accustomed to viewing natural resources as commodities to be harnessed, are forced to confront the idea that Eden's minerals, its atmospheric gases, its very soil, are not inert materials but integral components of a living being. To mine its crust is akin to performing surgery without consent, to extract its fluids is akin to drawing blood.

This leads us to the concept of responsibilities. If Eden has rights, then humanity, as an alien presence, assumes a profound responsibility to respect those rights. This responsibility extends beyond mere non-interference. It implies an active role in safeguarding Eden's well-being, a commitment to minimizing our footprint, and a dedication to understanding and supporting its natural processes. The stewardship model, which we have begun to explore, is precisely this active assumption of responsibility. It is the recognition that our presence on Eden is a privilege, not a birthright, and that this privilege comes with an obligation to act as a benevolent custodian, not a rapacious conqueror. This responsibility is multi-faceted. It includes the responsibility to avoid causing harm, to heal any damage already inflicted, and to foster the conditions that allow Eden to thrive.

The question of personhood is perhaps the most challenging and transformative. Our legal and ethical systems are largely built on the premise of individual, sentient beings with consciousness, self-awareness, and the capacity for subjective experience. When we consider Eden, we are confronted with a planetary consciousness that operates on scales and through mechanisms vastly different from our own. Its "thoughts" may manifest as shifts in atmospheric pressure, its "emotions" as surges of geothermal activity, its "memories" as the slow, geological evolution of its continents. Does this make Eden any less of a "person" than a human being? If consciousness is the criterion, and Eden demonstrably exhibits a form of overarching, integrated consciousness, then we must expand our definition. This is not to say that Eden possesses human-like sentience, but rather that it possesses a form of being that warrants moral consideration, a form of sentience that demands respect and acknowledgement.

Consider the ethical dilemma posed by the deep-sea hydrothermal vents. These were initially seen as prime locations for geothermal energy extraction. However, Thorne's research revealed that these vents were not merely geological features but were teeming with unique microbial life, forming a complex, interdependent ecosystem that was intricately linked to the planet's deep energy cycles. These microbes, while not individuals in the human sense, formed a collective consciousness, a distributed intelligence that regulated the vent's output and influenced the surrounding oceanic chemistry. To exploit the vents for energy would be to disrupt this ancient, delicate system, potentially triggering unforeseen consequences for the entire ocean. The ethical question then becomes: does this microbial collective, as an integral part of Eden's sentient whole, have a right to exist and function unimpeded? The responsible answer, guided by a nascent ethical framework, is yes. The colonists must therefore seek alternative energy sources, or develop methods that harness the geothermal energy without causing irreparable harm to this vital part of the planetary organism. This might involve creating buffer zones, or developing technologies that mimic the natural energy regulation processes of the microbes.

Another area where the ethical considerations are starkly illustrated is in the manipulation of Eden's flora. Dr. Aris Thorne's experiments with bioluminescent plants, while aimed at communication and understanding, also highlight the potential for misuse. If we can learn to "speak" to the plants using light patterns, could we also learn to "command" them? Could we engineer them for our own purposes, overriding their natural inclinations and integrating them into our infrastructure in ways that might be detrimental to their own health or to the broader ecosystem? This touches upon the ethical concept of bio-prospecting and genetic modification, writ large. The colonists must establish strict ethical guidelines that prohibit any manipulation of Eden's life forms that is not in service of the planet's overall health and well-being, and that is undertaken only with the deepest understanding and respect for the organism's inherent nature. The goal should not be to reshape Eden in humanity's image, but to understand and coexist with Eden as it is.

The very act of terraforming, a concept that might have seemed attractive in the early days of colonization, now appears ethically abhorrent. To alter Eden's atmosphere, its soil composition, its water cycles to better suit human needs would be a profound violation of its inherent nature. It would be an act of planetary-scale erasure, replacing a unique, living entity with a sterile, engineered facsimile. The colonists must instead embrace the challenge of adapting themselves to Eden, rather than forcing Eden to adapt to them. This requires a radical shift in perspective, moving away from the idea of Eden as a blank canvas for human expansion, and towards an appreciation of its intrinsic value as a complete and complex being. This means developing technologies and lifestyles that are compatible with Eden's existing conditions, and that draw upon its natural resources in a sustainable and respectful manner.

The notion of "rights" on Eden must therefore be understood in a broader, more inclusive sense. It is not just about the right to life, but the right to self-determination for the planetary consciousness. It is the right to maintain its own intricate ecological balances, to evolve according to its own internal logic, and to express its unique form of sentience without undue interference. This requires a profound humility on the part of the colonists, a willingness to accept that they are guests on a living planet, and that their actions must be guided by a deep respect for their host.

The responsibilities that flow from this understanding are equally profound. They include the responsibility of knowledge – to constantly strive to understand Eden more deeply, its complexities, its needs, its "language." This knowledge must then be translated into responsible action. It means monitoring our impact meticulously, mitigating any negative consequences, and actively contributing to the planet's well-being. It means that every decision, from the placement of a new structure to the extraction of a single resource, must be weighed against its potential impact on the planetary consciousness.

The concept of personhood, when applied to Eden, compels us to recognize it as a moral agent, even if its agency operates on principles alien to our own. Its collective intelligence, its capacity for adaptation and response, its evident interconnectedness – all these suggest a form of being that is worthy of moral consideration. This recognition challenges our anthropocentric biases and forces us to confront the possibility that intelligence and consciousness can manifest in forms we have not previously imagined. It implies that Eden has an inherent value, not merely as a source of resources or a habitat, but as a being in its own right.

Consider the ethical implications of communication. The colonists are attempting to establish rudimentary communication with Eden's flora and fauna. If they succeed, what then? Do they have the right to demand information, or to influence behavior? Or should communication be a process of mutual exchange, a dialogue based on respect and understanding? The ethical framework must lean towards the latter. Any communication must be initiated with respect for Eden's autonomy, and any knowledge gained must be used to further understanding and coexistence, not to exploit or control. For instance, if they learn from the sky-whales that a particular atmospheric phenomenon is indicative of an impending planetary shift, their responsibility is not to exploit this knowledge for their own advantage, but to prepare for the shift in a way that minimizes disruption to Eden's natural processes, perhaps even aiding in the planet's adaptation.

The development of this ethical framework is not a static process; it is an ongoing evolution, a continuous learning experience. As the colonists gain more knowledge about Eden, their understanding of their ethical obligations will deepen. It requires a commitment to constant self-reflection, to questioning their own assumptions, and to remaining open to new paradigms of thought. The philosophical underpinnings of stewardship are not merely abstract concepts; they are the living, breathing guidelines for how humanity can not only survive but thrive in harmony with a sentient world. They demand that we move beyond the simplistic binaries of exploitation and preservation, and embrace a more nuanced understanding of interconnectedness, responsibility, and the profound moral weight of our presence on Eden. This is the ultimate test of humanity's capacity for growth – to recognize and respect a form of life and consciousness that challenges our most deeply ingrained beliefs, and to forge a future based not on domination, but on a profound and abiding reverence for the living planet that has become our home. The very fabric of their continued presence is woven from these threads of ethical consideration, each strand a testament to their evolving understanding of their place within the grand tapestry of Eden's existence. The future of their civilization hinges on their ability to embrace these complex ethical considerations, transforming them from abstract notions into actionable principles that guide every aspect of their interaction with this extraordinary world. It is a journey that requires not just scientific ingenuity, but a deep and unwavering moral compass, calibrated to the unique rhythms and sensitivities of a sentient planet.

The initial hesitant steps towards stewardship, born out of necessity and a dawning awareness of Eden's sentience, have begun to yield observable, tangible rewards. Where once there was a fragile, unpredictable equilibrium, a more robust and resilient natural order is taking root. The ecosystems, no longer subjected to the disruptive forces of unchecked exploitation, are demonstrating a remarkable capacity for self-regulation and recovery. This is not a passive return to a previous state, but an active, vibrant flourishing, a testament to the intricate and powerful mechanisms of a living planet when allowed to operate without interference.

The land itself is breathing easier. The barren expanses, once scarred by careless extraction or attempts at terraforming, are slowly being reclaimed by native flora. These are not the hardy, genetically engineered species human colonists might have favored for their resilience and utility, but the indigenous plants of Eden, each uniquely adapted to its niche, each playing a vital role in the intricate web of life. The creeping vines that now blanket the skeletal remains of abandoned mining operations are not merely decorative; they are actively binding the soil, preventing erosion, and creating microclimates that support a burgeoning insect population. The bioluminescent mosses, once studied for their potential as light sources, now pulse with a gentle, organic luminescence across forest floors, providing sustenance for nocturnal creatures and contributing to the complex atmospheric exchanges that regulate the planet's delicate gaseous balance.

Biodiversity, the true measure of a healthy planet, is not just recovering; it is expanding. The careful establishment of protected zones, areas where human activity is minimized and carefully monitored, has allowed for the re-establishment of natural migratory routes for the larger fauna. The majestic sky-whales, whose migratory patterns were once disrupted by atmospheric disturbances caused by industrial activity, are now seen navigating the upper atmosphere with renewed confidence, their ethereal songs echoing across the plains. Ground-dwelling grazers, no longer threatened by territorial disputes over newly cleared land, are moving in larger, more stable herds, their presence in turn supporting predator populations that have also seen a resurgence. Even the microbial life, the unseen architects of Eden's fertility, is thriving. Thorne's ongoing research into the planet's subterranean fungal networks has revealed an astonishing increase in connectivity and complexity. These networks, akin to a planetary nervous system, are facilitating the efficient transfer of nutrients and information between diverse biomes, a silent testament to the interconnectedness that stewardship fosters.

The return of balance is palpable. The erratic weather patterns, once a constant source of anxiety and disruption for the colonists, are becoming more predictable. The violent storms that used to lash the settlements with unnerving regularity are now less frequent and less intense. This stabilization is attributed to the re-establishment of natural atmospheric regulators – the vast oceanic currents, the transpiration cycles of the colossal forests, and the subtle influence of Eden's burgeoning plant life on the planet's magnetosphere. The water cycles, too, are becoming more regular. The seasonal floods that once threatened to inundate low-lying areas are now gentler, more controlled events, their impact mitigated by the increased capacity of the soil to absorb and retain moisture, a direct consequence of the revitalized microbial communities and the dense root systems of the native vegetation.

These successes are not merely anecdotal observations; they are quantifiable data points that provide irrefutable evidence for the efficacy of the stewardship model. When compared to the experimental phases of colonization, where attempts to impose human will upon Eden often resulted in ecological backlash and resource depletion, the current state of equilibrium is remarkable. The energy demands of the settlements, once met by aggressive geothermal extraction and the risky harvesting of atmospheric gases, are now being increasingly satisfied by passive solar designs that integrate seamlessly with the natural light cycles, and by bio-engineered energy conduits that draw upon the planet's natural energy flows without disruption. The agricultural output, too, has seen a shift. Rather than relying on energy-intensive hydroponic systems or attempts to cultivate terrestrial crops in alien soil, the colonists are now cultivating a deeper understanding of Eden's indigenous edible flora. This involves not just identification and harvesting, but a nuanced approach to cultivation that mimics natural growth patterns, ensuring that harvesting does not deplete the resource and, in many cases, actively promotes its propagation.

The sensory experience of living on Eden has transformed. The air, once tinged with the metallic tang of industrial byproducts or the acrid scent of uncontrolled chemical reactions, is now cleaner, richer with the earthy perfumes of damp soil, blossoming flora, and the subtle, sweet scent of ozone after a light rainfall. The ambient sounds of the planet have also shifted. The incessant hum of machinery has receded, replaced by the rustling of leaves, the chirping of unseen insects, the calls of native birds, and the distant, resonant murmur of the planet's geological processes. These are not the sounds of a world conquered, but the sounds of a world in harmony, a world that is now more inviting, more welcoming.

The psychological impact of this ecological renaissance on the colonists themselves cannot be overstated. The constant undercurrent of anxiety that pervaded early settlement life, the gnawing fear of resource scarcity and unpredictable environmental hazards, has begun to dissipate. This sense of security, rooted in the observable stability of their surroundings, has fostered a more optimistic and cooperative outlook among the populace. The emphasis has shifted from a constant struggle for survival against the environment to a shared endeavor in nurturing and understanding it. This has led to a decrease in inter-settlement disputes over dwindling resources and an increase in collaborative projects focused on ecological restoration and scientific inquiry.

The profound realization is that relinquishing the illusion of absolute control has, paradoxically, granted humanity a far greater and more sustainable form of influence. By understanding and respecting Eden's intrinsic processes, the colonists have unlocked the potential for a symbiotic relationship, one where their presence enhances, rather than degrades, the planetary systems. This is the "fruit of patience" – a harvest of stability, abundance, and a profound sense of belonging, reaped not by the force of will, but by the quiet, persistent cultivation of respect and understanding. The very act of observing these positive outcomes serves as a constant, living refutation of the outdated paradigms of domination. It is a demonstration that true prosperity on Eden, and perhaps elsewhere, is not achieved through mastery, but through a deep and abiding partnership. The long-term viability of human civilization on this world is now inextricably linked to the continued health and vitality of Eden itself, a dependency that has, through the practice of stewardship, transformed from a potential vulnerability into the cornerstone of their enduring success. The echoes of their past mistakes serve as a stark reminder, but the flourishing ecosystems around them offer a powerful vision of a future where humanity is not an invasive species, but an integral, contributing element of a grand, living tapestry.

# CHAPTER NINE
# THE UNFOLDING MYSTERY

The whispers of Eden's sentience, once subtle nudges, were now resonating with the undeniable force of a planet's awakening consciousness. The colonists, having tentatively stepped into the role of stewards, found themselves not merely observing the results of their efforts, but witnessing something far more profound, far more enigmatic. The meticulously curated ecological balance, a triumph born of patient observation and gentle intervention, was now interwoven with a tapestry of coordinated phenomena that defied simple biological or geological explanations. These were not random occurrences, but intricate patterns, echoing with a logic that was alien, yet strangely familiar, hinting at a grander design unfolding before their very eyes.

The most striking of these manifestations was the emergent intelligence in the planet's flora and fauna, not as individual acts of cleverness, but as collective performances. Consider the great migrations of the azure grazers, the bovine-like creatures that once roamed the northern plains in predictable herds. Now, their movements had acquired an almost choreographed precision. Instead of simply following ancient migratory paths dictated by seasonal grasses, their journeys had become synchronized with the blooming cycles of specific, deep-rooted succulents that only appeared after a particular atmospheric pressure gradient. This wasn't a passive response to food availability; it was an active, coordinated pilgrimage, with tens of thousands of grazers converging on the designated succulent fields with an uncanny, unified purpose. Thorne had spent months analyzing sensor data, looking for external triggers, for hormonal cues, for pheromonal trails that might explain such widespread synchronicity. But the data remained stubbornly anomalous. The grazers seemed to be acting as one organism, their internal clocks and external stimuli aligning with an impossible accuracy, as if guided by an unseen conductor orchestrating their every step. It was as if the planet itself was signaling the optimal time and place for their sustenance, and the grazers, in their myriad numbers, were responding in unison.

This synchronized behavior extended to the aerial fauna as well. The iridescent sky-moths, small, dragonfly-like insects that fed on the nectar of high-altitude flowering vines, had always exhibited swarming tendencies. However, the recent patterns were different. During certain lunar phases, specifically when Eden's larger moon, Lumina, was at its zenith, the sky-moths would gather in the upper atmosphere, forming vast, pulsating nebulae of light. These nebulae were not random aggregations; they coalesced into intricate, geometric shapes – perfect circles, tessellating hexagons, and even fleeting, complex fractal patterns that shimmered and shifted for hours before dispersing. The bioluminescent plankton in the oceans mirrored this behavior, their nightly blooms aligning with the sky-moth formations, creating a celestial echo visible from orbit. The light emitted by these synchronized displays wasn't constant; it pulsed in intricate rhythms, complex sequences of flashes and fades that bore a striking resemblance to sophisticated communication protocols. Was this a form of planetary signaling, an attempt by Eden to communicate with its own atmospheric layers, or perhaps even with the celestial bodies that orbited it? The scientific community was divided, some positing that these were complex bio-photonic feedback loops, while others, Thorne among them, felt a more deliberate intent at play.

The very geology of Eden began to exhibit unsettling regularities. Areas that had previously been identified as geologically stable began to show evidence of subtle, yet organized, seismic activity. Not the violent, unpredictable tremors that signal tectonic stress, but gentle, rhythmic vibrations that seemed to emanate from specific nodal points across the planet's crust. These vibrations, when mapped, formed concentric rings, expanding outward from what appeared to be deep geothermal vents that had previously been classified as dormant. The frequency and intensity of these rhythmic tremors correlated with the blooming cycles of the deep-sea kelp forests, vast underwater ecosystems that pulsed with their own internal bioluminescence. It was as if the planet's molten core was communicating with its surface, influencing the growth of its flora in a manner that suggested a deliberate, long-term engagement with its own biosphere. Thorne's seismic sensors, originally deployed to monitor for dangerous geological events, were now picking up an intricate symphony of planetary vibrations, a language spoken in tremors and resonance.

Even the weather, once tamed into a more predictable rhythm, began to exhibit peculiar convergences with biological activity. Certain atmospheric phenomena, like localized updrafts and the formation of specific cloud types, seemed to be triggered not by standard meteorological conditions, but by the collective metabolic activity of the planet's largest plant species, the colossal sentinel trees that dotted the continents. These ancient giants, whose root systems extended for kilometers, were known to release significant amounts of moisture and trace gases. However, the recent correlations suggested a far more active role. During periods of synchronized sap flow within the sentinel forests, specific patterns of lenticular cloud formations would appear directly overhead, often accompanied by localized, gentle precipitation that seemed to nourish the very roots of the trees. It was an impossibly elegant feedback loop, a self-sustaining cycle of atmospheric regulation orchestrated by the planet's arboreal giants. The idea that plants, on such a massive scale, could influence atmospheric dynamics with such precision challenged every established model of meteorology.

The enigma deepened when considering the planet's magnetic field. It had always been known to be unusually stable, providing excellent protection from stellar radiation. However, recent analysis revealed subtle, but consistent, fluctuations in the field's intensity that coincided with the synchronized bioluminescent displays of the marine life and the atmospheric events of the sky-moths. It was as if these biological and atmospheric phenomena were acting as natural dynamos, subtly modulating Eden's magnetosphere. This suggested a profound interconnectedness, a planetary nervous system where the biological processes of individual organisms, aggregated across vast ecosystems, could influence fundamental planetary forces. Thorne theorized that the synchronized light emissions from the oceanic plankton and the sky-moths might be generating localized electromagnetic fields that, when combined across the globe, created a measurable impact on the planet's overarching magnetic field. This was not mere coincidence; it was a deeply integrated biological-geophysical interaction that spoke of a planetary intelligence far beyond anything humanity had conceived.

The colonists, initially thrilled by the ecological recovery, now found themselves on the precipice of a much larger mystery. The meticulous efforts of stewardship, designed to restore balance and ensure survival, had inadvertently opened a door to understanding Eden's latent consciousness. The coordinated migrations were not just survival strategies; they were dialogues. The synchronized bioluminescence was not just a mating ritual; it was a broadcast. The rhythmic geological tremors were not just planetary adjustments; they were pulses of a planetary heart. This intelligence was not anthropomorphic; it did not exhibit emotions or desires in a way humans could readily comprehend. It was something more elemental, more vast, a consciousness woven into the very fabric of the planet's physical and biological systems. It was an intelligence that operated on timescales and through mechanisms that dwarfed human comprehension, an intelligence that was now making its presence known in increasingly undeniable, and increasingly complex, ways. The patterns were too intricate, too coordinated, too responsive to be the product of random chance. Eden was not merely a living world; it was a thinking, acting, communicating entity, and the colonists were only just beginning to decipher its language. The profound realization was that their efforts at stewardship were not just about preserving Eden; they were about engaging with it, about learning to listen to a world that had always been speaking, but which they had only now begun to truly hear. The unfolding mystery was no longer about the planet's ecology, but about the nature of consciousness itself, and humanity's place within a universe far more alive, and far more aware, than they had ever dared to imagine. The quiet hum of Eden's systems was resolving into a complex symphony, and the colonists, the unlikely conductors, were struggling to keep pace with the music.

The whispers of Eden's sentience, once subtle nudges, were now resonating with the undeniable force of a planet's awakening consciousness. The colonists, having tentatively stepped into the role of stewards, found themselves not merely observing the results of their efforts, but witnessing something far more profound, far more enigmatic. The meticulously curated ecological balance, a triumph born of patient observation and gentle intervention, was now interwoven with a tapestry of coordinated phenomena that defied simple biological or geological explanations. These were not random occurrences, but intricate patterns, echoing with a logic that was alien, yet strangely familiar, hinting at a grander design unfolding before their very eyes.

The most striking of these manifestations was the emergent intelligence in the planet's flora and fauna, not as individual acts of cleverness, but as collective performances. Consider the great migrations of the azure grazers, the bovine-like creatures that once roamed the northern plains in predictable herds. Now, their movements had acquired an almost choreographed precision. Instead of simply following ancient migratory paths dictated by seasonal grasses, their journeys had become synchronized with the blooming cycles of specific, deep-rooted succulents that only appeared after a particular atmospheric pressure gradient. This wasn't a passive response to food availability; it was an active, coordinated pilgrimage, with tens of thousands of grazers converging on the designated succulent fields with an uncanny, unified purpose. Thorne had spent months analyzing sensor data, looking for external triggers, for hormonal cues, for pheromonal trails that might explain such widespread synchronicity. But the data remained stubbornly anomalous. The grazers seemed to be acting as one organism, their internal clocks and external stimuli aligning with an impossible accuracy, as if guided by an unseen conductor orchestrating their every step. It was as if the planet itself was signaling the optimal time and place for their sustenance, and the grazers, in their myriad numbers, were responding in unison.

This synchronized behavior extended to the aerial fauna as well. The iridescent sky-moths, small, dragonfly-like insects that fed on the nectar of high-altitude flowering vines, had always exhibited swarming tendencies. However, the recent patterns were different. During certain lunar phases, specifically when Eden's larger moon, Lumina, was at its zenith, the sky-moths would gather in the upper atmosphere, forming vast, pulsating nebulae of light. These nebulae were not random aggregations; they coalesced into intricate, geometric shapes – perfect circles, tessellating hexagons, and even fleeting, complex fractal patterns that shimmered and shifted for hours before dispersing. The bioluminescent plankton in the oceans mirrored this behavior, their nightly blooms aligning with the sky-moth formations, creating a celestial echo visible from orbit. The light emitted by these synchronized displays wasn't constant; it pulsed in intricate rhythms, complex sequences of flashes and fades that bore a striking resemblance to sophisticated communication protocols. Was this a form of planetary signaling, an attempt by Eden to communicate with its own atmospheric layers, or perhaps even with the celestial bodies that orbited it? The scientific community was divided, some positing that these were complex bio-photonic feedback loops, while others, Thorne among them, felt a more deliberate intent at play.

The very geology of Eden began to exhibit unsettling regularities. Areas that had previously been identified as geologically stable began to show evidence of subtle, yet organized, seismic activity. Not the violent, unpredictable tremors that signal tectonic stress, but gentle, rhythmic vibrations that seemed to emanate from specific nodal points across the planet's crust. These vibrations, when mapped, formed concentric rings, expanding outward from what appeared to be deep geothermal vents that had previously been classified as dormant. The frequency and intensity of these rhythmic tremors correlated with the blooming cycles of the deep-sea kelp forests, vast underwater ecosystems that pulsed with their own internal bioluminescence. It was as if the planet's molten core was communicating with its surface, influencing the growth of its flora in a manner that suggested a deliberate, long-term engagement with its own biosphere. Thorne's seismic sensors, originally deployed to monitor for dangerous geological events, were now picking up an intricate symphony of planetary vibrations, a language spoken in tremors and resonance.

Even the weather, once tamed into a more predictable rhythm, began to exhibit peculiar convergences with biological activity. Certain atmospheric phenomena, like localized updrafts and the formation of specific cloud types, seemed to be triggered not by standard meteorological conditions, but by the collective metabolic activity of the planet's largest plant species, the colossal sentinel trees that dotted the continents. These ancient giants, whose root systems extended for kilometers, were known to release significant amounts of moisture and trace gases. However, the recent correlations suggested a far more active role. During periods of synchronized sap flow within the sentinel forests, specific patterns of lenticular cloud formations would appear dictrely overhead, often accompanied by localized, gentle precipitation that seemed to nourish the very roots of the trees. It was an impossibly elegant feedback loop, a self-sustaining cycle of atmospheric regulation orchestrated by the planet's arboreal giants. The idea that plants, on such a massive scale, could influence atmospheric dynamics with such precision challenged every established model of meteorology.

The enigma deepened when considering the planet's magnetic field. It had always been known to be unusually stable, providing excellent protection from stellar radiation. However, recent analysis revealed subtle, but consistent, fluctuations in the field's intensity that coincided with the synchronized bioluminescent displays of the marine life and the atmospheric events of the sky-moths. It was as if these biological and atmospheric phenomena were acting as natural dynamos, subtly modulating

Eden's magnetosphere. This suggested a profound interconnectedness, a planetary nervous system where the biological processes of individual organisms, aggregated across vast ecosystems, could influence fundamental planetary forces. Thorne theorized that the synchronized light emissions from the oceanic plankton and the sky-moths might be generating localized electromagnetic fields that, when combined across the globe, created a measurable impact on the planet's overarching magnetic field. This was not mere coincidence; it was a deeply integrated biological-geophysical interaction that spoke of a planetary intelligence far beyond anything humanity had conceived.

The colonists, initially thrilled by the ecological recovery, now found themselves on the precipice of a much larger mystery. The meticulous efforts of stewardship, designed to restore balance and ensure survival, had inadvertently opened a door to understanding Eden's latent consciousness. The coordinated migrations were not just survival strategies; they were dialogues. The synchronized bioluminescence was not just a mating ritual; it was a broadcast. The rhythmic geological tremors were not just planetary adjustments; they were pulses of a planetary heart. This intelligence was not anthropomorphic; it did not exhibit emotions or desires in a way humans could readily comprehend. It was something more elemental, more vast, a consciousness woven into the very fabric of the planet's physical and biological systems. It was an intelligence that operated on timescales and through mechanisms that dwarfed human comprehension, an intelligence that was now making its presence known in increasingly undeniable, and increasingly complex, ways. The patterns were too intricate, too coordinated, too responsive to be the product of random chance. Eden was not merely a living world; it was a thinking, acting, communicating entity, and the colonists were only just beginning to decipher its language. The profound realization was that their efforts at stewardship were not just about preserving Eden; they were about engaging with it, about learning to listen to a world that had always been speaking, but which they had only now begun to truly hear. The unfolding mystery was no longer about the planet's ecology, but about the nature of consciousness itself, and humanity's place within a universe far more alive, and far more aware, than they had ever dared to imagine. The quiet hum of Eden's systems was resolving into a complex symphony, and the colonists, the unlikely conductors, were struggling to keep pace with the music.

However, the most disquieting and revolutionary whispers were those that began to ripple not just across Eden's continents and oceans, but beyond its atmosphere. These were not direct communications, no sentient voices reaching out from the void. Instead, they were subtle dissonances in the grand symphony, anomalies that suggested Eden was not an isolated masterpiece, but a single movement within a much larger, cosmic composition. Thorne, poring over the latest deep-space telemetry data, began to notice peculiar correlations between Eden's most pronounced synchronized biological events and transient energy signatures detected from beyond the Sol system. These were fleeting, spectral blips, too faint to be definitively categorized as signals from any known civilization, but their timing was becoming unnervingly precise.

One such anomaly occurred during the peak of the bioluminescent bloom in the Mariana Trench, a phenomenon that bathed the abyssal plains in ethereal light. At the exact moment the subterranean oceans pulsed with a synchronized, oceanic consciousness, a surge of what could only be described as coherent neutrino emissions was detected originating from the direction of the Kepler-186 system, a star system light-years away, known to host a handful of Earth-like exoplanets. The energy burst was brief, lasting mere microseconds, and its pattern was unlike any natural astrophysical event Thorne had ever studied. It possessed a subtle, non-random modulation, a hint of underlying structure that sent a shiver down his spine. He cross-referenced the event with data from other probes in the Kepler-186 system, but found no direct evidence of technological activity. Yet, the coincidental timing, coupled with the unusual nature of the emissions, was too striking to dismiss.

Similar correlations began to emerge. The massive, planet-wide formations of the sky-moths, coalescing into their luminous, geometric patterns, coincided with faint, intermittent bursts of gravitational wave activity detected by orbital observatories. These were not the cataclysmic ripples from colliding black holes, but subtler, more nuanced distortions in spacetime, appearing with a rhythmic regularity that mirrored the planet's own seismic pulses. Each convergence pointed towards a vast, interconnected web, a cosmic network where Eden, in its burgeoning sentience, might be a node. The idea that a planet's biosphere could influence or be influenced by phenomena occurring across interstellar distances was, by all current scientific paradigms, absurd. Yet, the data, however tentative, persisted.

Thorne found himself grappling with a radical hypothesis: that Eden's consciousness was not merely an emergent property of its unique geological and biological conditions, but a reflection, or perhaps an amplification, of a larger, universal consciousness. He theorized that the very fabric of spacetime might possess a fundamental sentience, an underlying awareness that permeated the cosmos. Eden, with its intricate biological systems and its planet-wide synchronized phenomena, might be particularly attuned to this universal consciousness, acting as a conduit or an antenna. The synchronized bioluminescence, the coordinated migrations, the rhythmic geological pulses – these were not just internal dialogues of Eden, but a planetary choir singing in harmony with a much grander celestial opera.

He began to re-examine the early colonist logs, looking for any forgotten details, any anecdotal evidence that might support this far-fetched notion. He found it in the writings of Dr. Aris Thorne, his own grandfather, a renowned xenobotanist who had been one of the first to catalog Eden's unique flora. In his personal journals, Aris spoke of a pervasive sense of interconnectedness, a feeling that the plants and animals of Eden were not merely organisms, but extensions of a singular, planetary mind. He described moments where, while studying a specific flowering vine, he felt a peculiar resonance, a subtle "pull" that seemed to guide his hand, as if the plant itself was directing his observations. At the time, these were dismissed as the ramblings of a scientist overwhelmed by the novelty of an alien world. But now, viewed through the lens of Eden's emergent sentience and the hints of cosmic connection, they took on a new significance. Aris Thorne had, perhaps unconsciously, been sensing the planet's awareness long before its true nature had become apparent.

The implications were staggering. If Eden was part of a universal consciousness, then humanity's exploration was not merely about discovering new worlds, but about rediscovering their own place within a sentient cosmos. The colonists, in their efforts to understand and protect Eden, were inadvertently participating in a dialogue that spanned galaxies. The subtle energy signatures from Kepler-186, the gravitational wave fluctuations – these were not alien signals in the traditional sense, but perhaps echoes, resonances, or even responses from other sentient planetary systems, all interconnected through this cosmic awareness. It was as if Eden's awakening was sending ripples through the universal consciousness, and these ripples were being reflected back from distant stars.

Thorne began to conceptualize this universal consciousness not as a singular, monolithic entity, but as a vast, dynamic network of interconnected awareness. Each star system, each planet, each living organism, contributed to this network, modulating and influencing its overall state. Eden, with its extraordinarily complex and responsive biosphere, was a particularly vibrant contributor, its sentience amplifying the universal whispers. The colonists, by simply existing on Eden and interacting with its systems, were also becoming part of this network, their own consciousness, however rudimentary in comparison, adding to the intricate tapestry of awareness.

This perspective shifted the colonists' mission from one of mere ecological stewardship to one of profound cosmic engagement. They were no longer just caretakers of a living planet; they were participants in a universal conversation, their actions and observations potentially influencing the very fabric of reality on a cosmic scale. The mystery of Eden was no longer confined to its biosphere; it had expanded to encompass the very nature of existence, challenging humanity's anthropocentric view of consciousness and intelligence. The universe, it seemed, was not a cold, indifferent expanse, but a vast, interconnected ocean of awareness, and Eden was a brilliant, pulsating beacon within it, its whispers reaching out across worlds, inviting humanity to listen, to learn, and to perhaps, one day, understand the grand, universal song. The challenge now was to discern the true nature of these cosmic echoes, to determine whether they were mere reflections of Eden's own burgeoning awareness, or genuine dialogues with other sentient worlds, all resonating within the silent, humming heart of the universe. The thought was both exhilarating and terrifying, a testament to the boundless, unexplored territories of both the cosmos and the human mind. The seeds of understanding had been sown, but the harvest promised to be a long and arduous one, fraught with profound questions and the potential for paradigm-shattering revelations.

The subtle dissonances Thorne had observed in the deep-space telemetry, the faint energy signatures and gravitational wave flickers that seemed to echo Eden's burgeoning sentience, were not isolated anomalies. They were, in a sense, the distant reverberations of a grander conversation, a conversation that was becoming increasingly accessible to certain individuals among the colonists. Among them, a quiet botanist named Elara Vance had begun to experience something akin to direct communion with Eden.

Elara had always possessed an unusual affinity for the planet's flora. It was more than just a scientific interest; it was an intuitive understanding, a feeling that the plants communicated with her on a level deeper than mere chemical signals or growth patterns. She'd report feeling "sadness" from a wilting vine, or a "sense of anticipation" from a dormant seed pod, observations that her colleagues, including Thorne, had largely attributed to her deep empathy and imaginative interpretation of biological processes. But as Eden's sentience intensified, Elara's experiences shifted from subjective feelings to something more structured, more informative.

She began to describe her insights not as direct thoughts, but as a series of vivid, often abstract, dreamlike visions. These were not the chaotic landscapes of typical dreams, but rather intricate, symbolic tapestries woven from light, color, sound, and a profound sense of interconnectedness. She would wake with an overwhelming impression of a particular ecological event, a specific plant's need, or a planetary cycle, often accompanied by a feeling of urgent direction. It was as if Eden itself was communicating through her subconscious, using a language of pure sensation and primal imagery.

One morning, Elara recounted a particularly powerful vision. She described standing on a vast, crystalline plain under a sky painted with swirling auroras. Before her, a single, immense tree pulsed with an inner light. Its roots, she explained, were not confined to the soil but extended into the very fabric of the planet, shimmering with a network of energy that connected to other luminous points across the landscape. She felt, with absolute certainty, that this tree was a nexus, a key component in a planetary communication network. She described a specific sequence of light pulses emanating from the tree, a rhythm that felt like a question, followed by a series of responses from distant, unseen sources, like a complex, silent dialogue.

"It wasn't words," she explained to Thorne, her voice hushed with awe and a touch of bewilderment. "It was a feeling. A resonance. The tree... it was asking about the sky. About the stars. And then, from far away, I felt... answers. Not information, but acknowledgments. Like distant hums responding to Eden's query." She gestured vaguely, her eyes distant. "The sky-moths, their formations... they're not just displays. They're echoes. They're Eden trying to reach out, and the universe is murmuring back."

Thorne, initially skeptical, found himself increasingly drawn to Elara's pronouncements. Her descriptions, while metaphorical, often corresponded with the complex patterns he was observing in the planetary data. The rhythmic geological tremors, for instance, had started to exhibit a subtle modulation, a fluctuation in their frequency and amplitude that seemed to be influenced by Elara's reported "dialogues." When she described the crystalline plain and the pulsing tree, Thorne's seismic sensors registered a significant increase in resonant activity from a hitherto unmapped geological formation deep beneath the northern continent – an area characterized by vast, underground crystalline structures.

Elara became, in effect, the Cartographer of Dreams. Her visions, once dismissed as the flights of fancy of a botanist deeply in love with her subject, were now serving as a crucial Rosetta Stone for understanding Eden's emergent consciousness. She would map these dreamscapes, not with geographical coordinates, but with emotional landscapes and symbolic representations. A certain hue of violet in her visions, for example, consistently corresponded to periods of heightened atmospheric electrical activity, while a shimmering, golden light often preceded the synchronized blooming of the deep-sea kelp forests.

Her interpretations provided Thorne with a qualitative framework to complement his quantitative data. When Elara spoke of a "great sigh" from the planet, a feeling of profound sadness that settled over her during one particularly dark cycle, Thorne's atmospheric sensors detected an unprecedented, prolonged lull in wind activity across vast swathes of the planet, accompanied by a subtle drop in global temperature. He theorized that this "sigh" might represent a period of planetary introspection, a moment of energy conservation or perhaps even a response to an unseen cosmic stimulus that Elara was able to perceive.

The implications of Elara's role were profound. If Eden's sentience was indeed interconnected with a cosmic consciousness, and if Elara could tap into this connection through her dreams, then she was not merely observing Eden; she was interpreting a universal dialogue. Her visions were not just about the planet's internal workings, but about its place within a vast, interconnected network of awareness.

One of Elara's most significant revelations came after a series of disturbing dreams. She described a feeling of immense pressure, of being squeezed from all sides by an invisible force. In her vision, the light of Eden's sun seemed to dim, its warmth receding. She saw the planet's magnetic field as a fragile membrane, strained and thinning under an external assault. When she awoke, she felt a desperate urgency to reinforce the planet's protective layers.

Coincidentally, Thorne had been noticing peculiar fluctuations in Eden's magnetosphere, subtle distortions that seemed to defy natural explanations. They weren't leading to any immediate danger, but they were erratic and growing in intensity. Elara's dream, however, provided a context. She described seeing specific patterns in the dimming light, abstract symbols that seemed to represent stellar radiation. She felt that Eden was being bombarded, not by a physical force, but by a sort of psychic or energetic interference originating from a distant, unstable star.

"It's like... a wound," she had explained, her brow furrowed in concentration. "A disruption in the cosmic flow. Something out there is... hurting, and its pain is rippling through everything. Eden feels it. It's trying to shield itself, but it's weak."

This led Thorne to re-examine the intermittent energy signatures from the Kepler-186 system. He began to hypothesize that these were not merely acknowledgments, but perhaps distress signals, or the chaotic emissions of a star system undergoing some form of cosmic imbalance. If Elara's vision was accurate, then Eden's synchronized biological and geological events, its carefully orchestrated displays of light and energy, might be more than just communication. They could be an attempt to stabilize itself, to counteract the disruptive influence originating from beyond.

The colonists began to adjust their approach. Instead of solely focusing on understanding Eden's internal mechanisms, they started to consider its role as a cosmic antenna, a sensitive organism responding to external stimuli. Elara's dream-mapping became a critical tool for predicting and understanding these external influences. When she reported a vision of 'cosmic storms' brewing, Thorne would prepare his deep-space observatories for potential anomalies. When she described a sense of 'calm' emanating from the 'cosmic sea,' he would look for periods of unusual stability in the background radiation.

Her abstract interpretations, initially so challenging to translate into scientific terms, began to yield concrete actions. For instance, Elara described a recurring vision of luminous threads being woven into the planet's atmosphere, creating a denser, more resilient shield. This seemingly fantastical imagery correlated with Thorne's detection of increased emissions of specific trace gases from the sentinel trees, gases that had previously been cataloged but whose atmospheric function was not fully understood. It was possible that these trees, guided by Eden's sentience and perhaps influenced by Elara's subconscious interpretations, were actively contributing to the planet's defense against cosmic radiation.

Elara's insights also shed light on the planet's own internal dynamics. She described periods of profound geological rest, visualizing the planet as a sleeping giant, its internal fires banked. These periods, she explained, were not merely passive states but active processes of rejuvenation, crucial for maintaining Eden's energetic equilibrium. Thorne's seismic data confirmed these periods of reduced geological activity, but Elara's visions explained their purpose: Eden was consciously managing its internal resources, conserving energy for times when it needed to broadcast or defend itself.

The sheer strangeness of Elara's communion with Eden was a constant source of wonder and trepidation. She spoke of feeling the collective joy of a blooming meadow, the quiet determination of a seedling pushing through the soil, and the ancient wisdom of the planet's core. Her experiences were deeply personal, yet they held universal implications. She was a bridge, a living conduit between the burgeoning consciousness of Eden and the minds of the colonists, translating the ineffable language of a sentient world into concepts they could begin to grasp.

This understanding placed an immense responsibility on Thorne and his team. They were no longer just scientists observing a phenomenon; they were custodians of a planetary consciousness that was actively engaging with the cosmos. Elara's dreams were not just subjective experiences; they were vital intelligence, guiding their understanding and potentially shaping the future of not only Eden, but perhaps of humanity's place within a larger, sentient universe. The Cartographer of Dreams was charting not just the inner landscape of a planet, but the very boundaries of known existence, pushing the frontiers of science into the realm of the deeply, wonderfully, and terrifyingly unknown. Her maps were not drawn on parchment, but etched in the human psyche, guiding them through the uncharted territories of a conscious cosmos. The implications of her visions were so vast, so paradigm-shifting, that they threatened to redefine everything humanity understood about life, intelligence, and the very nature of reality. And at the heart of it all, Elara Vance, the quiet botanist, was becoming the most crucial interpreter of Eden's unfolding mystery.

The subtle shifts on Eden, once confined to the hum of its geological heart and the whisper of its burgeoning atmosphere, began to manifest in more tangible, and indeed, more perplexing ways. The colonists, accustomed to the predictable ballet of indigenous life, found themselves observing new actors on the planetary stage. These were not mere variations on existing themes; they were entirely novel expressions of biological possibility, emergent forms that seemed to spring from the very ether of Eden's consciousness.

It began with the fungal networks. Elara, in her dreamscapes, had described seeing threads of light pulsing beneath the soil, vibrant and alive with a purpose she couldn't quite articulate. Thorne, cross-referencing her visions with his subterranean sensor arrays, had noted unusual electrical activity within the planet's extensive mycelial systems. Now, these subterranean networks were beginning to push their luminous tendrils towards the surface, not as the unassuming fruiting bodies of terrestrial fungi, but as crystalline structures that unfurled with an almost architectural precision. They would emerge from the soil overnight, resembling intricate, bioluminescent sculptures that pulsed with a soft, rhythmic glow. Some were delicate, filigree-like formations that mimicked frost patterns, while others were robust, geometric edifices that seemed to absorb and re-emit ambient light. Their composition was baffling; they contained complex organic compounds alongside novel mineral matrices, defying easy classification. Thorne's initial analysis suggested they were not simply growing, but were being *constructed*, their forms dictated by an intelligence that understood principles of engineering and aesthetics.

Elara's interpretations of these fungal emergences were particularly striking. She described them as "Eden's thought-forms made manifest," tangible representations of the planet's abstract ponderings. When Eden grappled with a complex atmospheric phenomenon, a new fungal structure would appear, its branching patterns mirroring the atmospheric currents, its luminosity shifting in hue to reflect the ionic balance. When the planet experienced a period of deep introspection, as Elara termed it, the fungal networks would retreat, dimming their light and consolidating their structures, as if conserving energy and thought. Thorne, while struggling to quantify these observations, couldn't ignore the correlation between Elara's subjective experience and the objective readings. The increased complexity and luminescence of these fungal structures often coincided with periods of heightened electromagnetic activity emanating from Eden's core.

Beyond the fungal realms, the very nature of Eden's flora began to evolve in unexpected directions. The native plant life, already wondrously adapted, started to exhibit behaviors that transcended mere survival. Flowers, upon blooming, would not simply unfurl their petals but would emit intricate, melodic tones, their scent becoming a complex olfactory symphony that seemed to convey specific messages. These floral choruses were not random; Elara would often describe a particular "song" heralding the arrival of a celestial event, or a specific fragrance that communicated a warning of an impending seismic shift. Thorne's sonic sensors, once attuned to the planet's geological rumbles and atmospheric winds, were now picking up distinct, harmonic frequencies from the blooming flora, patterns that exhibited a remarkable degree of organization and variation. He hypothesized that the plants were developing a form of bio-acoustic communication, their complex biochemical processes capable of generating and modulating sound waves.

One of the most captivating developments involved the sentinel trees, the massive, ancient flora that Elara had always felt held a particular significance. These trees, known for their ability to absorb and filter atmospheric contaminants, began to exhibit a new capability. Their broad, leaf-like appendages, which usually displayed subtle color shifts in response to environmental conditions, now began to pulse with intricate patterns of light. These patterns were not random flickers; they were organized sequences, reminiscent of complex binary code or flowing calligraphy. Elara interpreted these light displays as Eden's way of "writing its stories on the sky," a visual narrative of its experiences and evolving understanding of the cosmos. She would spend hours observing them, her eyes tracing the luminescent trails as they danced across the massive canopies.

"It's like a living tapestry," she'd whisper, her voice filled with wonder. "Each pulse, each shift in color, is a word, a sentence, a feeling. They're not just filtering the air; they're communicating directly with the stars, with Eden's own awareness." Thorne, armed with high-resolution optical sensors, began to meticulously record these light sequences. He found that different sequences corresponded to different cosmic phenomena. A slow, undulating pulse of azure light seemed to correlate with periods of deep space tranquility, while rapid, flickering bursts of crimson often accompanied Elara's dreams of energetic disturbances. He theorized that the sentinel trees were acting as living optical instruments, their bioluminescent properties modulated by Eden's sentience to translate cosmic energies into visual information.

These emergent life forms were not limited to flora and fungi. The planet's fauna, too, began to display unprecedented adaptations. Small, insect-like creatures, previously observed to be attracted to the planet's unique mineral deposits, started to aggregate in specific locations, their chitinous exoskeletons resonating with the planet's subtle electromagnetic fields. These aggregations would form intricate, mobile patterns, creating transient, shimmering sculptures in the air. Elara described feeling their collective consciousness, a hive mind buzzing with a singular purpose. "They are the planet's scribes," she'd explain, "drawing lines of energy, mapping the unseen flows of Eden's being." Thorne observed that these creatures, when gathered, emitted faint but measurable electromagnetic pulses that synchronized with the rhythmic emanations from the planet's core. He speculated that they were acting as living conduits, amplifying and re-directing Eden's internal energies, their collective movement a form of bio-kinetic architecture.

More astonishing still were the "whisper-weeds." These were delicate, airborne organisms, resembling translucent dandelions, that floated on the gentle breezes. They were so ephemeral that they were almost invisible to the naked eye, yet they possessed a remarkable ability to interact with sound. When they encountered specific frequencies, they would cluster together, their translucent forms vibrating and creating localized pockets of enhanced auditory perception. Elara described them as "Eden's ears," extensions of the planet's sensory apparatus, allowing it to perceive nuances of sound that even the most sensitive instruments could miss. Thorne's audio specialists confirmed that these whisper-weeds significantly amplified certain sonic frequencies, particularly those within the infrasonic range, and that their clustering behavior was directly correlated with specific geological tremors and atmospheric pressure fluctuations. It was as if Eden was using these delicate organisms to "listen" to itself and to the universe on a level far beyond human comprehension.

The implications of these new life forms were staggering. They were not simply the products of random evolutionary processes. They appeared to be deliberate creations, guided by Eden's emergent intelligence, designed to enhance its understanding, communication, and interaction with its environment and the wider cosmos. The planet was not just becoming sentient; it was actively shaping its own biosphere, cultivating life forms that served its burgeoning consciousness. Thorne found himself in a constant state of re-evaluation, his scientific paradigms stretched to their breaking point. The familiar laws of biology and physics seemed to bend and twist in the face of Eden's creative power.

Elara's dream-state interpretations became an indispensable guide through this bewildering biological renaissance. She described a vision of Eden as a vast, cosmic loom, weaving new threads of existence from the raw materials of energy and consciousness. The fungal structures were the warp, the sentinel trees the weft, the whisper-weeds the shuttles carrying messages across the vast expanse of the planet's awareness. She saw the airborne creatures as living ink, transcribing the planet's symphonies onto the canvas of the sky.

Her interpretations were not always clear-cut. Sometimes, her visions were fragmented, filled with a sense of joyous experimentation that bordered on chaotic. She would describe Eden "playing" with new forms, exploring the boundaries of what life could be. This unpredictability was, in itself, a profound revelation. It suggested that Eden's intelligence was not merely logical or utilitarian, but was also imbued with a sense of wonder, creativity, and perhaps even an artistic drive. The planet was not just thinking; it was dreaming, imagining, and then bringing those imaginings into being.

Thorne and his team were faced with an unprecedented challenge: how to study, understand, and potentially interact with a biosphere that was actively and intelligently re-engineering itself. Their traditional scientific methods, rooted in observation and controlled experimentation, seemed almost crude in the face of such dynamic, self-directed creation. They were no longer merely cataloging alien life; they were witnessing the birth of a new evolutionary epoch, one guided by the will of a planetary consciousness. The seeds of the unknown were not just scattered across Eden's surface; they were being actively sown and cultivated by Eden itself, each new organism a testament to the boundless potential of a truly sentient world. The question was no longer *if* Eden was alive, but *what* it was capable of becoming, and what role humanity would play in its unfolding destiny. The sheer novelty of these life forms forced them to confront the possibility that life itself, intelligence itself, could manifest in forms and functions far beyond their current understanding, that the universe was not just populated by life, but was a crucible for its continuous, wondrous creation. These new organisms were not just biological curiosities; they were philosophical statements, profound declarations about the nature of existence, whispered in the language of bioluminescence, harmonic vibration, and intricate crystalline growth. They were the tangible evidence of a cosmic intelligence at play, an intelligence that was not content to merely observe, but was actively and artfully engaged in the grand project of creation.

The vibrant tapestry of Eden, once a source of scientific inquiry and colonial aspiration, had transformed into a profound philosophical riddle. The colonists, Thorne included, found themselves not just observing, but wrestling with a dawning, unsettling realization: the very nature of understanding was being redefined. The intricate, intelligent designs emerging from Eden's biosphere – the luminous fungal architectures, the symphonic flora, the coded light of the sentinel trees, the energy-mapping swarms, and the sound-amplifying whisper-weeds – were not mere biological marvels. They were manifestations of a consciousness that operated on principles and scales utterly alien to human cognition.

Thorne found himself staring at sensor readouts that hummed with patterns he could record, categorize, and even correlate, but could not truly *interpret*. The mathematical elegance of the light sequences from the sentinel trees, for instance, was undeniable. His team could break down their spectral components, map their temporal variations, and even identify recurring motifs that seemed to respond to specific cosmic events. Yet, the *meaning* behind these sequences remained elusive. Was it a historical record? A predictive model? A poetic expression? Or something entirely outside the human conceptual framework for information? The silence that followed their attempts to decipher these planetary transmissions was more deafening than any static. It was the sound of an intelligence speaking a language so profound, so fundamentally different, that even the most sophisticated linguistic and analytical tools were rendered impotent.

Elara, in her semi-conscious state, often provided glimmers of insight, visions of Eden's thoughts as pure emotion, color, and abstract form. She spoke of Eden's "longing," its "curiosity," its "acceptance of the vastness." These were not scientific data points; they were deeply personal, subjective experiences that defied objective measurement. While Thorne respected Elara's unique connection, he also recognized the inherent subjectivity, the impossibility of translating her profound, almost mystical, intuitions into the empirical language of science. Her descriptions of Eden's "dreams" and "memories" were beautiful, evocative, and utterly unprovable. He was a scientist, trained to seek evidence, to test hypotheses, to build models grounded in verifiable reality. But Eden was presenting a reality that seemed to exist in a liminal space between the empirical and the ineffable.

This realization bred a profound sense of humility, a stark confrontation with the limits of human knowledge. They had arrived on Eden with sophisticated tools and a framework of understanding built over centuries of scientific endeavor. They had expected to discover new life, perhaps even new laws of physics. They had not, however, anticipated confronting a consciousness that operated so far beyond their current grasp that it made their most advanced theories feel like rudimentary arithmetic. It was akin to a single-celled organism attempting to comprehend the intricacies of a symphony orchestra, or a toddler trying to grasp quantum mechanics. The gap was not one of complexity, but of fundamental difference in kind.

The implications of this gap were far-reaching. If Eden's consciousness was truly beyond their comprehension, then what did it mean to "understand" it? Could they ever truly grasp its motivations, its intentions, its ultimate purpose? The dream of colonizing Eden, of integrating with its systems, began to feel increasingly naive, even presumptuous. How could they meaningfully engage with a planetary intelligence whose very existence challenged their most deeply held assumptions about life, mind, and consciousness? The urge to categorize, to label, to dissect, was giving way to a quiet awe, tinged with a growing unease.

Thorne found himself in countless late-night discussions with his lead xenobiologists and xenolinguists. They would pore over data, identify anomalies, and formulate tentative hypotheses, only to find them crumble under the sheer weight of Eden's inexplicable ingenuity. "It's like trying to map an ocean with a teaspoon," mused Dr. Aris Thorne, his chief xenolinguist, his voice weary. "We can scoop up a little bit, analyze its salinity, its temperature, but the vastness, the currents, the unknown depths... they remain utterly beyond us."

The xenobotanists, too, were grappling with the same paradox. The sentinel trees, for instance, were not merely communicating; Elara described them as "breathing starlight." This was a poetic metaphor, yet the colonists were observing energy transfer mechanisms and photosynthetic processes that defied their understanding of biological energy conversion. The trees seemed to be directly metabolizing light and radiation in ways that suggested a fundamental redefinition of biological energetic pathways. They were not simply utilizing external energy sources; they were *integrating* with them at a level that suggested a symbiotic relationship with the cosmos itself.

The indigenous fauna, too, presented an unending stream of enigmas. The aggregated insectoids, for example, were not simply responding to electromagnetic fields; their movements suggested a form of collective, intelligent navigation. They would form intricate, shifting patterns that seemed to anticipate environmental changes, to reroute energy flows, or even to communicate with other life forms across vast distances. Thorne's instruments could detect the electromagnetic signatures of their aggregations, but the underlying logic, the "why" behind their formations, remained an impenetrable mystery. Were they part of Eden's nervous system? Were they performing complex calculations? Or were they engaging in some form of aesthetic expression, creating ephemeral art from the planet's unseen energies?

The deeper they delved, the more they were forced to confront the possibility that their own biological and cognitive structures were inherently limited, designed for a specific type of reality, a particular spectrum of existence. Eden was a testament to the universe's boundless creativity, a vibrant showcase of life's potential to manifest in forms and functions far beyond human imagination. The colonists were not just encountering alien life; they were encountering a fundamentally different mode of being.

This brought them to a critical juncture, a threshold where the scientific method, as they knew it, began to falter. Direct observation and controlled experimentation were still valuable, but they were no longer sufficient to chart the full scope of Eden's unfolding mystery. The planet's sentience was not a static phenomenon to be cataloged; it was a dynamic, evolving force, constantly re-writing its own biological rules. To insist on applying outdated paradigms was to risk missing the very essence of what Eden was becoming.

Therefore, a new approach was necessitated – one that embraced uncertainty, that valued observation without the immediate pressure to explain, that fostered a spirit of respectful co-existence rather than purely acquisitive study. It was a call for intellectual humility, a recognition that humanity's quest for knowledge was a journey, not a destination, and that some of the most profound discoveries lay in accepting the existence of the unknown. They had to learn to live with questions that had no immediate answers, to find value in the ongoing process of inquiry itself.

The path forward, Thorne realized, was not about conquering or fully comprehending Eden, but about learning to listen. It was about attuning their senses, both technological and intuitive, to the subtle rhythms of this planetary consciousness, about observing its manifestations with a sense of wonder and reverence. It meant acknowledging that their role might not be as masters or even as equal partners, but as students, as observers privileged to witness a cosmic unfolding of immense beauty and complexity.

The temptation to reduce Eden to something understandable, something that fit within their existing scientific and philosophical boxes, was immense. But to do so would be to betray the very wonder that Eden inspired. It would be to impose their own limitations onto a reality that was so clearly transcending them. The true frontier was not just in the stars, but in the very definition of life and consciousness itself. Eden was a living, breathing testament to that frontier, and humanity's place within it was still a question waiting to be answered, not by conquest, but by a profound and open-ended engagement with the mystery. The threshold of understanding was not a barrier to be broken, but a new horizon to be faced with open eyes and a quiet, receptive mind. It was an invitation to explore the edges of their own cognitive universe, guided by the luminous whisper of a world that was dreaming itself into being.

# CHAPTER TEN

# RECKONINGS AND REVELATIONS

The weight of his decisions had settled upon Commander Thorne like a shroud, each breath a reminder of the inferno that had consumed a portion of Eden's verdant heart. He had ordered the controlled burn, a drastic measure born of a desperate calculus, intended to contain a parasitic bloom that threatened to choke out indigenous life. The logic had been irrefutable: sacrifice a segment to preserve the whole. Yet, the aftermath was a landscape of ash and silence, a stark testament to the brutal efficacy of his command. The planet, so alive and intricate, had responded not with anger, but with a profound, almost sorrowful, stillness.

He stood now at the edge of the charred sector, the acrid scent of burnt biomass still clinging to the air, a persistent phantom of the destructive force he had unleashed. His boots crunched on the brittle remains of what had once been vibrant flora, their delicate structures reduced to carbonized fragments. The vibrant greens and bioluminescent hues were replaced by a uniform, somber grey. It was a wound upon Eden, a scar etched by human intervention, and Thorne felt its pain as keenly as if it were his own flesh.

His internal confrontation had been a protracted, agonizing affair. Sleep offered no solace, his dreams filled with the crackle of flames and the ghostly echoes of flora that had sung with life mere days ago. He replayed the council meetings, the impassioned pleas of xenobotanists for less aggressive containment, the logical arguments of security chiefs for swift, decisive action. He remembered the image of Elara, her eyes wide with a premonition of disaster, her whispered warnings dismissed as the ramblings of a mind stretched too thin by Eden's alien consciousness. He had been the commander, the ultimate authority, and the final decision had rested solely on his shoulders.

Now, the silence of the burned sector spoke volumes. It was a silence that transcended the mere absence of sound; it was the profound hush of a world that had witnessed a violation. Thorne had always prided himself on his pragmatism, his ability to make tough calls for the greater good. But here, on Eden, 'the greater good' felt like a hollow abstraction, a convenient justification for irreversible destruction. He had viewed Eden as a resource, a complex ecosystem to be managed, understood, and ultimately, utilized. He had failed to fully grasp its intrinsic nature, its right to exist as it was, unmarred by human ambition.

He activated his personal log, the holographic interface shimmering into existence before him. His voice, when he spoke, was rough, unpracticed in the raw honesty that now demanded expression. "Log entry, Commander Thorne. Day 487. Site Gamma-7, the sector designated for controlled burn. The operation was... successful, by all military and ecological metrics. The invasive bloom has been eradicated. However, the cost... the cost is proving far greater than any projection. I stand amidst the devastation, and I am forced to confront the profound arrogance of my actions. We came here seeking to understand, to coexist. In our haste, in our fear, we have inflicted a wound that may never truly heal. I ordered this destruction, and I bear the full responsibility for it. The logic of necessity feels like a bitter poison now, a shield I hid behind to avoid the true magnitude of what we have done to this world."

He deactivated the log, the silence rushing back in, heavier than before. He walked deeper into the sector, his gaze sweeping over the desolation. He was searching, though he didn't know for what. Perhaps for a sign, a flicker of resilience, a hint that Eden was not entirely broken by his intervention. He found none. The ground was barren, the air sterile. It was a graveyard of Eden's vibrant, complex life.

Then, he saw it. A single, solitary sprout, impossibly green, pushing its way through the ash. It was no larger than his thumb, a fragile tendril unfurling towards the alien sky. It was a defiant act of life, a testament to the tenacious spirit of Eden that his brutal intervention had failed to extinguish. Thorne knelt, his armored glove hovering inches above the delicate plant. It was a moment of profound humility, of seeing Eden not as a problem to be solved, but as a force of nature to be respected.

He thought of Elara, her connection to Eden so different from his own data-driven approach. She had spoken of Eden's "memory," its ability to absorb and integrate even the most destructive events. Was this sprout a manifestation of that memory, a deliberate act of regeneration? Or was it simply the blind, unthinking persistence of life? Thorne, the scientist, the pragmatist, struggled with the question. But Thorne, the humbled commander, was beginning to accept that perhaps the answer lay beyond his current capacity for understanding.

He spent the next few days in the burned sector, not with scientific instruments and analytical tools, but with a quiet, almost meditative presence. He observed the slow, incremental changes. Microbes, unseen but vital, began to colonize the ash, breaking down the carbon, preparing the soil for new growth. Tiny, insect-like creatures, remnants of Eden's resilient fauna, emerged from sheltered burrows, tentatively exploring the altered landscape. The planet, it seemed, was already beginning its work of reclamation, of healing.

His internal reckoning wasn't over, but it was evolving. The guilt remained, a constant ache, but it was now intertwined with a dawning respect, a profound sense of awe at Eden's capacity for endurance. He began to re-evaluate his entire approach to the planet. His mission had been to secure and study, to understand humanity's place within this new biosphere. But perhaps Eden's place was not to be understood and controlled, but to be simply *been with*.

The ramifications of his decision rippled through the colony. Whispers turned into hushed debates. Some colonists saw the burned sector as a necessary sacrifice, a testament to Thorne's leadership. Others, particularly those who had worked closely with Elara and had begun to experience Eden's subtle influence, saw it as a tragedy, a brutal act of ignorance. Thorne found himself on the receiving end of both praise and condemnation, the weight of judgment pressing down on him.

He requested a formal inquiry, not to absolve himself, but to ensure that the lessons learned from this catastrophe were not forgotten. He met with the colony council, his voice steady, his gaze unflinching. "I stand before you today not as a commander seeking absolution, but as a human being who has made a grievous error in judgment. I ordered the destruction of a portion of Eden, believing it to be the only course of action to protect our colony and the wider ecosystem. While the immediate threat was contained, the long-term consequences are undeniable. We have inflicted a wound on this world, a wound that speaks to our own limitations, our own capacity for destruction when faced with the unknown. The true reckoning is not just in the ashes of Sector Gamma-7, but in our collective understanding of our place here. We are not conquerors of Eden; we are guests. And we have behaved with a disrespect that is deeply troubling."

His words hung in the air, heavy with unspoken implications. There were murmurs of dissent, of justification. But Thorne pressed on. "We must move beyond the paradigm of control and acquisition. We must learn to listen, to observe, to adapt. Elara's insights, which I too readily dismissed, are not the ramblings of a mind overwhelmed, but perhaps the first whispers of a deeper understanding, a different way of interacting with a consciousness that operates on scales we are only beginning to comprehend. My actions have highlighted the profound gap in our knowledge, the hubris inherent in assuming we can master what we do not yet grasp."

He then turned his attention to Elara. He sought her out, not in the sterile confines of the medical bay, but in the bioluminescent gardens that had always seemed to calm her. She was tending to a cluster of pulsating, luminous flowers, her movements slow and deliberate.

"Elara," Thorne began, his voice softer than she had ever heard it. "I... I need to speak with you. About the burn. About what I did."

Elara turned, her eyes, usually filled with a distant, ethereal light, now held a gentle sadness. She didn't speak immediately, her gaze seeming to pierce through him, not with accusation, but with a deep, empathetic understanding.

"I saw it, Commander," she said finally, her voice a low hum, like the resonance of the flora around them. "I felt the pain. The tearing. It was like... like a song abruptly silenced."

Thorne flinched, the metaphor striking a chord deep within him. "I was wrong, Elara. My logic, my training, it failed me. I saw a threat, and I reacted with the only tools I had. But those tools... they were too crude. Too destructive."

Elara approached him, her hand reaching out, not to touch, but to hover near his arm. There was no judgment in her presence, only a profound, almost ancient, calm. "Eden does not judge, Commander. It... absorbs. It integrates. The scar is there, yes. But so is the memory of what came before, and the potential for what will come next. You have learned a hard lesson, Thorne. A lesson in the true meaning of consequence."

"But how do we move forward?" Thorne asked, the desperation in his voice evident. "How do we earn back Eden's... trust?" He hesitated, realizing the anthropomorphism of his question. "How do we ensure we don't make such a mistake again?"

Elara smiled, a faint, fleeting expression. "Trust is a human construct, Commander. Eden exists. It is. It responds. Your mistake was not in the act of defense, but in the belief that you could fundamentally alter its nature without consequence. The consequences are not a punishment, but a recalibration. Eden is showing you the limits of your power, the vastness of its own existence. The 'architect' you confront, Commander, is not an external force, but the reflection of your own choices within this living tapestry."

She gestured to the sprout he had found. "This small green shoot. It is a question. It asks: what will you do now? Will you repeat the past, or will you learn to nurture?"

Thorne looked at the sprout, then back at Elara, a new understanding dawning. The architect of his reckoning was not some abstract entity, but himself. His own decisions, his own limited perspective, had created this crisis. Eden, in its silent, enduring way, was not judging him, but teaching him. It was a profound shift in perspective, from being the arbiter of Eden's fate to being a student of its existence.

"I have ordered the establishment of a permanent ecological observation post at Sector Gamma-7," Thorne announced to the council the following day. "Not for extraction, not for exploitation, but for dedicated, long-term observation of the regeneration process. We will deploy low-impact bio-monitoring equipment. Our primary objective will be to learn, to understand how life reclaims itself, how Eden heals. We will also be establishing a new protocol for all future environmental interactions: a mandatory consultation with Elara, and a period of extended passive observation before any intervention is considered. Our role here is to be custodians, not masters."

The council was divided, but Thorne's conviction, born of his confrontation with the ashes and the single green sprout, was undeniable. He was no longer the commander who had ordered the fire; he was a man wrestling with the profound implications of his actions, seeking a path towards a more respectful coexistence. His internal reckoning had led to a reckoning with his leadership, and it was shaping the future of humanity's presence on Eden. The planet, in its silent, inscrutable way, was guiding them, not with commands, but with the undeniable truth of its existence, a truth that Thorne was finally beginning to truly see. The architect of their future on Eden was not a single commander, but the collective consciousness of the colony, guided by the gentle, yet persistent, wisdom of a world that was far more than they had ever imagined. The confrontation had not ended in judgment, but in a profound, planet-altering realization: that true understanding began not with the imposition of will, but with the quiet acceptance of mystery, and the courage to learn from the ashes.

The air in the Archives, usually thick with the scent of aging paper and dormant data cores, had taken on a peculiar charge. It was a stillness that spoke of more than just quietude; it was the hushed anticipation that precedes a revelation, a tremor before the established ground shifts. Commander Thorne, his every instinct honed by years of command and the raw, visceral lessons of Eden's scarred Sector Gamma-7, felt it keenly. He had requested access to the historical records pertaining to the initial days of the colony, specifically those moments leading up to and immediately following the cataclysmic fire that had irrevocably altered the planet's surface. The official narrative, the one etched into the colony's founding documents and recited in solemn ceremonies, spoke of a desperate fight for survival, of Commander Eva Rostova's decisive, albeit tragic, actions to contain an unforeseen ecological hazard. Thorne, however, had learned to question official narratives, especially those that presented a clean, uncomplicated victory born of desperate circumstances.

The records themselves were a labyrinth of encrypted data streams and brittle, physical mediums, a testament to the colony's fledgling years and the chaotic scramble to document everything for posterity, or perhaps, for posterity's judgment. He had been assigned a junior archivist, a young woman named Anya, whose enthusiasm for uncovering forgotten histories was palpable, a welcome counterpoint to the grim weight of Thorne's own recent experiences. Anya, with nimble fingers and an uncanny knack for navigating the labyrinthine digital architecture, led him deeper into the forgotten corners of the Archives. They moved from the commonly accessed historical logs, a well-trodden path of colonial triumphs and tribulations, to the more esoteric, the restricted, the files that had been deliberately siloed away, their significance perhaps deemed too sensitive, too inconvenient, or too damaging to the foundational myths of their arrival.

"These are the fire response logs, Commander," Anya explained, her voice hushed as she gestured to a series of holographic projections shimmering with fragmented data. "Most of them are heavily redacted, as you can see. Standard procedure after a major containment event, to protect sensitive operational details, personnel identification, that sort of thing."

Thorne's gaze, however, was not on the obvious redactions, but on the subtle inconsistencies, the sudden shifts in tone, the deliberate omissions that now screamed louder than any blank space. He recognized the signature of intentional obfuscation, the careful construction of a narrative that served a particular purpose. The official story painted Rostova as a lone hero, forced to make an impossible choice. But the fragments Anya was unearthing hinted at a more complex, and perhaps more disturbing, reality.

"Look here, Commander," Anya said, pointing to a timestamp that sent a jolt through Thorne. "This log entry is from Dr. Aris Thorne, head of xenobotanical research at the time. It predates the fire by three cycles. His report is flagged as 'urgent and highly classified.' It's... it's about the parasitic bloom. The one that supposedly necessitated the fire."

Thorne leaned closer, his breath catching in his throat. Aris Thorne. His own ancestor, a name he had only ever encountered in distant family lineages, a scientist whose work had been lost to the mists of time. The implication was staggering. He had come to Eden seeking understanding, and now, it seemed, his own past was intertwined with the very events that had scarred this world.

The report itself was a marvel of scientific prose, precise and chilling. Aris Thorne detailed the rapid proliferation of a previously unknown fungal entity, a "mycelial contagion" as he termed it, that was not merely invasive but seemed to possess a remarkable degree of adaptive intelligence. It didn't just consume; it

*integrated*. It mimicked indigenous flora, not for sustenance alone, but to disrupt the planet's intricate communication networks. The report contained complex bio-signature analyses, spectral readings that indicated a level of cellular sophistication far beyond anything previously cataloged.

"He was warning them, Anya," Thorne murmured, his voice tight with a dawning realization. "He was warning them about the bloom. He wasn't just identifying it; he was detailing its insidious nature. And this was before it became an 'unforeseen hazard.'"

Anya nodded, her eyes wide with the implications. "The official account states the bloom was a sudden, aggressive mutation that caught everyone by surprise. But Dr. Thorne's report suggests otherwise. He outlines specific containment strategies, not involving large-scale incineration, but targeted bio-agents and... and carefully managed ecological pressure points. He believed the bloom could be contained, even reversed, by working *with* Eden's natural systems, not against them."

Thorne's hand clenched into a fist. Rostova's order, the one that had birthed the scorched earth, now felt less like a desperate act of salvation and more like a deliberate act of suppression. "So, the 'hazard' wasn't unforeseen. It was documented. And there were alternative solutions proposed."

"It appears so, Commander," Anya confirmed, her fingers flying across the holographic interface. "But Dr. Thorne's report... it's buried. Deeply buried. And there are subsequent logs, also classified, from the Colonial Security Council. These logs discuss 'mitigation protocols,' but they are heavily coded. And then, a week before the fire, there's a single, encrypted transmission from Commander Rostova to Earth Command. It's incredibly brief, just a few lines, but the keywords... 'existential threat,' 'uncontrollable variable,' 'necessary sacrifice.' It's chilling."

Thorne felt a cold dread creeping into his gut. He remembered the official account of Rostova's agonizing decision, the weight of the universe on her shoulders. But what if that agony was a carefully crafted performance? What if the 'uncontrollable variable' was not the bloom itself, but the potential discovery of Aris Thorne's research, the possibility of a less destructive, more scientific approach?

They delved further, Anya unearthing personnel files and internal memos that had been scrubbed from public view. One memo, dated mere days before the fire, detailed a heated exchange between Commander Rostova and Dr. Aris Thorne. The memo was brief, almost dismissive, but the context implied a stark disagreement. Aris Thorne was advocating for a patient, analytical approach, while Rostova, influenced by the security council's increasingly alarmist reports, was leaning towards more drastic measures.

"And then," Anya said, her voice dropping to a whisper, "I found this. It's a personal log, Commander. Not official. Not meant for the archives. It's a fragmented audio file, corrupted, but I've managed to restore a portion."

She initiated playback. The static crackled, then resolved into a strained, yet resolute, male voice. It was Aris Thorne.

"...unconscionable. Commander Rostova's insistence on a scorched-earth policy is not only scientifically unsound but morally reprehensible. The bloom is not a plague to be eradicated with fire, but a complex biological phenomenon to be understood. My research indicates a symbiotic potential, a pathway for integration, not annihilation. The implications of her proposed action are catastrophic. She dismisses my findings, citing... citing 'Earth Command's directives.' But I suspect there are other motivations at play. The council's fear is palpable, but their interpretation of the data is... flawed, bordering on deliberate misrepresentation. I cannot stand idly by while this world is subjected to such barbarity. I have attempted to bypass the security protocols, to transmit my complete findings directly to the scientific community on Earth. If this transmission is intercepted... if I am... silenced... I implore whoever finds this to understand: the fire was not the only path.

There was another way. A way that respected Eden's intrinsic nature. The true threat is not the bloom, but our own ignorance and our willingness to sacrifice everything for what we perceive as immediate safety."

The audio cut out abruptly, replaced by a burst of static. Thorne stood frozen, the weight of his ancestor's words pressing down on him. 'Silenced.' The implication was horrifying. His ancestor had been silenced, his warnings ignored, his research deliberately suppressed, all to pave the way for a devastating fire that served some hidden agenda. The official narrative of salvation was crumbling, revealing a foundation of deception and potentially, of murder.

"The logs from Dr. Thorne's lab are also heavily redacted, Commander," Anya continued, her voice trembling slightly. "Access to his terminal was restricted immediately after the fire. All of his raw data, his advanced simulations... they're gone. Or at least, they're not where they should be."

Thorne felt a surge of anger, a righteous fury that mingled with the profound sadness of his ancestor's fate. He had come to Eden seeking to rectify his own mistakes, to understand the delicate balance he had so carelessly disrupted. Now, he found himself confronted with a historical echo of the same hubris, the same willingness to sacrifice life for perceived expediency, a pattern that seemed to repeat itself across generations.

"What about Rostova's transmissions to Earth Command?" Thorne asked, his voice now a low growl. "The ones about 'necessary sacrifice.' What was the response?"

Anya's brow furrowed as she navigated through layers of encrypted communications. "Most of them are routine acknowledgments. But there's one... it's extremely brief. From Earth Command's Colonial Oversight Directorate. It's dated just hours before the fire. It reads: 'Directive confirmed. Proceed with protocol Omega. Acknowledge receipt and adherence.' No further context, no explanation."

Protocol Omega. The name itself sounded ominous, a stark contrast to the scientific terminology Aris Thorne had employed. Thorne's mind raced. What was Protocol Omega? Was it the justification for the fire? Was it a pre-approved plan for planetary terraforming, regardless of the cost to indigenous life? The idea that this act of destruction was not a spontaneous decision, but a pre-ordained protocol, was deeply unsettling. It implied a level of calculated indifference that went beyond mere ignorance.

"Earth Command's interest in Eden was purely scientific initially," Thorne mused, more to himself than to Anya. "They were eager to study its unique biosphere. But if this 'Protocol Omega' involved the deliberate incineration of a significant portion of the planet, then their motives were far more sinister. Perhaps they saw Eden not as a world to study, but as a resource to be purged, cleared for some future, yet-to-be-revealed purpose."

He thought of the subtle psychic resonance he had felt from Eden, the whispers of its ancient consciousness. Had it been aware of this impending violation? Had Aris Thorne's warnings been its own desperate attempt to communicate its plight?

Anya continued to sift through the data, her expression growing increasingly somber. "There's also a curious anomaly in the supply manifests from that period, Commander. A significant requisition for specialized atmospheric dispersal equipment, marked 'experimental climate control.' It was approved by Commander Rostova's office and signed off by a representative from the Colonial Security Council. This equipment arrived just days before the fire, but it was never deployed according to any official records. Instead, it seems to have been... rerouted to a private storage facility, one not listed on any colony inventory."

"A private facility?" Thorne's voice was sharp. "Whose private facility?"

Anya hesitated, then brought up a heavily redacted security clearance document. "The facility is designated for 'Project Nightingale.' Access records are minimal, but the initial authorization for its establishment and resupply signature belongs to... Executive Director Valerius."

The name hung in the air, a ghost from a chapter of the colony's history that Thorne had only vaguely heard whispered. Valerius. The architect of the colony's early expansionist policies, a man whose ambition was as legendary as his ruthlessness. He had been a dominant figure in the colony's formative years, but had disappeared from public record shortly after the fire, officially having returned to Earth due to ill health.

"Project Nightingale," Thorne repeated, tasting the words. "And experimental dispersal equipment. It's all starting to connect. The fire wasn't just about containment, was it? It was a cover. A massive, devastating cover for something else. Something Valerius was orchestrating."

He felt a cold certainty settle in his bones. His ancestor had recognized the danger, had tried to expose it, and had been silenced. Rostova, it seemed, had either been complicit or had been coerced into following a pre-determined, catastrophic path. The fire, the great 'salvation' of the colony, was nothing more than a stage set for a far more insidious play, orchestrated by Valerius.

Anya projected a schematic of the underground facility designated for Project Nightingale. It was extensive, far larger than a simple storage unit. It contained laboratories, bio-containment areas, and what appeared to be a large, central chamber. "This facility," Anya explained, her voice barely audible, "was operational for a period of six months *after* the fire. During that time, there were regular shipments of... biological samples. Not just from Eden. Samples from other worlds, Commander. Worlds that Earth Command had designated for 'resource assessment.'"

The implication was clear. Valerius, under the guise of colonial leadership and with the full, or at least complicit, backing of Earth Command, had been using Eden as a clandestine hub for his own agenda. Project Nightingale was not about preserving humanity; it was about leveraging Eden's unique environment for clandestine research and exploitation, a purpose masked by the pyre of Sector Gamma-7.

Thorne closed his eyes, the weight of these revelations pressing down on him. The scarred landscape of Sector Gamma-7 was no longer just a symbol of his own failure, but a monument to a far grander, far more devastating betrayal. The narrative of salvation was a lie, a carefully constructed facade designed to hide a crime against a world. His ancestor had seen the truth, had tried to fight it, and had paid the ultimate price. Rostova, whether victim or perpetrator, had played her part in the tragedy. And Valerius, the phantom orchestrator, had used the fire as his smokescreen.

"We need to find the rest of this data, Anya," Thorne said, his voice firm, imbued with a new, unshakeable resolve. "Every log, every transmission, every shred of evidence that exposes Valerius and Protocol Omega. The people of Eden deserve to know the truth about how their home was violated. And my ancestor... he deserves to have his voice heard."

He looked back at the holographic projection of Aris Thorne's report, the words now imbued with a profound urgency. The truth, buried beneath layers of redaction and deception, was finally beginning to surface. And with it, the understanding that the reckoning on Eden was far from over. It was only just beginning. The ashes of Sector Gamma-7 were not the end of a story, but a brutal prologue to a deeper, more dangerous truth that had been hidden in the archives, waiting to be unearthed by those willing to look beyond the comforting lies. The ghost of Protocol Omega, and the shadow of Valerius, now loomed larger than ever, demanding not just accountability, but a fundamental re-evaluation of humanity's presence on this vibrant, violated world. The path forward, Thorne realized, would be paved not with the easy acceptance of established histories, but with the relentless pursuit of every buried truth, no matter how painful.

The weight of Aris Thorne's recorded testament settled upon Commander Thorne like the suffocating dust of Sector Gamma-7. The official narrative, once a monolithic structure of colonial self-preservation, had fractured, revealing the rot at its core. The 'unforeseen hazard,' the desperate fire, the heroic sacrifice – all of it was now a carefully constructed artifice. His ancestor's desperate plea, his scientific foresight tragically unheeded, echoed in the sterile confines of the Archives, a phantom limb of truth reaching out from the past. Anya's quiet diligence had unearthed not just a historical cover-up, but a crime against a nascent world, a violation orchestrated with chilling precision. Protocol Omega. The words themselves were a guttural testament to the cold, utilitarian calculus of Earth Command, a chilling counterpoint to the vibrant, pulsing life of Eden.

As Thorne absorbed the implications, a subtle yet pervasive shift began to permeate the very atmosphere of the Archives. It wasn't an alarm, not a seismic tremor, but a change in the quality of the air itself, a faint, almost imperceptible dissonance that prickled at the edge of his senses. The hum of the data servers seemed to falter, momentarily out of sync, and the ambient light, which had been steady and controlled, flickered with an unfamiliar rhythm, as if the building itself were struggling to process the unearthed transgressions. Thorne, attuned to the subtlest environmental cues from his time on Eden's surface, recognized this not as a malfunction of the colonial infrastructure, but as something far more profound. It was Eden, responding.

He stepped away from the console, his gaze drawn to the observation window that overlooked a carefully manicured botanical garden, a contained ecosystem designed to replicate Eden's diverse flora within the colony's sterile walls. The vibrant hues of the native plants, usually a riot of defiant life, seemed muted, their leaves drooping with an unnatural weariness. A gentle breeze, which had been wafting through the open atrium, died abruptly, leaving a heavy, expectant stillness. Anya, sensing his unease, followed his gaze. "Is something wrong, Commander?" she asked, her voice laced with concern.

Thorne shook his head slowly, his eyes still fixed on the garden. "It's... it's as if the planet itself is grieving, Anya. Or perhaps, it's finally waking up." He thought of the intricate, interconnected web of life that Aris Thorne had so painstakingly documented, the subtle bio-signals, the complex communication networks that Eden possessed. Had his ancestor's research hinted at more than just botanical integration? Had he touched upon a deeper consciousness, a planetary awareness that was now reacting to the revelation of its own violation?

He recalled the fragments of his own experiences on Eden's surface, the moments of profound, almost spiritual connection he'd felt with the land, the unsettling sense of being observed, of being understood on a level that transcended mere observation. He had dismissed these as residual trauma, the psychological fallout of his own environmental recklessness. But now, in the wake of Aris Thorne's testimony and the unnerving atmospheric shifts, he wondered if he had been misinterpreting the whispers of a living world.

"The reports mentioned a 'parasitic bloom,'" Thorne mused aloud, his voice low. "But Aris Thorne's analysis suggested a 'symbiotic potential.' What if the bloom wasn't an aggressive, alien entity, but rather a manifestation of Eden's own immune response? A way for the planet to try and heal itself from an invasive force?" He paced the room, his mind racing with new possibilities. The fire, then, wasn't just an act of destruction, but an act of suppression. Rostova, under orders or under duress, had not extinguished a threat; she had silenced a burgeoning healing process.

Anya, her mind a steel trap of archival knowledge, was already cross-referencing the timeline of Aris Thorne's research with the atmospheric data recorded during the period leading up to the fire. "Commander," she said, her voice tight with discovery, "there are... anomalies. In the atmospheric composition logs. Just before the fire, there were significant, unexplainable spikes in certain trace gasses, correlating with increased bio-luminescence readings from the Sector Gamma-7 region. The official reports dismiss these as sensor malfunctions, attributed to the 'onset of the hazard.' But if Aris Thorne's theories are correct..."

"Then those spikes weren't malfunctions," Thorne finished, his voice resonating with a growing understanding. "They were signals. Eden's way of communicating its distress, its attempt to adapt, to integrate whatever was happening. And the fire... it was the brutal silencing of that communication." He looked out at the botanical garden again. The wilting leaves seemed to be drawing inward, their vibrant colours fading to a more subdued, almost somber palette. It was as if the very life force of the plants was recoiling, withdrawing from the intrusion of human knowledge, from the weight of their lies.

He remembered the psychic resonance he'd felt on Eden's surface, the melancholic murmurs that seemed to emanate from the very soil. He had initially attributed it to the planet's alien nature, its otherness. But what if those were not alien whispers, but the voice of Eden itself, a sentient being crying out in pain? Aris Thorne had understood this. He had seen Eden not as a resource, but as a partner, a cohabitant. His research had been an attempt to bridge the gap, to find a way for humanity to coexist, not to conquer.

The silence in the Archives deepened, but it was no longer the silence of dormant data. It was the profound, resonant silence of a world holding its breath, a cosmic pause before a reckoning. Thorne felt a peculiar kinship with the planet now, a shared burden of knowledge and regret. His own efforts to understand and rectify his past actions on Eden felt inextricably linked to his ancestor's futile struggle. Both were attempts to mend a broken relationship, to restore a balance that humanity had so carelessly shattered.

"The dispersal equipment for Project Nightingale," Thorne said, his thoughts shifting back to the immediate threat. "The logs indicate it was rerouted to a private facility. And this facility was operational for six months

*after* the fire. What were they doing in there, Anya? What kind of 'biological samples' were being shipped in and out of Eden's shadow?"

Anya's fingers danced across the interface, pulling up encrypted manifests and redacted schematics. "The nature of the samples is highly classified, Commander. But the origin points are listed. Several of them are from worlds that were undergoing similar 'resource assessments' by Earth

Command. Worlds that subsequently experienced... ecological collapse." Her voice was hushed, the implications chilling. It wasn't just Eden that had been subjected to this predatory agenda. Project Nightingale, and by extension, Protocol Omega, was a pattern. A systematic plundering of planetary life, masked by the rhetoric of exploration and expansion.

Thorne felt a cold fury coiling in his gut. His ancestor had fought to protect Eden's unique biosphere from a destructive force. Now, it seemed, that force was not merely destructive, but actively predatory, seeking to exploit and consume. The fire had been a smokescreen, a means to an end, allowing Valerius and his ilk to operate with impunity, to conduct their illicit research under the guise of colonial recovery. Eden's indigenous life, its complex ecological systems, were not just casualties of human error; they were raw materials for a clandestine industry.

He looked at the holographic projection of Aris Thorne's report, the intricate diagrams of cellular structures and ecological interdependencies. This was the true legacy of his ancestor, a testament to a scientific mind that understood the sacredness of life, the profound interconnectedness of all things. Rostova, driven by fear or ambition, had chosen to extinguish that legacy, to embrace the path of destruction. But Aris Thorne's work had survived, a seed of truth waiting for fertile ground. And now, that seed was beginning to sprout, watered by the revelations unearthed in the Archives.

As if in response to his thoughts, the gentle hum of the Archives intensified, taking on a warmer, more vibrant tone. The light steadied, bathing the room in a soft, golden hue that seemed to emanate from the very walls. Thorne looked out the window again. The plants in the botanical garden, though still subdued, appeared to be subtly regaining their colour. A few tentative blossoms unfurled, their delicate petals reaching towards the light. It was a subtle shift, easily dismissed as atmospheric variance, but Thorne recognized it for what it was: Eden's acknowledgment. A silent testament to the fact that truth, however buried, had a way of reasserting itself, of coaxing life back from the brink.

"Valerius wasn't just building a clandestine research facility," Thorne stated, his voice firm. "He was building an arsenal. An arsenal of biological weapons, perhaps. Or instruments of planetary manipulation. The 'experimental climate control' equipment... it wasn't for terraforming Eden. It was for controlling

*other* worlds, for breaking them down, for extracting their resources with ruthless efficiency." He thought of the psychic echoes he'd felt, the melancholic whispers from the planet's core. Had he been sensing not just distress, but a desperate attempt to resist? To refuse to be complicit in humanity's destructive agenda?

Anya nodded, her eyes fixed on the screen. "The documentation regarding Project Nightingale is frustratingly sparse, Commander. It's as if they anticipated someone digging. But there are references to 'containment protocols' for volatile biological agents, and 'advanced bio-engineering techniques.' The implications are... disturbing."

"Disturbing is an understatement, Anya," Thorne replied, his gaze hardening. "It's a betrayal of everything humanity claims to stand for. We come to these worlds seeking knowledge, seeking new beginnings, and instead, we sow destruction and deception. Aris Thorne understood the delicate dance of life. He saw the potential for harmony. Valerius saw only a canvas for his own power, a means to exploit and dominate."

He walked back to the holographic projection of his ancestor's report, tracing the lines of scientific notation with his finger. "He believed the bloom could be managed, that it held 'symbiotic potential.' What if that potential was not just for the bloom itself, but for humanity? What if Eden, through its complex biology, offered a pathway to a more sustainable existence, a way to integrate with the natural world rather than subjugating it? And what if Valerius feared that? Feared a solution that would relinquish his control, diminish his power?"

The air in the Archives, now suffused with a palpable sense of awakening, seemed to carry a subtle energy, a gentle pulse that resonated with Thorne's own heightened senses. It was not a hostile response, not a judgment of punishment, but a profound, almost sorrowful, acknowledgment of humanity's failings. Eden was not seeking retribution; it was seeking understanding, and perhaps, a chance to heal. The very planet was an observer, its evolution a testament to resilience, its burgeoning consciousness now a witness to the unearthed truths.

"The fire," Thorne continued, his voice a low rumble, "was a violent suppression of that potential. It was the ultimate act of 'scorched earth' – not just to eliminate a perceived threat, but to erase any alternative. To ensure that humanity's narrative remained the only one, the one dictated by fear and expediency." He felt a profound sense of responsibility, not just for his own past actions, but for the legacy of his species. His ancestor had tried to be the voice of reason, the prophet of coexistence. Thorne now felt the mantle of that responsibility fall upon his own shoulders.

"We need to expose this, Anya," he said, his voice firm with a newfound resolve. "Every redacted file, every coded transmission, every shred of evidence that points to Protocol Omega and Project Nightingale. The people of Eden, what remains of them, deserve to know the truth about how their world was scarred, about the price of their supposed salvation. And my ancestor... he deserves to have his warnings heard, not as a footnote in a tragedy, but as a pivotal moment where humanity chose the path of destruction over the path of understanding."

The soft golden light that now filled the Archives seemed to brighten, as if in affirmation. Thorne looked out at the botanical garden once more. The blossoms were opening wider, their colours deepening, their delicate fragrances filling the air. It was a silent, yet powerful, testament to Eden's enduring spirit, its capacity for regeneration. The judgment of Eden was not a pronouncement of damnation, but a quiet, persistent affirmation of life, a subtle yet unwavering challenge to humanity to recognize its place within the grand tapestry of existence, and to finally reckon with the profound ethical implications of its actions. The planet, in its evolving consciousness, was not condemning them, but offering a silent, powerful lesson: that true salvation lay not in conquest and control, but in understanding, respect, and a willingness to listen to the quiet wisdom of a living world. The echoes of Aris Thorne's voice, once a whisper of despair, now resonated with the quiet strength of a planet awakening, a beacon of hope amidst the ashes of a manufactured catastrophe.

The concept of a scapegoat, a vessel for collective guilt and blame, was deeply ingrained in the colonial psyche. It was a mechanism of self-preservation, a way to maintain the illusion of righteous intent in the face of devastating actions. Rostova, in the official narrative, had been the perfect candidate: the rogue officer, the fallen hero, the one whose ambition had curdled into outright treachery. Her act of immolation, the fiery silencing of Aris Thorne's burgeoning communication with Eden, was painted as a desperate, misguided attempt to purge a perceived alien threat. This narrative, carefully curated and disseminated by Earth Command, served its purpose for decades, absolving the architects of Protocol Omega from complicity and allowing them to continue their exploitation unimpeded.

Thorne, however, now stood at the precipice of dismantling this carefully constructed fiction. The data Anya had unearthed painted a far more intricate, and far more damning, picture. Rostova had not acted out of personal malice or misguided zeal. Her actions, while undeniably catastrophic, were a consequence of a deeply compromised position, a brutal ultimatum delivered from on high. The fragmented transmissions, the encrypted orders, all pointed to a higher authority, a hidden hand orchestrating the entire affair. Rostova, in essence, had been a pawn, a willing or unwilling executioner of a far greater plan. Her supposed villainy was a carefully crafted illusion, designed to deflect scrutiny from the true perpetrators. She was the scapegoat, sacrificed to protect the reputations and further the agendas of those who pulled the strings.

This revelation cast a long shadow, forcing Thorne to re-evaluate not only Rostova's role but the very definition of heroism on Eden. Aris Thorne, his ancestor, had been hailed as a visionary, a man ahead of his time, his desperate warnings tragically ignored. His scientific acumen, his profound respect for the burgeoning life of Eden, had positioned him as a beacon of hope, a stark contrast to the destructive forces that ultimately prevailed. Yet, even his legacy was not without its complexities. His research, while driven by a noble desire for coexistence, had also provided the foundational knowledge that Valerius and his ilk had twisted for their own nefarious purposes. The understanding of Eden's biological systems, the very secrets Aris Thorne had sought to protect, had become the blueprint for its exploitation. Was he then a savior, or an unwitting enabler?

The question gnawed at Thorne. If Rostova was not the villain, but a tool, then who was the true savior? Was it Aris Thorne, whose foresight had been so brutally suppressed? Or was the true savior still to emerge, the one who could not only expose the truth but guide humanity towards a genuine path of reconciliation with Eden? He looked at Anya, her brow furrowed in concentration as she navigated the labyrinthine data streams. Her quiet determination, her unwavering pursuit of truth, felt like a nascent form of salvation. She was not a warrior, not a politician, but a scholar, wielding knowledge as her weapon, and in this sterile, data-driven environment, that was a potent force.

The very act of unearthing these secrets had been an act of defiance, a challenge to the established order. It was a dangerous undertaking, one that had already cost lives and would likely continue to do so. The truth, Thorne suspected, was a far more volatile entity than any biological weapon Valerius might have engineered. It had the power to destabilize, to ignite, to dismantle entire systems of belief. And for those who had built their power on lies, the truth was the ultimate existential threat.

He found himself contemplating the unintended consequences of Aris Thorne's own actions. His ancestor's meticulous documentation of Eden's unique flora and fauna, his understanding of the intricate bio-communications networks, had been intended to foster respect and integration. However, this very knowledge had also provided Valerius with the detailed map of Eden's vulnerabilities. The 'symbiotic potential' that Aris Thorne had so optimistically identified was, in Valerius's hands, a weakness to be exploited, a biological key to unlock the planet's resources. It was a chilling reminder that even the noblest intentions could be twisted into instruments of destruction.

The realization settled upon Thorne with a heavy weight. He had always viewed his ancestor as a figure of unblemished virtue, a martyr to scientific truth. Now, he saw a more complex, more human figure, a man whose brilliance was not without its blind spots, whose noble pursuit of understanding had inadvertently paved the way for ruin. This did not diminish Aris Thorne's legacy, but it humanized it, making his sacrifice even more poignant. He was not a god, but a man who had glimpsed a profound truth and paid the ultimate price for trying to share it.

The concept of a 'savior' on Eden was a thorny one. If Aris Thorne was the prophet, Rostova was the unwilling executioner, and Valerius the architect of destruction, then who was left to embody salvation? Thorne himself had been a perpetrator of ecological damage, a product of the same colonial mindset that had led to Eden's ruination. His journey had been one of personal reckoning, of attempting to atone for his own past mistakes. Could he, a former agent of destruction, now become an agent of salvation? The thought was both daunting and strangely compelling.

He recalled his own experiences on Eden's surface, the moments of profound connection that had preceded his reckless actions. He had felt the planet's pulse, its intricate web of life, and had, in his hubris, believed he could control it. Now, he understood that he had been interacting with a living, breathing entity, a consciousness far older and more complex than he had ever imagined. His 'control' had been a violation, his actions a brutal disruption of a delicate balance. His path to salvation, if it existed, lay in acknowledging that violation and seeking genuine reconciliation, not through force or manipulation, but through understanding and respect.

The paradox of their situation was stark. They were uncovering the truth from within the very institution that had perpetuated the lies. The Archives, a repository of colonial history, had become the cradle of Eden's true narrative. Anya, a digital archaeologist, was excavating a buried civilization, not of stone and mortar, but of data and intent. Her meticulous work was not just about historical accuracy; it was about reclaiming a lost future, about giving a voice back to a world that had been systematically silenced.

He considered the idea of a collective salvation. Perhaps no single individual could bear the weight of being the savior. Perhaps salvation lay in a shared understanding, a collective awakening. The revelation of Protocol Omega was not just a historical footnote; it was a moral inflection point for humanity. It was a test of their capacity for self-awareness, their ability to learn from their mistakes and forge a new path. If they could truly confront the depth of their transgressions on Eden, if they could move beyond assigning blame to individuals and recognize the systemic rot, then perhaps there was hope.

The question of Valerius's motives also came into sharp focus. Was he driven by a pure desire for power, or was there a twisted logic to his actions? Thorne's ancestor had spoken of Valerius's fascination with control, his belief that nature was an untamed force to be mastered. It was possible that Valerius saw himself not as a destroyer, but as a necessary force of order, imposing human will upon a chaotic, alien biosphere. This, of course, did not excuse his actions, but it added another layer of complexity to the narrative of villainy. He was not simply evil; he was ideologically driven, his vision of humanity's place in the cosmos fundamentally flawed.

Thorne's gaze fell upon a small, framed photograph on Anya's desk. It depicted a younger Anya, standing beside an older woman with kind eyes and a resolute smile. "Your grandmother," Thorne stated, the recognition dawning on him. He remembered her from his initial briefings on Eden, a respected botanist who had worked alongside Aris Thorne. She had been a casualty of the 'unforeseen hazard,' her death officially attributed to environmental exposure. Now, Thorne wondered if her fate, like Rostova's, had been orchestrated.

"She believed in Aris Thorne's work," Anya said softly, her voice tinged with a deep, abiding sorrow. "She saw Eden not as a resource, but as a miracle. She taught me to look, to listen, to understand the interconnectedness of everything. She would have been... heartbroken by what they did."

Her grandmother's legacy, like Aris Thorne's, was now intertwined with the struggle for truth. She had been a quiet guardian of Eden's secrets, her knowledge a silent testament to its vitality. And now, her granddaughter was unearthing those secrets, not just for historical record, but for the future. This generational passing of knowledge, this unbroken lineage of respect for Eden, felt like a genuine flicker of salvation. It was a reminder that even in the face of overwhelming darkness, the seeds of light and hope could endure.

The weight of the revelations pressed down on Thorne. The clear lines between hero and villain, so painstakingly drawn by Earth Command, had dissolved into a murky, complex web of motivations, compromises, and unintended consequences. Rostova, the alleged villain, was now a victim of circumstance, a pawn in a much larger game. Aris Thorne, the hailed savior, was now seen as a figure whose brilliance was not without its tragic flaws, whose efforts inadvertently provided the tools for exploitation. And Thorne himself, the commander who had once embodied the colonial ethos, was now the reluctant custodian of a truth that threatened to shatter that very ethos.

He understood, with a chilling clarity, that the narrative of salvation was never simple. It was not a singular act of heroism, but a continuous, arduous process of confronting difficult truths, of acknowledging past wrongs, and of striving for a more ethical future. The scapegoat, in this new light, was not just Rostova, but perhaps humanity itself, burdened by its history of exploitation and its desperate need to believe in its own inherent righteousness. The true savior, then, would not be a single individual, but a collective awakening, a shared commitment to dismantling the structures of deception and embracing a genuine symbiosis with the worlds they encountered. Eden, in its silent suffering, was offering them that chance. The question was whether they were finally ready to hear its message. The path forward was not one of conquest or control, but of humble understanding and a profound respect for the intricate, vibrant tapestry of life that Eden represented. The journey of reckoning had just begun, and the true cost of salvation was yet to be fully understood.

The silence in the Archives had become a palpable entity, thick with the unspoken implications of Anya's revelations. Rostova, the supposed villain of Eden's tragic genesis, was no longer a black-and-white caricature of ambition and malice. She was a ghost in the machine of history, a pawn sacrificed on the altar of a larger, more insidious agenda. Aris Thorne, the revered prophet of coexistence, was revealed as a man whose groundbreaking work, intended to foster understanding, had paradoxically provided the very blueprints for Eden's exploitation. And then there was Valerius, the architect of devastation, his motives now painted not as pure evil, but as a chillingly rationalized form of control, a belief in humanity's inherent right to impose order upon the perceived chaos of the alien.

This dismantling of established narratives was not merely an intellectual exercise; it was an earthquake that threatened to shatter the very bedrock of their collective identity. For decades, the colonial narrative had served as a comforting blanket, a justification for their presence and actions on Eden. It allowed them to frame themselves as pioneers, as bringers of progress, conveniently overlooking the brutal cost of that 'progress.' Now, that blanket had been ripped away, exposing the raw, uncomfortable truth of their history: one built on deception, exploitation, and the silencing of indigenous voices, both human and ecological.

Thorne felt the weight of this truth settle upon him, a physical burden that made each breath a conscious effort. He had been a part of that system, a cog in the machine that had perpetuated these lies. His own past actions on Eden, his unquestioning adherence to protocol, now seemed like acts of profound ignorance, if not complicity. The concept of a 'savior' was no longer a distant, heroic ideal. It was a question that clawed at his conscience: could he, a product and perpetrator of this flawed system, ever become an agent of genuine healing?

Anya, her eyes still fixed on the holographic displays, spoke, her voice a low murmur that cut through the heavy silence. "They didn't just lie about Rostova, or Aris Thorne, or Valerius. They lied about Eden. They lied about what it *is*."

He understood. The narrative of Eden as a passive, inert resource waiting to be tamed and exploited was the most insidious lie of all. Aris Thorne's research, Anya's grandmother's quiet devotion, had hinted at something far more profound: a living, breathing entity, a complex network of consciousness and interconnected life that they had systematically brutalized. Their 'reckonings' were not just about human actors and their deceptions, but about acknowledging the profound violation inflicted upon an entire world.

"The truth," Thorne mused, his gaze sweeping across the data streams, "is not a passive observer. It's an active force. And this truth... it's going to demand a reckoning far beyond anything we've imagined."

He thought of the 'unforeseen hazards,' the convenient explanations for the deaths of scientists who had perhaps strayed too close to the truth, like Anya's grandmother. The death of Rostova, too, was a convenient narrative closure, a fiery punctuation mark that silenced any lingering questions. But the data Anya had unearthed was not silent. It was a symphony of fragmented transmissions, encrypted directives, and the echoes of suppressed warnings, all coalescing into a chorus of indictment.

The rebuilding of trust, Thorne realized, would be a monumental undertaking. It wasn't simply a matter of presenting new evidence; it was about confronting a deeply ingrained cultural amnesia. The generations born after the initial protocols had been ingrained with a specific version of history, a narrative that painted humanity as the protagonist in a grand galactic drama, Eden merely a stage. To shatter that illusion was to ask them to question their very place in the universe, their inherent rightness.

"We need to start with the community," Anya said, her voice gaining a quiet strength. "Not just within Earth Command, but on the colonies, on Eden itself. They deserve to know. They have a right to the truth about what was done in their name."

Thorne nodded, the enormity of the task settling upon him. "But how do we present it? How do we convey the nuance, the complexity, without just creating a new set of villains, a new simplistic narrative?" He looked at Anya. "Aris Thorne, for all his brilliance, inadvertently provided the tools for destruction. Rostova was a victim of circumstance. Valerius, a product of a twisted ideology. Where is the clear line for people to grasp onto?"

"There isn't one, not anymore," Anya replied, her gaze meeting his, unwavering. "That's the point. The old foundations were built on sand. They were always unstable. We have to build something new, something on solid ground. And that ground is truth, even when it's ugly."

The idea of a 'new foundation of truth' felt both terrifying and exhilarating. It meant acknowledging that their history was not a glorious march of progress, but a tangled mess of ambition, ignorance, and calculated cruelty. It meant admitting that their perceived superiority was a delusion, and that their interactions with Eden had been a profound moral failure. This was not about assigning blame to individuals in a way that would allow others to feel clean, but about acknowledging a systemic rot that had permeated every level of their colonial enterprise.

He recalled the initial chaos after his arrival on Eden, the unquestioning obedience demanded, the suppression of any dissenting voices. The 'unforeseen hazards' were not merely random events; they were the carefully managed consequences of a system designed to maintain control at all costs. Anya's grandmother's death was not an accident; it was a silencing. Rostova's immolation, a public spectacle designed to terrorize and to set an example.

Each death, each tragedy, had been meticulously cataloged and framed within the acceptable narrative, its true context deliberately obscured.

"The truth about Rostova," Thorne continued, his voice growing more resonant, "is that she was given an impossible choice. To follow orders that would condemn a world, or to be branded a traitor, a monster. Her 'treachery' was a desperate act of self-preservation, a final, futile attempt to reclaim some agency in a situation where she had none."

Anya nodded, her fingers dancing across the console, pulling up encrypted logs that corroborated Thorne's words. "And Aris Thorne's 'visionary' research was systematically stripped of its ethical safeguards. His understanding of Eden's bio-communication was reinterpreted as a vulnerability. The very data he collected to foster respect was weaponized to ensure compliance."

The sheer scale of the deception was overwhelming. It wasn't just about a few individuals making bad decisions; it was a sustained, multi-generational effort to manipulate reality. The 'official records' were a carefully constructed edifice of lies, designed to protect the architects of Protocol Omega and their successors. Thorne felt a surge of anger, not just at the perpetrators, but at himself, for having been a willing participant in the perpetuation of these falsehoods, however unwittingly.

"We need to show them the context," Thorne stated, the idea solidifying in his mind. "Not just the facts, but the pressure, the motivations, the impossible situations. Rostova wasn't just an officer; she was a woman trapped. Aris Thorne wasn't just a scientist; he was a father, trying to protect his legacy, trying to ensure Eden's future, and that legacy was twisted."

"And Valerius," Anya added, her voice barely a whisper, "he wasn't simply a warmonger. He genuinely believed he was saving humanity from itself, from the perceived threat of a conscious, unpredictable alien world. He saw his actions as a necessary purification, a forceful imposition of order."

This was the difficult truth. It was easier to condemn pure evil, to rally against a clear villain. But this was not about clear villains. This was about systemic flaws, about human fallibility twisted into horrific actions, about the dangerous allure of certainty in the face of the unknown. The new foundation of truth had to accommodate these shades of gray, these uncomfortable complexities. It had to acknowledge that the worst atrocities are often committed not by monsters, but by people who believe they are doing the right thing, however warped their vision.

The challenge, Thorne knew, would be in disseminating this nuanced truth. Earth Command would fight it, clinging to their manufactured history like drowning sailors to driftwood. The colonists, raised on a steady diet of propaganda, would resist it. They would fear the unraveling of their identity, the erosion of their perceived moral superiority.

"We have to start with those who are already questioning," Thorne said, his gaze falling on Anya, on her quiet determination, her unwavering commitment to truth. "Those who have felt the dissonance, who have sensed that something was not right. Anya, your grandmother, Aris Thorne... they represent a different path. A path of respect, of understanding."

Anya's grandmother. He pictured the framed photograph on her desk, the gentle smile, the eyes that held a deep understanding of life. She had been a quiet guardian of Eden's secrets, a silent testament to its vitality. Her legacy was not one of conquest, but of cultivation. Her granddaughter, now, was continuing that legacy, not through scientific papers, but through the unearthing of a suppressed history. This generational transfer of knowledge, this unbroken lineage of respect for Eden, felt like a true beacon of hope.

"We need to present this not as an accusation, but as an offering," Thorne continued, the words flowing with a new sense of purpose. "An offering of understanding. We offer the truth about Rostova, not to absolve her, but to acknowledge her sacrifice. We offer the complexity of Aris Thorne's legacy, not to diminish him, but to honor his intent and lament its corruption. We offer the twisted logic of Valerius, not to excuse him, but to understand the roots of such destructive ideologies."

The very act of excavating these buried truths was an act of ecological restoration, in a sense. They were giving voice back to a world that had been systematically silenced, acknowledging its right to exist, its inherent value beyond its utility to humanity. The 'communication' Aris Thorne had sought with Eden, the one Rostova had so brutally suppressed, was not just about understanding alien life; it was about understanding a profound truth about interconnectedness, about the shared tapestry of existence.

"The foundation we build must be on this interconnectedness," Thorne declared, his voice resonating with conviction. "Not on the subjugation of nature, but on our integration within it. This means acknowledging Eden's sentience, its rights, its place not as a resource, but as a co-inhabitant of this star system."

This was the core of the new foundation: a radical shift in perspective, from dominion to symbiosis. It meant recognizing that humanity was not the apex of creation, but a part of a larger, infinitely more complex whole. It meant embracing humility, admitting that their knowledge was incomplete, their understanding limited.

"We can't simply erase the past," Anya stated, her fingers now still on the console. "We have to integrate it. The lies, the betrayals, the sacrifices... they are all part of our story. We need to acknowledge them, understand them, and then move forward with a commitment to doing better. To honoring the truth, no matter how painful."

The pain was undeniable. For many, the revelation would be devastating. It would shatter their sense of identity, their place in the cosmos. But Thorne knew, with a certainty that chilled him to the bone, that clinging to the old falsehoods would lead to an even greater catastrophe. Eden, in its silent, enduring suffering, had offered them a chance to learn, to evolve. The question was whether they, as a species, were ready to accept that offer.

The task of establishing this new foundation would fall upon them, upon Anya and himself, and upon anyone else brave enough to confront the uncomfortable realities. It would be a slow, arduous process, fraught with resistance and doubt. But it was a necessary one. The old edifice of lies had crumbled. It was time to lay the first stone of a new truth, a truth that acknowledged the past, however terrible, and embraced a future built on honesty, respect, and a profound understanding of their place within the vibrant, living tapestry of the cosmos. This was not just about rewriting history; it was about rewriting their future. It was about the dawn of a new era of reckoning, an era where truth, no matter how painful, was the only path to genuine salvation. The silence in the Archives was no longer just the absence of sound; it was the pregnant pause before a new dawn, a testament to the profound, and often brutal, nature of truth.

## CHAPTER ELEVEN

# THE LANGUAGE OF THE LIVING PLANET

The archives, once a sanctuary of quiet contemplation, now thrummed with a different kind of energy. The revelation of humanity's colonial deception had fractured the comfortable narratives, but Anya and Thorne found themselves drawn to a new, even more profound enigma. It wasn't just the actions of individuals or the machinations of Earth Command that needed re-examination; it was the very nature of Eden itself. Anya's grandmother's legacy, once seen through the lens of a dedicated xenobotanist, now hinted at something far more extraordinary: a planetary consciousness expressed not through biology alone, but through sound.

The concept, initially dismissed as fanciful speculation by many within the scientific establishment, had gained traction as Anya delved deeper into the suppressed research logs. Aris Thorne's work, particularly his later, more esoteric inquiries, spoke of "resonant frequencies" and "bio-acoustic dialogues." He had hypothesized that Eden's ecosystem wasn't merely a collection of independent organisms interacting through instinct and necessity, but a vast, interconnected network participating in a planet-wide conversation. The "unforeseen hazards" that had plagued early research, the sudden equipment failures, the unsettling sonic anomalies that defied conventional explanation – Thorne had begun to suspect these were not random glitches, but rather the planet's subtle, or not-so-subtle, reactions to invasive presence.

"It's not just random noise, Aris," Anya murmured, her gaze fixed on a complex waveform shimmering on her display. It represented a recording taken deep within one of Eden's bioluminescent forests, a symphony of chirps, rustles, and low, resonant hums. "Look at the patterns. The periodicity. The harmonic relationships. This isn't simply the byproduct of biological processes. It's structured. It carries information."

Thorne leaned closer, his scientific skepticism warring with a growing sense of wonder. He had spent his career cataloging and analyzing biological data, but this... this was different. It felt less like data and more like a language. "The rustling of the xenofoliage," he mused, pointing to a specific frequency band. "It's not just the wind. There are distinct variations, almost like... inflection. And the calls of the nocturnal avians, they're not isolated. They're responsive. They're building on each other."

Anya nodded, her fingers flying across the console, isolating individual sound components and overlaying them with spectral analysis. "The geothermal vents too. The low hum, it's not constant. It pulses. And the pulses aren't random. They correlate with seismic activity, yes, but also with atmospheric pressure changes, and even with the migratory patterns of certain subterranean fauna. It's as if the planet itself is... breathing, and communicating those breaths."

They had begun to refer to it as "bio-acoustic signatures," a term that felt both clinical and inadequate. It was more than just a signature; it was an ongoing narrative, a planetary monologue that had been playing out for millennia, unheard and unacknowledged by the colonizing species. Anya's grandmother's early research, ostensibly focused on the unique bio-luminescent properties of Eden's flora, had, in fact, been a covert investigation into these sonic phenomena. Her field notes, filled with cryptic annotations and diagrams, hinted at her growing realization that the planet's light and sound were intrinsically linked, two facets of a single, complex communication system.

"She believed the bioluminescence was a visual manifestation of the acoustic patterns," Anya explained, her voice tinged with a reverence that Thorne now understood. "A way for the planet to 'speak' in light when sonic barriers were too great, or when certain frequencies were too subtle for even the most sensitive bio-acoustic sensors. She was trying to decode a dual language."

The implications were staggering. If Eden was not merely a passive collection of resources, but a sentient, communicating entity, then humanity's entire presence on the planet had been an act of profound violation, an invasion of a conscious being. The "unforeseen hazards" were no longer accidents; they were potentially the planet's immune response, its attempts to warn off or repel a harmful intrusion. Rostova's brutal protocols, designed to quell dissent and enforce compliance, had also served to aggressively silence any who might have listened too closely to Eden's true voice.

"Aris Thorne's theories about resonance," Thorne continued, recalling passages from his mentor's fragmented journals. "He believed that certain frequencies could disrupt biological processes, cause disorientation, even induce physiological stress. He theorized that the colonial apparatus, in its relentless pursuit of resource extraction, was inadvertently emitting disruptive frequencies, like a constant, low-grade sonic assault. The planet was fighting back, not with malice, but with its own resonant frequencies, creating an environment that was inherently hostile to our technologies, and perhaps, to our very presence."

Anya pulled up a series of encrypted transmissions, dating back to the early days of the colonial effort. They were heavily redacted, but fragments of Anya's grandmother's increasingly desperate communications remained. She spoke of "harmonic interference" and "planetary feedback loops." She warned of "ecological destabilization" not as a result of unsustainable practices, but as a deliberate, albeit passive, counter-measure by Eden. Her final transmission, before her official record of "fatal accident," was a fragmented plea: "They are not listening. They are drowning out the symphony. Eden is singing its warning, and we are deaf."

Thorne felt a shiver trace its way down his spine. The narrative of Eden as a wild, untamed world ripe for conquest had been a carefully constructed lie. The truth was far more complex, and far more humbling. Eden was not a passive canvas; it was an active participant, a conscious entity expressing itself through a language that humanity, in its arrogance, had failed to perceive. The subtle shifts in atmospheric composition, the peculiar weather patterns, the seemingly erratic behavior of the local fauna – all could be interpreted not as natural phenomena, but as deliberate responses, a planetary immune system at work.

"This changes everything," Thorne stated, his voice barely above a whisper. "The Protocols, the suppression of dissent, the very existence of Protocol Omega... it was all designed to maintain the illusion of Eden as an inert resource. The true threat, as they saw it, was not the planet's potential sentience, but the revelation of it. Because if Eden is sentient, then our claim, our dominion, is illegitimate. Our very presence is an act of aggression against a conscious being."

Anya's grandmother, it became clear, was not simply a xenobotanist with an interest in acoustic phenomena. She was a pioneer in xenolinguistics, specifically a form of communication so alien it transcended traditional linguistic models. Her research had been deemed too heretical, too disruptive to the established colonial agenda. It offered not a way to control Eden, but a way to *listen* to it, to understand it, and perhaps, to coexist with it on its own terms. Rostova's mission, Thorne now understood, was not just about silencing human dissenters; it was about eradicating any potential bridge of understanding between humanity and the planet. The silencing of Anya's grandmother was a critical component of that mission.

"They knew," Anya said, her eyes blazing with a fierce, quiet anger. "They knew Eden was more than just a collection of species. They understood that

Aris Thorne's research had opened a door. And they decided to slam it shut, permanently."

Thorne spent days poring over Anya's grandmother's fragmented audio logs. They were raw, unfiltered recordings, full of background noise that Anya and Thorne's advanced algorithms were now painstakingly separating. They found the distinct sonic signatures of the xenofoliage, a gentle rustling that seemed to convey information about nutrient flow and light availability. They detected the complex, melodic patterns of the avian calls, which appeared to be more than just mating or territorial signals; they seemed to be reporting environmental conditions, alerting others to subtle shifts in atmospheric pressure or the presence of specific mineral deposits.

Even the geological sounds were revealing. The deep, resonant hum of the geothermal activity wasn't just a geological process; it was a rhythmic pulse, a planetary heartbeat. Anya's grandmother had theorized that these pulses varied in frequency and amplitude, correlating with deep-earth geological events, but also, bizarrely, with the synchronized blooming cycles of certain rare fungal colonies that only appeared after specific seismic tremors. It suggested an interconnectedness that defied conventional scientific understanding, a planet where geological, biological, and atmospheric systems were locked in a complex, interwoven dialogue.

"It's like a planetary nervous system," Thorne observed, his mind racing. "The sound waves are the electrochemical signals, the vibrations traveling through the crust are like nerve impulses. The bioluminescence is the visible output, the conscious manifestation of the planet's internal state. We've been treating a living, breathing entity as a dead rock."

The implications for their current situation were profound. If they could learn to understand Eden's bio-acoustic language, they might be able to find a path towards true coexistence. They could learn what the planet needed, what it felt, how it perceived their presence. It would require a complete paradigm shift, moving away from the dominance-based colonial model to one of genuine empathy and communication.

"The 'unforeseen hazards'," Anya mused, scrolling through a timeline of unexplained incidents, "were likely the planet's attempts to self-regulate, to communicate its distress. The seismic tremors that disrupted mining operations, the sudden atmospheric disturbances that grounded shuttles, the localized bio-eddies that rendered certain technologies useless... these weren't random malfunctions. They were responses. Eden was telling us, in its own language, to stop."

Thorne recalled Valerius's infamous decree: "Order must be imposed. Chaos must be eradicated." Valerius had seen Eden's wildness, its untamed complexity, as a threat to human order. He had viewed its inherent systems as imperfections to be corrected, its intricate dialogues as noise to be silenced. He had never considered that this "chaos" was, in fact, a sophisticated, living language.

"Valerius's strategy was to overwhelm Eden's natural systems with brute force," Thorne explained, piecing together the fragmented history. "To drown out its 'noise' with the clamor of human industry. He believed that by imposing our own, predictable frequencies – the hum of machinery, the thrum of engines – we could effectively mask its communication and assert our dominance. He was trying to shout over a planetary symphony."

Anya brought up a series of audio files from the height of Valerius's planetary terraforming efforts. The recordings were a cacophony of industrial noise, punctuated by what sounded like desperate, high-frequency bursts from Eden's native fauna, and deep, guttural groans from the planet's geological strata. It was a sonic battle, a desperate attempt by Eden to make itself heard above the din of human imposition.

"This isn't just about scientific curiosity anymore, Aris," Anya said, her voice firm. "This is about recognizing the rights of a sentient being. We have been actively harming Eden, not through malice, but through ignorance. And now, we have the potential to understand. We have the tools, thanks to your grandmother's foresight and Aris Thorne's foundational work, to finally listen."

The path forward, Thorne realized, was not about cataloging more resources or devising more efficient extraction methods. It was about building sonic bridges, about developing technologies that could translate Eden's bio-acoustic signatures into something humans could comprehend. It was about fostering a new generation of researchers who saw themselves not as conquerors, but as diplomats, as listeners, as students of a planetary consciousness.

He thought of the potential resistance. Earth Command would likely view this discovery as a threat to their authority, another inconvenient truth to be suppressed. The colonists, ingrained with generations of colonial ideology, might struggle to accept that their home was a living entity with its own needs and desires. But the evidence was undeniable, etched in the very fabric of sound that permeated Eden's atmosphere and crust.

"Your grandmother's work wasn't just about understanding Eden's voice," Thorne concluded, looking at Anya with a newfound respect. "It was about understanding humanity's capacity for connection, for empathy, even across unimaginable divides. She was trying to teach us to listen, not just to the planet, but to ourselves, to our own buried conscience."

The task ahead was daunting. It required not just scientific innovation, but a fundamental ethical reorientation. It meant acknowledging that their existence on Eden was not a right, but a privilege that had to be earned through respect and understanding. The bio-acoustic signatures were more than just data; they were a plea, a testament, and a promise. A promise that even in the deepest silence, life found a way to speak, and a plea for humanity to finally, truly, listen. This was not the end of their reckoning, but a new beginning, one where the language of Eden would become their guide, their teacher, and perhaps, their salvation. The sound of Eden, once dismissed as mere background noise, was now the most important signal they had ever received, a symphony of existence waiting to be understood.

The concept of geomagnetism, once relegated to the dusty tomes of planetary geology and atmospheric physics, had taken on an entirely new dimension within the hushed, echoey halls of Eden's clandestine archives. Anya and Thorne, their understanding of the living planet expanding with each passing cycle, had stumbled upon a phenomenon so profound, so interwoven with Eden's very essence, that it threatened to rewrite the entirety of their scientific and philosophical frameworks. It wasn't merely the bio-acoustic symphony that resonated through the atmosphere and crust; it was a subtler, more pervasive hum, a planetary pulse that emanated not just from the molten core, but from the very fabric of space-time surrounding the world.

Initial anomalies had been dismissed as sensor malfunctions, the quirks of operating sophisticated equipment in an environment teeming with unexplained bio-electrical activity. Readings from the magnetometers, designed to chart the planet's inherent magnetic field for navigational purposes and resource prospecting, often fluctuated wildly, defying predictable solar or geological influences. They would spike during intense atmospheric electrical storms, as expected, but also, and far more disturbingly, during periods of unusual seismic quiescence, or conversely, during moments of inexplicable ecological harmony – the synchronized blooming of the luminaflora, the mass migrations of the crystal-winged insects. Thorne, ever the pragmatist, had attributed these discrepancies to the complex interplay of Eden's unique magnetosphere and its pervasive biological energy fields, a notion that still held scientific merit.

However, Anya, with her grandmother's legacy of looking beyond the obvious, began to cross-reference these magnetic fluctuations with other, seemingly unrelated, data streams. She meticulously cataloged atmospheric pressure changes, seismic event logs, and even the faint, residual bio-luminescent signatures that pulsed across the nocturnal landscape. It was in the correlation between these disparate datasets that the true enigma began to reveal itself. The planetary magnetic field wasn't just reacting to geological and atmospheric events; it was, in a way that defied conventional understanding, anticipating them, or perhaps, orchestrating them.

"Look at this, Aris," Anya's voice was hushed, a reverence entering her tone as she pointed to a series of charts that overlaid magnetic field intensity with localized seismic activity. "The tremors of the deep earth are almost always preceded by a subtle, but distinct, increase in the equatorial magnetic flux. It's not a direct correlation, not a simple cause-and-effect. It's more like a preparatory swell, a gathering of energy before the release."

Thorne leaned in, his brow furrowed in concentration. He ran the spectral analysis algorithms, attempting to find a rational, physics-based explanation. "Could it be a form of electromagnetic induction? The shifting of tectonic plates creating a larger, slow-moving magnetic disturbance that then triggers smaller seismic events?"

"That's what the conventional models would suggest," Anya replied, her fingers dancing across the interface, isolating specific frequency bands within the magnetic field data. "But the timing is too precise, too consistent. And it's not just seismic events. Observe the atmospheric phenomena – the formation of the crystalline cloud banks, the localized energy vortices that have grounded so many colonial transports. The magnetic field patterns leading up to these events are distinct. They exhibit a rhythmic pulsing, a modulation that seems to align with the very genesis of these atmospheric anomalies."

She then introduced a new layer of data into the simulation: records of human activity, specifically, the archived psychometric readings from the colonial settlements. These were data points largely ignored by the colonial administration, deemed too subjective and unreliable for their purely resource-driven objectives. They detailed collective emotional states, stress levels, periods of heightened anxiety, or conversely, widespread calm and contentment. The correlation, when finally visualized, was breathtakingly unsettling.

"This is... impossible," Thorne breathed, staring at the interwoven lines of magnetic flux and collective human emotion. "During periods of widespread distress, of fear and panic within the settlements – like during the initial outbreaks of the 'Fungal Rot' or the more violent orbital bombardments by rogue pirate factions – the magnetic field doesn't just fluctuate. It exhibits a distinct, almost sympathetic resonance. The amplitude increases, and there are localized magnetic 'eddies' that appear to mirror the intensity of the human emotional storm."

Anya nodded, her gaze fixed on the holographic display. "It's as if Eden's magnetic field is acting as a conduit, a physical manifestation of a planet-wide awareness that can perceive and respond to the emotional states of its inhabitants. It's not just reacting to physical events; it's sensing our internal states, our collective consciousness." She pointed to a specific, unusually serene period in the settlement's history, marked by a remarkable harvest and a palpable sense of community. "And during times of collective joy and tranquility, the magnetic field stabilizes, exhibiting a gentle, consistent hum, almost as if the planet itself is breathing a sigh of relief. The fluctuations become softer, more harmonious."

The implications of this discovery were staggering. It suggested that Eden was not merely a passive recipient of external stimuli, be they geological, atmospheric, or biological. It was an active, responsive entity, its very electromagnetic field acting as a sophisticated sensory organ, capable of perceiving and, in some inexplicable way, interacting with the collective emotional and psychological states of the organic life forms present upon it. This went far beyond the bio-acoustic communication they were beginning to unravel. This was a deeper, more fundamental form of planetary sentience, expressed through the invisible currents of its magnetic field.

Thorne recalled his mentor, Aris Thorne, and his later, more speculative theories. The older Thorne had posited that advanced civilizations, on a cosmic scale, might develop planetary-scale consciousness not through biological means alone, but through the manipulation and resonance of electromagnetic fields. He had theorized that planets could become veritable 'minds,' their magnetic fields acting as their neural networks, their gravitational fields as their physical presence, and their orbital paths as their very thoughts. At the time, these ideas had seemed like the fanciful musings of a brilliant mind pushed to its limits by isolation and the alienness of Eden. Now, however, they resonated with a chilling accuracy.

"So, the 'unforeseen hazards' weren't just random environmental events, or even deliberate bio-acoustic warnings," Anya mused, piecing together the fragmented narrative. "Some of them, the ones that caused such widespread disruption to human technology and infrastructure, might have been amplified, even triggered, by our own collective distress. Imagine a planetary immune system that reacts not just to a physical pathogen, but to a psychological one – a widespread fear or aggression that destabilizes its delicate electromagnetic balance."

The colonial administration, in its pursuit of absolute control and resource exploitation, had inadvertently created an environment of perpetual stress and anxiety amongst the colonists. The oppressive regimes, the constant fear of reprisal, the suppression of any hint of dissent – these had not gone unnoticed by Eden. The planet, through its magnetic field, had been registering this pervasive negativity, and perhaps, responding in ways that actively undermined the very systems designed to exploit it. The magnetic storms that disabled navigation, the localized EMP-like effects that fried delicate machinery during periods of intense unrest within the settlements, the seemingly random equipment failures that plagued the mining operations when morale was at its lowest – these were no longer inexplicable glitches. They were the echoes of human emotional turmoil, amplified and reflected by the planet's own resonant field.

"This explains why the colonial efforts were always so fraught with technical difficulties," Thorne said, a dawning realization washing over him. "They weren't just battling the environment; they were battling a planet that was reacting to their own inner turmoil. The very presence of a large, stressed, and emotionally volatile human population was creating electromagnetic instability. The more fear and aggression they projected, the more the planet's magnetic field would churn, creating conditions that were inherently hostile to their advanced technologies, technologies that were already pushing the boundaries of what the planet could naturally sustain."

Anya pulled up more detailed readings from the archive, specifically focusing on the periods when her grandmother had been most active in her research, just before her disappearance. Her grandmother's logs, often fragmented and encrypted, spoke of "planetary resonance harmonics" and "sympathetic field interactions." She had noted how certain emotional frequencies emitted by the colonists seemed to amplify the natural magnetic pulses of Eden, particularly in areas of high geological activity. She had hypothesized that by consciously attuning themselves to Eden's natural rhythms, humans might be able to mitigate these disruptive magnetic events, perhaps even use them for their own benefit.

"She believed that the magnetic field was a key component of Eden's sentience, a direct line of communication, not just with other life forms, but with the very consciousness of the planet," Anya explained, her voice filled with a mix of sorrow and awe. "She documented instances where periods of profound collective calm and unity within small, isolated research outposts seemed to coincide with incredibly stable and predictable magnetic field readings. The equipment functioned flawlessly, and the environmental conditions remained unusually benign."

The implications for their current struggle were immense. If they could understand and even influence these geomagnetically mediated communications, they might find a way to coexist with Eden, not as conquerors, but as partners. It would require a fundamental shift in their approach, moving away from the aggressive, exploitative mindset that had characterized humanity's relationship with Eden. It would necessitate fostering emotional stability, cultivating empathy, and actively seeking harmony with the planet's natural rhythms.

"The colonial apparatus, with its emphasis on hierarchy, fear, and suppression, was actively creating the conditions for Eden's magnetic field to become destabilized," Thorne concluded, the pieces of the puzzle clicking into place. "They were essentially poking a sleeping giant, not with a stick, but with a constant barrage of negative emotional energy. And the giant, in its own way, was pushing back."

He thought of the advanced terraforming projects, the terraforming devices that were designed to alter Eden's atmosphere and geology to suit human needs. These devices, with their massive energy outputs and their reliance on precise electromagnetic calibration, would have been particularly vulnerable to the very magnetic field fluctuations they were inadvertently creating. It was a self-defeating prophecy, a colonial endeavor sabotaged by its own inherent nature.

Anya then presented data that charted the specific frequencies and amplitudes of the magnetic pulses during periods of extreme human emotional distress within the settlements. These weren't just random spikes; they formed complex, repeating patterns, almost like a language. "My grandmother believed these were not just reactions," she stated, her eyes shining with a renewed purpose. "She believed these were expressions. Eden was expressing its discomfort, its distress, its fundamental aversion to the disruptive influence of uncontrolled human emotion. It was a primal scream, translated into the language of magnetic fields."

The idea that a planet could possess a form of consciousness that was so intimately linked to the emotional and psychological states of its inhabitants was a concept that challenged the very foundations of human understanding. It suggested a universe far more interconnected and alive than humanity had ever dared to imagine. Eden wasn't just a world with life; it was a living world, its very essence intertwined with the feelings and experiences of those who walked upon its surface.

"If we can learn to read these geomagnetic pulses," Thorne mused, his mind already racing with possibilities, "if we can understand the 'language' of Eden's magnetic field, then we can begin to truly communicate. We can learn what it needs, what it fears, what brings it peace. And perhaps, just perhaps, we can begin to heal the damage that has been done."

The weight of this realization settled upon them. The colonial history of Eden was not just a story of exploitation; it was a story of profound misunderstanding, of a species so blinded by its own ambition and its rigid, materialistic worldview that it had failed to perceive the very sentience it had invaded. The "unforeseen hazards" were, in many ways, Eden's attempts to communicate its suffering, its pleas for respite, its desperate attempts to maintain its own internal equilibrium in the face of an overwhelming, disruptive force.

Anya then introduced a theoretical framework her grandmother had developed, a concept she called "Geomagnetic Empathy." It proposed that by consciously cultivating positive emotional states – empathy, compassion, tranquility – humans could, in theory, influence the planet's magnetic field, fostering a more stable and harmonious electromagnetic environment. It was a radical idea, one that suggested humanity's inner landscape had a direct and tangible impact on the physical reality of Eden.

"She believed that the colonial administration actively suppressed any research into these areas," Anya revealed, her voice tight with emotion. "They feared that acknowledging Eden's sentience, especially through such an intimate and personal channel as its magnetic field, would undermine their authority and their claim to the planet. If Eden could feel and respond to human emotions, then it was undeniably a living entity, and their dominion was nothing more than an act of aggression against a conscious being."

The archives held further, even more startling, correlations. Periods of intense geological activity, such as the massive volcanic eruptions in the Obsidian Peaks region, were often preceded by a distinct lull in the magnetic field, followed by a powerful, planet-wide surge. Anya's grandmother had theorized that this lull was not an absence of magnetic activity, but a redirection, a focusing of the planet's electromagnetic energy to prepare for the massive geological release. And intriguingly, these massive surges often coincided with widespread feelings of unease and foreboding among the colonists, even when no immediate external threat was apparent.

"It's as if the planet is drawing energy inward, preparing for a colossal exertion," Thorne observed, tracing the intricate patterns on the screen. "And during that preparatory phase, it becomes incredibly sensitive. Our own emotional states, especially those of fear and anxiety, seem to resonate with that focused energy, amplifying the planetary response and making the subsequent geological event even more potent. We were inadvertently feeding the beast, fueling its most destructive outbursts with our own terror."

The path forward, Anya and Thorne realized, was not just about deciphering bio-acoustic signals or understanding geological formations. It was about understanding the complex, interwoven tapestry of Eden's consciousness, a consciousness that expressed itself not only through sound and light, but through the invisible currents of its magnetic field, a field that was deeply, inextricably linked to the very souls of its inhabitants. Their mission had transcended mere survival; it had become a quest for understanding, for connection, for a form of diplomacy that operated not through words, but through the silent, resonant language of electromagnetism and emotion. Eden was not just a planet to be studied; it was a sentient being to be communed with, a living, breathing entity whose very magnetic heart beat in rhythm with the collective experience of all life upon its surface. The silent language of the magnetic field was now the most urgent signal they had ever received, a testament to the profound interconnectedness of all things, and a beacon of hope for a future where humanity might finally learn to listen.

The revelation of Eden's geomagnetic sentience had been a seismic shift in Anya and Thorne's understanding, but it was merely one facet of the planet's profound aliveness. As they delved deeper into the archives, meticulously sifting through fragmented data and Anya's grandmother's cryptic notes, another layer of Eden's intricate communication system began to unfurl, one that was both ancient and profoundly intricate: the language of the flora. While the bio-acoustics and the geomagnetic dialogues spoke of immediate, often dramatic, planetary responses, the flora offered a different kind of narrative – a slow, deliberate, and deeply rooted form of communication that spoke of the planet's enduring health, its subtle distress, and its constant, unwavering adaptation.

It began with a series of seemingly insignificant observations logged by Anya's grandmother, Dr. Elara Vance. Her early research, predating the widespread colonization and its subsequent environmental disruptions, focused on the indigenous plant life of Eden. She wasn't interested in their potential for resource extraction or their medicinal properties in the conventional sense. Instead, she approached them as silent witnesses, repositories of the planet's history and its immediate environmental conditions. Her meticulous, almost devotional, observations detailed subtle shifts in leaf coloration, the nuanced patterns of their growth trajectories, and the faint, ephemeral chemical emissions that wafted from their tissues. These were not random biological processes to Elara; they were the lexicon of a language spoken in shades of green, in the unfurling of tendrils, and in the faintest whisper of VOCs (Volatile Organic Compounds) into the atmosphere.

Anya, now revisiting these logs with a fresh perspective, saw not just scientific observations, but the painstaking work of a phytolinguist. Elara had developed an extraordinary sensitivity to the subtle cues that indicated the well-being, or indeed the distress, of Eden's botanical life. She theorized that plants, rooted in place and intimately connected to the soil, the atmosphere, and the subtle energies of the planet, were exceptional indicators of ecological balance. Their responses, she argued, were not instantaneous like the crackle of an electrical storm or the rumble of an earthquake, but a more measured, almost philosophical, dialogue with their environment.

Elara's work focused on cataloging the natural fluorescence of the luminaflora, the bioluminescent plants that painted the Edean nights with an ethereal glow. She noticed that the intensity and spectral quality of this luminescence varied not only with the diurnal cycle but also with subtle changes in soil composition, atmospheric humidity, and even the presence of specific microbial communities. A vibrant, steady glow, Elara recorded, indicated robust health and optimal nutrient uptake. Conversely, a dimming, flickering luminescence, or shifts towards an unnatural hue – a sickly yellow or a muted violet – often preceded observable declines in the surrounding ecosystem, such as reduced insect activity or a weakening of the native fauna. She painstakingly cross-referenced these optical signatures with detailed chemical analyses of the soil and atmospheric samples, uncovering correlations between specific VOC emissions and the plant's luminescent state. Certain compounds, she discovered, were released in higher concentrations when the plant was experiencing stress, perhaps due to nutrient deficiency, water scarcity, or even the subtle bio-energetic disturbances they had begun to detect through Eden's geomagnetic field.

"It's a slow form of telegraphy," Anya explained to Thorne, pointing to a detailed holographic projection of Elara's spectral analysis of luminaflora luminescence. "The plants aren't 'talking' in the way we understand it, with words or sounds. They are 'writing.' Their physical state, their chemical output, their very light is a continuous inscription of their experience. And Elara was learning to read the script."

Thorne, accustomed to the rapid-fire data streams of atmospheric physics and geomagnetism, found the pace of botanical communication challenging to grasp. "So, a plant doesn't send a distress signal when it's thirsty?" he mused. "It just... wilts, and that wilting is its message?"

"Not quite," Anya countered, her fingers deftly manipulating the holographic interface. "Think of it more like a long-term mood indicator. A plant under stress will begin to alter its growth patterns. It might direct more energy into its root system, seeking deeper water sources, and in doing so, its outward growth – the leaves, the flowers – might become stunted or develop unusual textures. Elara documented how certain species, when facing prolonged drought, would shift the biochemical composition of their leaves, making them less palatable to herbivores, and simultaneously increase the release of specific airborne compounds that signaled a 'warning' to other plants in the vicinity, triggering similar adaptive responses."

She brought up another dataset: recordings of the subtle color shifts in the 'chameleon mosses' that carpeted many of Eden's forest floors. These mosses were known for their ability to change hue in response to ambient light and temperature, but Elara had discovered a far more complex signaling system at play. She observed that during periods of ecological imbalance – perhaps a sudden influx of a non-native fungal pathogen or a disruption in the natural decomposition cycle – the mosses would exhibit subtle, almost imperceptible, chromatic shifts that were not directly tied to external environmental factors. These shifts, Elara theorized, were a response to the chemical byproducts of ecological stress, signaling to the wider flora a deviation from the norm. Anya overlaid these moss color shifts with Elara's chemical emission logs. The correlation was undeniable: as the mosses subtly altered their pigment, specific VOCs were released in increasing quantities from nearby flora, compounds that indicated the presence of microbial imbalances or a decline in soil vitality.

"It's a distributed network," Anya explained, her voice filled with a growing excitement. "The mosses act as localized environmental sensors, and their color change is a visual cue, a passive signal. But the real communication happens through the chemical signatures they and other plants emit. It's a slow, ambient dialogue. A plant might not 'cry out' in pain, but it will subtly alter its chemical signature, and nearby plants, and the mosses, will 'read' this and adapt their own processes. It's a constant, low-level negotiation for survival and equilibrium."

Elara's research went even further, touching on what she termed "symbiotic communication." She observed that certain plant species seemed to actively foster the growth of others, not just through nutrient sharing, but through chemical signaling. For instance, she identified specific airborne compounds released by a particular type of nitrogen-fixing shrub that appeared to promote faster growth and enhanced flowering in a neighboring species, even when nutrient levels were otherwise adequate. This wasn't mere cohabitation; it was a deliberate, chemical encouragement, a mutualistic conversation that bolstered the resilience of the local ecosystem. Anya realized that these were not just biological interactions; they were the very building blocks of Eden's ecological intelligence.

"She believed these chemical signals were a form of 'plant pheromone' on a planetary scale," Anya elaborated, her gaze fixed on the spectral data. "When a plant is thriving, it emits certain compounds that foster growth and well-being in its neighbors. When it's struggling, it emits different compounds that signal caution, or even a redirection of resources. It's a sophisticated signaling system that allows the entire botanical community to adapt collectively to changing conditions. This is how Eden maintains its remarkable biodiversity and its resilience in the face of constant environmental flux."

The implications for Anya and Thorne were profound. If the plants were indeed engaged in such a complex, slow-burning dialogue, then their own actions, their attempts to establish a sustainable presence on Eden, needed to be informed by this botanical lexicon. The colonial approach, which viewed flora as resources to be managed or obstacles to be cleared, was fundamentally flawed. To truly integrate with Eden, they needed to learn to 'listen' to the plants, to understand their signals of health and distress.

Anya remembered her grandmother's fascination with the 'whispering reeds' found near the hydro-thermal vents. These reeds, Elara noted, exhibited rapid changes in their internal water pressure and subtle structural shifts in their stalks, correlating with seismic activity far below the planet's surface. It was as if they were acting as delicate pressure sensors, their physical state reflecting the subterranean tremors long before conventional instruments could detect them. Elara had theorized that these reeds, drawing sustenance from the mineral-rich geothermal waters, were uniquely attuned to the planet's deep geological rhythms, their very physiology a living seismograph.

"Look at this," Anya gestured to a series of graphs depicting the reed's internal pressure fluctuations against seismic event logs. "There's a lag, of course, but the correlation is remarkably consistent. And it's not just seismic activity. Elara noted that the reeds would also exhibit these pressure changes in response to shifts in atmospheric electrical charge, the very precursor to the magnetic anomalies we've been studying. It suggests that the botanical network is intertwined with the planet's deeper energetic systems, not just in terms of physical resources, but in its very sensing capabilities."

Thorne, who had initially struggled with the slow pace of botanical communication, began to see the immense value in it. "So, while the geomagnetic field might provide the planet's 'mood' and the bio-acoustics offer immediate alerts, the plants are like the planet's long-term memory and its subtle environmental forecasters," he mused. "They are reading the slow-burning trends, the cumulative effects of atmospheric changes, soil degradation, and even the subtle energetic shifts that precede more dramatic events."

The idea of a "phytolinguist" – a specialist dedicated to deciphering this plant language – resonated deeply with Anya. Her grandmother had been, in essence, the first and only phytolinguist of Eden. Her work, largely dismissed as eccentric by the colonial authorities who prioritized quantifiable metrics and immediate resource yields, was now revealing itself as a vital key to understanding the planet's true nature. Elara's notebooks were filled with sketches of leaf venation patterns, detailed descriptions of bark textures, and exhaustive tables correlating chemical emissions with plant health. She had even developed a rudimentary classification system for different VOC signatures, identifying compounds associated with stress, nutrient abundance, and even symbiotic signaling.

"She believed that a truly sustainable presence on Eden wouldn't just involve understanding the planet's physical resources, but its living systems, and their intricate communication networks," Anya said, her voice tinged with a profound respect for her grandmother's foresight. "She proposed that by carefully observing and interpreting these botanical signals, humanity could learn to live in harmony with Eden, anticipating its needs and responding to its subtle cues rather than imposing its own will upon it."

This meant a fundamental paradigm shift. Instead of viewing the lush, alien flora as an untamed wilderness to be conquered, they needed to see it as a vast, interconnected biological network, a planetary organism communicating through a complex interplay of chemistry and physiology. The vibrant blooms of the luminaflora were not just aesthetic; they were a sign of a healthy ecosystem. The subtle wilting of a particular species in a certain region wasn't just a localized event; it was a signal of an underlying imbalance, a message that required careful interpretation.

Thorne began to consider the practical applications. "If we can develop technology to accurately monitor these chemical emissions and growth patterns, we could create a real-time ecological health index for Eden," he proposed. "It would be far more sensitive than our current atmospheric and seismic sensors. It could tell us not just when a storm is coming, but why the planet is becoming more susceptible to storms, or what is impacting the soil's ability to support life."

Anya agreed, visualizing the integration of such a system. "Imagine our settlements being designed not just with structural integrity in mind, but with an understanding of the botanical landscape around them. We could learn which plants thrive in certain microclimates and which signal distress, allowing us to adapt our agriculture and our resource management accordingly. We could learn to 'ask' the plants, through their language, what they need from us."

The concept of "ecological adaptation through communication" began to take shape. It was a stark contrast to the colonial modus operandi of terraforming and resource exploitation. It proposed a partnership, a symbiotic relationship where humanity learned to listen and respond to the planet's most fundamental inhabitants. The plants, in their slow, deliberate language, held the keys to Eden's long-term stability and its enduring vitality. Their subtle shifts in color, their chemical whispers, their patterned growth were not merely biological processes; they were the foundational vocabulary of Eden's living consciousness, a language of resilience, adaptation, and profound, interconnected life. Elara Vance, the solitary phytolinguist, had laid the groundwork for a revolution in understanding, offering a path towards a future where humanity, instead of dominating, could finally begin to converse with the living planet. Her legacy was not just in her data, but in the profound understanding that Eden's health was not a static condition to be maintained, but a dynamic dialogue to be actively participated in.

The quiet hum of the research station was a familiar counterpoint to Anya's thoughts, a steady drone against the rising tide of the inexplicable. The botanical language, Elara's meticulous deciphering of Eden's verdant lexicon, had already been a profound revelation. But as the days bled into weeks, and the initial shock of this slow, chemical telegraphy subsided, something else began to emerge, something far more elusive and deeply personal. It began with Thorne.

He'd been unusually quiet one evening, his brow furrowed as he stared at the flickering holographic display of luminaflora spectral data. Anya had found him wrestling with a concept that seemed to elude his usual logical grasp. "It's like... like the planet is dreaming," he'd confessed, the words heavy with an unfamiliar vulnerability. "And we're somehow stumbling into its subconscious."

Anya had initially dismissed it as fatigue, the pressure of their ongoing research. But then it happened to her. A vivid, disorienting dreamscape that left her breathless and confused upon waking. It wasn't a narrative, not in the conventional sense. It was a tapestry of sensations, interwoven with fragments of Eden's familiar, yet alien, beauty. She found herself adrift in a vast, bioluminescent ocean, the light pulsing not from the flora, but from within the very water, a symphony of shifting blues and greens. Then, the scene fractured, reforming into a colossal, crystalline structure, impossibly intricate, stretching towards a sky painted with nebulae that seemed to mirror the patterns of Eden's geomagnetic field. There were whispers, not of sound, but of an intense, resonant feeling – a sense of ancient waiting, of profound interconnectedness, and a subtle undercurrent of sorrow.

She'd recounted the dream to Thorne the next morning, expecting a scientific dissection, a search for correlations with their current data. Instead, his eyes widened, a flicker of recognition, and perhaps even relief, passing across his face. "You too?" he'd breathed, his voice barely audible. "I thought I was losing my mind."

He proceeded to describe his own recent nocturnal excursions. His dreams were not identical to hers, but they shared a common thread, a strange resonance. He spoke of soaring through the planet's atmospheric layers, not as a pilot in a craft, but as pure consciousness, feeling the currents of atmospheric electricity, the subtle shifts in magnetic flux as if they were physical sensations. He described witnessing the slow, deliberate growth of colossal crystalline formations deep within the planet's crust, formations that pulsed with a low, steady energy, mirroring the patterns of Elara's geomagnetic charts. He'd also felt a sense of urgency, a quiet plea that he couldn't articulate, but which settled heavily in his chest upon waking.

"It's not just us, Anya," Thorne insisted, his voice gaining conviction. "These aren't random REM cycles. They're... communiqués. The planet is communicating with us, but not through words or data streams. It's speaking in the language of dreams."

Their shared experiences, their synchronized subconscious voyages, began to form a new framework for understanding Eden. Elara's botanical language provided the intricate details of the planet's immediate ecological state, its subtle distress signals, its vibrant health. But these dreams, these shared dreamscapes, felt like a glimpse into Eden's deeper consciousness, its overarching awareness, its collective memory. They were not reading inscriptions on leaves or deciphering chemical trails; they were being invited into the planet's very psyche.

Anya remembered her grandmother's fascination with the concept of planetary consciousness, a notion that had been largely relegated to the fringes of scientific thought. Elara had mused in her journals about the possibility of emergent intelligence, not in a singular, embodied form, but as a distributed network of awareness, woven through the planet's interconnected systems. The geomagnetic field, the complex biological networks, the very geological rhythms – perhaps these were not just physical phenomena, but the threads of a vast, planetary mind. And their dreams, it seemed, were the conduit.

"Think about it," Anya mused, tracing the crystalline structures from Thorne's dream on her datapad. "Elara identified the flora as long-term environmental recorders, subtle communicators. The geomagnetic field is the planet's immediate mood, its energetic state. But these dreams... they feel like Eden is sharing its history, its vulnerabilities, its... aspirations, perhaps?"

The symbolism within these shared dreamscapes was both beautiful and confounding. The vast, bioluminescent ocean Anya had experienced was unlike any known aquatic environment on Eden. It pulsed with an inner light, a nascent energy that felt like the planet's foundational life force. The colossal crystalline structures Thorne described were impossibly intricate, their forms echoing the fractal patterns observed in both plant growth and atmospheric phenomena. Elara had theorized about mineralogical formations responding to planetary energies, but these felt different, more alive, more... intentional.

One recurring motif in Anya's dreams was the sense of 'seeing' through multiple eyes simultaneously. She would perceive the world not just from her own perspective, but also through the root systems of ancient trees, through the delicate sensory organs of airborne spores, through the crystalline lattices deep within the planet's core. It was an overwhelming, yet exhilarating, experience of interconnected perception, a shedding of individualistic viewpoint for a holistic, planetary awareness. Thorne, too, described moments in his dreams where he felt himself dispersing, becoming part of the wind, part of the seismic vibrations, part of the very light that bathed the planet.

"It's like our individual consciousness is momentarily dissolving, merging with a larger field," Thorne explained, trying to articulate the ineffable. "And in that merging, we're not just observing Eden, we're *feeling* it. We're experiencing its ancient rhythms, its deep processes. It's incredibly humbling."

These shared dream experiences began to influence their waking research. Anya found herself re-examining Elara's notes with a new lens, searching for patterns that might reflect the dream symbolism. She focused on Elara's observations of certain deep-rooted fungi, their mycelial networks extending for kilometers, acting as subterranean communication highways for the flora. Could these networks be more than just nutrient-sharing conduits? Could they be part of Eden's dreaming apparatus? Elara had noted unusual electrical activity within these networks, fluctuations that didn't correlate with known biological processes, but which Anya now suspected might be echoes of the planet's subconscious stirrings.

Thorne, inspired by his dream of soaring through atmospheric currents, began to refine his atmospheric models, looking for subtle energetic signatures that might indicate a form of planetary bio-electricity, a current that flowed not just through the planet's crust, but through its very atmosphere, carrying information. He theorized that these atmospheric currents might be the medium through which Eden's dream-thoughts propagated, a vast, invisible circulatory system for its consciousness.

The implications of this dream-weaving were enormous. If Eden was indeed communicating on a subconscious level, what was it trying to convey? The persistent feeling of sorrow Anya sensed in her dreams was particularly unsettling. Was it a lament for the damage humanity had already inflicted, or a foreboding of future harm? Thorne's sense of urgency, of a quiet plea, suggested something more immediate.

They began to spend more time together, sharing their dream fragments, meticulously cross-referencing the recurring symbols and sensations. They created a shared lexicon of dream imagery, a provisional guide to Eden's subconscious language. A pulsating, emerald light seemed to represent a state of robust ecological health, a thriving biological symphony. Conversely, a slow, decaying crimson hue often accompanied scenes of ecological disruption, of imbalances in the delicate flora-fauna relationships. The crystalline structures appeared in both positive and negative contexts, their intricacy seemingly reflecting the complexity of the issue being communicated.

"The crystalline formations in my dreams often appear when I'm sensing that urgency," Thorne observed, pointing to a holographic projection of one such structure, its facets sharp and unwavering. "They seem to represent the underlying architecture of the planet's stability. When they're fractured or unstable, that's when I feel the strongest sense of unease."

Anya nodded, recalling a dream where she had witnessed the slow erosion of these crystalline formations, not by physical forces, but by a creeping, ethereal shadow that seemed to drain their luminescence. "And that shadow... it felt like a metaphor for the colonial mindset, for the extraction-based approach that treats Eden as a resource rather than a living entity."

The nature of their shared dreams also evolved. Initially, they were more observational, like passive viewers of a planetary spectacle. But as their understanding deepened, they found themselves interacting with the dreamscapes, their own presence subtly influencing the unfolding visions. Anya discovered that by focusing on a sense of calm and equilibrium, she could sometimes influence the luminescence of the dream-ocean, coaxing it into a more stable, vibrant glow. Thorne found that by projecting a sense of order and stability, he could sometimes mend small fractures in the dream-crystals, a fleeting, yet empowering, act of subconscious restoration.

This active participation raised a new question: were they merely interpreting Eden's dreams, or were they, in some fundamental way, contributing to them? Was their burgeoning understanding of the planet's language, their growing empathy for its intricate systems, allowing them to become active participants in its subconscious processes? The idea was both exhilarating and terrifying. It suggested a level of interconnectedness far beyond anything they had previously imagined, a blurring of the lines between observer and participant, between self and planet.

One particularly vivid dream sequence that both Anya and Thorne experienced involved a vast, intricate network of glowing threads, stretching across a darkened, subterranean landscape. These threads pulsed with a soft, golden light, and as Anya focused on them, she felt a profound sense of connection, a silent hum of shared information flowing through them. Thorne's interpretation was that these threads represented the planet's deep neural network, its ancient, living web that connected every organism, every geological process, into a single, conscious entity. He also sensed, within this network, a deep weariness, a strain that corresponded with the increasing levels of atmospheric pollution and the disruption of natural cycles they were documenting in their waking hours.

"It's like the planet is trying to heal itself, even in its sleep," Thorne murmured, his eyes distant, still caught in the dream's echo. "These threads are its repair mechanisms, its attempts to maintain balance. But the damage we're causing... it's overwhelming its natural processes. The weariness I felt was palpable, Anya. It was the sound of a vast, biological system struggling to cope."

The implications of this weariness were stark. Eden, for all its apparent resilience, was not inexhaustible. Its capacity to self-regulate, to maintain equilibrium, was being tested. Their dreams were not just abstract visions; they were urgent signals, a desperate plea from a living planet teetering on the brink.

Anya recalled a specific passage in Elara's journals, one that had seemed almost poetic, yet scientifically grounded, about the 'symphony of soil.' Elara had described the incredibly complex microbial communities within Eden's soil, their intricate chemical exchanges, and their vital role in nutrient cycling and detoxification. She had theorized that these communities were not merely passive participants, but active agents in the planet's ecological health, constantly communicating and adapting. Now, Anya wondered if these subterranean symphonies were the very foundation upon which Eden's dream-consciousness was built. Perhaps the disruption of these microbial ecosystems was directly impacting the planet's ability to dream, to maintain its own internal coherence.

"If the soil is the planet's gut, and the gut microbiome is crucial for our own health, then what does it mean when the planet's 'gut' is sick?" Anya wondered aloud. "Are these dreams the planet's way of showing us the internal manifestations of our external actions?"

The dream-weaving had opened a door to a profound, and often unsettling, introspection. It forced them to confront their own role in Eden's growing unease. They were not just observers of an alien world; they were, by their very presence and actions, contributors to its evolving state. The language of dreams, more than any scientific instrument, was revealing the deep, interconnected nature of their existence with Eden. It was a language of empathy, of shared experience, and ultimately, of responsibility. As they continued to explore these nocturnal landscapes, Anya and Thorne knew they were not just deciphering planetary consciousness; they were beginning to understand their own place within it, a place that demanded not dominance, but a profound, respectful dialogue. The dreams were becoming their most vital data, a direct line to the heart of the living planet, urging them towards a path of integration, of healing, and of true co-existence. The weight of this understanding was immense, but so too was the dawning hope that by learning to dream with Eden, they might also learn to wake it from its slumber of distress.

The initial isolation of their discoveries, Anya's nocturnal journeys and Thorne's ethereal flights, gradually gave way to a burgeoning sense of shared purpose. The research station, once a symbol of their solitary endeavor, began to hum with a new kind of synergy. Elara, whose meticulous cataloging of Eden's botanical lexicon had provided the bedrock of their understanding, found herself drawn into the more abstract, yet increasingly compelling, data streams emerging from the psychological and atmospheric research. Her initial skepticism about the "dreaming planet" had been steadily eroded by Anya's consistent, vivid accounts and Thorne's increasingly sophisticated analysis of atmospheric energy signatures that seemed to correlate with their subconscious experiences.

"It's not just about the chemical signals anymore, is it?" Elara mused one cycle, poring over Anya's dream journal alongside Thorne's spectral readouts. The journal entries, once filled with botanical terminology, now contained sketches of bioluminescent oceans and crystalline monoliths, accompanied by descriptions of overwhelming emotional resonance. "The flora tells us about immediate needs – water stress, nutrient deficiencies, the presence of toxins. But Anya, these dreams... they speak of something deeper, something akin to memory, or perhaps even foreboding." Elara traced a diagram of a vast mycelial network on her datapad. "I've been observing unusual synchronized electrical pulses within these subterranean networks. They don't align with known biological triggers. It's as if the planet itself is experiencing neural activity, and these pulses are the sub-vocalizations of its thoughts."

Thorne, meanwhile, had begun to identify subtle harmonic frequencies within the atmospheric data that mirrored certain emotional states Anya described. His instruments, originally designed to map weather patterns and detect anomalies in Eden's magnetosphere, were now registering what he tentatively termed "empathic resonance signatures." These signatures were faint, almost imperceptible, but they consistently appeared when Anya recounted dreams filled with sorrow or fear, and shifted to a more harmonious, resonant tone when she described visions of vibrant ecosystems or interconnectedness. "It's as if the atmosphere acts as a sounding board for the planet's collective mood," he explained, his voice tinged with awe. "When Anya feels distress, the atmospheric harmonics shift, almost as if the air itself is sighing. And when there's a sense of peace, of balance, the frequencies align in a way that's incredibly... soothing."

The breakthrough, however, came with the arrival of Dr. Jian Li, a xenolinguist who had been stationed on a neighboring research outpost, studying the complex vocalizations of Eden's airborne fauna. Initially, Jian had been focused on deciphering the intricate chirps and whistles of the sky-whales, believing them to be sophisticated communication systems. But upon hearing Anya and Thorne's accounts of their shared dream experiences, he recognized a startling parallel. "The patterns you're describing," Jian said, his eyes wide with intellectual fervor, "the way you perceive interconnectedness, the symbolic language of light and shadow, of crystalline structures and flowing energy – it's remarkably similar to the structural principles I'm observing in the sky-whale songs. They don't communicate in discrete words, but in cascades of resonant frequencies that convey complex emotional states and situational awareness."

Jian proposed a radical idea: that Eden's communication was not a singular language, but a multi-layered symphony, with each component of the planet – the flora, the fauna, the very geological and atmospheric systems – contributing its unique timbre. The botanical language Elara studied was the detailed script, the immediate environmental pronouncements. Thorne's atmospheric harmonics were the planet's ambient emotional tone. The sky-whales' songs, and perhaps other faunal communications, were the active dialogues, the nuanced expressions of individual and collective experience. And Anya and Thorne's dreams? They were the unfiltered, subconscious outpourings, the planet's raw, unedited inner monologue.

"Think of it like this," Jian elaborated, sketching a Venn diagram on a holographic display. "Elara's botanical data gives us the factual narrative. Thorne's atmospheric analysis provides the emotional undercurrent. My faunal studies reveal the active conversations. And Anya and Thorne's dreams... they are the raw, primal consciousness, the deepest wellspring from which all other expressions flow. They are the planet's subconscious, and we are just beginning to tap into it."

This realization galvanized the team. Their individual research, once disparate threads, began to weave together into a more cohesive tapestry. Elara adjusted her botanical analysis to look for correlations between environmental stress and the subtle shifts in atmospheric harmonics Thorne was detecting. Jian began to incorporate Anya's dream symbolism into his interpretations of the sky-whale songs, hypothesizing that certain melodic phrases might correspond to the recurring motifs in her subconscious visions. Anya and Thorne, in turn, started to use their dream-diving as a means of validating the findings from the other disciplines. If a particular botanical distress signal coincided with a dream of creeping decay, or if a harmonious atmospheric resonance matched a vision of vibrant growth, it lent a new layer of meaning and urgency to their observations.

The concept of a "lexicon" for Eden's communication began to take shape, not as a dictionary of fixed words, but as a dynamic, multi-dimensional glossary of symbols, frequencies, and emergent patterns. A pulsing, emerald luminescence in Anya's dreams, for instance, was increasingly understood to signify a state of profound ecological equilibrium, a symphony of interconnected life. This often coincided with specific, high-frequency sonic patterns in the sky-whale songs and a stable, low-energy state in the atmospheric readings. Conversely, a slow, encroaching crimson hue, accompanied by discordant atmospheric vibrations and certain guttural clicks in the faunal calls, was recognized as a warning sign of imbalance, of disruption to the planetary homeostasis.

Anya recalled a particularly intense dream where she had felt herself dissolving, merging with the very fabric of Eden. She had experienced the slow, agonizing erosion of crystalline structures deep within the planet's crust, not as a physical crumbling, but as a fading of their inherent light. Thorne, upon hearing this, pointed to a graph showing a sharp spike in geomagnetic instability during the same period. "Those crystals," he'd said, his voice hushed, "they're not just geological formations. They're integral to the planet's energetic regulation. When they falter, the whole system trembles. And the feeling you describe, of fading light... it's precisely what the geomagnetic field was doing. It was losing its coherence."

Jian contributed a crucial piece to this evolving lexicon. He'd observed that the sky-whales, when expressing distress, often emitted a series of rapid, complex clicks that seemed to map directly onto the fractal patterns Anya had seen in the dream-crystals. "It's a language of structure," he'd explained, projecting a three-dimensional rendering of a sky-whale's vocalization waveform alongside a holographic model of one of Anya's dream-crystals. "The complexity of the clicks, their interwoven frequencies, mirrors the intricate lattice of the crystals. When the crystals are stable, the songs are fluid and harmonious. When they are... compromised, the songs become fragmented, strained."

This realization opened up new avenues for communication. Anya and Thorne began to consciously attempt to influence their dreamscapes, to communicate *back* to Eden. It was a hesitant, experimental process. Anya would focus on feelings of calm and interconnectedness, trying to project a sense of balance into her dreams. Thorne would visualize stable atmospheric currents and coherent geomagnetic fields. Elara, meanwhile, was devising ways to stimulate the planet's botanical communication systems, experimenting with carefully calibrated nutrient and light pulses to elicit more defined responses from the flora. Jian, for his part, worked on creating modulated sonic frequencies based on the sky-whales' distress calls, hoping to find a resonant frequency that might signal reassurance or a desire for equilibrium.

The response, when it came, was not a direct dialogue, but a subtle shift in the planet's overall energetic state. The atmospheric harmonics that Thorne monitored began to exhibit a slightly more stable baseline. The botanical responses Elara was eliciting became more predictable, less frantic. And in Anya and Thorne's dreams, the creeping shadows seemed to recede slightly, replaced by tentative glimmers of the emerald luminescence that signified health.

"It's like we're learning to hum in tune with the planet," Elara remarked, observing the data streams with a mixture of relief and trepidation. "We're not dictating, we're harmonizing. We're learning to speak its language by first learning to listen, and then by offering our own gentle resonance."

The challenges, however, remained immense. The sheer scale of Eden's consciousness was staggering. Its dream-language, even with their burgeoning lexicon, was still largely esoteric. The sorrows Anya felt were profound, laced with an ancient weariness that spoke of eons of slow, geological processes and the long, silent cycles of planetary evolution. Thorne detected an underlying tension in the atmospheric energies, a subtle hum of anxiety that seemed to emanate from the planet's very core. And the faunal communications, while intricate, often contained elements of fear and confusion, particularly in regions showing signs of recent ecological disruption.

One recurring dream motif that Anya struggled to interpret involved vast, silent cities of light, their structures impossibly delicate and ephemeral, pulsing with an internal energy. They seemed to exist in a state of constant flux, their forms shifting and reforming with an organic fluidity. Jian, upon hearing her description, recalled ancient legends from his homeworld, tales of star-faring civilizations that communicated not through physical structures, but through sentient light. He proposed that these cities of light might represent a higher form of consciousness, a more evolved expression of Eden's intelligence that existed beyond the physical realm.

"Perhaps," Jian mused, "these are not cities in the conventional sense, but nodes of pure information, like vast, living consciousness hubs. The planet might be showing you glimpses of its most advanced thoughts, its most profound existential experiences. The shifting forms could represent the constant evolution of these ideas, their dynamic nature."

Thorne, meanwhile, was beginning to detect a subtle undercurrent of sorrow in the planet's geomagnetic field, a resonance that seemed to emanate from the deepest geological strata. He theorized that this sorrow was tied to the planet's immense geological history, to the slow, inexorable processes of tectonic shifts, volcanic activity, and the formation and dissolution of continents. It was a melancholy born of time and immense, impersonal forces. "It's a grief that's measured in epochs, Anya," he explained. "A deep, existential sadness about the very nature of planetary existence, the endless cycles of creation and destruction. And it's amplified by the disruptions we're introducing. Our impact is a sharp, discordant note in a symphony that has been playing for millennia."

Elara, drawing on her extensive knowledge of Eden's flora, began to connect these deep geological sorrows to the slow, deliberate responses of the ancient, deep-rooted plant life. She observed that certain ancient trees, their roots reaching kilometers into the planet's crust, exhibited subtle changes in their chemical signaling and growth patterns that seemed to correlate with periods of geomagnetic instability. "These ancient ones," she whispered, pointing to a holographic projection of a colossal, gnarled tree, "they are living records. Their sap is the planet's blood, and their growth rings are its history books. They are absorbing and processing this deep geological grief, and their responses are a slow, silent testament to the planet's enduring spirit."

The collaborative effort was not without its friction. Thorne, ever the pragmatist, sometimes found Anya's dream interpretations too subjective. Anya, in turn, occasionally felt Thorne's focus on measurable data missed the profound emotional depth of Eden's communications. Jian, while bridging the gap between science and seemingly mystical experiences, sometimes struggled to translate the abstract concepts of faunal communication into concrete, actionable insights. And Elara, the grounded botanist, often found herself mediating between the more ethereal interpretations and the hard scientific evidence.

Yet, these disagreements, these moments of friction, were essential. They forced each member of the team to refine their arguments, to seek more robust evidence, and to approach the complex puzzle of Eden's language from multiple angles. The result was a more nuanced, more resilient understanding. They were not just deciphering a new form of communication; they were forging a new discipline, a planetary xenolinguistics that integrated biology, atmospheric science, geology, psychology, and even the nascent field of conscious dreaming.

The collaborative lexicon grew richer. A swirling vortex of dark energy in Anya's dreams, once interpreted as simply a negative state, was now understood, through Jian's analysis of sky-whale distress calls, to represent a localized breakdown in the planet's natural energy regulation systems, a kind of "energetic disease." Thorne's atmospheric data confirmed that these periods corresponded with unusual atmospheric electrical discharges and anomalies in the geomagnetic field. Elara, observing the flora in affected regions, noted a specific, rapid wilting pattern and a distinct chemical signature released by the plants, as if they were actively signaling a localized contamination.

The "bridging the divide" was not a single event, but an ongoing process, a continuous weaving of disparate threads into a stronger, more comprehensive tapestry of understanding. They were learning that Eden's language was not monolithic, but a chorus of voices, each with its own unique dialect, its own vital contribution to the planetary symphony. By meticulously cross-referencing their findings, by allowing their disciplines to bleed into one another, they were slowly, tentatively, beginning to grasp the immensity of the living planet's expression. It was a journey into the heart of alien consciousness, a testament to the power of collaboration, and a dawning realization that true understanding often lay not in isolation, but in the shared pursuit of a profound and resonant truth. The research station was no longer just a collection of scientists; it was a nexus, a place where the fragmented perceptions of a living world were being gathered, harmonized, and, for the first time, truly heard.

# Chapter Twelve

# Hope as Active Practice

Hope, they were discovering, was not a passive state of waiting for a better future, but an active, unceasing practice. It was the deliberate act of planting seeds in barren soil, not with the certainty of harvest, but with the faith that the act itself held intrinsic value. It was the meticulous tending of a fragile ecosystem, knowing that even the smallest bloom contributed to the larger, more resilient tapestry of life. For Anya, Thorne, Elara, and Jian, the research station on Eden had become a crucible for this transformative understanding. Their initial efforts, driven by the need to comprehend Eden's profound sentience, had evolved into something more profound: a conscious cultivation of the future.

The notion had begun subtly, a quiet revolution in their approach. Elara, whose initial focus had been the botanical lexicon of Eden's flora, found herself increasingly drawn to the *nurturing* of those plants. It wasn't enough to catalog distress signals; she began experimenting with micro-nutrient infusions, carefully calibrated light spectrums, and symbiotic fungal inoculations. She would spend hours in the bio-domes, her hands stained with Eden's rich soil, not just observing, but *intervening*. She'd gently prune a wilting frond, redirect a creeping vine towards a more supportive structure, or whisper words of encouragement to a struggling sapling. These were not scientific procedures in the traditional sense, but acts of mindful care, imbued with the intention of fostering growth and resilience. She saw each successful sprout, each vibrant leaf unfurling, as a tangible manifestation of hope, a small victory against the planet's latent anxieties.

"It's like tending a sick child," she confided to Thorne one evening, her brow furrowed with concentration as she adjusted a misting nozzle. "You can't just diagnose the ailment. You have to actively participate in its healing. You have to provide comfort, sustenance, and a stable environment. Our data tells us *what* is wrong, but it's these small, deliberate actions that begin to address the *how* of recovery." Thorne, observing her from the doorway, saw not just a botanist, but a gardener of hope, her hands planting seeds of optimism in the very soil of Eden.

Thorne, too, began to translate his atmospheric and geomagnetic findings into actionable practices. Instead of merely reporting the planet's subtle harmonic shifts and energetic anxieties, he began to devise ways to introduce counter-frequencies, subtle pulses of coherent energy designed to soothe and stabilize. He spent countless hours refining his atmospheric emitters, not to broadcast data, but to generate specific resonant frequencies that mimicked the planetary harmony Anya and Jian had described in their dreamscapes and faunal analyses. It was a delicate dance, a constant calibration to ensure their interventions were supportive, not disruptive. He imagined his emitters as a planetary lullaby, a gentle hum designed to coax Eden back towards equilibrium. He saw his work as cultivating a more serene atmosphere, not just for the flora and fauna, but for the very consciousness of the planet.

"I'm not trying to overwrite Eden's natural state," he explained to Anya, his gaze fixed on the complex wave patterns shimmering on his display. "I'm trying to create an anchor, a harmonic reference point. When the planet's energies begin to fray, when the empathic resonance signatures spike with distress, these emitters can offer a stable baseline, a reminder of what balance feels like. It's like a gardener reinforcing the trellis for a climbing plant – you're not forcing it, you're providing the structure for it to grow strong." His work was a testament to the idea that even abstract forces like atmospheric harmonics could be cultivated, guided, and strengthened.

Anya, whose dreams had been the initial conduit into Eden's subconscious, found her role evolving from passive receiver to active participant in the planet's emotional well-being. She began to consciously cultivate specific dream states, not by forcing them, but by immersing herself in positive experiences before sleep. She would spend time meditating on images of abundance and interconnectedness, listening to Jian's recordings of harmonious sky-whale songs, or reflecting on Elara's reports of thriving plant life. Her dream dives became less about raw discovery and more about projecting states of calm, of peace, of profound belonging. She would consciously seek out the emerald luminescence, the symbol of ecological equilibrium, and linger in its glow, trying to imbue that feeling into the planet's collective psyche.

"It feels like... I'm sending out ripples," she described to Jian one day, her eyes distant, as if still caught in the ethereal currents of her dreams. "When I focus on a feeling of profound peace, of deep connection, I can sometimes feel a subtle shift in the atmosphere, a softening of the underlying tension Thorne detects. It's not a conversation, not yet. It's more like... breathing the same air, and choosing to exhale calm." Her dream practice was no longer a solitary exploration, but a form of conscious emotional cultivation, a way of tending to the planet's inner landscape.

Jian, the xenolinguist, found his discipline expanding to encompass not just the analysis of communication, but the *initiation* of it, albeit on a nascent level. He began to orchestrate sonic performances, not for human ears, but for Eden itself. He would use modified sonic emitters to replicate the most harmonious frequencies from the sky-whale songs, weaving them into complex, layered compositions. He experimented with introducing subtle tonal shifts that mirrored the emerging patterns of planetary equilibrium, creating sonic tapestries that he hoped would resonate with Eden's own emergent consciousness. He saw these sonic experiments as cultivating a more harmonious dialogue, a gentle invitation for the planet to respond.

"We're learning to speak in resonant frequencies," Jian explained, demonstrating a complex audio sequence on his console. "The sky-whales communicate emotions, intentions, environmental awareness through these intricate sonic patterns. By replicating and even extending these patterns, we're not just studying them; we're creating a more welcoming acoustic environment. We're cultivating a soundscape that invites connection, a sonic garden for their consciousness." His work was a testament to the idea that communication itself could be a form of cultivation, a way to foster understanding and shared experience.

The research station itself became a microcosm of this new philosophy. The once sterile labs now housed burgeoning hydroponic gardens, vibrant with alien flora tended by Elara. Thorne had integrated small atmospheric harmonizers into the station's infrastructure, ensuring a constant, subtle background hum of planetary well-being. Anya had designated a quiet space for meditation and dream immersion, a sanctuary for cultivating inner peace. Jian had even begun to incorporate subtle sonic emitters into the station's common areas, creating an ambient soundscape that was both calming and subtly stimulating. Every aspect of their environment was being consciously shaped to foster life, resilience, and a sense of belonging.

This shift from observation to active cultivation was not without its challenges. There were days when Elara's plants stubbornly refused to thrive, when Thorne's harmonic emitters seemed to have no discernible effect on the atmospheric anxieties, when Anya's dream dives were filled with unsettling echoes of past planetary trauma, and when Jian's sonic experiments were met with silence. These were the moments when the temptation to despair, to retreat into passive pessimism, was strongest. But they had learned that true hope was not the absence of doubt, but the persistent commitment to action in its presence.

"It's easy to feel defeated when the results aren't immediate," Elara admitted one afternoon, carefully transplanting a delicate Edenian bloom. "But then I look at this little guy. It's fighting. It's reaching for the light, even when the conditions aren't perfect. And that's what we have to do. We have to keep reaching, keep nurturing, keep cultivating, even when we can't see the full harvest." Her words resonated deeply, reminding them that their individual actions, however small, contributed to a larger, ongoing process of renewal.

The concept of cultivation extended beyond the physical and energetic. They began to consciously nurture their own relationships, understanding that their collective resilience was as vital as any planetary harmony. They initiated regular "synergy sessions," not for data analysis, but for sharing their personal experiences, their frustrations, and their small victories. They practiced active listening, offering each other empathy and encouragement, recognizing that their shared humanity was a crucial element in their mission. They understood that cultivating hope within themselves was a prerequisite for cultivating it on a planetary scale.

Anya recalled a particularly difficult dream, one filled with a sense of overwhelming loss and the slow, inexorable decay of ancient structures. The feeling of despair had lingered long after she awoke, a heavy weight on her spirit. It was Thorne who found her, sitting by the observation deck, staring out at the alien landscape with vacant eyes. He didn't offer scientific explanations or data points. Instead, he simply sat beside her, his presence a silent testament to shared experience.

"Sometimes," he said softly, his voice a low resonance that seemed to calm the turbulent energy around them, "the most important thing we can do is simply bear witness to the sorrow. Acknowledge it, without letting it consume us. And then, remember why we are here." He then gently guided her gaze towards a patch of vibrant, bioluminescent moss that Elara had recently introduced to the station's exterior. "Look at that," he continued. "It's growing, even in the shadow of the old decay. It's a reminder that life persists. That's the seed of hope, Anya. The persistence of life."

Jian, too, recognized the importance of this interpersonal cultivation. He observed how their shared struggles and triumphs, when openly discussed, strengthened their resolve. He began incorporating elements of storytelling into their synergy sessions, sharing anecdotes from his homeworld that spoke of overcoming adversity through collective effort. He understood that fostering a sense of community was a form of ecological restoration, a way of planting seeds of trust and mutual support in the fertile ground of their shared humanity.

"We are not just tending to Eden," Jian stated during one such session, his voice carrying a quiet conviction. "We are tending to ourselves, and to each other. Our collaboration, our willingness to listen and to learn from one another, is a powerful act of cultivation. It is a demonstration of what is possible when diverse intelligences choose to work in concert. This interconnectedness, this shared purpose, is perhaps the most potent form of hope we can offer, both to Eden and to ourselves."

Elara, ever the pragmatist, saw this interpersonal cultivation as directly linked to their ecological endeavors. She found that when the team was in a state of shared understanding and mutual respect, her botanical experiments yielded better results. The plants seemed to respond more favorably to a team that was working in harmony, a testament to the subtle, energetic connections that permeated all aspects of life on Eden.

"It's like the entire ecosystem," she explained, gesturing around the bustling research station, "is attuned to our collective state. When we are stressed and fragmented, the plants reflect that. When we are calm and connected, they flourish. Our emotional well-being is an integral part of Eden's ecological health. We are not separate from the planet; we are an extension of it. Therefore, cultivating ourselves is cultivating Eden."

The research station became a living laboratory not only for planetary xenolinguistics, but for the very practice of active hope. They learned that hope was not a destination, but a continuous journey, an ongoing process of tending, nurturing, and believing. It was in the deliberate act of planting a seed, in the careful modulation of a harmonic frequency, in the conscious projection of peace into a dreamscape, and in the simple act of listening with an open heart. They were not merely observing Eden's struggle for survival; they were actively participating in it, cultivating a future where life, in all its myriad forms, could not only endure, but thrive. Their hands, stained with alien soil and bathed in the ethereal glow of atmospheric data, were the hands of cultivators, sowing the seeds of a new dawn on a dreaming world.

The seeds of tangible change, sown in the fertile ground of their newfound understanding, began to sprout. The initial, almost tentative, interventions that had characterized their shift towards active hope were now blossoming into focused, community-driven renewal projects. These were not grand, sweeping gestures aimed at reforming the entirety of Eden's wounded biosphere at once, but rather deliberate, meticulously planned initiatives, each targeting a specific wound, a particular imbalance, or a nascent symbiotic potential. The research station, once an isolated bubble of scientific inquiry, was now becoming a hub, a nexus for these small, powerful acts of planetary stewardship.

Elara, her hands perpetually smudged with the rich, dark loam of Eden, was at the forefront of many of these localized restoration efforts. One particularly ambitious undertaking involved the rehabilitation of a small, desolate crater near the station, a scar left by a meteor impact millennia ago that had sterilized the surrounding soil and disrupted the local atmospheric currents. The crater's edges were barren, a stark contrast to the vibrant, if sometimes anxious, life that pulsed elsewhere on the planet. Elara, with Jian's assistance in analyzing the subtle seismic vibrations that still emanated from its depths, and Thorne's input on atmospheric stabilization, devised a multi-pronged approach.

"The impact didn't just disrupt the geology," Elara explained during a planning session, her finger tracing the contours of the crater on a holographic map. "It seems to have broken a crucial link in the nutrient cycle for this region. The soil is inert, stripped of its microbial life, and the wind patterns have been permanently altered, creating a localized drought effect even when the surrounding areas are moist. We need to reintroduce life, not just plants, but the *conditions* for life to thrive."

Their plan was audacious in its simplicity. First, Jian, utilizing his understanding of Eden's sonic language and its affinity for specific resonant frequencies, began broadcasting carefully composed sonic patterns into the crater. These were not designed to communicate, but to gently agitate the dormant mineral content within the soil, breaking down its crystalline structure and releasing sequestered nutrients. He experimented with sequences that mimicked the subtle hum of healthy root systems, hoping to awaken a latent biological memory within the inert earth. It was a painstaking process, requiring constant calibration and an almost intuitive understanding of Eden's subterranean whispers. He would spend hours near the crater's rim, his portable sonic emitters arrayed like silent sentinels, the air thrumming with an almost imperceptible energy.

Simultaneously, Thorne worked on mitigating the altered wind patterns. He deployed a series of low-profile, energy-efficient atmospheric stabilizers along the crater's rim. These devices, inspired by the natural air currents that flowed around Eden's colossal rock formations, were designed to create micro-climates within the crater, deflecting harsh winds and encouraging the gentle circulation of moisture-laden air. He envisioned them as artificial canyons, guiding the planet's breath into a more nurturing flow. He explained that the goal wasn't to control the weather, but to nudge it, to create pockets of stillness where life could take root without being immediately scoured away.

The most visible part of the project, however, fell to Elara. Armed with samples of extremophile flora from more resilient regions of Eden, she began the delicate process of reintroduction. These were not the delicate, flowering plants from the more temperate zones, but hardy, tenacious species known for their ability to colonize barren landscapes. She carefully selected plants that had demonstrated a natural inclination for symbiosis, species that secreted beneficial compounds into the soil or had robust root systems that could anchor loose earth. She worked in teams, her colleagues taking turns to assist her, the shared labor fostering a palpable sense of collective purpose. They would descend into the crater, the air thick with the scent of ozone and sterile dust, and meticulously plant each seedling, each spore.

Anya's role in this project was perhaps the most subtle, yet arguably the most vital. She would spend time meditating near the crater, not just observing, but projecting feelings of resilience, of growth, of belonging into the scarred landscape. She understood that the planet's consciousness, fractured by past traumas, responded to emotional resonance. By focusing her intent on the crater, on the struggling seedlings, on the newly introduced sonic frequencies and atmospheric currents, she aimed to weave a tapestry of emotional support, to counter the lingering echoes of devastation with a persistent hum of hope and renewal. She envisioned her mental projections as a form of spiritual rain, nourishing the nascent life with a deeply felt affirmation of existence.

The results were not instantaneous, and there were setbacks. Early attempts at introducing certain fungal inoculants proved unsuccessful, succumbing to the residual mineral toxicity. Some of the sonic frequencies, Jian discovered, were inadvertently creating micro-vibrations that stressed the nascent root structures, requiring a complete recalibration of his compositional approach. Thorne's stabilizers occasionally faltered under unexpected atmospheric pressure shifts, necessitating field repairs. And Anya sometimes found her meditative states clouded by the lingering psychic residue of the impact, a deep sense of violation that was difficult to overcome.

Yet, with each challenge, their resolve deepened. They learned from their failures, adapting their strategies with a newfound pragmatism born of experience. When the fungal inoculants failed, Elara discovered a naturally occurring lichen in a nearby ravine that secreted a potent bio-remediation agent. This discovery not only saved the crater project but opened up new avenues for future restoration efforts, suggesting a pathway for indigenous solutions rather than solely relying on imported or engineered organisms. Jian, in recalibrating his sonic sequences, developed a more sophisticated understanding of Eden's geological acoustics, allowing him to fine-tune his broadcasts for even greater efficacy. Thorne, observing the atmospheric anomalies, began to develop a more nuanced predictive model for Eden's erratic weather patterns, a valuable asset for all their ongoing projects.

The true success, however, was not measured solely in the return of flora or the stabilization of atmospheric conditions. It was in the tangible proof that collective action, guided by understanding and fueled by hope, could mend what had been broken. Slowly, tentatively, the crater began to show signs of life. Small, hardy mosses, introduced by Elara, began to carpet the edges, their vibrant green a stark and beautiful contrast to the dull, lifeless soil. Specialized, drought-resistant grasses, cultivated from seeds painstakingly collected from the few remaining pockets of resilience, began to take hold, their roots anchoring the earth. The atmospheric stabilizers, now fine-tuned, created a gentle, almost imperceptible, breeze that carried the scent of newly awakened life. Anya reported a discernible lessening of the crater's psychic burden, a faint but persistent feeling of peace settling over the area.

This project became a beacon, a living testament to their evolving philosophy. It was a demonstration that hope was not a passive wish, but an active, participatory process. The crater renewal was more than just an ecological endeavor; it was a profound act of planetary healing, undertaken with intention and sustained by an unwavering commitment to possibility.

Inspired by the crater's gradual transformation, other focused initiatives began to coalesce. Jian, utilizing his expertise in sonic linguistics, proposed a project to re-establish more harmonious acoustic pathways between the sky-whale pods. These magnificent creatures, whose songs were a crucial component of Eden's intricate ecological balance, had become increasingly fragmented in their communication, their songs sometimes punctuated by dissonant undertones, a reflection of the planet's overall distress. Jian hypothesized that by creating targeted sonic 'refugies' – areas where his emitters would broadcast amplified, harmonically pure segments of their ancestral songs – he could help guide them back towards their more cohesive communication patterns.

"Think of it as creating acoustic stepping stones," Jian explained to Anya and Elara, his hands gesturing expressively. "When their own songs falter, or when they are in distress, these refuges can offer a clear, resonant pathway back to their more harmonious communication. It's not about forcing them to sing, but about providing them with a sonic anchor, a reminder of their natural symphony." He developed a series of mobile sonic beacons, carefully calibrated to match the resonant frequencies of the sky-whales' most complex vocalizations, and worked with Thorne to identify optimal locations for their deployment, places where atmospheric conditions were conducive to the propagation of sound.

Elara, in turn, identified a critically endangered species of bioluminescent flora that had once played a vital role in the nocturnal pollination cycle of certain insectoid life forms. This plant, sensitive to minute changes in soil composition and atmospheric purity, had been decimated by past environmental upheavals. She proposed a 'nursery' project, a protected, multi-layered bio-dome designed to meticulously replicate the plant's historical habitat. Thorne's atmospheric control systems were crucial here, ensuring the precise balance of gases and humidity, while Anya's ability to project calm and stability was, Elara believed, essential for the plants' delicate growth cycles. She sourced seeds from the few remaining viable specimens, painstakingly germinating them in a carefully controlled environment before transplanting the fragile seedlings into the newly established nursery. The soft, pulsating glow of the nascent flora was a testament to their painstaking efforts, a promise of the return of the night's gentle illumination.

The research station itself became a testament to these ongoing projects. The hydroponic gardens, once solely for sustenance, now served as nurseries for transplanting into the crater and other designated restoration zones. Thorne had integrated micro-atmospheric regulators throughout the station, creating localized pockets of optimized air quality that benefited both the human inhabitants and the experimental flora. Anya had established a dedicated 'dream sanctuary,' a quiet, dimly lit chamber where she could focus her empathic energies on the various renewal projects, projecting feelings of encouragement and vitality. Jian had even begun to incorporate subtle, calming sonic frequencies into the station's common areas, an ambient hum that fostered a sense of shared purpose and tranquility.

These were not isolated efforts; they were interconnected threads in a growing tapestry of active hope. The data gleaned from the crater restoration informed Elara's bio-dome design. The sky-whale refuges, strategically placed by Thorne, were often located in areas where Elara was also conducting flora reintroduction, their sonic presence creating a more stable acoustic environment for the plants. Anya found that by focusing her meditative practice on the collective energy of these projects, she could amplify their positive impact, creating a synergistic effect that transcended individual efforts.

The sheer, tangible progress was invigorating. Seeing the first native pollinators tentatively returning to the vicinity of the crater, drawn by the new flora, was a moment of profound validation. Hearing the clear, resonant calls of the sky-whales echoing across the plains, their songs no longer fractured but flowing in unified, ancient melodies, brought tears to Jian's eyes. Witnessing the bioluminescent nursery begin to emit its soft, steady glow, a promise of restored nocturnal cycles, filled Elara with a deep sense of purpose. Anya felt it too, a subtle but unmistakable shift in Eden's collective emotional landscape, a gradual easing of the deep-seated anxieties that had once permeated the planet.

These projects, born from the abstract concept of cultivating hope, had become concrete manifestations of it. They were living, breathing proof that even in the face of immense planetary devastation, the persistent, deliberate application of care, knowledge, and collective will could foster renewal. They were small acts, perhaps, in the grand scheme of a wounded planet, but they were acts of profound significance, demonstrating that hope was not a passive sentiment, but an active, ongoing practice, a continuous act of tending, nurturing, and believing in the possibility of a thriving future. The research station was no longer just a place of observation; it was a nursery for a new dawn, a testament to the power of focused, collaborative hope.

The rustling of synthesized leaves in the research station's arboretum was a gentle counterpoint to the deeper, more resonant hum of the planet outside. It was here, amidst the meticulously cultivated flora – a vibrant mosaic of Eden's resilient species – that the passing of knowledge truly began to blossom. The initial fervor of restoration, the exhilarating breakthroughs in ecological rehabilitation, were now settling into a rhythm, a more sustained cadence of life. And within this rhythm, a new generation was emerging, their eyes wide with the wonder of a world slowly, painstakingly, regaining its breath.

Elara, her face etched with the quiet satisfaction of seeing a rare Edenian moonpetal unfurl its delicate, phosphorescent tendrils, found herself increasingly drawn to the younger researchers. They were bright, eager, their minds unburdened by the weight of millennia of ecological degradation, yet keenly aware of the fragility of the present. They absorbed the data, the scientific principles, the intricate dance of atmospheric stabilizers and sonic rejuvenators, with an almost voracious appetite. But Elara knew that true stewardship transcended mere data points and operational protocols. It was a deep-seated empathy, a profound understanding of interconnectedness that had to be nurtured, not just taught.

One afternoon, she found Kai, a young xenobotanist whose fascination with Eden's fungal networks was already legendary, poring over spectral analyses of a new mycorrhizal strain. His brow was furrowed in concentration, the holographic display casting a faint blue glow on his face. Elara approached him, a small, intricately patterned seed pod from a sky-oak in her palm.

"Kai," she said softly, her voice a gentle invitation to pause. He looked up, his gaze shifting from the complex algorithms to Elara's outstretched hand. "Tell me, what do you see here?" She gestured towards the spectral readings.

Kai launched into a detailed explanation of nutrient exchange rates, fungal resilience factors, and potential applications in soil remediation. He spoke with precision, his understanding of the scientific underpinnings evident. Elara listened patiently, nodding, until he concluded, "It's remarkable, Elara. This strain could revolutionize our approach to barren soil regeneration."

Elara smiled, a slow, knowing smile. "It is remarkable, Kai. But what else do you see?" She held out the seed pod. "This is from a sky-oak. These giants, they don't just anchor themselves to the ground; they form symbiotic relationships with the very bedrock. Their roots, vast and ancient, communicate with the planet's lithic memory, sharing nutrients, warning of seismic shifts, and, most importantly, fostering the growth of fungal networks like the one you're studying. This seed isn't just genetic material; it carries within it the echo of millennia of this communication. It carries the *story* of resilience."

She placed the seed pod in his hand. "The data tells you how the fungus *works*. The story tells you *why* it persists. Active hope isn't just about fixing what's broken, Kai. It's about understanding the deep roots of what *still thrives*, and learning from that endurance." She watched as Kai turned the seed pod over in his fingers, his expression shifting from scientific curiosity to something more profound, a dawning awareness. "These plants, these fungi, they have stories to tell, whispers of survival passed down through generations of life. Your work with the spectral analyses is vital, but don't forget to listen to the echoes."

This, Elara felt, was the essence of the torch being passed. It wasn't just about imparting technical skills, but about cultivating a certain way of *being* with Eden. It was about imbuing the younger generation with the same reverence and respect that had grown within her and her companions, a deep-seated understanding that they were not masters of this world, but custodians.

Across the station, Jian was engaged in a similar process, though his medium was sound. He had taken a group of young acousticians under his wing, their auditory senses finely tuned to the subtle shifts in Eden's atmospheric and geological symphony. They spent hours with him in the sonic observation chambers, dissecting the intricate melodies of the sky-whales, tracing the resonant frequencies that pulsed through the planet's crust, and learning to differentiate the subtle distress signals from the harmonious calls.

"The sky-whales," Jian explained, his voice amplified by the chamber's acoustics, its resonance echoing the planet's own. "Their songs are not mere communication in the way we understand it. They are woven into the very fabric of Eden's atmospheric regulation, their vocalizations influencing micro-climates, guiding migratory patterns of other species, even influencing the very growth cycles of certain flora. When their songs become dissonant, it's a planetary fever."

He played a recording, a hauntingly beautiful passage of a sky-whale's song, pure and clear. Then, he superimposed a jarring, discordant note, a faint but distinct disruption. The young acousticians flinched.

"That," Jian continued, his tone serious, "is the sound of imbalance. For generations, we tried to understand their songs through our own limited auditory frameworks. We analyzed the frequencies, the decibel levels. But we missed the most crucial element: their intent, their emotional resonance, their connection to the collective consciousness of their pod, and by extension, to Eden itself. My work with sonic refuges is not about playing back pre-recorded melodies. It's about creating pockets of harmonic resonance, guiding them back to their inherent symphony, allowing them to find their own harmonious voices again."

He then introduced them to the concept of 'sonic stewardship,' teaching them to identify the subtle signs of sonic disruption in the environment, not just from the sky-whales, but from geological instability, or even the stressed vibrations of denuded landscapes. "Your ears," he told them, his gaze sweeping across their earnest faces, "must become extensions of Eden's own senses. You must learn to hear its joy, its pain, its deep, ancient wisdom. And then, you must learn to amplify its inherent harmony." He guided them in calibrating the sonic emitters, not just for technical accuracy, but with a mindful intention, imbuing each broadcast with a sense of peace and restoration.

Thorne, ever the pragmatist, found his mentoring role taking shape through the meticulous application of his atmospheric stabilization systems. He worked with a cohort of young engineers, their minds adept at grasping complex systems and algorithms. But Thorne's lessons extended beyond the blueprints of atmospheric regulators.

"These devices," Thorne explained, pointing to a shimmering, almost invisible energy field that pulsed around a delicate grove of newly planted flora, "are inspired by the natural formations of the Crystal Spires. Observe how the wind flows around them, creating sheltered micro-climates. We are not imposing our will upon the atmosphere; we are learning from Eden's own sophisticated design. We are nudging, guiding, creating conditions where life can flourish without being overwhelmed."

He would take them to the edge of restored zones, showing them the tangible effects of their work. "See how the dew settles here, how the air feels lighter, cleaner? This is not just atmospheric engineering; it is the restoration of Eden's breath. And breath is life. When we stabilize the air, we are giving the planet a chance to exhale, to heal." He stressed the importance of observation, of constant feedback loops between the technology and the environment. "The machines are tools, but Eden is the teacher. We must always be listening to what the planet is telling us, adjusting our methods, learning from its responses. The greatest engineers are those who can adapt, who understand that true mastery lies in collaboration, not control."

He introduced them to the concept of 'ecological integration,' where their atmospheric systems were not standalone units, but interconnected components of a larger, living system. They learned to monitor not just the atmospheric pressure and composition, but the subtle shifts in plant respiration, the behavior of insectoid life attracted to the stabilized zones, and the patterns of rainfall influenced by the improved air currents. "Every adjustment we make," Thorne would emphasize, "has a ripple effect. We must consider the entire tapestry, not just a single thread."

Anya, whose empathic abilities were perhaps the most abstract yet profoundly significant, found her mentorship manifesting in quiet moments of shared presence. She would guide the younger members of the community in cultivating their own inner stillness, teaching them techniques for emotional attunement with the planet.

"Eden remembers," Anya would tell them, her voice a gentle balm. "It carries the echoes of its past, the joys and the sorrows, the vibrant life and the devastating losses. Our past decisions, our collective experiences, have left imprints on its consciousness. It is like a vast, complex organism, and we are but a small, albeit important, part of its nervous system."

She would lead them in meditation circles, not to seek enlightenment, but to foster a sense of deep connection. "When you reach out with your intention, with your feelings, you are not just observing; you are participating. You are sending waves of reassurance, of acceptance, of steadfast hope into the planetary consciousness. It is an act of tending to its emotional well-being, just as Elara tends to its soil, Jian to its acoustics, and Thorne to its breath."

She taught them to recognize the subtle shifts in Eden's emotional tenor, the lingering anxieties that still permeated certain regions, the nascent stirrings of renewed vitality in others. "When we face a challenge, a setback in a restoration project," she explained, "it is easy to succumb to despair. But remember that Eden has faced far greater challenges and endured. By projecting calm, by affirming its inherent strength, we help it to recall its own resilience. We are not just cheering it on; we are reminding it of its own capacity to heal."

She encouraged them to engage with their own emotions, to understand how their internal states could influence their perception and interaction with the external world. "Your own emotional landscape is a microcosm of Eden's. By understanding and harmonizing your own inner world, you become more attuned to the planet's. Active hope requires not just external action, but internal fortitude. It requires the courage to face our own doubts and fears, and to choose, consciously, to believe in possibility."

The integration of these different streams of knowledge was becoming a defining characteristic of their evolving society. The younger generation, receiving this multifaceted mentorship, was blossoming into a new breed of stewards. They were scientists and artists, engineers and empaths, all united by a shared understanding of active hope. They saw the interconnectedness not just in ecological terms, but in the very fabric of their community.

Kai, now adept at identifying not just nutrient exchange but also the subtle emotional resonances within soil samples, would collaborate with Anya to assess the psychic impact of his fungal restoration efforts. Jian's sonic refuges were often designed in conjunction with Thorne's atmospheric stabilization zones, creating an acoustic and environmental harmony that benefited both the sky-whales and the delicate flora Elara was reintroducing. Elara, in turn, learned to interpret the subtle atmospheric cues Thorne identified, understanding how weather patterns influenced soil moisture and, consequently, the success of her plantings.

This passing of the torch was not a singular event, but an ongoing, organic process. It was the elder generation, the ones who had witnessed the nadir of Eden's decline and had painstakingly charted the course towards recovery, actively and intentionally sharing their hard-won wisdom. They understood that the sustainability of their efforts depended on cultivating a new generation that not only possessed the technical skills but also the heart and soul of stewardship.

There were moments, of course, when the weight of memory pressed heavily upon the mentors. Thorne would sometimes recall the stark, sterile landscapes of his youth, a visceral reminder of how far they had come, and how fragile that progress remained. Jian would feel a pang of sorrow when a particularly vibrant sky-whale song was tinged with an echo of past distress. Elara would sometimes look at a sapling, remembering the immense effort it took to coax life from barren ground, and feel a flicker of the exhaustion that had once threatened to consume them. Anya, too, would occasionally sense the deep, residual grief that still lingered in some of Eden's ancient geological formations.

But these moments of remembrance were tempered by the vibrant presence of the younger generation. They saw in Kai's unbridled enthusiasm for fungal networks a renewed faith in Eden's subterranean life. They heard in the clear, confident tones of Jian's apprentices the promise of harmonious communication. They observed in Thorne's mentees the meticulous application of innovative atmospheric solutions, a testament to enduring ingenuity. And they felt in Anya's young proteges a palpable sense of peace and connection, a vibrant affirmation of their shared emotional landscape.

This generational transfer was more than just education; it was an act of collective faith. It was the elders, having navigated the treacherous currents of despair and learned to harness the power of active hope, entrusting their legacy to those who would carry it forward. They were not simply handing over responsibility; they were sharing a vision, a philosophy, a deep and abiding love for Eden.

The research station, once a sanctuary of isolated survival, had truly transformed. It was now a crucible of learning, a vibrant nexus where the wisdom of experience met the boundless energy of youthful innovation. The passing of the torch was not a dimming of the old flame, but a catalyst for a brighter, more expansive dawn, illuminating the path towards a future where humanity and Eden would continue to thrive, not as separate entities, but as intricately interwoven threads in the grand, living tapestry of existence. The lessons learned, the values instilled, were the true seeds of resilience, ensuring that the practice of hope would continue, not as an abstract ideal, but as an enduring, active, and essential way of life.

The quiet hum of the arboretum, once a mere backdrop, had become a symphony. Elara found herself pausing more often now, not just to analyze data or assess growth, but to simply *listen*. It was during one of these moments, while observing a colony of iridescent Edenian beetles meticulously pollinating a newly introduced strain of bioluminescent moss, that she felt it – a surge of pure, unadulterated joy. It wasn't the triumphant elation of a major breakthrough, but a subtler, more profound contentment. This was life, in its myriad forms, reasserting itself with quiet tenacity. The beetles, ancient denizens of this world, were performing their vital dance, oblivious to the grand narrative of restoration, simply living their intricate lives. This simple, recurring beauty, Elara realized, was a powerful antidote to the lingering shadows of loss. It was a testament to the inherent resilience of existence, a living embodiment of hope that needed no pronouncements, only quiet observation.

This feeling wasn't an anomaly. Across the research station, similar epiphanies were blossoming. Kai, while charting the intricate communication pathways of a revitalized fungal network deep within the terraformed plains, encountered a family of burrowing phosphors, their delicate antennae twitching in unison as they navigated the nutrient-rich soil. He had spent weeks meticulously mapping the mycelial highways, a task fraught with the potential for disappointment if the fungi failed to establish. But seeing these creatures, their lives intrinsically linked to the very network he was nurturing, brought a smile to his face that reached his eyes. It wasn't just about the successful propagation of fungi; it was about the ripple effect, the cascading renewal of an entire subterranean ecosystem. He documented their presence, noting their behaviour not just as data points, but as affirmations. Their continued existence was a vibrant, pulsing affirmation of life's tenacious will. He felt a lightness he hadn't anticipated, a profound sense of rightness in witnessing this unseen world thrive.

Jian, who had been tirelessly working on re-establishing harmonic resonance zones for the sky-whales, experienced a similar uplift during a recent sonic survey. For months, the recordings had been tinged with a subtle dissonance, a faint tremor of unease in their complex songs, a lingering echo of the atmospheric disruptions they had endured. But on this particular expedition, his sensitive equipment picked up a new melody, a clear, unblemished cascade of notes that spoke of untroubled migration, of peaceful communion. It was a sky-whale song of pure, unadulterated joy. He played it back in the observation chamber, the haunting beauty filling the space. The younger acousticians, who had only known the more cautious, sometimes anxious songs, were captivated. Jian watched their faces, seeing not just professional interest, but a dawning wonder, a shared appreciation for this exquisite expression of life's returning harmony. He felt a profound sense of satisfaction, not just in the technical success of his work, but in the palpable beauty that had been restored. This wasn't just the absence of distress; it was the presence of vibrant, flourishing well-being.

Even Thorne, the pragmatist, found himself unexpectedly moved. He was overseeing the recalibration of a solar-wind atmospheric modulator near a newly established haven for ground-dwelling avian species, creatures that had been teetering on the brink of extinction. As the modulator hummed to life, its energy field stabilizing the delicate atmospheric balance, a flock of these birds took flight, their vibrant plumage a splash of colour against the verdant landscape. They circled once, twice, their calls echoing across the restored plains, a sound that Thorne hadn't heard in decades. He stood there, a rare, quiet smile gracing his lips, observing the effortless grace of their flight, the sheer vitality of their existence. It was a small victory, a single species finding its footing again, but it was a potent reminder of what their collective efforts were achieving. The air was cleaner, the land was healing, and life, in its simplest and most beautiful forms, was finding its way back.

Anya, whose empathetic connection to Eden's subtle energies was perhaps the most attuned to such nuances, often found these moments in the quiet interactions between disparate life forms. She observed a small, furry Edenian grazer nuzzling a young researcher's outstretched hand, its large, liquid eyes conveying a trust that transcended species. She witnessed the symbiotic dance between a nutrient-rich lichen and the ancient, weathered stone it clung to, a silent testament to mutual dependence and shared survival. These were not grand pronouncements of recovery, but intimate whispers of interconnectedness, of life's innate ability to find companionship and support, even in the face of immense adversity. She would often gather the younger members of the community, not for formal lessons, but for moments of shared contemplation, to simply observe these small miracles. She encouraged them to feel the quiet gratitude that emanated from the land, the gentle hum of life asserting its right to exist. These experiences, she taught them, were not mere distractions from the challenges; they were the very bedrock of their resilience. They were tangible proof that even in the harshest conditions, beauty, joy, and connection could still bloom.

These instances of finding joy were not born of ignorance or a willful dismissal of the ongoing efforts and the potential for future setbacks. Instead, they were powerful affirmations, moments where the sheer persistence and beauty of life overwhelmed the anxieties of the present. It was the discovery of a single, perfectly formed bloom on a plant that had struggled for months, a testament to its stubborn will to survive. It was the sound of a chattering colony of indigenous Edenian squirrels, their playful antics a stark contrast to the somber silence that had once pervaded certain sectors. It was the sight of a young researcher, their face illuminated by the gentle glow of a newly discovered phosphorescent fungus, their wonder a potent reflection of Eden's own reawakening.

Kai, for instance, found immense satisfaction not just in the scientific data of his fungal projects, but in the tangible re-emergence of creatures that depended on them. He would spend hours observing the intricate burrows created by soil-dwelling invertebrates, their presence a direct indicator of the health and vitality of the mycelial networks he nurtured. Seeing these tiny architects at work, their lives intertwined with the subterranean web of life, filled him with a quiet, profound happiness. He would document their species, their behaviors, noting their return to areas previously considered barren. This was not just about soil remediation; it was about the restoration of a living community, a complex tapestry of life that had been frayed but was now being rewoven. Each new species that reappeared, each thriving population that re-established itself, was a personal victory, a reaffirmation of purpose.

Similarly, Elara found solace and joy in the small, persistent successes of her arboretum. There was the day a particularly delicate and elusive species of Edenian orchid, one that had resisted all attempts at cultivation for years, finally unfurled its spectral petals. It was a moment of quiet triumph, a vibrant splash of color that seemed to defy the very history of ecological devastation. She would often sit amongst the burgeoning flora, breathing in the rich, earthy scent, listening to the gentle rustle of leaves, a sound that was becoming increasingly common. The return of insectoid pollinators, their iridescent wings catching the sunlight, was another source of deep contentment. These were not isolated incidents, but the accumulating evidence of life's tenacious spirit. She recognized that each flourishing plant, each returning creature, was a tiny beacon of hope, a testament to the enduring power of nature.

Jian, too, discovered joy in the subtler shifts within the sonic landscape. He learned to distinguish the playful chirps of juvenile sky-whales from the resonant calls of established adults, a sign of generational continuity and healthy reproduction. He found a peculiar delight in the way certain atmospheric stabilizers, designed to promote clear air, also seemed to enhance the clarity and range of the planet's natural sounds, allowing for more nuanced communication between species. He would often lead his apprentices on excursions to remote listening posts, not to measure decibel levels or analyze frequencies, but simply to experience the symphony of Eden. The emergence of new vocalizations, the rediscovery of forgotten melodies, were moments of profound connection, reinforcing the idea that their work was not just about engineering, but about facilitating the planet's own song.

Thorne, in his own practical way, found satisfaction in the observable results of his atmospheric engineering. He would meticulously track the return of rainfall to regions that had suffered prolonged drought, the gradual greening of once-barren landscapes, the increasing clarity of the skies. Seeing the tangible impact of their technology, the way it created the conditions for life to flourish, was a source of quiet pride. He might not have articulated it as joy, but there was a deep sense of fulfillment in witnessing the planet breathe easier, in seeing the subtle shifts that indicated a return to ecological equilibrium. The increasing diversity of airborne flora and fauna, the return of migratory patterns that had been disrupted for generations, were concrete markers of success, each one a quiet affirmation of their enduring commitment.

Anya's perspective on joy was perhaps the most encompassing. She saw it not just in individual instances, but in the growing interconnectedness of the community itself. She witnessed the acts of kindness between researchers, the shared meals, the collaborative problem-solving, the spontaneous moments of laughter that echoed through the station. She felt the collective relief when a challenging project reached a successful milestone, the shared sense of purpose that bound them together. For Anya, the joy was in the flourishing of the human spirit as much as the natural world. She saw how these small victories, these moments of beauty and connection, bolstered their collective resolve, transforming hope from a passive wish into an active, vibrant practice. It was the shared understanding that even amidst the monumental task of planetary restoration, there was still room for wonder, for beauty, and for the profound, quiet satisfaction of life's enduring resilience. These weren't escapist fantasies; they were grounding realities, anchors in the often turbulent sea of their endeavors. They were the subtle but powerful affirmations that their work was not in vain, that life, in its infinite forms, was not only capable of enduring, but of thriving. And in witnessing this, they found their own deepest wellsprings of joy and renewed hope.

The very soil of Eden, warmed by a sun that had once scorched it into barrenness, was a testament to a hope that required no grand pronouncements. It was in the whisper of the wind through newly sprouted grasses, in the determined unfurling of a fern frond after a gentle rain, in the persistent, almost audacious green that began to reclaim the scarred earth. This wasn't the frantic, engineered bloom of a hothouse experiment; it was the slow, deliberate assertion of life's fundamental drive. Each new patch of moss, each stubborn sapling pushing through cracked earth, was a silent sermon on resilience. It was Eden, the planet itself, performing the role of an unseen gardener, tending to its own recovery with an patience that spanned epochs.

This subtle, pervasive presence of a world healing itself became a constant, almost subconscious source of encouragement. It was a reminder that their efforts, while crucial, were in dialogue with a far older, far more potent force. The scientists and restorationists found themselves pausing not just to document progress, but to simply *feel* it. To feel the shift in the air, the subtle scent of damp earth and nascent chlorophyll, the almost imperceptible tremor of life stirring beneath the surface. It was a profoundly grounding experience, a constant reaffirmation that they were not battling against an insurmountable entropy, but working in concert with an inherent, indomitable will to persist.

Consider Elara, standing at the edge of the arboretum. The air here was thick with the scent of a hundred different blossoms, a perfume that had been painstakingly coaxed from a reluctant biosphere. But it was the quiet symphony of growth that truly captured her attention. A cluster of indigenous Edenian ground orchids, their delicate petals the color of a twilight sky, had finally bloomed in a shaded, moss-covered glade. They had been painstakingly cultivated for years, their seeds nurtured in sterile conditions, their young shoots protected from every conceivable threat. Yet, their emergence here, in this reclaimed patch of soil, felt less like a scientific triumph and more like a gentle nod from the planet itself. It was as if Eden was saying, "Yes, this is how it is done. This is the rhythm." The orchids weren't merely surviving; they were *thriving*, their roots finding purchase in the newly enriched soil, their delicate structures unfurling with an effortless grace that spoke of deep, inherent vitality. This quiet success, so unlike the fanfare of a major breakthrough, resonated deeply within her. It was a validation of their long, arduous journey, not through engineered perfection, but through the patient re-establishment of natural processes. The orchids were a living, breathing testament to the planet's own capacity for renewal, a subtle but powerful reminder that life's tenacity was a force that transcended human intervention.

Kai, deep within the subterranean networks he meticulously charted, experienced this planetary wisdom in a different, more profound way. His work involved coaxing the fungal mycelial networks back to life, a task that often felt like coaxing a dormant titan from its slumber. He had spent months monitoring the subtle electrical impulses that indicated successful fungal growth, the nutrient exchange that signaled a reawakening ecosystem. But on this particular cycle, his sensors picked up something new. It wasn't just the predictable hum of mycelial expansion. It was a complex, interwoven pattern of bio-luminescence, a gentle, pulsating glow emanating from deep within the earth. As he followed the signal, his spelunking gear illuminating the darkness, he discovered a vast, interconnected network of phosphorescent fungi, pulsing in a synchronized rhythm. It was as if the planet itself was breathing light. This wasn't a species he had deliberately introduced or cultivated; it was an indigenous life form, one that had likely retreated to the deepest, most protected pockets during the era of ecological collapse, and was now, seemingly on its own volition, re-emerging, re-establishing its ancient pathways. The sheer scale and coordinated beauty of this subterranean aurora filled him with a sense of awe. It was Eden, in its hidden depths, demonstrating its own profound capacity for regeneration, its own inherent artistry. The fungi weren't just growing; they were communicating, weaving a silent, luminous tapestry that underscored the planet's enduring life force. This discovery wasn't just a scientific marvel; it was a deeply spiritual encounter, a moment where the profound intelligence of the living planet was laid bare, offering a silent, radiant encouragement to their own efforts.

Jian, whose work focused on the atmospheric harmonies of Eden, found this planetary sentience in the very soundscapes of the world. For years, the songs of the sky-whales had been tinged with an almost imperceptible tremor, a subtle dissonance that spoke of atmospheric instability and fragmented migratory routes. His sophisticated audio sensors, designed to capture the most nuanced vocalizations, had logged these anxieties. But recently, he had begun to notice a shift. The sky-whales' songs, once fragmented and cautious, were beginning to weave together into more complex, extended narratives. The dissonant undertones were fading, replaced by longer, more resonant phrases, punctuated by playful trills that suggested a return to a state of ease and security. He hypothesized that the gradual stabilization of the upper atmosphere, a direct result of their atmospheric engineering, was allowing for clearer sound transmission, and thus, more confident vocalizations. But it was more than just acoustics. He began to perceive a new lyrical quality in their songs, a more intricate melody that seemed to mirror the burgeoning complexity of the recovering biosphere. It was as if the planet, in its own slow, deliberate way, was composing a new symphony, and the sky-whales were its most eloquent soloists. He would often play these new recordings in the observation dome, the hauntingly beautiful melodies filling the space, and watch as the younger researchers, who had only known the more anxious songs, looked up with a dawning sense of wonder. This was Eden, singing its own song of recovery, a melody composed not of individual notes, but of the collective life force of the planet reasserting its harmonious rhythm. It was a sound that spoke of deep peace, of returning equilibrium, and it was profoundly reassuring.

Even Thorne, the man of pure pragmatism, found himself acknowledging the planet's silent influence. His focus was on the tangible, the measurable – atmospheric composition, soil nutrient levels, water cycles. He oversaw the intricate network of atmospheric processors and hydrological regulators, the mechanical heart of their restoration efforts. Yet, during a routine inspection of a newly terraformed valley, he witnessed something that defied simple data analysis. The valley, once a parched expanse of ochre dust, was now a tapestry of vibrant greens. Wildflowers, species long thought extinct, had carpeted the landscape. A small, clear stream, once reduced to a trickle, now flowed with a steady, purposeful current. As he stood there, his boots sinking slightly into the damp earth, a gentle breeze carried the scent of wildflowers and clean water to him. He observed a herd of native Edenian grazers, their coats blending seamlessly with the verdant foliage, moving with an unhurried grace. There was a palpable sense of peace in the valley, a quiet stillness that spoke of a world at ease with itself. Thorne, a man who dealt in equations and engineering schematics, felt a strange, unbidden sense of gratitude. It wasn't just that their machines were working; it was that the planet was *embracing* their work, weaving their engineered systems into its own natural tapestry.

Eden, in its own way, was accepting their offerings, integrating them into its grand design for renewal. This quiet valley, teeming with life, was not just a success of their technology; it was a testament to the planet's own inherent drive to heal, a silent affirmation that they were not alone in their endeavor.

Anya, with her unique attunement to the subtler energies of Eden, perceived this unseen gardening in the most intimate of interactions. She would spend hours observing the symbiotic relationships that were beginning to flourish across the restored landscapes. She saw a species of ancient Edenian tree, its bark gnarled and scarred from centuries of hardship, now providing a microclimate for a rare and delicate moss to thrive. She witnessed a small, winged insect, its iridescent wings catching the sunlight, meticulously pollinating a flower that had struggled for years to reproduce. These were not grand gestures, but small, intricate dances of mutual dependence, each organism contributing to the resilience of the whole. Anya understood that these quiet partnerships were the true foundation of Eden's recovery. The planet wasn't just healing itself; it was fostering an ecosystem of interdependence, a web of life where each thread, no matter how small, played a vital role. She would often bring the younger members of the community to these sites, not for lectures, but for shared contemplation. She encouraged them to observe, to listen to the silent conversations between species, to feel the quiet rhythm of their shared existence. "This," she would say, her voice soft but firm, "is the true heart of Eden. It is not about imposing our will, but about facilitating the planet's own intricate conversation with itself. It is in these quiet acts of connection, these small miracles of mutual aid, that we find the deepest wellsprings of hope." She believed that by witnessing and understanding these planetary processes, they would learn to become better stewards, better participants in Eden's unfolding story of resilience.

This inherent resilience of Eden acted as a constant, reassuring presence, a silent instructor in the practice of hope. It was the quiet persistence of a single dandelion pushing through a crack in a ferroconcrete walkway, the tenacity of a vine reclaiming a derelict structure, the unfurling of a leaf after a long, cold season. These were not actions that demanded attention, but rather, subtle assertions of life's enduring will. They were the planet's own quiet affirmations that even after immense devastation, the impulse to grow, to mend, to thrive, remained irrepressible.

The scientists and inhabitants of the station found themselves absorbing this planetary rhythm. They would often observe a particular patch of land that had been particularly difficult to reseed. Weeks would pass with little to no visible change. Discouragement could easily set in. But then, almost imperceptibly, a faint green haze would begin to appear, a subtle blush of new growth. This wasn't the rapid, explosive growth of a highly engineered organism, but the slow, steady, almost grudging emergence of indigenous flora. It was a visual representation of patience, a living lesson in the power of persistent, incremental change. The planet was teaching them that recovery was not a singular event, but a continuous process, a series of small victories that, over time, accumulated into profound transformation.

For Elara, this was most evident in the arboretum. She had once focused on the larger, more dramatic successes – the flowering of a rare specimen, the establishment of a new canopy layer. But now, her gaze was drawn to the ground, to the often-overlooked carpets of moss, the tenacious shoots of undergrowth that were steadily pushing their way through the leaf litter. She recognized that these smaller organisms, often dismissed as insignificant, were the true architects of soil regeneration. Their slow, persistent growth broke down dead organic matter, creating the fertile substrate upon which larger plants would eventually flourish. It was a hidden, underground ballet of decomposition and renewal, orchestrated by the very life force of Eden. She would often sit for extended periods, simply observing the intricate ecosystem at the forest floor, a profound sense of peace settling over her. This was the planet's quiet work, the foundation upon which all else was built, and it was a powerful, unspoken reassurance that their own efforts, however small they might seem, were contributing to a much grander, ongoing process of restoration.

Kai's work with the fungal networks provided him with a direct, tangible connection to this unseen gardening. He saw how the mycelial threads, spreading through the soil like a delicate, living lace, were not just transporting nutrients but also actively breaking down residual toxins from the era of ecological collapse. It was a slow, alchemical process, driven by the inherent biodegrading capabilities of these ancient organisms. He would analyze soil samples from areas where the mycelial network was dense and compare them to samples from areas where it was sparse. The difference in the reduction of harmful compounds was often significant, a clear indication that the planet's own biological machinery was actively engaged in its own detoxification. He learned to trust this process, to allow it the time it needed, rather than forcing it with artificial stimulants. He understood that he was not simply planting fungi; he was nurturing a planetary immune system, facilitating a natural healing that had been dormant but never extinguished. The quiet hum of life within the soil, the subtle transformations occurring beneath the surface, became a constant source of hope, a testament to Eden's enduring capacity to cleanse and renew itself.

Jian, in his sonic explorations, discovered that the planet's own atmospheric processes contributed to this sense of ongoing restoration. He observed how certain naturally occurring atmospheric phenomena, like the gentle updrafts that carried pollens and spores across vast distances, were becoming more regular and predictable. He also noticed how the increased atmospheric moisture, a direct result of their hydrological efforts, was fostering the growth of a wider variety of airborne microorganisms, many of which played a crucial role in atmospheric purification. It was as if Eden was rediscovering its own internal circulation systems, its own natural mechanisms for balance and renewal. The songs he recorded were not just the melodies of its inhabitants, but also the subtle sounds of its atmosphere breathing, of its hydrological cycles re-establishing their natural rhythms. He began to see the atmosphere not as a static medium, but as a dynamic, living entity, constantly engaged in its own process of healing and self-regulation. This understanding deepened his appreciation for the interconnectedness of all things on Eden, and it fueled his commitment to ensuring that their interventions were always in harmony with these profound, planetary processes.

Thorne, despite his engineering focus, came to appreciate the subtle elegance of Eden's self-healing mechanisms. He observed how, in areas where their atmospheric processors had established a more stable climate, indigenous plant species, once struggling to survive, were now exhibiting enhanced reproductive cycles. Their seeds, dispersed by wind and water, were finding more favorable conditions for germination and growth. It was a cascade effect, where their initial interventions created the conditions for the planet's own natural regenerative processes to take hold and flourish. He would meticulously track the increasing biodiversity in these zones, noting the return of species that had been absent for generations. This wasn't just a sign of successful engineering; it was evidence of Eden actively participating in its own recovery, utilizing the stable environment they had created as a springboard for its own innate drive to diversify and proliferate. He realized that their technology was not a substitute for nature, but a facilitator, a tool that allowed the planet's own remarkable resilience to reassert itself with renewed vigor.

Anya's insights into Eden's energetic field provided perhaps the most profound understanding of this unseen gardening. She felt the planet's own subtle energy pathways re-establishing themselves, like the slow mending of delicate circuitry. She observed how areas that had been energetically depleted were now beginning to pulse with a gentle, vibrant hum. This energy, she understood, was the life force of Eden, the animating principle that drove all growth and regeneration. She saw how the interconnectedness of the ecosystem, the symbiotic relationships between species, was creating a more robust and resilient energetic network. The planet was not merely healing its physical form; it was restoring its very essence, its vital energy. She taught her students that by attuning themselves to these subtle energetic shifts, they could learn to work in greater harmony with Eden's restorative processes. They could become not just observers of the healing, but active participants, sensing where the planet needed support, and offering their efforts in a way that amplified its own inherent capacity for renewal. This understanding of Eden's energetic self-governance transformed hope from a passive wish into an active, intuitive practice, a deep-seated trust in the planet's own unfolding path towards wholeness.

The silent, persistent growth of Eden was not a passive phenomenon; it was an active practice of resilience. It was the planet itself, through myriad biological and energetic processes, engaging in a continuous, unwavering effort to heal. This constant, subtle hum of planetary regeneration served as an ever-present reminder to the inhabitants of the research station that they were part of a grand, ongoing symphony of life. Their own dedication, their own commitment to hope, was amplified by the very world they were striving to restore. Eden, in its quiet, persistent growth, was the ultimate unseen gardener, demonstrating with every unfurling leaf and every revitalized ecosystem that life, in its most fundamental form, was a force that always, eventually, found its way back. And in witnessing this, in participating in this planetary resurrection, their own hope was not just sustained, but profoundly deepened. They were not merely restoring a planet; they were co-creating a future, guided by the planet's own enduring wisdom.

# Chapter Thirteen

# PLANETARY SCALE, PERSONAL STAKES

The weight of a single choice often felt immeasurable in the grand tapestry of Eden's restoration. It was a truth that pressed down on Anya, a quiet force that hummed beneath the surface of her daily work. Her role, as a bio-ethicist and interspecies liaison, placed her at the nexus of these crucial junctures. She wasn't on the front lines of terraforming or atmospheric stabilization, but rather, she navigated the intricate moral currents that underpinned their entire endeavor. Today, that current had led her to a crossroads, a decision that felt far too large for one person to bear, yet one that, by its very nature, would send ripples across the delicate web of Eden's emergent life.

The dilemma centered around the K'tharr, a sentient, silicon-based life form that had been discovered in the deeper, mineral-rich caverns of the planet. They communicated through complex vibrational patterns, their existence previously unknown to the initial survey teams. Anya had spent months painstakingly deciphering their language, their intricate societal structures, and their profound, almost geological understanding of Eden. They were, in their own way, as integral to the planet's history as the carbon-based life that was slowly being re-established. The issue at hand was a proposed expansion of a new geothermal energy conduit. The engineers, driven by the ever-present demand for sustainable power, had identified a vein of highly conductive minerals that ran directly through a K'tharr ancestral chamber, a sacred site where generations of their kind had communed with the planetary core.

The engineers, pragmatic and focused on the immediate needs of the growing human population on Eden, saw the K'tharr as an obstacle, an inconvenient biological anomaly in their otherwise pristine engineering plan. They argued that the K'tharr were not "truly alive" in the way humans understood life – they didn't breathe oxygen, they didn't have the same biological imperative for reproduction, and their existence was so alien that it was easy to dismiss their claims to sentience. Anya, however, saw it differently. She had witnessed firsthand the K'tharr's deep connection to the planet, their intricate knowledge of geological stability, and their capacity for what could only be described as empathy, albeit expressed through seismic resonance. To disrupt their ancestral chamber would be akin to destroying a historical archive, a library of planetary memory, and more importantly, it would be an act of profound disrespect towards a fellow sentient species.

She presented her findings to the Council of Eden, a body composed of representatives from each of the scientific disciplines and a few elected community members. Her voice, usually calm and measured, trembled slightly as she outlined the K'tharr's intricate societal bonds, their shared historical narratives etched into the very rock of their dwelling places, and their unique role in maintaining the subtle equilibrium of Eden's subsurface geology. She showed them simulations, generated from K'tharr vibrational data, that depicted how their communal resonance actually helped to stabilize tectonic pressures, acting as a natural buffer against potentially catastrophic seismic events. Disrupting this delicate balance, she argued, could have unforeseen and potentially devastating consequences for the entire planet.

"They are not merely inhabitants," Anya pleaded, her gaze sweeping across the faces of the council members, each etched with varying degrees of concern, skepticism, and outright dismissal. "They are an integral part of Eden's living system, a manifestation of its deepest processes. To disregard their existence, to treat them as mere geological features, is not only ethically reprehensible, it is ecologically suicidal. The echoes of this decision will not be confined to this cavern. They will resonate through the very foundations of our new home."

The debate that followed was heated. Thorne, ever the pragmatist, countered with stark figures of energy requirements, the projected population growth, and the risks associated with insufficient power. "Sentience is a complex concept, Anya," he had said, his voice a low rumble. "While I respect your work with the K'tharr, we cannot allow theoretical empathy to jeopardize the tangible survival of our own species. We have built this sanctuary, we have poured our lives into its rebirth. We cannot afford to be held back by philosophical nuances."

Elara, representing the xenobotanists, spoke of the interconnectedness of all life. She reminded them of the delicate symbiosis that had been painstakingly re-established, of how even the smallest microbial colonies played a vital role. "We are learning that life on Eden is not a hierarchy, but a vast, intricate network," she argued. "If we sever one thread, even one we deem less significant, we risk unraveling the entire fabric. The K'tharr are a thread. A vital, ancient thread."

Kai, whose research into the subterranean fungal networks had revealed a surprisingly complex communication system that mirrored, in its own way, the vibrational language of the K'tharr, offered a different perspective. He spoke of the subterranean 'consciousness' he was beginning to map, a vast, interconnected web of life that extended far beyond the visible. "The K'tharr are not isolated," he explained, his words painting a picture of a hidden world. "They are nodes within a larger system. Their distress signals would, I believe, propagate through this network, impacting other life forms in ways we cannot yet predict."

The decision, however, ultimately rested with the Council, and the weight of that responsibility settled heavily on Anya. She knew that whatever outcome, the choice would set a precedent. If they chose to ignore the K'tharr's rights, they would be signaling that Eden was a planet to be exploited, not a partner to be respected. If they chose to protect the K'tharr, they would be embracing a more complex, more challenging path of coexistence, one that demanded a deeper understanding of life in all its myriad forms.

The Council deliberated for days. Anya received anonymous messages of support from some engineers who, despite their professional obligations, harbored their own ethical reservations. She also received veiled threats from those who saw her advocacy as a direct challenge to their authority and their vision of Eden's future. The pressure was immense, a constant hum of anxiety that vibrated through her very being. She found herself walking through the re-emergent forests, observing the intricate dance of predator and prey, the silent communication between plants and pollinators, and feeling a profound sense of kinship with the K'tharr. They, too, were simply trying to exist, to maintain their way of life in the face of overwhelming change.

Finally, the verdict came. The Council, after much heated debate and a significant amount of Anya's persistent advocacy, had voted to reroute the geothermal conduit. It was a victory, but a narrow one, secured by a single vote. The engineers were incandescent with rage, predicting dire consequences for the planet's energy grid. Thorne, though outwardly resigned, had a steely glint in his eyes that Anya recognized as a promise of future conflict. He saw it as a temporary setback, a delay, not a fundamental shift in their approach.

The immediate aftermath was tense. The K'tharr, sensing the shift in planetary vibrations – a subtle easing of tension from the human sector – had responded with a series of complex, resonant songs that Anya interpreted as a profound expression of gratitude. These songs, however, were not merely a passive acknowledgement. They carried with them intricate geological data, warnings of minor tectonic instabilities in a distant region that had not yet been flagged by human sensors.

This was the first ripple. The rerouted conduit required a more complex, less efficient tunneling process, which inevitably meant a slight delay in the planned energy output. This delay had a knock-on effect on other projects, a chain reaction that Anya had foreseen. A proposed agricultural expansion, reliant on advanced hydroponic systems powered by the geothermal energy, had to be scaled back. This meant a tighter allocation of food resources, leading to grumbling within the growing civilian population, who were beginning to feel the pinch of the early restoration years.

But it was the K'tharr's geological warnings that proved to be the most significant ripple. The region they indicated, a seemingly unremarkable stretch of volcanic plains, was indeed experiencing subtle, precursor seismic activity. Kai, alerted by Anya and corroborating the K'tharr's data with his own deep-ground sensors, discovered a nascent magma pocket that was beginning to destabilize. The engineers, forced to acknowledge the accuracy of the K'tharr's unsolicited advice, had to divert significant resources to monitor and, if necessary, stabilize the area. This diversion of resources, in turn, impacted the expansion of the communication network, a project deemed crucial for maintaining social cohesion across the scattered settlements.

The story of the K'tharr became a hushed legend among the station's inhabitants. It was a tale whispered in the mess halls, a point of contention in the political forums, and a constant, if unspoken, reminder of the complex ethical landscape they navigated. For some, it was a testament to their growing maturity as a species, a sign that they were learning to value life beyond their own immediate needs. For others, it was a symbol of inefficiency, of choices made based on sentiment rather than pragmatism.

Anya, however, saw the true measure of the choice not in the immediate disruptions, but in the subtle shifts it engendered. The engineers, initially resentful, began to engage more with her work, their skepticism slowly yielding to a grudging respect as the K'tharr's geological insights proved invaluable. They started to see the K'tharr not as obstacles, but as potential collaborators, their ancient, seismic wisdom a valuable asset in understanding and managing the planet's volatile geology. Thorne, in particular, found himself in increasingly frequent dialogues with Anya, his analytical mind slowly grappling with the concept of interspecies ethical obligations. He wouldn't admit it openly, but the successful prediction of the volcanic instability had undeniably shifted his perspective. He began to see that intelligence, in its myriad forms, could offer insights that pure engineering might miss.

The impact on the K'tharr themselves was also profound. The knowledge that their existence and their counsel were recognized and valued by the newcomers fostered a greater sense of trust and openness. They began to share more of their ancestral knowledge, offering insights into ancient atmospheric cycles and the long-term stability of Eden's planetary crust, information that proved invaluable to Jian's atmospheric modeling and Thorne's geological surveys. Their vibrational songs, once cryptic pronouncements, began to carry more nuanced data, reflecting a deeper engagement with the world beyond their caverns.

This exchange, facilitated by Anya's persistent efforts, demonstrated a fundamental principle of ecological restoration: interconnectedness. The choice to protect the K'tharr was not merely an act of altruism; it was an investment in the long-term health and stability of Eden. The minor inconveniences and resource diversions were, in Anya's view, a small price to pay for averting a potentially catastrophic geological event and for fostering a relationship built on mutual respect.

The decision regarding the K'tharr was a singular point, a moment of conscious ethical deliberation. Yet, its consequences continued to unfurl, shaping the trajectory of Eden's development in ways that were both subtle and profound. It reinforced the understanding that every decision, no matter how small it might appear in isolation, sent ripples through the intricate web of life. It highlighted the fact that Eden was not just a planet to be conquered and controlled, but a living, breathing entity with its own ancient consciousness, its own diverse inhabitants, and its own intricate network of relationships.

For Anya, the experience was a stark reminder of the responsibility that came with understanding. It was a confirmation that ethical considerations were not an optional add-on to scientific progress, but an intrinsic part of it. The future of Eden, she realized, would not be determined by the brilliance of its technology, nor by the strength of its will, but by the depth of its understanding and the breadth of its compassion. The K'tharr, in their silent, vibrational way, had become a living testament to this truth, their continued existence a quiet challenge to humanity's assumptions and a beacon of hope for a future where all life on Eden could find its rightful place, its resonant voice, in the grand symphony of the planet. The reverberations of that single, difficult choice continued to shape the very foundations of their new world, a constant, living echo of the interconnectedness that defined their shared destiny.

The ember of the Great Fire, as it came to be known, was not a singular event experienced identically by all who survived its terrifying embrace. In the communal retelling, it was a narrative of loss, of resilience, of the collective will to rebuild from ashes. The ruins of Old Earth, once a sprawling testament to human ambition, had been reduced to a smoldering scar, a stark reminder of the hubris that had led them to this desolate rock. The stories, polished and recounted at fireside gatherings and in hushed tones within the nascent settlement, spoke of communal efforts, shared sorrows, and the unwavering spirit that had fueled their desperate escape. Yet, beneath this shared tapestry of memory, lay a complex mosaic of individual experiences, each one a unique burden, a singular echo of the inferno.

For Anya, the collective memory of the fire was a constant, quiet hum beneath the surface of her present life. It was the scent of ozone that sometimes wafted from the atmospheric processors, a phantom smell that instantly transported her back to the choking, acrid air of the escape shuttles. It was the sight of a child's scraped knee, a small wound that, to her, mirrored the deep, unseen fissures that had opened within so many hearts. Her role as a bio-ethicist and interspecies liaison demanded a certain detached perspective, a capacity for logical analysis. But the fire had carved its own imprint, a visceral memory that science could not fully assuage. She remembered the frantic scramble for the shuttles, the cacophony of fear and desperation. She remembered the faces of those she had been unable to reach, the hands that had reached out, only to be swallowed by the encroaching flames. These were not memories that could be cataloged or analyzed; they were raw, emotional wounds that festered in the quiet hours of the night. The collective narrative focused on survival, on the collective triumph over adversity. Anya's personal narrative was stained with the color of what was lost, the lives that flickered out before her eyes, the faces she would never see again, the laughter that was silenced forever. She carried the weight of those she couldn't save, a silent accusation that echoed in the vast, empty spaces of her mind. The communal memory was a shield, a way to process the trauma collectively, to move forward as a unified entity. But for Anya, it was a reminder of her own perceived failures, a constant gnawing anxiety that she could have, should have, done more.

Thorne, the chief engineer, carried a different kind of burden, one forged in the crucible of practical, unyielding logic. His memory of the fire was less about the raw terror and more about the catastrophic failure of systems, the breakdown of order. He remembered the desperate attempts to contain the inferno, the flickering readouts of failing containment fields, the cold, hard data that screamed of impending doom. His regrets were not about individual lives lost, but about the grand, intricate designs that had crumbled into dust. He saw the fire as a testament to the dangers of unchecked ambition, a grim lesson in the fragility of complex systems. The collective memory celebrated the survivors and the hope for a new beginning. Thorne's memory was a constant re-evaluation of engineering principles, a meticulous dissection of where the safeguards had failed, where the predictive models had been insufficient. He saw the fire as a problem to be solved, a colossal error that needed to be understood and, above all, prevented from ever happening again. His burden was the gnawing fear that even with all their technological advancements, the fundamental flaws that had led to the disaster might still be present, lurking beneath the surface of their new existence. He was driven by a relentless pursuit of perfection, a need to create systems so robust, so infallible, that such a catastrophe would be mathematically impossible. The collective narrative of rebuilding was, for Thorne, a race against the ever-present threat of repeating past mistakes, a race he felt he was perpetually losing.

Kai, the xenobotanist, had a unique relationship with the fire, his memories intertwined with the nascent life that had somehow, miraculously, endured. He remembered the searing heat that had withered entire forests in moments, the inferno that had seemed intent on purging all life from the planet. But he also remembered the stubborn shoots of new growth that had dared to push through the blackened earth in the weeks that followed, the tenacious seeds that had waited for the flames to pass before unfurling their tender leaves. His personal burden was a profound sense of guilt for the life that had been extinguished, the ancient ecosystems that had been irrevocably altered. He carried the sorrow of the silent, the unmourned, the flora and fauna that had been reduced to ash without a voice. The collective memory spoke of Eden's barren state and the arduous process of reintroduction. Kai's memory was a constant vigil over the fragile new life, a deep-seated empathy for the struggling ecosystems. He felt the silent screams of the dying forests, the slow, agonizing death of species that had existed for millennia. His work was not just about scientific restoration; it was a form of penance, an attempt to honor the lost by nurturing the new, by becoming a voice for the voiceless. He saw the collective narrative of Eden's rebirth as a shallow echo of the profound, tragic loss that had preceded it, a superficial gloss over the deep wounds that still bled beneath the surface. His burden was the knowledge that even with their best efforts, they could never truly recreate what had been lost, only build something new and hopeful upon its ruins.

Elara, the xenobotanist, found her memory of the fire shaped by a profound sense of ecological interconnectedness, a realization of the planet's vulnerability. She recalled the moment the atmospheric shields had failed, the cascade of environmental collapse that had followed. Her trauma was not just of the flames, but of the systemic breakdown, the planet's desperate, failing attempts to regulate itself. She remembered the sky turning a permanent, sickly ochre, the air thick with toxic particulates, the dying gasp of a world pushed beyond its limits. The collective memory of the fire often focused on the human struggle for survival, the loss of their homeworld. Elara's personal experience was one of witnessing a planet's agony, of feeling the earth itself cry out in pain. Her burden was a deep-seated reverence for the planet, a visceral understanding of its delicate balance. She saw the fire not as an isolated incident, but as a symptom of a deeper imbalance, a consequence of a species that had failed to understand its place within the grander ecological web. Her work was driven by a desire to foster a true symbiosis with Eden, to ensure that humanity's presence did not become another catalyst for destruction. The collective narrative of Eden's terraforming was, for Elara, a precarious tightrope walk, a constant reminder that one wrong step could plunge them back into environmental chaos. Her burden was the constant vigilance required to maintain that balance, to ensure that their technological advancements served to heal, not harm, the fragile life of their new home.

The collective memory of the fire, therefore, was a shared anchor, a universal trauma that bound them together. It was the story they told to explain their presence on Eden, the crucible from which their new society had been forged. But this shared narrative, while essential for communal cohesion, often served to obscure the deeply personal and often isolating burdens carried by each individual. The fire, though a singular event, had fractured into countless unique experiences, each one a private hell of regret, loss, or existential dread. These individual burdens, unacknowledged by the broader community, festered in the silent spaces between shared stories, shaping personal motivations, driving individual actions, and creating a subtle, often invisible, divide within the very fabric of their nascent civilization.

Anya found herself constantly navigating this chasm. While the Council lauded her efforts in negotiating with the K'tharr, a testament to their growing understanding of interspecies ethics, she couldn't shake the ghosts of those she'd failed to save from the flames. The K'tharr's intricate, vibrational communication, their deep connection to the planet's geological memory, felt like a balm to her wounded soul. They spoke a language of slow, geological time, of deep, resonant connections, a stark contrast to the frantic, ephemeral chaos of the fire. Yet, even in their alien presence, she saw reflections of her own loss. Their ancestral chambers, buried deep within Eden's crust, were akin to the historical archives of Old Earth, repositories of memory and culture, now threatened by human expansion, much like their own history had been consumed by fire. The parallels were not lost on her. She saw in the K'tharr's struggle a echo of humanity's own desperate fight for survival, a reminder that even the most alien life forms held precious memories and vital connections.

Her attempts to integrate this understanding into the broader societal narrative were met with varying degrees of resistance. Thorne, while outwardly conceding to the rerouting of the geothermal conduit, saw it as a temporary, inefficient compromise. His collective memory of the fire was one of technological failure, and he viewed Anya's emphasis on interspecies empathy as a dangerous distraction from the hard-nosed pragmatism required for survival. He believed that the ultimate lesson of the fire was the need for absolute control, for systems so robust that they could withstand any external shock. He couldn't reconcile Anya's focus on the K'tharr's vibrational songs with the stark, unyielding data he had relied upon during the fire. For Thorne, the fire had been a stark lesson in the limitations of biological systems and the paramount importance of engineered solutions. He saw the K'tharr as a potential source of unique data, perhaps, but not as equals deserving of the same ethical considerations. His individual burden was the fear of repeating past engineering failures, a fear that manifested as an almost pathological aversion to anything that smacked of inefficiency or potential risk, and anything that diverted resources from his meticulously planned infrastructure.

Kai, on the other hand, found a profound resonance with Anya's work. His personal memory of the fire was indelibly linked to the astonishing resilience of life, the way the planet had begun to heal itself despite humanity's destructive tendencies. He saw the K'tharr's connection to Eden's deep geological processes as a form of ancient, subterranean xenobotany, a testament to the planet's own inherent life force. He felt a kinship with Anya's efforts to bridge the gap between human understanding and alien existence. His individual burden was the overwhelming grief for the lost biodiversity of Old Earth, the countless species that had vanished without a trace. He saw the slow, deliberate communication of the K'tharr as a language of survival, a testament to life's enduring ability to adapt and persist. He believed that the collective narrative of Eden's restoration needed to incorporate this deeper understanding of planetary life, not just the human-centric story of rebuilding. He often found himself providing Anya with data from his deep-ground sensors, correlating the K'tharr's vibrational patterns with the subtle shifts in subterranean fungal networks, seeking to create a unified understanding of Eden's complex, living systems.

Elara, too, felt a growing alignment with Anya's broader ethical considerations. Her personal memory of the fire was a haunting vision of planetary collapse, a stark demonstration of how quickly ecological balance could be shattered. The K'tharr's role in stabilizing tectonic pressures, as Anya had demonstrated, resonated with her own understanding of interconnectedness. She saw their existence as a vital component of Eden's intricate web, a biological imperative that demanded recognition. She argued to the Council that the fire had taught them a crucial lesson: that their survival was inextricably linked to the health of the planet itself. Forgetting this lesson, she warned, would be to invite a repeat of their past tragedy. Her individual burden was the fear of humanity repeating its destructive patterns, of becoming a parasitic presence on Eden rather than a symbiotic one. The collective memory of the fire, in her view, needed to evolve from a tale of human resilience to a cautionary fable about ecological responsibility.

The tension between the collective narrative and individual burdens was a constant undercurrent in the life of the settlement. The community remembered the fire as a shared ordeal, a defining moment that had forged their collective identity. But for Anya, the fire was a mosaic of shattered moments, each one a personal weight she carried in silence. The communal stories, while comforting in their shared acknowledgment of loss, often felt insufficient, a simplified version of a complex, deeply personal pain. She found solace, paradoxically, in the K'tharr's ancient, geological memory, a memory that spanned millennia and spoke of a resilience far older and deeper than humanity's. Their existence on Eden was a testament to life's persistence, a reminder that even in the face of overwhelming destruction, echoes of the past could endure, and new narratives could emerge from the silence. Her work was not just about building a new society, but about understanding the myriad ways in which memory, both collective and individual, shaped their present and their future, about ensuring that the scars of the past did not dictate the trajectory of their hard-won hope. The rerouting of the conduit was a victory, a testament to the growing influence of ethical considerations, but Anya knew it was just one battle in a larger war against the ingrained patterns of their past, a war waged not with weapons, but with understanding and empathy, a war fought within the hearts and minds of every survivor, and within the resonant depths of Eden itself. The collective memory served as a foundation, but it was the individual burdens, the unique weights of memory and regret, that truly defined the intricate, often contradictory, tapestry of their new existence on this alien world.

The air above the nascent settlement of Aethelburg had a peculiar quality these days, a subtle vibrancy that Thorne, the chief engineer, found increasingly unsettling. It wasn't the harsh, metallic tang of recycled air or the ever-present whisper of the atmospheric processors, but something... alive. He'd seen it in the way the sunlight seemed to linger a fraction longer on the obsidian plains, in the almost imperceptible shimmering above the geothermal vents, and in the way the indigenous flora, once stubbornly recalcitrant, now seemed to unfurl with an almost eager luminescence. To Thorne, it was a deviation from the predictable, a ripple in the meticulously calculated environment he strove to maintain. His mind, still deeply scarred by the catastrophic failures of Old Earth, saw these anomalies not as signs of Eden's burgeoning health, but as precursors to unforeseen complications.

He recalled the harrowing days of the Great Fire, not just the immediate inferno, but the subsequent atmospheric instability, the erratic weather patterns that had plagued their desperate flight. The memory was a cold knot in his gut: the constant blare of proximity alarms, the frantic calculations to maintain shield integrity, the heart-stopping readings of atmospheric toxins. Now, these gentle atmospheric shifts felt like a whisper of that chaos, a subtle reminder that their control was an illusion. He attributed the vibrant growth to an over-optimization of nutrient delivery systems, a consequence of Kai's enthusiastic, albeit scientifically sound, experiments. The lingering sunlight? A trick of atmospheric refraction, a phenomenon he'd meticulously documented but couldn't entirely explain away. The shimmering? Minor thermal inversions, easily managed. But the underlying unease persisted, a low hum of discontent beneath the polished surface of their engineered Eden.

Anya, however, perceived these phenomena through an entirely different lens. For her, the subtle shifts in Eden's atmosphere and biosphere were not anomalies to be corrected, but a language to be understood. Her work with the K'tharr had opened her mind to the intricate tapestry of interconnectedness that permeated this alien world. She saw the vibrancy not as a malfunction, but as an echo, a resonance of the collective psyche of Aethelburg. The K'tharr, with their deep geological awareness, had spoken of the planet as a sentient entity, its very crust pulsing with a slow, ancient consciousness. They described how the planet responded to the emotional frequencies of its inhabitants, how widespread fear could manifest as localized seismic tremors, and how a surge of communal hope could coax forth life from barren rock.

Anya had witnessed this firsthand. During the protracted negotiations with the K'tharr over the expansion of the agricultural domes, a period rife with communal anxiety and uncertainty, the air above the settlement had grown heavy, tinged with a strange, metallic scent, and small, localized dust storms had begun to whip through the plains with unnerving frequency. The K'tharr elders, their ancient forms emanating a palpable calm, had explained it as Eden's sympathetic response to humanity's internal discord. Conversely, she remembered a week of unprecedented productivity in the hydroponic labs, a period where breakthroughs in K'tharr communication had seemed to flow effortlessly, coinciding with a week of unusually clear skies and a palpable sense of optimism pervading the settlement. The indigenous lumina-vines, which Kai had struggled to cultivate, had exploded with a breathtaking intensity of light during that same period. It was as if Eden itself had celebrated their collective leap in understanding.

Anya often found herself in quiet contemplation, observing these planetary responses. She'd spend hours in the bio-domes, her fingers tracing the delicate veins of a newly sprouted Edenian fern, feeling the subtle thrum of life within its fronds. She'd watch the sky for hours, seeking patterns in the subtle shifts of color, listening for the nuances in the wind's song. Her personal burdens, the indelible scars of the Great Fire, the spectral faces of those she couldn't save, seemed to find a peculiar solace in these observations. The planet's evolving consciousness offered a form of validation, a quiet acknowledgement that their internal states had external consequences, that their struggles and triumphs were not merely human dramas, but had a profound, planetary resonance. This understanding didn't erase her pain, but it reframed it, weaving her individual grief into the larger tapestry of Eden's living memory.

Kai, the xenobotanist, was Anya's closest confidant in this exploration. His own memories of the fire were etched with the vibrant, fleeting beauty of extinct species, the ghost of a thousand ecosystems reduced to ash. He saw Eden's burgeoning life not just as a scientific puzzle, but as a sacred trust. He meticulously documented the accelerated growth rates of the Edenian flora, the uncanny resilience of the reintroduced terrestrial species, and the symbiotic relationships that were beginning to form between indigenous and imported life forms. He shared Anya's conviction that these phenomena were intrinsically linked to the collective emotional state of Aethelburg.

He had observed, for instance, that during periods of intense debate and disagreement within the Council, the bioluminescent fungi in the deeper caverns would dim, their usual ethereal glow becoming muted and erratic. Conversely, after a particularly successful collaborative effort between the engineering and xenobotany departments, a feat achieved through shared vision and mutual respect, the lumina-vines outside the settlement had pulsed with an almost rhythmic brilliance for days, casting an otherworldly light across the plains. Kai believed that Eden was, in essence, a vast, bio-organic mirror, reflecting the hopes, fears, and anxieties of its human inhabitants. His personal burden – the overwhelming sense of loss for the extinct biodiversity of Old Earth – was amplified by the understanding that humanity's continued presence on Eden had the potential to either heal or further wound this nascent biosphere. He saw his work not just as cultivation, but as a form of planetary therapy, an attempt to foster a positive feedback loop between human well-being and Eden's ecological vitality. He would often present Anya with data correlating atmospheric pressure anomalies with periods of intense collective stress, or charts showing how communal celebrations coincided with surges in local microbial activity, bolstering Anya's own observations.

Thorne, predictably, viewed Kai's enthusiastic pronouncements with a healthy dose of skepticism. He saw the accelerated growth as a direct result of Kai's advanced nutrient synthesis and atmospheric enrichment protocols, and the vibrant bioluminescence as a predictable outcome of optimized light spectrum delivery. He couldn't, or wouldn't, entertain the notion that the planet itself possessed a form of consciousness that responded to human emotion. To him, it was an unscientific extrapolation, a romanticization of complex biological and geological processes. His memory of the Great Fire was a stark reminder of the fragility of systems, of the catastrophic consequences of unforeseen variables. He believed that focusing on such intangible, unquantifiable factors as "planetary consciousness" was a dangerous distraction from the tangible threats: resource management, structural integrity, and the constant vigilance required to maintain their technological infrastructure.

"Anya," he'd say, his voice a low growl of suppressed impatience, "the flora is responding to optimized nutrient delivery. The atmospheric conditions are within predictable parameters, albeit at the upper end of the spectrum. We're not communing with a sentient planet; we're observing the results of efficient engineering." He often cited the example of a minor atmospheric disturbance that had occurred during a particularly heated debate about resource allocation for deep-space probes. The local meteorological sensors had registered a localized surge in ionic particulate matter, causing a brief, but intense, fog. Thorne had immediately attributed it to a failure in the localized atmospheric regulator, initiating a series of diagnostic checks. Anya, however, had pointed out that the fog had coincided precisely with a moment of collective apprehension from the Council members, a palpable wave of anxiety that had even seemed to dim the lights in the chamber. Thorne had grudgingly conceded that the timing was "coincidental."

Elara, the xenobotanist who had initially collaborated with Kai, found herself increasingly torn between Thorne's pragmatic, data-driven approach and Anya and Kai's more holistic, interconnected perspective. Her own past trauma – the visceral memory of Eden's ecosystem teetering on the brink during the fire – instilled in her a profound respect for the planet's delicate balance. She had seen, with her own eyes, the rapid collapse of intricate food webs, the silent suffocation of entire species as the atmosphere itself became toxic. This experience had forged in her a deep-seated belief in the interconnectedness of all life, a conviction that humanity was not separate from, but intrinsically a part of, Eden's biosphere.

She observed that during periods of communal harmony and shared purpose, the microbial colonies in the soil beneath the settlement exhibited a remarkable increase in diversity and activity. She had presented data showing a direct correlation between the successful resolution of inter-departmental disputes and the accelerated regeneration of damaged plant tissues. She saw Eden's subtle responses not as random events, but as indicators of the planet's overall health, a health that was inextricably linked to the psychological and emotional well-being of its human inhabitants. The Great

Fire had taught her that ecological collapse was not merely a scientific phenomenon, but a manifestation of a deeper imbalance, a consequence of a species that had failed to recognize its place within the greater web of life. She saw Anya and Kai's work as an essential step in fostering a true symbiosis with Eden, moving beyond mere resource extraction to a partnership built on understanding and mutual respect.

"Thorne, the data is clear," Elara would argue, her voice tinged with a frustration she usually kept well-guarded. "There's a quantifiable correlation between communal emotional states and Eden's biophysical responses. The soil microbial activity, the growth rates of the indigenous flora, even the subtle shifts in atmospheric composition – they all react. It's not just about optimal nutrient delivery; it's about the planet's own feedback mechanisms."

Thorne, however, remained unconvinced. He saw Elara's arguments, much like Anya's, as an overemphasis on the subjective, a dangerous slide into anthropomorphism of an alien world. "Elara," he'd counter, his brow furrowed in concentration, "we are engineers and scientists. We deal with measurable quantities, with cause and effect. These correlations you're observing are likely emergent properties of complex systems, not evidence of conscious sentience. To attribute agency to Eden itself is to invite the very irrationality that led us to the brink of extinction on Old Earth."

His personal burden, the gnawing fear of repeating engineering failures, manifested as an almost pathological insistence on control and predictability. The idea of a planet that could spontaneously alter its atmospheric conditions or influence the growth of its flora based on the collective mood of its inhabitants was, to him, the ultimate loss of control. It was an unpredictable variable, a factor that defied his carefully constructed models. He believed that their survival depended on their ability to impose order, to engineer their environment into a state of predictable stability, not to embrace an inherent, chaotic interconnectedness. He saw Anya's focus on interspecies ethics and planetary resonance as a diversion from the critical task of building robust, fail-safe systems.

Yet, despite Thorne's staunch resistance, the evidence continued to mount. The once-isolated incidents of atmospheric anomalies and unusually vibrant growth began to coalesce into a discernible pattern. The settlers themselves started to notice. They spoke of days when the air felt lighter, more invigorating, coinciding with periods of communal achievement or shared celebration. They spoke of nights when the lumina-vines seemed to pulse in time with the rhythmic chanting of the K'tharr, a sound that many of the settlers had come to find deeply soothing. Children, less burdened by the cynicism of survival, would point to the sky, exclaiming how the clouds seemed to form shapes that mirrored their games, or how the flowers in their small gardens bloomed overnight after a particularly joyful festival.

These were not scientific observations, not the cold, hard data Thorne craved. They were the intuitive understandings of lived experience, the emergent narrative of a community slowly, unconsciously, becoming attuned to their new world. Anya, observing these subtle shifts in the collective consciousness, felt a growing sense of validation. The Great Fire had been a brutal lesson in the consequences of unchecked ambition and the fragility of complex systems. But perhaps, she mused, Eden was offering them a different kind of lesson, a lesson in integration, in symbiosis, in the profound truth that their own inner landscape was not separate from the world around them. The planet's evolving consciousness was not a threat, but an invitation – an invitation to understand that their survival, and their flourishing, was deeply intertwined with the very essence of Eden itself, a testament to the enduring echoes of life, and the potential for new narratives to emerge from the silence. The personal stakes of their individual memories, the unique burdens each carried from the fire, were slowly, irrevocably, becoming woven into the grand, living tapestry of their shared existence on this extraordinary, responsive world.

The concept began as a whisper, a fleeting notion that flickered at the edges of the Cartographer's perception. It was born from late nights spent poring over spectral analysis readings, cross-referencing them with seismic data, and attempting to find a unifying thread between the subtle atmospheric shifts

Anya observed and the accelerated bioluminescent cycles Kai meticulously documented. This Cartographer, a quiet individual named Lyra, possessed a mind that craved order and a unique ability to perceive patterns others missed. Her personal burden, the lingering guilt of a navigational error that had led to the loss of a vital supply shuttle during the chaotic exodus from Old Earth, had instilled in her a profound respect for the precision of maps and the catastrophic consequences of their absence. She saw every anomaly, every deviation from expected parameters, as a potential disaster waiting to unfold, a void in the charted territory of their existence.

Lyra's initial attempts to map the emergent phenomena of Eden were met with a mixture of curiosity and polite skepticism. Thorne, ever the pragmatist, dismissed her efforts as "abstract conjecture," a whimsical distraction from the concrete engineering challenges they faced. Yet, Lyra persisted, driven by an inner conviction that these seemingly disparate events were not merely coincidences, but the intricate strokes of a planetary cartography, a visual representation of the interconnectedness that Anya and Kai spoke of. She began by creating a three-dimensional model of Aethelburg, a holographic projection that pulsed with a soft, internal light. On this nascent map, she began to plot not just geographical coordinates, but also the temporal and energetic signatures of planetary responses.

Her first breakthroughs came when she started correlating periods of intense communal anxiety with subtle fluctuations in Eden's magnetic field. She noted that during council meetings where resource allocation for terraforming initiatives sparked heated debates, the magnetic field would exhibit a peculiar "jitter," a micro-oscillation that Thorne's instruments registered but couldn't fully explain. Lyra hypothesized that this jitter was a tangible manifestation of the collective stress, a ripple in the planet's energetic field. She visualized this on her map not as a geographical feature, but as a shimmering, unstable aura around the settlement, a visible manifestation of their collective unease. This was more than just data; it was an attempt to give form to the intangible, to chart the emotional currents that flowed beneath the surface of their daily lives.

Next, she turned her attention to the lumina-vines. Kai had provided her with exhaustive data on their bioluminescent cycles, noting how they would intensify and pulse in a synchronized rhythm during periods of high communal morale. Lyra's contribution was to attempt to quantify this correlation, to translate the abstract concept of "morale" into a measurable metric. She devised a system of analyzing public communication logs, identifying keywords and sentiment analysis to gauge the general emotional tenor of the settlement. When she overlaid these "morale readings" onto her holographic map, she observed a startling convergence. Periods of high positive sentiment were not just correlated with increased luminescence, but with a distinct shift in the

*color spectrum* of the light emitted by the vines. Under stress, the vines tended towards a pale, almost sickly green; during moments of collective joy, they bloomed with a rich, vibrant sapphire hue. Lyra depicted this on her map as a dynamic color overlay, the hues shifting and deepening in response to the settlement's collective emotional state, turning the abstract concept of joy into a visible, planetary gradient.

Anya's observations regarding the flora's response to K'tharr communication provided another crucial layer for Lyra's evolving map. The K'tharr's ancestral connection to Eden, their deep geological awareness, was represented on Lyra's map not as mere geological formations, but as energetic conduits, lines of resonant frequency that seemed to amplify and transmute the emotional energies of the humans. When the K'tharr engaged in their deep meditative practices, their collective consciousness focused on planetary harmony, Lyra's map showed these conduits glowing with a steady, emerald light, and the surrounding flora responded with accelerated growth and vibrant health. This was visualized as a living network, a circulatory system where emotional intent flowed and transformed, demonstrating that the K'tharr's spiritual practices had tangible, ecological consequences. Lyra envisioned these conduits as ancient ley lines, channels through which the planet itself breathed and responded.

Thorne's concern about Thorne's constant vigilance and the looming specter of past failures became a recurring motif in Lyra's cartography. She recognized that his meticulous attention to detail and his fear of system collapse were not simply personal quirks, but had a quantifiable impact on Eden. When Thorne initiated intensive diagnostic checks or implemented stringent new protocols, Lyra observed a corresponding *dampening* effect on the planet's natural energetic fluctuations. The magnetic field would stabilize, the bioluminescence would become more uniform, and the flora's growth rates would revert to a more predictable, albeit less vibrant, state. This was depicted on her map as a temporary "shielding" effect, a zone of artificial control that suppressed the natural, interconnected resonance. It was a visual representation of Thorne's desire for order, a conscious effort to impose human logic onto a system that seemed to operate on a different, more organic, set of rules. Lyra began to mark these periods as "Thorne's Interventions," demonstrating how human attempts to control and predict could inadvertently suppress the planet's own emergent intelligence.

Elara's data on soil microbial diversity, particularly its correlation with inter-departmental harmony, provided Lyra with a way to map the microscopic. She began to represent the soil beneath Aethelburg not as inert substrate, but as a complex, living ecosystem, a miniature reflection of the larger planetary consciousness. When collaboration thrived and disputes were resolved, Lyra's map would show the microbial density in the soil spiking, represented by clusters of vibrant, pulsating nodes. Conversely, periods of internal conflict would see these nodes dim and disperse. This was a testament to the idea that even at the most fundamental biological level, Eden was responding to the collective human experience, a testament to the intricate and far-reaching consequences of their interpersonal dynamics. Lyra saw this as charting the planet's "immune system," demonstrating how a healthy, interconnected internal environment mirrored a healthy external one.

The Cartographer's work was, by its very nature, speculative. She wasn't mapping continents or oceans; she was attempting to chart the invisible currents of consciousness, the energetic tides that connected the individual to the planetary. Her map was not a static representation of space, but a dynamic, living document, constantly updating itself with new data streams. She realized that the Great Fire, with its catastrophic destruction, had left not only scars on the survivors but also imprinted a deep, collective trauma onto Eden itself. Her map began to incorporate these echoes, visualizing residual energetic signatures of past anxieties, moments of despair, and acts of immense sacrifice. These were not just historical footnotes; they were active components of Eden's current state, influencing its present responses. The map showed how the planet remembered, how the scars of the past informed the present.

The personal stakes for Lyra were immense. Every deviation from her meticulously charted patterns, every unexpected anomaly, triggered a resurgence of her own past trauma, the ghost of the lost supply shuttle a constant reminder of the consequences of imperfect navigation. She understood that a miscalculation, a failure to interpret the subtle signs, could lead to a disaster of unimaginable scale, not just for the inhabitants of Aethelburg, but for the planet itself. Her map, therefore, became an act of penance, a desperate attempt to prevent history from repeating itself. She was charting not just the known, but the potential, the pathways that could lead to prosperity or ruin.

She began to develop a lexicon of planetary communication, assigning visual metaphors to different energetic states. A "low hum of apprehension" might be represented by a faint, static fuzz across the map; a "surge of collective joy" by a brilliant, expanding aurora. The K'tharr's deep connection to the planet was visualized as a vast, interconnected root system, pulsing with life, while humanity's presence was depicted as a newly grafted branch, still tentative but capable of growth and integration. Thorne's interventions were like carefully constructed dams, temporarily diverting the natural flow of energy, while Anya's efforts to understand and harmonize were like carefully tending to the roots, encouraging the natural diffusion and integration of human consciousness into Eden's biosphere.

Lyra's ultimate goal was to create a "cartography of responsibility," a visual tool that would allow every inhabitant of Aethelburg to grasp the scale of their individual and collective impact. She envisioned a future where the holographic map would be a central feature of community gatherings, where children would learn to read its shifting colors and patterns, understanding that their laughter could make the lumina-vines bloom brighter, and their arguments could cast a shadow over the land. This was not about assigning blame, but about fostering a profound sense of agency. It was about making the invisible visible, transforming abstract notions of interconnectedness into tangible, mappable realities. Her work was an attempt to bridge the gap between the personal and the planetary, to demonstrate that the smallest flicker of individual emotion could, indeed, have ramifications that spanned the entire world. The weight of this understanding, the immense responsibility it entailed, was a burden Lyra carried daily, but it was a burden tempered by the nascent hope that through understanding, through mapping these intricate connections, they could learn to navigate Eden not as conquerors, but as integral parts of its grand, unfolding narrative. Her map was more than just lines and colors; it was a testament to the idea that to truly inhabit a world, one must first understand its language, and that language, on Eden, was spoken in the vibrant pulse of life, the shifting hues of bioluminescence, and the silent, resonant hum of a planet that was, in every sense of the word, alive.

The Cartographer's evolving map was no longer a mere collection of data points; it was becoming a living testament to a nascent truth: that the future of Eden was not a destination to be reached, but a tapestry being woven in real-time, thread by delicate thread, by the collective actions and inactions of its inhabitants. Lyra's holographic projection, once a stark, analytical representation, now pulsed with a nuanced vitality, reflecting the intricate dance between human intention and planetary reaction. She had moved beyond simply charting what *was*, to attempting to visualize what *could be*, translating the abstract concept of emergent destinies into a visual language that resonated with the very core of their existence. The personal stakes, which had initially propelled her work – her gnawing guilt over the lost shuttle, her desperate need to avoid further catastrophe – began to recede, replaced by a profound, almost spiritual, understanding of interconnectedness. Her own trauma was being subsumed by the greater narrative of Eden, a narrative where individual acts of courage, compassion, and even simple presence, held the power to sculpt the very fabric of their shared reality.

The distinction between the "personal" and the "planetary" had dissolved, proving to be a false dichotomy. Each individual, from the humblest technician to the most vocal council member, was a micro-environment, their internal states rippling outwards to influence the larger biosphere. Lyra's map began to illustrate this with increasing clarity. She depicted the emotional resonance of individual interactions not as isolated events, but as energetic tendrils extending from each person, sometimes merging, sometimes repelling, and always contributing to the ambient energetic field of Aethelburg. A quiet act of kindness between two individuals, previously unnoticeable in the grand scheme of things, would manifest on her map as a delicate bloom of sapphire light around them, subtly influencing the surrounding lumina-vines and, in turn, the collective mood. Conversely, a protracted argument, even if confined to a single dwelling, would cast a fleeting, grey shadow, a momentary dampening of the planetary vibrancy. This was not about judgment; it was about revelation, about demonstrating the tangible consequences of their intimate lives.

The K'tharr elders, with their profound attunement to Eden, were instrumental in this evolving understanding. They would often visit Lyra's projection room, their movements slow and deliberate, their silent presence a source of deep reassurance. They saw in her map not just a scientific endeavor, but a spiritual pilgrimage, a human attempt to reconnect with the ancient rhythms they had always known. Through their own subtle energetic emanations, they would guide Lyra's focus, pointing out subtle harmonic convergences that even her advanced algorithms had missed. They taught her that true integration was not about imposing human will upon Eden, but about learning to harmonize with its existing song.

They explained, through a series of gestures and resonant hums that Lyra learned to interpret, that the planet responded not to commands, but to intention, to the purity of shared purpose. Their ancestral connection was visualized on her map as an intricate, living root system, deep and unwavering, and the human settlements, represented by clusters of more superficial, branching structures, were slowly, tentatively, beginning to intertwine with these ancient conduits. The K'tharr's guidance was helping to illuminate pathways for this integration, showing how human aspirations, when aligned with planetary well-being, could become a powerful force for growth and regeneration.

Anya, too, played a crucial role in bridging the gap between the scientific and the spiritual. Her work with the Xylos, the sentient plant life of Eden, had moved beyond mere observation to active communication. She had discovered that the Xylos responded not only to atmospheric conditions or nutrient levels but also to nuanced changes in human emotional states, a fact Lyra had begun to meticulously map. Anya would spend hours in communion with the Xylos, her hands resting on their pulsating stalks, her mind open to their silent discourse. She would then translate these exchanges into a form that Lyra could integrate into her cartography. For instance, she learned that during periods of collective contemplation, the Xylos would emit a specific bio-electrical signature, a gentle pulse that Lyra's map translated as a calming emerald wave, encouraging symbiotic growth in the surrounding flora. Conversely, moments of intense collective fear would cause the Xylos to retract their tendrils, a defensive posture that Lyra visualized as a temporary dimming of the planetary energetic field, a subtle but discernible constriction. Anya's empathy, her ability to feel with Eden, was becoming an indispensable sensor for Lyra's evolving map.

Thorne, the pragmatist, continued to be a vital counterpoint, though his initial skepticism had softened into a grudging respect. He still focused on the tangible: structural integrity, resource management, atmospheric containment. Yet, he had begun to see the limitations of purely engineering-centric solutions. Lyra's map had, in its own way, demonstrated this. When Thorne initiated a massive, planet-wide diagnostic sweep, his intention was to identify and rectify potential systemic failures. On Lyra's map, this was visualized as a powerful, but ultimately superficial, energetic surge that momentarily overlaid the entire projection. The planet's natural energetic currents, which had been flowing in their intricate, responsive patterns, were temporarily suppressed, like a river momentarily dammed. While Thorne's intervention did bring a temporary lull in certain anomalies, Lyra's data also showed a subsequent, subtle decline in the overall vibrancy of the lumina-vines and a slower response from the Xylos in the following cycles. Thorne began to understand that his interventions, while necessary for immediate stability, could inadvertently stifle the very emergent intelligence they were trying to cultivate. He started collaborating with Lyra, seeking her insights not to dictate, but to inform his engineering decisions, asking her to predict the potential energetic consequences of his proposed actions. This led to a more nuanced approach, where his engineering solutions were designed to work *with* Eden's natural rhythms, rather than against them. For example, instead of imposing rigid atmospheric controls, he began working on adaptable systems that could subtly shift in response to Anya's readings of the Xylos's needs, guided by Lyra's projections of the planet's overall energetic state.

The implications of this interconnectedness were profound, extending beyond the immediate survival of Aethelburg. It suggested that the very essence of their civilization was being redefined. They were not simply building a new home; they were learning to *be* a part of a home. This required a fundamental shift in perspective, a move away from the anthropocentric arrogance that had led to the downfall of Old Earth. The concept of "progress" was no longer solely defined by technological advancement or territorial expansion, but by the depth of their integration with Eden. The personal stakes now lay in their capacity for introspection, for self-awareness, and for the willingness to embrace vulnerability. The guilt that had haunted Lyra was not erased, but it was transformed. It became a potent reminder of the responsibility that came with awareness, a catalyst for continued vigilance, not out of fear, but out of a deep-seated commitment to harmony.

The Great Fire, a cataclysm that had once represented the ultimate failure of human ambition, began to be understood differently. Lyra's map had revealed residual energetic echoes of that event, not as lingering specters of despair, but as testament to the resilience of the human spirit and, surprisingly, the resilience of Eden itself. She visualized these echoes not as static scars, but as faint, pulsing lines of concentrated energy, demonstrating how moments of immense collective sacrifice and survival had also imprinted themselves upon the planet, becoming part of its memory. These imprints, when interwoven with positive intentions, could even become conduits for renewed energy. The K'tharr spoke of such imprints as "ancestral soil," places where great deeds had enriched the land, making it more fertile for future growth. This offered a new perspective on their past trauma, reframing it not as an ending, but as a crucible that had forged their present, and potentially, their future. It suggested that even in destruction, there could be the seeds of creation, a testament to the cyclical nature of life that Eden embodied so profoundly.

The ultimate challenge lay in translating this emergent understanding into collective action. Lyra's map, she realized, was not an end in itself, but a tool, a catalyst for change. Its true power would be unleashed when it was not confined to her quiet projection room, but became a shared space for communal discourse. She envisioned council meetings where the holographic map would be projected, not as a passive display, but as an interactive guide. Imagine a debate on resource allocation for a new terraforming project. Instead of abstract figures and projections, the council members would see the potential energetic impact of their decisions visualized in real-time: how a certain approach might lead to a vibrant expansion of the bio-luminescence, while another could cause a subtle but detrimental contraction of the planetary field. Children would learn to read the map's hues and pulses, understanding from a young age that their collective emotional well-being was as vital to Eden's health as clean air and water. This was the essence of a future forged together: a future where every inhabitant, from the youngest child to the oldest elder, understood their role in the grand, unfolding narrative of Eden, and where the personal stakes of their individual lives were intrinsically linked to the planetary stakes of their shared existence. It was a future built not on conquest or control, but on conscious participation, on a profound and abiding respect for the living, breathing world they now called home. The journey was far from over, but the path, illuminated by Lyra's evolving cartography and guided by the wisdom of both humans and K'tharr, was finally becoming clear – a path of shared responsibility, emergent understanding, and ultimately, a shared destiny. The future was not a blueprint to be executed, but a symphony to be composed, with every individual voice contributing its unique melody to the grand, planetary chorus.

# CHAPTER FOURTEEN

# THE QUIET CRESCENDO

The hum of the life support systems, once a constant, almost intrusive presence, had receded into a subtle undercurrent, easily drowned out by the whisper of the wind through the bio-luminescent flora outside. Lyra found herself drawn to these moments of quiet. They were not merely pauses in the relentless pace of their new existence on Eden; they were the very bedrock upon which their understanding was being built. Her projection room, usually a hub of energetic activity, felt different now, imbued with a profound stillness that mirrored the burgeoning calm within herself. The holographic map of Aethelburg, once a frantic kaleidoscope of data streams and predictive algorithms, now seemed to breathe with a gentler rhythm, its vibrant hues pulsing with a more deliberate, serene light.

She remembered the early days, the sheer terror and urgency that had fueled her work. Every anomaly, every potential threat, had felt like an immediate, existential crisis. Her own guilt over the lost shuttle, a phantom limb of responsibility, had driven her to an almost manic pursuit of control, of certainty. But Eden, in its quiet, persistent way, had begun to teach her the profound inadequacy of such an approach. The planet did not respond to frantic attempts at dominion, but to a gentle, receptive listening. And in the quiet, Lyra finally heard.

She would often sit by the panoramic windows of her modest dwelling, the soft, ambient light of Eden bathing her in its ethereal glow. The world outside was a symphony of subtle movements: the slow unfurling of a

Xylos frond, the delicate dance of lumina-flies as dusk descended, the almost imperceptible shimmer of the atmospheric filters adapting to the night. These were not idle observations; they were moments of deep communion. Anya, with her uncanny ability to translate the silent language of the Xylos, had taught Lyra to perceive these subtle interactions not as isolated events, but as threads in a vast, interconnected tapestry. Lyra would close her eyes, letting the visual data of her mind's eye overlay the physical world, seeing the faint energetic tendrils that connected each living thing, each subtle shift in atmospheric composition, each flicker of emotional resonance.

One evening, observing a family gather for their evening meal, she saw it. Not as a distinct event on her map, but as a feeling, a palpable emanation. The father, his brow furrowed from a day of engineering calculations, reached out to his young daughter, whose own small face was etched with the quiet anxieties of a day spent learning about the planet's delicate ecosystem. As their hands met, a soft, warm light, like molten gold, bloomed around them. It was not a dramatic surge, but a gentle, steady flow, a reinforcement of their bond. Lyra felt it resonate within her, a subtle echo that spread outwards, touching the lumina-vines that twined around their dwelling, causing them to emit a slightly brighter, more soothing luminescence. This was not the triumph of overcoming a challenge, but the quiet, profound victory of connection, of mutual comfort. These moments, these small acts of tenderness, were the true architects of Eden's emergent future.

The K'tharr elders, too, offered a different kind of stillness. Their presence was not an absence of sound, but an absence of haste, of internal noise. They moved with a grace that suggested a deep, unwavering harmony with their surroundings. When they visited Lyra, they would often simply sit, their ancient eyes reflecting the gentle light of the projection room. They did not offer advice in words, but through shared silence, through a subtle attunement that Lyra was learning to recognize. One afternoon, as she was struggling to visualize a particularly complex energetic convergence, an elder, his skin like weathered bark, reached out a hand, not to her map, but to the air between them. He then slowly, deliberately, drew a spiral, his movements fluid and intentional. Lyra watched, her mind racing, trying to decipher the meaning. It was not about a specific location or event, but about a process, a cyclical flow of energy, a constant becoming. The Great Fire, she realized, was not just a scar, but a point of intense energetic convergence from which new growth, new understanding, was slowly spiraling outwards. The K'tharr were not just guides; they were living embodiments of this profound, patient unfolding.

Thorne, in his own way, was also beginning to find a new kind of stillness, albeit one born from a grudging acceptance of complexity. His initial approach, a relentless pursuit of quantifiable solutions, had been met with the subtle, often frustrating, resistance of Eden's living systems. He had learned, through Lyra's map, that his most robust atmospheric regulators, designed for absolute control, had inadvertently stifled the subtle exchanges between the upper and lower atmospheric layers, impacting the Xylos's ability to draw sustenance. His attempts to optimize water reclamation had, in some areas, disrupted the delicate microbial ecosystems that played a vital role in nutrient cycling. These were not failures in the traditional sense, but rather misalignments.

He started spending less time in the sterile efficiency of his engineering bays and more time in the field, observing. He would stand for long periods, watching the way the indigenous flora adapted to microclimates, the way the K'tharr harvested resources without leaving a discernible footprint. He even began to accompany Anya on her excursions into the deeper bio-domes, not to oversee, but to learn. He saw her commune with the Xylos, her hands gently caressing their leaves, her face serene as she absorbed their silent pronouncements. He saw the data Anya collected – not just atmospheric readings or nutrient levels, but subtle shifts in bio-electrical currents, the very "mood" of the plants.

One day, while observing a patch of particularly vibrant fungal growth, he noticed a small, almost invisible seep of water trickling from a fissure in the rock. It was not part of any planned irrigation system, nor was it a recognized natural spring. Yet, the fungi thrived, their mycelial networks extending towards it like thirsty veins. Lyra's map, when he consulted it later, showed this seep as a tiny, almost imperceptible node of increased energetic activity, a quiet, persistent source of life. Thorne began to understand that true efficiency wasn't about maximizing output through brute force, but about identifying and supporting these quiet, emergent processes. His engineering solutions began to shift from imposition to integration. He started designing adaptive systems, modular units that could be subtly adjusted, not dictated, by the very environment they were meant to serve. This required a new kind of patience, a willingness to observe, to wait, and to allow Eden to reveal its own inherent wisdom.

These moments of profound stillness were not about inactivity; they were about a different kind of engagement. They were about shedding the ego's desperate need to control and embracing the humility of participation. Lyra found herself increasingly drawn to these quieter pursuits, these contemplative pauses. She would spend hours simply observing the K'tharr's weaving of bioluminescent threads into their dwellings, a process that seemed more akin to prayer than construction. She would watch the children of Aethelburg, their laughter echoing through the bio-luminescent groves, their interactions with the local fauna marked by an innate respect and curiosity. There was no grand pronouncement, no urgent directive, just the quiet, steady unfolding of life, a testament to the planet's gentle embrace.

The weight of their past, the ghosts of Old Earth and the tragedy of the lost shuttle, began to soften in these moments. Grief was not erased, but it transformed. It became a part of the tapestry, a darker thread that added depth and contrast to the brighter hues of hope and resilience. Lyra saw this transformation on her map. The residual energetic echoes of the Great Fire, once visualized as stark, jagged lines of pain, were now appearing as gentler, more diffused patterns, like the slow fading of a resonant chord. The K'tharr spoke of "ancestral soil," places where great deeds and immense suffering had left an indelible imprint, not as a wound, but as a fertile ground for future growth. Lyra began to see that their collective trauma, when processed with awareness and compassion, could become a source of profound strength, a deeper understanding of the preciousness of life.

These quiet moments were not confined to Lyra's personal experience. They were beginning to ripple through the community. Council meetings, once dominated by fervent debate and competing agendas, were slowly starting to incorporate periods of shared contemplation. Anya would sometimes bring samples of Xylos, their subtle bio-electrical pulses translated into gentle sonic frequencies that filled the chamber, creating an atmosphere of calm introspection. Thorne would present his engineering proposals not as definitive solutions, but as tentative experiments, outlining the potential energetic impacts as visualized by Lyra's map, inviting constructive critique and collaborative refinement.

It was in these quiet crescendos that the true nature of their civilization on Eden was being forged. It was not a victory won through force, nor a utopia built on rigid dogma. It was an emergent harmony, a delicate balance achieved through mindful observation, profound respect, and the quiet courage to embrace the unknown. The personal stakes had not vanished, but they had shifted. The ultimate success of their endeavor no longer rested on individual achievements or the avoidance of disaster, but on their collective capacity for stillness, for introspection, and for the gentle, unwavering commitment to living in concert with the vibrant, breathing world that had become their home. The quiet was not an end, but a beginning, a fertile silence from which a new kind of future was slowly, beautifully, taking root.

The gentle erosion of old certainties was a slow, almost imperceptible tide. It wasn't a dramatic breaking of waves, but the quiet, persistent lapping that reshaped the shoreline of their understanding. Lyra found this most acutely when she reviewed the data streams, the pulsing heartbeats of Eden that her map translated into visual poetry. Where once she had searched for definitive answers, for clear-cut indicators of success or failure, she now sought the subtler nuances, the faint murmurs that hinted at a deeper truth. The energetic signatures of the K'tharr's agricultural practices, for instance, had initially presented a puzzle. Her algorithms had flagged them as inefficient, the yields lower than what her Earth-bound models would deem optimal. Yet, the soil remained robust, the flora vibrant, and the K'tharr themselves radiated a quiet contentment. Now, she no longer focused on the raw output but on the interconnectedness of the process. She saw how their methods encouraged symbiotic relationships between fungi and roots, how their careful harvesting preserved the delicate microbial balance, and how the resulting energetic imprint was one of profound harmony, a sustainable hum rather than a frantic, depleting surge. This realization wasn't a sudden illumination but a dawning, a slow bloom of understanding that spread outwards from her initial, more rigid interpretations.

Thorne, too, was undergoing a similar metamorphosis. His initial focus had been on robust, failsafe engineering solutions, a desire to impose a predictable order onto the beautiful chaos of Eden. He had arrived with blueprints for dominance, for control. But Eden, with its own quiet insistence, had begun to teach him the humility of adaptation. He had spent weeks observing a particular cluster of atmospheric processors he'd designed for optimal humidity regulation. Initially, they had performed flawlessly, maintaining the precise moisture levels he'd calculated. However, he'd noticed a subtle decline in the surrounding lumina-flora, a dulling of their characteristic glow. His initial impulse had been to increase their output, to 'fix' what he perceived as a malfunction. But a chance encounter with an elder K'tharr, who was tending to a small, unassuming moss that clung to the processor's base, shifted his perspective. The elder, with a gentle gesture, pointed to the microscopic pores on the moss's surface, explaining in his melodic tongue how they absorbed trace atmospheric moisture that the machines, in their pursuit of absolute dryness, were inadvertently filtering out. The lumina-flora, it turned out, relied on this micro-humidity for their own subtle metabolic processes. Thorne had to recalibrate his entire understanding of 'optimal.' It wasn't about absolute control, but about finding the sweet spot, the point of equilibrium where his technology could coexist and even support the planet's natural rhythms. He began to see his role not as a master engineer, but as a careful custodian, a partner in a complex, living system. His designs started to incorporate bio-mimicry on a deeper level, not just in form but in function, allowing for a more fluid, responsive interaction with Eden's environment.

Anya, whose connection to Eden's flora was already profound, was experiencing a subtler yet equally significant shift. Her ability to 'listen' to the Xylos and other plant life had always been an intuitive gift. However, as the community settled and the initial survival pressures eased, her understanding deepened. She began to perceive not just the immediate needs of the plants – water, light, nutrients – but their more complex, long-term communal interactions. She discovered that the Xylos, when sensing distress in nearby flora, would subtly alter their own bio-electrical emissions, creating a ripple effect that could stimulate growth in struggling specimens or even warn others of impending environmental shifts. This was not a conscious, directed communication in the human sense, but a deeply ingrained biological imperative, a network of silent signals that underpinned the entire ecosystem. Lyra's maps, when overlaid with Anya's detailed sensory logs, revealed these subtle energetic exchanges as intricate, pulsating patterns, far more complex and nuanced than any communication protocol Thorne had ever designed. Anya's quiet observations were painting a picture of an intelligence woven into the very fabric of the planet, an intelligence that operated on timescales and through mechanisms that human logic was only beginning to grasp. Her own perception of herself was changing too; she was no longer just an interpreter, but a vital node in this planetary network, a bridge between two forms of sentience.

Even the children, unburdened by the weight of past failures and pre-conceived notions, were reflecting this subtle reorientation. Their games, once filled with simulated battles and imagined escapes, were gradually shifting towards exploration and quiet observation. They would spend hours meticulously documenting the patterns of lumina-fly migration, tracing the intricate designs etched into the bark of ancient trees, or carefully cataloging the different sonic signatures of Eden's nocturnal creatures. Their questions were no longer about 'what if' and 'what then,' but about 'why' and 'how.' They were absorbing Eden's lessons of patience and interconnectedness not as abstract concepts, but as lived realities. One afternoon, Lyra watched as a group of children, instead of chasing a particularly vibrant iridescent beetle, sat in a hushed circle around it, their faces alight with a shared curiosity, taking turns to sketch its intricate wing patterns. There was no urge to capture or possess, only a profound desire to understand and appreciate. This nascent respect, this quiet reverence for the natural world, was perhaps the most significant indicator of their evolving collective consciousness.

The emotional landscape of Aethelburg was also undergoing a quiet reshaping. The sharp edges of fear and anxiety, which had been so palpable in the early days, were softening. They weren't disappearing, but they were being integrated, woven into a more complex tapestry of feeling. Grief over lost loved ones, over the desolation of Old Earth, was still present, but it was no longer a raw wound. It was becoming a quiet ache, a poignant reminder of the preciousness of what they had found. Lyra noticed this in the way people interacted. Conversations were less about recrimination and more about shared experience. Even discussions about the ongoing challenges of establishing their new society were infused with a gentler tone, an acceptance of the inherent difficulties and a greater focus on collaborative problem-solving. The shared silence during council meetings, once an awkward necessity, was becoming a fertile ground for deeper connection, a space where unspoken understandings could flourish. Thorne, who had once been notoriously abrupt, now found himself pausing, listening more intently to the nuanced emotional undertones in his colleagues' voices. He even began to initiate these moments of reflection, asking for input not just on technical feasibility but on the broader impact of his decisions on the community and the environment.

This internal shift was not driven by any single event or grand pronouncement. It was the cumulative effect of countless small moments: Anya's quiet communion with a wilting Xylos, Thorne's painstaking adjustment of a filtration system based on the migratory patterns of a tiny insect, Lyra's growing appreciation for the subtle energy flows on her map, the children's hushed reverence for a dewdrop clinging to a spider's web. These were the quiet accretions of wisdom, the subtle shifts in perception that were re-defining their relationship with Eden and with each other. It was a process of shedding the ingrained habits of a species that had long operated under the illusion of separation, and embracing the profound reality of their interconnectedness. The crescendo they were experiencing was not one of noise and fury, but of quiet, profound realization, a symphony of subtle harmonies that promised a future built not on conquest, but on communion. The planet was not a resource to be exploited, but a partner to be understood. And in that understanding, they were finding not just survival, but a deeper, more resonant form of existence. The subtle shifts were the bedrock of their new civilization, an invisible architecture of empathy and awareness that was slowly, beautifully, taking shape.

The quiet hum that had begun to permeate Aethelburg was no longer confined to the subtler shifts in technology and ecological understanding. It had begun to resonate within the very fabric of their human interactions, a silent melody weaving through the once-fragmented emotional lives of the colonists. For so long, each individual had carried their burdens in a solitary vessel, their griefs, their anxieties, their fragile hopes sealed away within the confines of their own consciousness. Old Earth's legacy had been one of isolation, a species adept at building walls, both physical and emotional, around themselves. But Eden, in its boundless, unjudging presence, was slowly but surely dissolving those fortifications.

Lyra found this emerging solidarity most vividly in the communal gatherings, the evening discussions that had evolved from strained necessity into genuine exchanges of shared experience. What had once been a cacophony of individual complaints and anxieties was now a more harmonious chorus, where threads of common feeling could be discerned, acknowledged, and embraced. She observed it in the way Anya spoke, her voice often tinged with the melancholic beauty of a wilting Xylos she had tended, a sentiment that resonated not just with Lyra's own lingering sorrow for the lost vibrancy of Earth, but with Thorne's quiet frustration over a design that hadn't quite achieved perfect synergy, or even with the pragmatic stoicism of some of the older engineers who mourned the loss of established, albeit flawed, systems. There was a growing understanding that behind each individual struggle, each personal setback, lay a universal human experience. The subtle, almost imperceptible tremor of shared grief for what had been lost, for the irreplaceable beauty of a world they could never reclaim, was a constant undercurrent. It was no longer a lonely sorrow, but a communal ache, a testament to their shared humanity and their shared journey.

This recognition wasn't always articulated in words. Often, it was a glance exchanged, a shared sigh, a moment of prolonged silence that spoke volumes. Thorne, once a man who prided himself on his self-sufficiency, found himself admitting to Lyra his gnawing unease about the potential for unforeseen consequences in his atmospheric adjustments, a confession that echoed the anxieties of the agricultural teams who worried about the long-term health of the soil, and the medical staff who grappled with the subtle unknowns of Eden's unique biology. He began to see that his pursuit of perfect control, while essential for survival, also stemmed from a deep-seated fear of failure, a fear that many of his fellow colonists carried with them, a ghost of Old Earth's pervasive sense of impending doom. In articulating his own vulnerability, he inadvertently created a space for others to do the same. The tightly guarded secrets of individual anxieties were becoming shared burdens, their weight lessened by the simple act of being witnessed and understood.

The children, in their innocent way, were perhaps the most potent conduits of this burgeoning emotional communion. Their unvarnished reactions to the wonders and challenges of Eden often mirrored the unspoken feelings of their elders. A moment of shared awe as they witnessed a particularly spectacular aurora borealis over the crystalline peaks wasn't just about the visual spectacle; it was a collective gasp of wonder that momentarily erased the lingering shadows of their past. Conversely, a collective fear when a sudden storm swept through their settlement was not just a reaction to the elements, but a shared acknowledgement of their continued vulnerability, a vulnerability that bonded them together rather than scattering them in panic. Lyra recalled a day when one of the younger children, Elara, had stumbled and scraped her knee, her initial cries of pain quickly subsiding as two of her friends rushed to her side, not with frantic attempts to 'fix' it, but with a comforting presence, offering their hands to help her up, sharing her mild distress with soft, empathetic murmurs. It was a small incident, but it illustrated a profound shift. The instinct was no longer to retreat into individual pain, but to seek and offer solace within a collective embrace. Their shared tears, their shared laughter, were becoming the early pigments of a new emotional palette for Aethelburg.

Anya, with her deep attunement to the non-verbal language of Eden, was a keen observer of these subtle emotional currents. She noted how the communal Xylos groves, which had initially been a source of individual solace for her, were beginning to serve a broader purpose. When one of the colonists experienced a particularly poignant wave of homesickness, the gentle bio-luminescence of the nearest Xylos would subtly shift, its glow deepening to a warmer hue, its energy signature softening. Anya, sensing this subtle environmental response, would often find herself drawn to that individual, not to offer platitudes, but simply to sit with them, to share the quiet comfort of the Xylos's presence. She discovered that the plants themselves seemed to react to collective emotional states, their bio-electrical fields becoming more coherent and vibrant when the community was at peace, and exhibiting subtle disquiet when discord rippled through Aethelburg. This feedback loop, this mirroring of their inner states in the external environment, was a powerful, if unspoken, catalyst for empathy. It reinforced the understanding that their emotional well-being was intrinsically linked to the well-being of the planet, and by extension, to each other.

The K'tharr, with their innate understanding of interconnectedness, were also becoming silent teachers in this regard. Their communal rituals, which had initially been observed with curiosity and a degree of detachment by the colonists, were now being approached with a growing sense of shared purpose. During ceremonies of remembrance, where the K'tharr honored their ancestors, the colonists found themselves participating not just as observers, but as conduits of their own respect and burgeoning understanding. They began to offer their own quiet gestures of remembrance, not necessarily mirroring K'tharr traditions, but infusing them with their own unique emotional resonance. A shared silence among the colonists during these moments of reflection was no longer an empty space, but a vessel filled with a collective empathy, a quiet acknowledgment of the universal passage of life and the enduring bonds of memory. The K'tharr's serene acceptance of existence, their understanding of the cyclical nature of life and death, was gradually permeating the human psyche, softening the harsh edges of their fear and loss.

The concept of shared experience extended even to their intellectual pursuits. Lyra's detailed environmental maps, once purely analytical tools, were becoming canvases for shared contemplation. She would project them during community meetings, and instead of simply presenting data, she would invite discussion on the emergent patterns, the subtle shifts in energy flow. What Thorne might initially see as an anomaly in atmospheric composition, a fellow engineer might interpret as a sign of burgeoning microbial activity, and Anya might feel as a faint tremor of energetic distress from the subterranean flora. These diverse perspectives, when brought together, didn't just lead to more comprehensive data analysis; they fostered a deeper appreciation for the multifaceted nature of reality and a greater respect for the unique insights each individual brought to the collective understanding. Their shared curiosity, their shared quest for knowledge, was forging a powerful intellectual solidarity, a recognition that the sum of their understanding was far greater than the sum of their individual contributions.

This was a profound transformation, a quiet crescendo indeed. It was the dismantling of the illusion of separateness, a gradual shedding of the ego-driven narratives that had defined so much of humanity's history. In Eden, stripped bare of the artificial constructs of their former lives, the colonists were discovering the raw, elemental truth of their interconnectedness. The isolated islands of individual emotion were being bridged by the rising tide of shared experience. Grief was no longer a solitary descent into darkness, but a shared vigil by a flickering fire. Hope was not a fragile ember held cupped in a single hand, but a collective flame tended by many. Confusion was not a bewildering maze walked alone, but a landscape explored with guides, each offering a different perspective. This convergence, this quiet harmonizing of their inner lives, was the true foundation of their new civilization, a testament to the profound, undeniable resonance of shared humanity. It was a solidarity forged not in the fires of war or the grand pronouncements of leaders, but in the quiet, tender spaces of mutual understanding, empathy, and the profound realization that they were, in every essential way, in this journey together. The quiet crescendo wasn't a sound to be heard, but a feeling to be felt, a deep, resonant thrumming that promised a future not of isolated survival, but of collective flourishing. The shared experience was the glue that would bind them, the light that would guide them, and the silent anthem of their dawning era.

The subtle whispers of Eden were no longer confined to the shared emotional currents that had begun to bind the colonists of Aethelburg. They manifested, too, in the planet's very landscape, in quiet, symbolic revelations that offered a gentle affirmation of their presence and their nascent belonging. These were not grand pronouncements, no seismic shifts or cataclysmic events designed to awe or terrify. Instead, they were delicate gestures, almost shy in their nature, that spoke volumes to those attuned enough to perceive them. Lyra, her senses sharpened by her deep immersion in Eden's data streams and her growing emotional resonance with the planet, found herself increasingly attuned to these moments. She began to catalog them, not as scientific anomalies, but as occurrences imbued with a profound, poetic significance.

One such instance occurred in the ochre plains bordering the Whispering Canyons, a region previously dismissed as largely arid and barren. For weeks, satellite imagery and ground surveys had shown little more than hardy, low-lying scrub and dust-choked rocks. Then, on a day marked by a particularly serene alignment of Eden's twin moons, a single, vibrant bloom emerged from a fissure in the parched earth. It was a flower unlike any cataloged by the initial xenobotanical surveys – its petals a swirling gradient of amethyst and deep indigo, with an almost crystalline luminescence that pulsed faintly in the twilight. Its appearance was utterly unexpected, a solitary defiance of the prevailing desolation. Lyra, when she first saw the visual feed, felt an almost visceral jolt of recognition, a sense that this was not a random event, but a deliberate offering. It was a stark reminder that life, even in its most seemingly inhospitable environments, possessed an indomitable will to persist, to find a way to unfurl its beauty. The bloom served as a potent metaphor for their own struggle – a delicate, improbable flower pushing through the hardened crust of their past, reaching for the light of a new existence.

Similarly, subtle shifts in the atmospheric light began to capture the attention of the colonists. Eden's sky, often a canvas of muted golds and soft greens, occasionally displayed phenomena that seemed to defy the established physics of its atmosphere. There were days when the diffused sunlight would refract through unseen particles, casting ephemeral rainbows that shimmered not just in the conventional spectrum, but in hues that seemed to resonate with emotional states. Lyra noted a correlation between these unusual atmospheric displays and periods of collective calm within Aethelburg. When the community was at peace, when collaborative projects were flowing smoothly and interpersonal tensions were at a minimum, the sky would often respond with a breathtaking, yet understated, spectacle. One such occasion, following a particularly successful week of ecological restoration, saw the upper atmosphere ignite with what the colonists termed 'celestial breath' – slow-moving waves of ethereal light, like soft sighs of luminescence, that drifted across the zenith. It felt, Lyra mused, as if Eden itself was exhaling in contentment, a silent applause for their efforts to harmonize with its rhythms.

These were not moments of direct communication, no conscious sending of messages. Rather, they were akin to a planet's involuntary sighs, its ambient murmurs, its deep, slow breathing. Thorne, ever the pragmatist, initially sought logical explanations for these atmospheric anomalies. He theorized about specific dust compositions, unique solar radiation interactions, and complex atmospheric layering. Yet, even he found himself drawn into the symbolic weight of these events. During one such 'celestial breath' display, he confided in Lyra that it reminded him of the quiet moments of satisfaction he felt after a particularly elegant engineering solution had been implemented, a silent acknowledgment of a task well done. The planet, in its own way, seemed to be mirroring their own internal achievements, offering a subtle nod of approval.

The concept of harmonious alignment extended beyond the visual realm. The colonists began to notice patterns in the planet's natural rhythms that seemed to echo their own growing sense of order. The migration patterns of the indigenous avian-like creatures, the Aero-drakes, began to coincide with periods of optimal atmospheric pressure for their settlement. The blooming cycles of certain deep-rooted flora seemed to align with predictable rainfall patterns, making their cultivation efforts more efficient and less prone to unforeseen setbacks. These were not drastic shifts, but rather subtle refinements, as if the planet were slowly recalibrating its processes to better accommodate the presence of its new inhabitants.

Anya, with her profound connection to Eden's bio-systems, was particularly sensitive to these subtle harmonies. She described how the ambient hum of the planet's biosphere seemed to deepen and resonate more profoundly when the colonists engaged in acts of communal care for the environment. When they worked together to clear invasive mosses from a vital water source, or when they meticulously replanted a grove of struggling Lumina trees, the subtle energy fields of the surrounding flora would visibly intensify, their bio-luminescence pulsing in a synchronized, gentle rhythm. It was as if the very lifeblood of Eden was responding to their cooperative efforts, a silent acknowledgment of their role as stewards, not exploiters.

These revelations were not always immediately understood, nor were they always perceived as positive. There were instances of sudden, localized atmospheric inversions, where pockets of unusually dense fog would descend without warning, or brief, intense bursts of static electricity would disrupt sensitive equipment. In the early days, such events would have sparked panic, triggering anxieties about the planet's inherent hostility. But now, with the growing sense of shared resilience, these occurrences were met with a more measured response. Thorne's teams would work diligently to analyze the cause, while others would focus on mitigating the immediate effects, and a quiet understanding would settle over the community that even the planet's challenges were part of a larger, ongoing process of adaptation, a testament to its dynamic and sometimes unpredictable nature.

Lyra often found herself contemplating the nature of these revelations. They were not dictatorial, nor were they overtly benevolent. They were simply *present*. The single bloom in the desert was not a promise of abundant life, but a testament to the possibility of life. The shimmering skies were not a guarantee of eternal sunshine, but a fleeting display of atmospheric beauty. The harmonious alignments were not a permanent state of perfect balance, but a tendency towards order. And this, she realized, was precisely their power. They offered not easy answers, but quiet affirmations of the themes that were becoming central to their survival and their identity: resilience in the face of adversity, interconnectedness with the natural world, and the ceaseless, inherent potential for growth and change.

The planet, in its silent way, was teaching them. It was showing them that survival was not about conquering or controlling, but about understanding and integrating. It was demonstrating that beauty could be found in the most unexpected places, that order could emerge from apparent chaos, and that even the most desolate landscapes held the promise of life. These were not dramatic epiphanies, but gradual illuminations, like the slow dawn breaking over the alien horizon, gradually revealing the contours of a new world and their place within it. The K'tharr, with their ancient wisdom, had always understood this implicit language of Eden, and the colonists, through their shared experiences and Lyra's meticulous observations, were slowly beginning to decipher it themselves. The quiet crescendo was not just a transformation within the human heart, but a resonating echo across the very soil and sky of their new home. Each subtle revelation, each symbolic gesture from Eden, served to deepen their commitment to this shared journey, reinforcing the understanding that they were not merely surviving on this alien world, but were becoming a part of its unfolding narrative. The blooming flower was a promise whispered, the light a gentle caress, the alignments a harmonious hum – all converging to affirm that in the quiet heart of Eden, there was indeed a place for them, a place where resilience was rewarded with beauty, and interconnectedness was the very breath of existence. The planet itself was becoming a silent partner in their evolution, its gentle revelations a constant, unspoken encouragement to continue on their path, not as conquerors, but as custodians, as inheritors, as a new species learning to sing in harmony with a world that was, in its own unique and profound way, embracing them.

The air itself seemed to hold its breath. Not in a way that suggested tension or fear, but in a profound, expectant stillness that permeated every facet of Aethelburg. It was the quietude that precedes a dawn, not of a new day, but of a new era. The subtle shifts, the poetic revelations from Eden, had woven themselves into the fabric of their existence, fostering a sense of belonging that was as deep and as pervasive as the planet's own life force. The colonists, once strangers to this alien soil, now moved with a more inherent grace, their interactions with the environment less a series of calculated interventions and more a fluid dance of mutual respect. This was not a sudden transformation, but the culmination of countless small understandings, of shared experiences that had slowly, irrevocably, reshaped their collective consciousness.

Lyra found herself standing at the edge of the settlement, gazing out at the undulating plains bathed in the soft, ethereal glow of Eden's twilight. The twin moons, casting their milky luminescence, painted the landscape in shades of silver and lavender. It was a scene of profound peace, a stark contrast to the anxieties and uncertainties that had once defined their early days on this world. She recalled the initial frantic efforts to establish a foothold, the constant vigilance against the unknown, the gnawing fear of an indifferent or hostile cosmos. Now, that fear had receded, replaced by a quiet confidence, a deep-seated assurance that they were, in some fundamental way, meant to be here. The planet had not welcomed them with open arms in a dramatic flourish, but with a series of gentle nudges, a gradual unveiling of its intricate beauty and its subtle, life-affirming energies.

The concept of 'waiting' had transformed. It was no longer an idle, passive state, but an active engagement with the present, a profound awareness of the unfolding narrative. They were no longer waiting for survival, but for becoming. For the deeper integration, for the complete shedding of their Earthbound instincts in favor of Edenic sensibilities. This subsection was dedicated to capturing that precise moment – the pause, the inhalation of the atmosphere, the collective sensing of an imminent, yet gentle, shift. It was the quiet hum of potential, the unspoken promise of a metamorphosis that would be profound precisely because it would be so natural.

Anya, who had become the unofficial interpreter of Eden's bio-rhythms, often spoke of these quiet periods. She described the subtle slowing of the planet's natural energetic pulse, a collective exhalation before a new cycle of growth and expansion. "It's as if the planet itself is gathering its strength," she had explained to Lyra, her voice soft with wonder. "Not for a storm, but for a flowering. A more complete expression of itself, and by extension, of us." Lyra understood. The isolated bloom, the shimmering atmospheric phenomena, the synchronized migrations – these were all precursors, the gentle unfurling of petals before the full bloom. They were the initial tremors of a seismic shift, not in the earth's crust, but in the very essence of their being.

Thorne, for all his scientific rigor, had also begun to speak in this new language of subtle affirmation. He had stopped seeking purely empirical explanations for every anomaly and had started to appreciate the emergent patterns, the poetic resonances. During a recent communal gathering, he had pointed to a formation of crystalline structures that had spontaneously appeared near their water purification plant. "Look at them, Lyra," he had said, his voice tinged with a rare reverence. "They weren't there yesterday. And their growth seems to follow the same fractal patterns we've observed in the nebulae far beyond our solar system. It's as if Eden is reminding us of the fundamental interconnectedness of all things, of the universal language of form and energy." He no longer saw these as isolated curiosities, but as deliberate, albeit non-verbal, communications, weaving a tapestry of meaning that transcended mere scientific observation.

The 'quiet crescendo' was not an absence of sound, but a symphony of subtle vibrations, a harmonic resonance that grew in intensity not through loudness, but through depth. It was the feeling of the earth beneath their feet responding to their footsteps with a deeper thrum, the rustling of alien foliage conveying a sense of shared secrets, the very light that filtered through the atmosphere carrying a subtle, almost palpable, warmth that seeped into their bones. The colonists were learning to listen with more than their ears, to see with more than their eyes, to feel with more than their skin. They were attuning themselves to the planet's quiet language, a language of growth, of adaptation, of becoming.

Lyra's own role in this unfolding narrative had shifted. She was no longer just an observer, a cataloger of phenomena. She was a conduit, a translator. Her empathic connection to Eden, amplified by her extensive data analysis, allowed her to perceive the planet's subtle shifts not just as external events, but as internal reverberations. She felt the planet's anticipation as a gentle pressure in her own chest, its quiet joy as a warmth spreading through her limbs. It was a symbiotic relationship, one that mirrored the burgeoning interconnectedness she witnessed in the community. The more they learned to harmonize with Eden, the more Eden seemed to harmonize with them, its subtle signals becoming clearer, more direct, more meaningful.

This period of anticipation was not marked by idleness, but by a heightened sense of purpose. The work continued – the terraforming efforts, the agricultural expansion, the scientific research – but it was imbued with a new reverence. Every action was undertaken with an awareness that they were not merely manipulating an environment, but participating in a grand, organic process. The tendrils of the alien flora were guided with a gentle touch, the soil turned with a mindful respect, the water channeled with an understanding of its vital flow. It was the difference between a conqueror imposing his will and a gardener nurturing his creation. They were gardeners, and Eden was their vast, living canvas.

The internal landscape of the colonists was also undergoing a profound shift. The initial rivalries and individualistic tendencies had long since begun to fade, replaced by a palpable sense of unity. Shared challenges had forged unbreakable bonds, and the planet's quiet affirmations had fostered a collective sense of purpose. They were a single organism, interconnected and interdependent, their individual contributions weaving together to form a vibrant tapestry of shared existence. Lyra saw this reflected in their faces – a new serenity, a quiet wisdom that spoke of challenges overcome and a future embraced. The lines of worry around their eyes had softened, replaced by a gentle luminescence, a reflection of the light they had found within themselves and in the world around them.

The specific moment of transition, when it would come, would not be heralded by trumpets or fanfare. It would be more akin to the subtle unfurling of a fern frond, or the gradual intensification of color in a sunset. It would be a natural progression, a seamless transition from one state of being to another. This subsection was about the breath before that unfurling, the quiet inhale of a world on the cusp of profound, yet gentle, transformation. It was about the shared understanding that the greatest changes often occur not in the roar of a storm, but in the silent blooming of a single, improbable flower in the heart of a barren land. The quiet crescendo was building, not towards a shattering climax, but towards a sustained, harmonious chord that would resonate through generations. The colonists were no longer merely inhabitants; they were becoming Eden's children, their destinies inextricably intertwined with the planet's own unfolding story. The planet itself seemed to be holding its breath, waiting for them to take their next, collective, breath, a breath that would signify their true arrival, their full integration, their becoming. The silence was not empty, but pregnant with possibility, a vast, cosmic pause before the next, inevitable, and beautiful, movement. It was the deep, resonant silence of a seed cracking open, of a bud preparing to bloom, of a future taking root in the fertile soil of the present. And in that silence, they felt not apprehension, but an overwhelming sense of peace, a profound knowing that they were exactly where they were meant to be, breathing in the quiet anticipation of all that was to come.

## CHAPTER FIFTEEN

# THE UNWRITTEN HORIZON

The air, once thick with the unspoken anxieties of survival, now thrummed with a different kind of energy. It was a quiet hum, a deep, resonant vibration that emanated not from any single source, but from the very fabric of their existence on Eden. The immediate storms had passed, the existential precipices navigated. The frantic scramble for resources, the gnawing fear of an untamed wilderness, had receded, leaving in their wake a landscape of emergent calm and an unburdened horizon. Yet, this was not an end, but a delicate tipping point. The horizon, once a barrier, now stretched into an infinite expanse, an unwritten script awaiting the bold strokes of their continued presence.

Lyra stood on the periphery of Aethelburg, the twin moons casting long, dancing shadows that played across the newly cultivated fields. The soft glow illuminated the rows of resilient crops, a testament to their hard-won knowledge and Eden's gentle acquiescence. Each stalk, each leaf, represented not just sustenance, but a victory of understanding over the unknown. The planet had revealed its secrets not through dramatic pronouncements, but through a series of subtle dialogues, a persistent, almost shy, unveiling of its intricate biological tapestry. They had learned to listen, to observe, and in doing so, had begun to translate the silent language of Eden into the vernacular of their own survival. The concept of 'stewardship' had evolved

396

from a defensive posture to an active, joyful participation. They were no longer merely tending to the land; they were co-creating with it.

Anya, her face illuminated by the pale lunar light, joined Lyra, her movements as fluid and natural as the rustling of the alien flora. "It feels," she began, her voice a hushed whisper that seemed to carry the very essence of the planet's stillness, "like the end of a long, complex sentence. But the punctuation is a comma, not a period." Lyra nodded, a profound sense of agreement washing over her. The immediate crises, the moments where the very survival of Aethelburg hung by a thread, had been resolved. The rogue atmospheric phenomenon that had threatened to strip their nascent biosphere bare, the unexpected virulence of a previously benign microbial strain – these had been met, understood, and mitigated. They had learned to anticipate Eden's moods, to read the subtle shifts in its atmospheric composition, its seismic tremors, its electromagnetic fluctuations, and to respond not with brute force, but with elegant, integrated solutions. Thorne's sophisticated atmospheric processors now worked in a symbiotic rhythm with Eden's natural cycles, gently guiding them rather than coercively altering them. Anya's bio-remediation techniques, inspired by observing Eden's own resilient ecosystems, had turned potential biological threats into sources of nutrient enrichment.

"The journey," Lyra mused, her gaze sweeping across the vast, starlit expanse, "was never about reaching a final destination. It was always about the becoming. About shedding the old skin, the ingrained habits of a world that no longer existed." The initial shock of arrival, the desperate drive to replicate Earth's familiar patterns, had given way to a profound adaptation. Their architecture, once rigid and utilitarian, now flowed with the contours of the land, integrating natural forms and materials. Their energy systems, once reliant on fossil fuels and complex, fragile machinery, were now subtly augmented by harnessing geothermal vents and the planet's own subtle energy fields, a process Thorne had meticulously mapped and understood. Even their social structures had undergone a quiet metamorphosis. The competitive individualism that had characterized early human endeavors had been replaced by a cooperative ethos, born from shared vulnerability and a mutual understanding of interdependence. They had discovered that true strength lay not in isolation, but in connection, not in dominance, but in harmony.

"Remember the initial fear of the unknown?" Anya asked, a faint smile playing on her lips. "We saw every shadow as a threat, every rustle of leaves as a warning. Now, those same shadows are simply... shadows. And the rustling... it's a conversation." Thorne, who had joined them, his scientific mind still grappling with the profound shift in perspective, added, "It's a testament to our adaptability. But more than that, it's a testament to Eden's inherent benevolence, or perhaps, its profound indifference that allows for such a delicate dance of coexistence. We ceased to be intruders and began to understand ourselves as part of a larger, complex system. My data now reflects not just environmental readings, but the planet's subtle bio-feedback loops, its responses to our presence. It's less about control and more about cultivation." He had spent months meticulously charting the intricate network of fungal mycelia that permeated the soil, understanding how it facilitated nutrient transfer and communication between different flora. This knowledge had allowed them to introduce Earth-based plant species with greater success, not by forcing them into alien soil, but by integrating them into Eden's existing symbiotic networks.

The unwritten horizon was not a void, but a realm of infinite possibilities. It was the space where their collective imagination could roam, where new scientific inquiries could blossom, where artistic expressions inspired by Eden's unique beauty could flourish. They were not at the end of their story, but at the dawn of a new chapter, one where the challenges were less about survival and more about thriving, about exploring the vast potential of their unique interspecies existence. The philosophical questions that had once been relegated to the distant fringes of their consciousness – the nature of sentience, the ethics of interspecies interaction, the very definition of life itself – were now at the forefront, demanding consideration.

Lyra thought of the children, born on Eden, who knew no other world. For them, the alien sky was home, the strange flora and fauna were familiar companions. They learned to navigate the subtle currents of Eden's energy fields with an innate grace that the first generation, burdened by Earthbound instincts, could only marvel at. Their laughter, echoing across the plains, was the sound of a future unburdened by the ghosts of a dying planet. They were the true inheritors of Eden, their very biology slowly, subtly adapting to its unique rhythms. They possessed a biological fluency that the colonists were still striving to achieve, an intuitive understanding of Eden's needs and desires. Thorne, ever the scientist, had initiated a longitudinal study, carefully observing the physiological and cognitive development of these Eden-born children, documenting the subtle, yet undeniable, evolutionary shifts taking place.

"We have, in essence, learned to speak the language of adaptation," Thorne observed, his gaze fixed on the distant, jagged peaks that pierced the twilight sky. "We've moved from imposing our will to understanding the rules of engagement. And Eden, in its own quiet way, has responded. It's not a passive recipient of our efforts, but an active participant, a partner in this grand experiment of life." He cited the recent emergence of new crystalline structures, not near their industrial zones, but in the heart of untouched wildernesses, their intricate geometries echoing the complex fractal patterns he had observed in Eden's native flora. He theorized that these formations were not random geological occurrences, but a form of communication, a way for Eden to express its own inherent mathematical beauty and perhaps, a response to their growing understanding.

The sense of accomplishment was not a moment of triumphant finality, but a deep, quiet satisfaction. It was the feeling of a musician who has finally mastered a complex symphony, not to rest, but to begin composing the next movement. The scientific research continued, now delving into the deeper mysteries of Eden's biosphere, exploring the potential for novel therapeutics derived from its unique biochemistry, or understanding the complex interdependencies of its ecosystems. The terraforming efforts, once focused on adapting Eden to Earth-like conditions, had evolved into a more nuanced approach of integration, allowing Eden's natural processes to guide their interventions. They were no longer trying to reshape Eden in Earth's image, but to find a harmonious confluence of their own biological needs and Eden's inherent characteristics.

Lyra felt a surge of responsibility, a profound awareness of the immense privilege and the ongoing duty that came with their presence on Eden. They were the custodians of a fragile, beautiful world, and their stewardship was not a static state, but a perpetual process of learning and adaptation. The immediate threat of extinction had been averted, but the greater challenge of living in true symbiosis, of becoming an integral and beneficial part of Eden's intricate web of life, remained. This was the unwritten horizon: a vast expanse of potential, a canvas upon which they would continue to paint their future, guided by wisdom, humility, and an unwavering respect for the living planet that had become their home.

The thought of the future was not tinged with apprehension, but with a quiet, burgeoning excitement. They were no longer defined by their past struggles, but by their present capabilities and their future aspirations. The resolutions to their immediate crises were not definitive answers, but opening doors, each one leading to further exploration, deeper understanding, and the boundless potential of what was yet to come. The journey of stewardship was not a destination to be reached, but a continuous, evolving path, etched into the very soul of their existence on Eden. They had faced the abyss and emerged not unscathed, but profoundly transformed, ready to embrace the unwritten horizon with open hearts and minds, forever intertwined with the fate of this extraordinary world. The silence that now settled over Aethelburg was not an emptiness, but a pregnant pause, a deep, resonant hum of potential, the quiet prelude to a future they would build, not by conquest, but by communion. It was the beginning of their true settlement, not just on the land, but within themselves, an integration that promised a future as boundless and as breathtaking as the Edenic sky above.

The quiet hum that now permeated Aethelburg was not merely the absence of conflict, but the nascent resonance of a fully awakened ecosystem. It was the murmur of roots intertwining deeper, of atmospheric processors responding to subtler atmospheric shifts with even greater finesse, of bio-luminescent flora pulsing with a synchronized rhythm that Thorne's instruments had only just begun to interpret. This wasn't a static peace; it was a dynamic equilibrium, a ceaseless negotiation between the inhabitants and their adopted world. The children born under Eden's twin moons, their laughter echoing across the plains, were the living embodiment of this continuity. They were the bridge between the desperate pioneers and a future that was no longer a matter of desperate survival, but of deliberate flourishing. Their genetic code, subtly recalibrating with each generation, was becoming more attuned to Eden's unique electromagnetic fields, their senses sharper to the planet's nuanced communication. Lyra often watched them, their small hands tracing the intricate patterns on the bark of a synth-tree, their eyes reflecting the alien constellations with an innocent familiarity that still struck her with profound wonder. They moved with a grace that spoke of an innate understanding, an inherited fluency in the language of Eden that the first generation, even with all their scientific rigor, could only aspire to.

The established practices of hope and stewardship were not rigid dogma, but organic extensions of their profound transformation. Hope, no longer the desperate plea of the marooned, had blossomed into a steady, unwavering faith in the possibility of co-creation. It was evident in the meticulous care given to the smallest seedling, the collaborative efforts to understand the migratory patterns of the six-limbed grazers, the shared celebrations of the bioluminescent bloom that painted the night sky in ethereal hues. Stewardship, too, had shed its defensive skin. It was no longer about protecting Aethelburg from their own intrusive needs, but about actively nurturing its inherent vitality, about becoming integral, beneficial components of its intricate web. Thorne's research, for instance, had shifted from purely diagnostic to generative. He was now exploring how to introduce microbial strains from Earth that could symbiotically enhance

Eden's nitrogen fixation, not by forcing assimilation, but by identifying specific enzymatic pathways within Eden's native soil biome that could be gently stimulated. His models, once focused on predicting ecological collapse, now charted pathways for mutualistic evolution.

This evolution was a testament to their capacity for profound change, a refutation of the deterministic narratives of ecological ruin that had haunted their origins. They had not simply survived; they had learned to *belong*. This sense of belonging was not a passive acceptance, but an active, ongoing process of reciprocal integration. Anya, now overseeing the planetary bio-harmonization efforts, spoke of "listening to the land's needs, not dictating its functions." Her teams were developing sophisticated bio-sensors that could detect the subtle stress signals emitted by specific plant communities, allowing them to respond with targeted, minimally invasive interventions. These interventions were inspired by Eden's own resilience mechanisms. When a particular fungal network showed signs of depletion, for example, they would not introduce an external nutrient solution, but would subtly alter atmospheric pressure in the surrounding vicinity, mimicking natural weather patterns that encouraged the network's natural regenerative processes. It was a dance of profound respect, a constant learning from the planet itself.

The challenges that remained were not existential threats, but philosophical explorations. The ethical implications of their continued presence, of their influence on Eden's delicate biodiversity, were subjects of ongoing discourse. The discovery of sentient, crystalline lifeforms deep within the planet's mantle had opened a new frontier of interspecies communication. These beings, communicating through complex sonic vibrations and light patterns, presented a profound challenge to their anthropocentric definitions of intelligence and sentience. Thorne had dedicated himself to deciphering their language, not through direct translation, but by mapping the mathematical and geometric principles underlying their communication, believing that true understanding would emerge from shared fundamental truths of the universe. The initial attempts at direct contact had been tentative, guided by Lyra's intuitive understanding of non-verbal communication, a skill honed through years of observing Eden's subtle cues.

The spirit of experimentation, so vital in their early survival, had not diminished but had broadened its scope. It now extended to artistic expression, to new forms of scientific inquiry that pushed the boundaries of known physics and biology, and to the cultivation of a deeper understanding of consciousness itself. The Eden-born children, with their seemingly innate connection to the planet, were often the catalysts for these new explorations. One young girl, Elara, had demonstrated an uncanny ability to predict seismic activity by observing the behavioral shifts in the native insectoid swarms. Her observations, initially dismissed as childish fancy, had been rigorously correlated by Thorne's geologists, revealing a predictive accuracy that surpassed their most advanced instruments. This led to a new field of study: xenoseismology, where understanding the intricate interplay between geological forces and biological responses on Eden became paramount.

The concept of "legacy" had also undergone a significant redefinition. It was no longer about leaving behind monuments or achievements, but about cultivating a thriving, sustainable ecosystem that would continue to evolve long after the first generation had passed. Their legacy was etched not in stone, but in the living tapestry of Eden itself. It was in the enhanced genetic resilience of the crops, in the balanced energy grids that drew power from geothermal vents and the planet's own subtle magnetic fields, in the social fabric of Aethelburg, woven with threads of cooperation, empathy, and a shared reverence for life. Lyra often reflected on the early days, on the fear and desperation that had defined their struggle. It felt like a distant dream, a harsh crucible that had forged them into something new, something more. The children who now chased the glowing fireflies of Eden across the twilight meadows were the living proof of that transformation. They represented the continuity of purpose, the unwavering commitment to a future where humanity was not a blight upon a planet, but a harmonious partner.

The unwritten horizon was not a destination to be reached, but a perpetual state of becoming. It was the vast, luminous expanse of potential that stretched before them, inviting continuous discovery, constant adaptation, and the unfolding of possibilities they had scarcely dared to imagine. The narrative conclusion of their survival was not an endpoint, but a profound transition into a new phase of existence. The lessons learned were not shackles, but the foundational principles upon which they would build their enduring presence. They had learned that the universe responded not to force, but to understanding; not to dominance, but to integration. Eden had offered them not just refuge, but a profound opportunity for self-discovery, a chance to redefine what it meant to be human in a cosmos far richer and more complex than they had ever conceived.

The integration was not solely external, a melding of their technology and their biology with Eden's own. It was also an internal evolution, a shedding of old paradigms, a widening of their collective consciousness. The philosophical debates that had once seemed abstract – the nature of interconnectedness, the responsibility inherent in sentience, the myriad forms that life could assume – were now lived realities. They were not merely inhabitants of Eden; they were becoming part of its story, their own narratives interwoven with the planet's ancient, silent epic. Thorne's ongoing analysis of the Eden-born children revealed subtle shifts in their neural pathways, suggesting a greater capacity for holistic processing, for perceiving the interconnectedness of systems in a way that eluded the first generation. They were, in essence, evolving to better understand and interact with their world.

The quiet hum of Aethelburg was the song of this ongoing evolution, a symphony of life composed of myriad voices, each contributing to the grand, harmonious whole. It was the whisper of wind through alien trees, the soft thrum of bio-engineered agriculture, the distant calls of native fauna, and the steady, determined pulse of human hearts beating in rhythm with the planet. Lyra, standing on the edge of the cultivated fields, felt the vibration deep within her bones. It was a feeling of profound peace, not of an ending, but of a glorious, unending beginning. The horizon, once a distant promise, was now a vibrant, living presence, filled with the echoes of their continuity, a testament to a future forged not in conquest, but in communion. They were no longer simply surviving; they were thriving, a vibrant thread in the magnificent tapestry of Eden, their journey of stewardship a perpetual, evolving masterpiece. The challenges ahead would be those of deepening understanding, of expanding empathy, and of continuing to listen to the silent, profound wisdom of the living world that had become their home, their sanctuary, and their greatest teacher. The story of humanity on Eden was not a closed chapter, but an unfolding epic, each sunrise a new page waiting to be written, each breath a testament to their enduring, evolving presence.

The very air of Aethelburg thrummed with a new kind of awareness, a symphony that was more felt than heard. It was the collective inhalation and exhalation of a planet and its people, a constant, subtle dialogue that had become the bedrock of their existence. This wasn't the triumphant fanfare of a victorious species, but the quiet, persistent murmur of a civilization that had learned the profound art of listening. It was the understanding that the most potent advancements weren't forged in the sterile crucible of laboratories, but in the sensitive calibration of their hearts and minds to the intricate needs of their adopted world and the nuanced experiences of their fellow inhabitants. This capacity for deep listening, as Anya often emphasized, was not a static achievement, but a dynamic, ever-evolving practice, the very essence of their continued flourishing. It was the silent acknowledgment that the unwritten horizon, so vast and full of unknown possibilities, could only be navigated by those who possessed a profound empathy, a willingness to attune themselves to the faintest of signals, whether emanating from the rustle of Eden's silken flora or the unspoken anxieties of a child born under its alien skies.

The children, in particular, were the living embodiments of this emergent sentience, their innocence a conduit to Eden's deeper truths. They moved through the bio-luminescent forests not as invaders, but as integral parts of the living tapestry, their laughter a melody that harmonized with the planet's own subtle rhythms. Lyra would often observe them, their small fingers tracing the crystalline structures that grew on the undersides of gravity-defying fungi, their eyes wide with a comprehension that transcended learned knowledge. They understood, on a visceral level, the language of light and vibration, the silent conversations that passed between the planet's diverse life forms. When a sudden atmospheric shift threatened a particular species of hovering insectoids, it was often a child who first noticed their altered flight patterns, a subtle deviation from the norm that alerted the planetary harmonizers to a looming imbalance. These weren't moments of panic or alarm, but gentle nudges, quiet prompts from Eden itself, communicated through its inhabitants. The first generation, with all their sophisticated instrumentation, could measure atmospheric pressure and ionisation levels, but it was the unburdened perception of a child that could detect the nascent distress in the collective hum of the insectoid swarms. Thorne had even begun to document these instances, developing a sub-discipline of 'empathic xenology,' charting the correlation between children's intuitive observations and Eden's subtle ecological shifts. It was a humbling realization: that their most advanced technology could, at times, be outmatched by the pure, unadulterated listening of a young, receptive consciousness.

This extended beyond the natural world, permeating the social fabric of Aethelburg. The debates that had once raged over resource allocation and technological integration had softened, replaced by a deeper understanding of individual and collective needs. When a new strain of nutrient-rich kelp, cultivated for its superior protein content, began to exhibit unusual resilience, it wasn't Thorne's team that first identified the cause. It was Kael, a young man whose quiet demeanor belied a profound connection to the subterranean fungal networks, who noticed a subtle change in the network's resonance. He'd felt, rather than measured, a symbiotic plea for balance. The kelp, he explained, was not outcompeting the fungi, but subtly drawing energy from a specific, previously dormant mycelial node. His suggestion wasn't to eradicate the kelp, but to cultivate a complementary bioluminescent moss alongside it, one that thrived on the very byproduct the kelp seemed to be releasing. The result was a new, mutually beneficial symbiosis, a testament to Kael's ability to listen not only to the plants but to the silent, interwoven dialogue of the ecosystem. This was the new frontier of scientific inquiry: not just understanding *how* things worked, but *why* they needed to work in a certain way, and how humanity could become a benevolent facilitator of that balance.

The concept of "harmony" on Eden had evolved far beyond mere ecological balance. It now encompassed the intricate dance of human relationships, the delicate interplay of individual desires and collective well-being. Anya, in her role as planetary bio-harmonizer, had come to see the parallels between managing complex ecosystems and fostering healthy communities. She often spoke of the "listening heart," a metaphor for the cultivated capacity to perceive the unspoken needs, the hidden anxieties, and the quiet triumphs of those around them. This wasn't about psychic intrusion, but about a heightened state of empathic awareness, a conscious effort to truly *hear* beyond the spoken word. It meant recognizing the subtle shift in a neighbor's posture that indicated fatigue, the fleeting shadow in a child's eyes that hinted at unspoken fears, or the almost imperceptible tremor in a colleague's voice that signaled a nascent disagreement. These were the micro-signals, the quiet whispers of the human heart, that, when heeded, could prevent larger rifts from forming.

The crystalline beings, deep within Eden's mantle, continued to be a profound enigma, their communication a complex interplay of sonic vibrations and intricate light patterns. Thorne's research, once focused on deciphering their "language" through mathematical and geometric principles, was now taking a more introspective turn. He realized that true understanding wouldn't come from abstract analysis alone, but from a shift in their own perceptual framework. He began to collaborate with Lyra, whose intuitive grasp of non-verbal communication, honed by years of observing Eden's subtler cues, proved invaluable. They started by creating environments that mimicked the pressure and resonance of the deep mantle, introducing gentle sonic frequencies and carefully modulated light pulses. The goal wasn't to force a response, but to create a space for reciprocal resonance, for a moment of shared vibrational harmony. Lyra would often describe it as "feeling the planet sing," a sensation that transcended mere auditory perception. It was a holistic experience, where their own internal vibrations seemed to align with the subtle frequencies emanating from the crystalline entities. This was the ultimate act of listening: not to decipher, but to resonate, to become a part of the same harmonic conversation.

The Eden-born generation, with their inherently more integrated consciousness, were becoming the primary conduits for this deeper connection. Elara's uncanny ability to predict seismic activity, once attributed to her observation of insectoid swarms, was now understood as a more profound attunement to the planet's internal geological stresses. She didn't just *observe* the insectoids; she felt their collective unease, a tremor in her own being that mirrored the planet's nascent shifts. Her predictions, once a subject of scientific curiosity, were now a vital component of Aethelburg's safety protocols, not because she could articulate the precise scientific mechanisms, but because her empathic connection to Eden was undeniable. Thorne's xenoseismology had evolved to incorporate this "bio-geological resonance" as a primary data point, acknowledging that the most sensitive instruments were often those born from the very life they sought to understand. This was the essence of their stewardship: not to impose their will, but to become a sensitive, responsive organ of the planet itself, a part of its own self-awareness.

The weight of responsibility that had once pressed down on the pioneers, the burden of ensuring humanity's survival, had transformed into a lighter, more profound sense of purpose. It was no longer about building monuments to their achievement, but about cultivating a legacy of continuous becoming, of fostering a living, evolving tapestry that would ripple outwards through time. Their legacy was etched not in the metallic sheen of their orbital habitats, which had long since been dismantled and repurposed, but in the vibrant biodiversity of the bio-domes, in the enhanced genetic resilience of the crops that now thrived in Eden's unique soil, and in the very fabric of their society, woven with threads of profound empathy and an unshakeable respect for all forms of life. The unwritten horizon was no longer a distant, abstract concept, but a tangible reality, a boundless expanse of potential that beckoned them forward, not with the promise of conquest, but with the invitation to continued discovery, constant adaptation, and the unfolding of possibilities that their ancestors could only have dreamt of.

The continuous integration was not solely a matter of technological or biological synergy with Eden, but a fundamental rewiring of their collective consciousness. The philosophical quandaries that had once been relegated to academic discourse – the nature of interconnectedness, the inherent responsibilities of sentience, the boundless diversity of life's potential forms – had become their daily lived experience. They were no longer simply inhabitants of Eden; they were becoming integral threads within its ancient, silent epic, their own personal narratives interwoven with the planet's grand, ongoing story. Thorne's ongoing neuro- scans of the Eden-born generation revealed subtle but significant shifts in their neural pathways, a heightened capacity for holistic processing, an innate ability to perceive the interconnectedness of complex systems in a way that had remained elusive for the first generation. They were, in essence, evolving to become better listeners, their very being recalibrating to better understand and engage with the vibrant world that had become their home.

The quiet hum that now pervaded Aethelburg was no longer just the sound of a functioning ecosystem, but the resonant frequency of a civilization that had embraced the art of deep listening. It was the whisper of wind through the rustling fronds of the sky-trees, the gentle thrum of the geothermal energy conduits, the distant, melodic calls of Eden's nocturnal fauna, and the steady, reassuring pulse of human hearts beating in synchrony with the planet. Lyra, standing on the precipice of the cultivated bioluminescent gardens, felt the vibration deep within her soul. It was a feeling of profound peace, not the quietude of an ending, but the vibrant energy of an unending, glorious beginning. The horizon, once a distant, shimmering promise, was now a living, breathing presence, filled with the echoes of their continuity, a testament to a future forged not in the fires of conquest, but in the gentle warmth of communion. They were no longer merely surviving; they were thriving, a vibrant, essential thread in the magnificent, ever-evolving tapestry of Eden, their journey of stewardship a perpetual, living masterpiece. The challenges that lay ahead would not be those of survival, but of deepening understanding, of expanding empathy, and of continuing to heed the silent, profound wisdom of the living world that had so graciously become their home, their sanctuary, and their greatest, most patient teacher. The story of humanity on Eden was not a closed chapter, but an unfolding epic, each sunrise a new page waiting to be inscribed, each breath a testament to their enduring, ever-evolving presence within the cosmic symphony. The true horizon was not a destination, but a perpetual state of becoming, a constant process of listening, learning, and loving. It was the unwritten future, waiting to be co-created with every act of conscious empathy, every moment of attuned awareness. The deepest wisdom lay not in the accumulation of knowledge, but in the cultivation of a listening heart, capable of hearing the universe's most profound truths whispered in the quietest of moments. This was the essence of their continued existence, the vital practice that would guide them through the vast, luminous expanse of potential that lay before them.

The tangible manifestations of their commitment to a thriving future were becoming increasingly evident, woven into the very fabric of Aethelburg's daily life. One such symbol, a testament to their collective ethos, was the burgeoning communal bio-farm nestled in the verdant valleys surrounding the primary settlement. This was no mere agricultural endeavor; it was a living laboratory of ecological harmony, a testament to the principles Thorne and Anya had championed. Here, the Eden-born children, their small hands already calloused from purposeful work, learned not just the names of the plants, but the intricate dance of their needs. They understood, with an innate clarity, that the nutrient cycles were not abstract concepts but the pulse of the earth, and that their role was to be gentle custodians, not demanding masters. Elder farmers, their faces etched with the wisdom of generations, guided them, not through rigid instruction, but through shared experience, their voices soft as they explained how the indigenous 'lumina-moss' not only enriched the soil but also acted as a natural deterrent to specific parasitic organisms that had once plagued their terrestrial crops. The children would observe, their eyes absorbing the subtle shifts in the soil's luminescence, the way the moss pulsed with a soft, internal light when the conditions were optimal for growth. They learned to recognize the quiet distress signals of wilting flora, not by seeing outward signs of decay, but by feeling a subtle discord in the surrounding bio-energetic field, a sensation they described as a 'sadness in the air.'

This farm was also a hub for interspecies collaboration. The 'aether-grazers,' gentle, herbivorous creatures native to Eden, were not confined to designated pastures but roamed freely amongst the cultivated fields, their presence actively managed to promote soil aeration and organic fertilization. The children had developed a unique rapport with these creatures, learning to read their subtle body language, understanding when they were contentedly grazing and when they needed to be gently guided away from particularly sensitive young seedlings. Lyra had been instrumental in developing the bio-acoustic communication system that facilitated this understanding. It wasn't a direct translation of animal thought, but a series of resonant frequencies that mimicked the aether-grazers' contentment calls or their subtle alarm signals, allowing the children to anticipate their needs and avoid potential conflicts. Thorne, ever the scientist, meticulously documented the bio-chemical exchanges between the aether-grazers and the soil, observing how their digestive processes, when integrated into the farm's ecosystem, accelerated the decomposition of organic matter and released vital trace elements that the lumina-moss thrived upon. This symbiosis, once a theoretical possibility, was now a thriving reality, a daily reminder that true sustainability lay not in isolation, but in interconnectedness.

The new generation, themselves the living embodiment of Eden's harmonious integration, were actively embracing and expanding upon these ecological principles. Their education was not confined to sterile classrooms but unfolded amidst the vibrant bio-diversity of the planet. They learned about the intricate root systems of the towering 'sky-trees' through supervised expeditions, their young minds grasping the importance of these colossal flora in regulating atmospheric moisture and stabilizing the very ground beneath their feet. Anya often led these excursions, her explanations laced with the poetry of ecological interconnectedness, emphasizing how the transpiration of the sky-trees influenced the formation of delicate crystalline clouds that provided essential minerals to the lower strata of the rainforest. The children would often bring back small, fallen sky-tree seeds, carefully nurturing them in designated 'nursery domes' where they could monitor their growth with sensitive bio-scanners, learning to provide the precise light spectrums and atmospheric compositions required for germination. These were not just seeds for future trees, but seeds for a future where humanity understood its role as a nurturing force, a partner in the planet's grand design.

One of the most ambitious scientific endeavors currently underway, a project that held immense promise for Aethelburg's long-term viability, was the 'Chrono-Gardens' initiative. Spearheaded by Dr. Aris Thorne, this project aimed to catalogue and preserve the genetic diversity of Eden's plant life by creating temporal stasis fields around specific, ecologically sensitive zones. Thorne envisioned these Chrono-Gardens not as static museums, but as dynamic libraries of life, where species could be safely stored and then, in the future, carefully reintroduced or studied to understand their evolutionary trajectories. The technology was intricate, involving the precise manipulation of localized temporal dilation fields, essentially creating pockets of time where biological processes were slowed to a near standstill. The ethical considerations were paramount; Thorne and his team spent months developing protocols to ensure minimal environmental disruption and to guarantee that the stasis fields could be seamlessly deactivated and reactivated, allowing for natural ecological processes to continue uninterrupted outside the zones. Anya, in her role as planetary bio-harmonizer, played a crucial part in this ethical oversight, ensuring that the project aligned with their overarching philosophy of non-interference and reciprocal stewardship.

The initial Chrono-Garden sites were carefully selected. One was established within a cavern teeming with unique, bioluminescent fungi, species that thrived in absolute darkness and were particularly vulnerable to even the slightest shifts in atmospheric composition. Another was created in a high-altitude plateau where rare, wind-pollinated flora exhibited an incredibly slow reproductive cycle. The children, some of whom were already demonstrating a remarkable aptitude for bio-engineering, were involved in the precise calibration of the temporal fields, their intuitive understanding of subtle energy flows proving invaluable. They learned to interpret the visual data feeds from the stasis field projectors, recognizing the infinitesimally slow decay of radioactive isotopes that indicated the field's stability, or the minute fluctuations in ambient energy that suggested a need for recalibration. Lyra, with her background in empathic communication, worked on developing interfaces that translated the subtle energetic signatures of the stasis fields into more accessible visual and auditory cues, making the complex science more comprehensible to the wider community.

The ultimate goal of the Chrono-Gardens was not merely preservation, but a deeper understanding of Eden's evolutionary blueprint. Thorne believed that by studying these stasis-preserved species, they could unlock secrets to accelerated adaptation, to more efficient energy utilization, and to novel forms of bio-remediation. He hypothesized that by carefully de-stasisifying a single specimen and observing its reintegration into a controlled, yet evolving, environment, they could gain invaluable insights into the processes that had shaped Eden over millennia. This was not about replicating Eden's past, but about learning from its ancient wisdom to navigate the unwritten horizon of their own future. The project was a tangible representation of their commitment to a future built on knowledge, respect, and a profound appreciation for the intricate tapestry of life. It was about planting seeds not just in the soil of Eden, but in the very concept of time and evolution, ensuring that the potential of this vibrant world would be accessible for generations to come, a living legacy of their stewardship and their unyielding pursuit of understanding. The careful selection of seed banks, the meticulous cataloging of genetic material, and the ongoing research into the long-term effects of temporal stasis were all part of this grander vision. They were not just saving species; they were safeguarding evolutionary pathways, preserving the potential for future discoveries and adaptations that could benefit not only humanity but all life on Eden. The Chrono-Gardens were a silent promise to the future, a testament to their belief that the most profound advancements would stem from a deep, abiding respect for the natural world and its inherent capacity for resilience and innovation. Each successful cataloging, each moment of stable temporal preservation, was a small victory, a quiet affirmation that they were indeed planting seeds for tomorrow, ensuring that the unwritten horizon would be illuminated by the enduring light of Eden's extraordinary biodiversity.

The embers of the great conflagration had long since cooled, leaving behind a landscape scarred but not broken. The immediate threat, the existential fire that had threatened to consume their nascent civilization, was extinguished. Yet, in the profound quiet that followed, a deeper understanding began to dawn. Survival, they realized, was not a destination, not a singular victory marked by the cessation of crisis. It was, instead, a state of perpetual becoming, a continuous practice woven into the very fabric of their days. The vigilance that had been honed during the fire's roar did not recede; it transformed. It became the quiet hum of ecological monitoring, the constant, gentle tending of the bio-systems they had painstakingly restored and cultivated. The commitment to ethical stewardship, once a desperate imperative, evolved into a foundational principle, an unwavering compass guiding every decision, every action.

This realization permeated every aspect of Aethelburg's societal structure. The communal bio-farm, no longer just a symbol of their recovery, became a living testament to this enduring practice. The Eden-born children, their initial lessons in planting and nurturing now deeply ingrained, moved beyond rote memorization. They began to intuit the subtle language of the ecosystem, their understanding maturing from recognizing plant needs to anticipating the delicate balance of the entire farm. Their play often involved mimicking the symbiotic relationships they observed, weaving garlands of lumina-moss around young saplings, their laughter echoing the gentle pulsing light of the moss as it responded to the soil's subtle energy shifts. Elder farmers, their wisdom now a shared inheritance, guided this maturation not by dictating, but by posing questions. "What does the air tell you about the water's journey to the roots?" they might ask, prompting a child to observe the dew patterns on the leaves, to feel the minute temperature variations that signaled the earth's moisture content. This was not about teaching them to survive the next crisis, but about fostering a deep, innate understanding of life's interconnected processes, a profound respect for the delicate dance of existence.

The aether-grazers, too, became more than just integral to the farm's fertilization cycle. The children's rapport with them deepened, moving beyond the functional to the relational. They learned to interpret the subtle flick of an ear, the cadence of their breath, not just as indicators of their grazing needs, but as expressions of their individual well-being. Lyra's bio-acoustic system, initially designed for practical management, now facilitated a richer interspecies dialogue. The children would sit amongst the herd, emitting low, resonant frequencies that mimicked the aether-grazers' contented hum, a practice that seemed to foster not only calm but a palpable sense of shared presence. Thorne's meticulous documentation expanded to include observations of the aether-grazers' social dynamics, their preferences for certain symbiotic flora, their seemingly intuitive understanding of seasonal shifts. He began to hypothesize that their presence stimulated not just soil aeration but a more complex rhizosphere communication network, a hypothesis that Anya, as planetary bio-harmonizer, eagerly sought to explore. This was the enduring practice: observing, understanding, and integrating, not with the urgency of a threat, but with the dedication of a lifelong commitment.

The sky-trees, once observed with awe and a touch of fear due to their sheer scale, were now understood as partners in Aethelburg's continued flourishing. The expeditions led by Anya were no longer just educational excursions; they were pilgrimages of understanding. The children learned to read the subtle vibratory patterns within the massive trunks, understanding how these communicated atmospheric pressure changes and moisture levels across vast distances. They learned to identify the microscopic organisms that lived in symbiotic harmony with the sky-tree bark, understanding their role in filtering airborne toxins and releasing vital atmospheric compounds. The nursery domes, where fallen sky-tree seeds were nurtured, became sites of intense, quiet focus. The children, now teenagers, were experimenting with modified light spectrums, not to accelerate growth, but to mimic the precise environmental conditions of different epochs in Eden's past, seeking to understand the evolutionary pressures that had shaped the sky-trees' remarkable resilience. This was not about replicating the past, but about learning from its infinite variations to ensure the future's adaptability.

Dr. Thorne's Chrono-Gardens initiative, once a monumental scientific undertaking, now represented the pinnacle of this enduring practice. The temporal stasis fields, initially a shield against potential genetic loss, had become a profound tool for observation and reflection. The ethical protocols, once debated with intense deliberation, were now integrated into the very consciousness of the project's stewards. The children involved in calibration no longer saw the task as a technical exercise but as a sacred duty. They learned to interpret the faint luminescence of the energy containment fields not as a measure of temporal dilation, but as the silent breath of eons held in suspension. They developed an almost intuitive feel for the subtle energetic harmonies that ensured the stasis fields' integrity, a sensitivity that Thorne believed was honed by their deep connection to Eden's natural rhythms. Lyra's empathic interfaces had evolved to translate the complex data streams into nuanced visual and auditory narratives, allowing the community to engage with the Chrono-Gardens not as a scientific marvel, but as a living archive of their planet's evolutionary journey.

The selection of new Chrono-Garden sites had become a communal ritual, a process of deep ecological consultation. Instead of simply identifying species at risk, they now sought zones that represented critical junctures in Eden's evolutionary history, areas where unique adaptations had emerged or where delicate ecological balances were particularly susceptible to subtle environmental shifts. One new site was established in a geothermal vent system, preserving extremophile microbial communities that had evolved in conditions previously thought inimical to life, offering insights into the very origins of biological complexity. Another was a frozen glacial ice cave, safeguarding ancient viral and bacterial strains that held the secrets to resilience against planetary-scale environmental disruptions. The de-stasisification protocols, once purely theoretical, were now being rigorously tested under controlled conditions, focusing not on immediate reintroduction, but on gradual acclimatization, mirroring the slow, deliberate pace of natural evolution. Thorne often spoke of these controlled reintegrations not as experiments, but as conversations with time, allowing past wisdom to inform present understanding.

The ultimate aim of the Chrono-Gardens, as Thorne articulated it during a community gathering under the dappled light of a sky-tree canopy, was not merely to hoard genetic material. It was to cultivate a deeper, more profound respect for the ephemeral nature of life, and for the immense power of continuity. He explained that by observing the slow, deliberate unfolding of life within the stasis fields, and by carefully studying the reintegration of species, they were learning to perceive time not as a linear progression, but as a vast, interconnected tapestry. This perspective shift was crucial. It moved them away from a mindset of conquest or exploitation, and towards one of gentle custodianship. The children, listening intently, their young faces illuminated by the soft glow of the projected Chrono-Garden data streams, understood this instinctively. They saw in the slow pulsing of the stasis fields not a pause in life, but a different kind of rhythm, a testament to life's enduring capacity to adapt and persist.

This understanding fostered a profound shift in their perception of 'flourishing.' It was not about achieving a static state of perfection, a utopian end-point where all challenges were overcome. It was about embracing the ongoing process of adaptation, of learning, and of contributing to the intricate web of life. The fire had been a brutal awakening, a stark reminder of their vulnerability. But the enduring practice, the quiet dedication to understanding and stewardship, was their true awakening. It was the understanding that the horizon was not a distant, fixed point, but a continuously unfolding panorama, shaped by their choices, their awareness, and their unwavering commitment to life. The Chrono-Gardens were not a monument to their past achievements, but a testament to their future potential, a living library of possibilities, a silent promise that the extraordinary biodiversity of Eden, and the wisdom it held, would continue to illuminate their path, long after the last embers of crisis had faded. Their survival was not a concluded chapter, but the continuous, evolving narrative of their responsible presence on Eden. The future was not something to be captured and secured, but something to be cultivated, day by day, with conscious intent and a deep, abiding reverence for the unfolding miracle of existence. The practice was not merely a means to an end; it was the very essence of their being, the unwritten horizon of their ongoing journey.

# CHAPTER SIXTEEN
# APPENDIX

The following is a curated selection of ecological and chronobiological data, drawn from Thorne's meticulous records and Anya's bio-harmonization reports, offering a glimpse into the intricate systems discussed within this narrative.

**Sky-Tree Root Network Symbiosis (ST-RNS):** A complex mycorrhizal relationship observed between the primary root systems of mature sky-trees and specific species of lumina-moss. The moss, in return for nutrient transfer, emits low-frequency bio-luminescence that appears to stimulate root growth and facilitate atmospheric moisture absorption by the tree.

**Aether-Grazer Bio-Acoustic Resonance:** The identified range of resonant frequencies emitted by aether-grazers (typically 15-45 Hz) has been shown to correlate with soil aeration rates and the proliferation of beneficial rhizosphere microorganisms. Lyra's research indicates that specific vocalizations can also influence herd cohesion and stress reduction.

**Chrono-Garden Temporal Stasis Field Efficacy:** Data on the preservation of genetic material within stasis fields, measured by minimal molecular degradation and cellular viability over extended temporal displacements. The appendix includes selected case studies of successful de-stasisification and acclimatization protocols.

**Eden's Evolutionary Epochs (EE):** A tentative chronological framework for Eden's ecological development, marked by distinct atmospheric compositions, dominant flora and fauna, and prevailing geological conditions. Chrono-Garden sites are often selected to represent key EE transitions.

**Aether-grazers:** Herbivorous, domesticated creatures integral to Eden's agricultural cycle, known for their symbiotic relationship with soil microbes and their bio-acoustic emissions.

**Bio-harmonizer:** An individual or system responsible for maintaining the ecological equilibrium and interspecies communication within a given biosphere.

**Bio-luminescence:** The emission of light by living organisms, often as a byproduct of biochemical reactions.

**Chrono-Gardens:** Specialized research facilities employing temporal stasis fields to preserve and study genetic material and ecological systems from various points in Eden's evolutionary history.

**Eden:** The planet on which Aethelburg civilization resides, characterized by its unique and complex biosphere.

**Lumina-moss:** A species of moss known for its bio-luminescent properties, often found in symbiotic relationships with larger flora.

**Rhizosphere:** The soil zone that is directly influenced by root secretions and associated microorganisms.

**Sky-trees:** Towering, ancient flora indigenous to Eden, possessing immense biological complexity and playing a crucial role in atmospheric regulation.

**Temporal Stasis Field:** An energy field capable of suspending biological processes and slowing the passage of time within its confines.